D. E. WHITE started writing fifteen years ago, scribbling ideas on napkins at work on the night shift. After various jobs, including working as cabin crew, in a hospital, a supermarket, and as a 999 call handler for the ambulance service, she began writing full time in 2018.

She is a multi-award winning entrepreneur, and was part of a small business delegation speaking at Number 10, Downing Street in 2015.

Having spent a lot of time travelling the world, she now lives with her husband and two sons on the south coast of the UK, with a growing assortment of animals and several stick insects.

Remember Me is her debut psychological thriller.

Visit D. E. White at daisywhiteauthor.co.uk

Remember Me

D. E. WHITE

ONE PLACE. MANY STORIES

HQ
An imprint of HarperCollins*Publishers* Ltd
1 London Bridge Street
London SE1 9GF

This paperback edition 2019

1

First published in Great Britain by
HQ, an imprint of HarperCollins*Publishers* Ltd 2019

ISBN: 9780008330804

MIX
Paper from
responsible sources

FSC
www.fsc.org   FSC® C007454

This book is produced from independently certified FSC™ paper
to ensure responsible forest management.

For more information visit: www.harpercollins.co.uk/green

Typeset by Palimpsest Book Production Ltd, Falkirk, Stirlingshire
Printed and bound in Great Britain by
CPI Group (UK) Ltd, Melksham, SN12 6TR

In memory of Brian Crocker
'Gorffwys mewn heddwch'.

Chapter 1

I'd give everything to be back at the first square on the board, with all still to play for...

In the beginning, I was just another kid, with just another unlucky family. I used that bad luck, as I used my good looks and confidence. Nobody knew I'd already killed once. In the games I play, I have always used the charm I was born with – along with various other, less admirable, skills I have had to acquire along the way.

There are a few golden days, bottled and stored at the back of my mind, that bring a comforting glow of nostalgia when uncorked. I inhale, eyelids drooping, and allow my thoughts to drift back...

The grass of the school playing field was warm and smelled pleasantly of hay. It was scratchy on my bare legs and under my spread palms. I remember that day so clearly that I can summon the laughter, the scent of cut grass, the bumpy feeling of a packet of pills in my pocket. I leaned back until the sun enveloped my face in a wave of burning fire, and I enjoyed the dizziness evoked by blood-red patterns on my closed eyelids. Sprawled lazily in a semicircle facing me, a few of the other kids were idly chucking empty Coke cans at an old oak stump. Someone was passing round an illicit cigarette, and the curling blue smoke teased my senses.

I had already discovered how to play with my pack – how to get them into a ball game, climbing trees at the far end of the field, or even a bit of joyriding when darkness fell. That day I had less innocent activities planned. It was the first true test of my power over my players and I relished that tingle of excitement. It buzzed through my veins like a drug hitting home. I could never have guessed how that day and night would shape my life, or how my need for revenge would become everything – a tearing, ravenous hunger I could never satisfy.

I can see us all now, as though I am soaring above the school, floating like a bird, arms outstretched. It's where I belong. The boys and the girls, so bright and alive against the scorched summer grass. The laughing, teasing group of friends and enemies, and the drifting smell of sweat and chips. Someone was singing that stupid little song we'd had since primary school:

'Three little girls, sitting up a tree,
Kissed all the boys,
But no one wants me.'

I knew exactly what was happening in my life, and some might say I could have stopped it at any time – but I didn't. I watched, and I waited. It turned out better than I could ever have imagined. That's one of the things about being a gamer – you have to know when to let fate dip a finger into your spit. It doesn't mean losing control, it just means loosening the reins for a moment.

It has always paid to be smart and, looking back, that was more important than anything. It still is. I know I'm smarter than all of them, and that will be my legacy. Before that day at school, everything in my life was just a blurred rehearsal. My heartbeat thumps deep and strong – a jungle drum to my prey. It's been a few years since I last played for real, but things have changed.

I can hear music from another room. It's a lilting, joyous sound, and it brings me back to the present. Time to play again.

I pick up a phone, scroll down, type a message and hit the send button.

'*Ydych chi'n cofio fi, Ava Cole?*'

'**Do you remember me, Ava Cole?**'

Chapter 2

There was no marker on the grave. Not an impressive carved headstone, nor even a crude nailed cross.

Even the swathes of early wildflowers avoided the leafy mound. Ava knelt, ignoring the damp that seeped through her jeans, the icy wisps of April breeze slicing through the quiet woodland. Her comfort was not important. Ellen, in her lonely bed of leaves and soil, could feel nothing now.

The earth was cold and gritty under her palms, and she stirred the faded leaves with the toe of her boot. An overgrown holly branch scraped glossy fingers across the grave, and overhead the larger trees creaked and moaned. The sour smell of winter death and decay fought with the delicate sweetness of the first bluebells.

Fifteen years of self-imposed exile, and she was finally back in Wales, huddled in a thick jacket and oversized boots, crying over her best friend's grave. Not back home, but just *back*.

Awkwardly, slowly, she stood, wiping the tears away with her sleeve. It didn't take long to find the vast, triple-trunked oak, and the gnarled bark still bore the scars. Just their initials and two scrawled words:

'*COFIWCH FI.*'

Remember me.

A sudden glimmer of red and gold, lighting the wood with the last rays of a winter sun, softened the path of early darkness. Ava left the grave and headed west, stamping through the twists of dead bramble cables, blowing on her hands to warm them again. As the trees thinned, she found a path winding steeply towards the village.

Ellen's bungalow had a light in her bedroom window. Her parents would have gone into her room, turned the immaculate bed covers down, laid a flower on her pillow, and turned on her nightlight. Just as they had done every evening since her death, Ava caught herself remembering. Or maybe not. Perhaps they had finally moved on, and all traces of Ellen had been removed. They might even have a lodger in her old bed. Tomorrow, Ava thought grimly, she would have to go and see them. Everything had changed, and she wasn't back by choice. But since she *was* here, she needed to make her peace with Ellen and her family. She told herself it was respectful and courteous, but the pain that burned on the inside was conjured from both fear and shame. Trying to make amends, she had always fallen back on cheap promises. *If I can just get this grade, solve this case, take out this drug dealer...* The list went on and on, and she had only ever done it for two people – her best friend and her son.

She crested the hill, panting slightly from the climb, and then spun around as the noise of someone else stamping through the wood penetrated her thoughts. It was a man, his face in shadow, shoulders hunched under his own bulky jacket. He was moving fast, along the same winding path she had just climbed. As she strained to see, the last of the light disappeared and the raw chill of darkness fell across the woodland.

Common sense told her to call out a greeting, to be adult and begin as she meant to go on. But she was still drifting, jolted out of her usual efficiency, lost in the past – her past and Ellen's. In her mind, back in the valleys, she was no longer a successful detective working the streets of Los Angeles, but

5

a teenage screw-up returning to the scene of the crime. Returning fifteen years too late. The man was coming swiftly now, his breath twisting smoky clouds into the darkness. As he came close enough for her to make out his face, he looked up, deliberately searching out her gaze. He was smiling.

Ava squared her shoulders, fists clenched and chin up. Still in fighting stance, she walked towards him, determined to gain the upper hand. Two long strides before her boot caught in a tussock of grass. She was down, sprawled like a helpless child, while he laughed. Time spun back, and embarrassment trailed burning tendrils along her spine, flushing her face. Their lives had been hopelessly entwined throughout her childhood. Every new experience, every memory, was filled with his laughter, his energy. Until that last night, when she'd fled towards the bridge, passport and cash stuffed in her jeans pocket, crouched low over the motorbike, praying to every angel in Wales that she would make it to the other side. He belonged to the drug-drenched memories of adolescence, not the gritty reality of her carefully constructed, and very grown-up, world.

'Hallo, Ava. Remember me?' Leo Evans was still laughing, still charming. Even in the shadows, he was all carved cheekbones and piercing blue eyes. He ran a gloved hand through his messy crop of dark hair as she climbed slowly to her feet.

'Don't be stupid, Leo. I'm not in the mood for games.' She was not fourteen years old again, and it pissed her off that he was still a good-looking bastard. A successful bastard too, from what she had heard. Embarrassed at her primitive reaction to his appearance, she was snappy and defensive. Her legs were shaky and her stupid heart was pounding far too fast. She licked her dry lips and rubbed a bruised elbow.

'Well, that's a welcome. Shame. You used to love them.' The blue eyes glinted with mischief and two dimples appeared in the stubbly cheeks. The darkness wiped away any signs of ageing, and his face was that of the manipulative, charming boy who shared his sandwiches with her on her first day at school.

'It really doesn't bother you, does it?' Ava indicated the wood below them with a vague wave of her hand. The hand was shaking, a fact which he couldn't fail to miss, even in the semi-darkness.

He didn't pretend to misunderstand, 'Should it? We were stupid kids. It's over and done with, Ava. I think we've all moved on. Who would have thought you'd turn out to be a copper? LAPD no less. I gather you're Detective Ava Cole, now. And you specialise in narcotics investigations? Narcotics! That is an absolute classic, darling, don't you think? I also heard you were involved in the John Wayland case last year as well. Triple homicide, wasn't it? Clever old you.'

So he kept tabs on her. She wasn't sure how to feel about that, except to take it that he had never outgrown that urge to control everyone, to have power over his friends and enemies alike. Anger bubbled in her chest, but she shrugged with forced nonchalance, 'Quite. I'm only back because of Stephen, and then I'll be going home. We don't have to run into one another, Leo. Paul said you turned your nana's old place into a holiday home…'

'Holiday home sounds like a grotty caravan – no offence, darling. I only come back for business, but luckily your visit has coincided with one of my stays in the village.' He smiled at her, a swift upward look from under his lashes, all charm and sincerity. It was an adult version of his teenage smoulder, and without doubt an important part of his rise to fame.

'Lucky me.' God, she really had to stop reverting to pissed-off teenager. She was an adult now. Ava took a deep, steadying breath, and studied her ex-boyfriend as he continued. The strong Welsh accent of his boyhood was now a mere lilt dancing across some of his words, and she knew hers was long gone.

'I know Paul hasn't got long, and I know that he might have been a bit brusque when he asked you to come home, but he needs you, Ava. Penny went crazy when they found out he only had a few months to live. I've never seen her lose it, but she was crying like he was already gone. She needs you too. I'm sorry you had to come back for this,' he added gently. To anyone else, he would have been an old friend offering condolences. But to Ava, struggling to knit past and present, the mischief was still there, despite the apparent sincerity of his words.

Ava shrugged. 'I'm sorry too. But he's your friend before he's my ex-husband anyway. Shit happens. I wouldn't wish that on anyone, but the fact that it's Paul dying of cancer doesn't make it any worse or any better.'

'You've changed. Not just your accent, and your hair, but something else... you're a hard woman now, Ava Cole.'

'I'm impressed you could deduce that after a few minutes, and no, I'm not – I've just grown up. I found a way out a long time ago, and now I'm just here to tie up loose ends.' She could smell his sweat, disturbingly familiar, nudging other memories to the forefront of her mind. Ava deliberately turned her head away and took a gulp of the night air.

He scuffed a boot on the wet grass, staring down as though it was the most interesting thing in the world. 'Actually, we probably will run into each other. As you say, Paul is still a friend, and I'm filming the new series of my show this month.' Leo looked up now, a glimmer of a smile tugging at his lips. 'I'm sure you must know about my show. Unless the weather's really bad we film up near Cochran Hill. Or at Big Water.'

'Yeah, I heard about it. Clever old you.' Big Water was an eerie place – a huge sheet of shining water that concealed a drowned village. The reservoir had flooded the bones of a rural civilisation and in the summer months, it was a magnet for the bored teenagers of Aberdyth and nearby Cadrington.

'Touché.' Leo sighed, and took out a packet of cigarettes, seemingly in no hurry to move on.

He didn't offer one to Ava, and she ignored the tantalising aroma of smoke as it curled into the darkness. She had quit smoking four years ago, and she wasn't about to start again.

'*Tough Love* has the highest ratings of any reality show in the last five years. It is the ultimate blend of sex and survival.' Leo sounded as if he was reciting a press release or a well-rehearsed publicity line. 'You really should watch it, Ava. It was inspired by our childhood.'

'I'm not some investor, or your producer. You don't have to pitch it to me,' she snapped. Of course, she had seen Leo's handsome face on magazine covers, caught him being interviewed on television, and she had even watched an episode of *Tough Love*, because her friends loved it. But she was damned if she was going to admit that it was a bloody clever concept, and one that had clearly had huge financial rewards for those involved, if the media was to be believed.

Whilst she had been burying her head in studies, graduating second in her class, and then fighting for promotion in the NYPD, Leo had risen to fame on a reality show about Welsh teenagers. His stunning good looks and fiery outbursts had guaranteed his popularity. Unlike many reality stars, though, Leo had built a thriving business empire from simply appearing on TV. 'Leo, have you been sending me text messages?'

His cigarette end glowed orange in the shadows. 'I don't even have your number, Ava. How could I possibly do that?'

'I just wondered…' She studied his face for a moment longer. As always, it was impossible to tell when Leo was lying. The whispers that lay below the surface of her mind grew louder for a moment, but she forced them away. 'I thought Paul might have given it to you. Or Penny?'

'No. They haven't really mentioned you in ages – I thought you all communicated strictly by email, and only then when absolutely essential. Just another happy Aberdyth family. Until we knew about Paul, of course.'

The note of sarcasm was so subtle it might have been lost on someone who didn't know him, but Ava caught it. Happy families.

She swung away, abruptly ending their conversation. 'I need to go.'

He didn't try to stop her, and she didn't look around. But she knew he was standing in the shadows, watching her all the way back to the village. It had happened so many times before. Well, this time was different.

The main street was deserted, even so early in the evening, and her boots echoed hollowly on the tarmac. The neat, ugly rows of pebbledash houses were decorated with yellow-lit windows, and the pub doors were flung open despite the cold. The roar of laughter and clink of glasses mingled with luscious scents of fish and chips and roast lamb. Ava's stomach growled, but she could just imagine the sensation if she marched up to the bar and demanded dinner and a beer. She'd probably get a punch in the face – and she probably deserved one.

Ava pushed on past the lights and the company, turning instead up a dirt track to her left. A few rusty car wrecks decorated the roadside, and she forced her cold, aching legs faster up the hill. She was fit enough, and back home in LA she hiked in the hills, did spin classes and kickboxing. But she'd lost that innate childhood toughness and grit required to tackle the countryside around Aberdyth. That, and the fact she was jetlagged up to her eyeballs, and sick with worry about her imminent first meeting with her now-teenage son.

Despite her good intentions, her mind was flickering back over the events of the past week. Fuck, she couldn't wait to get back to LA. Here in Wales, the sickly mix of emotions was like a box of dead weights lodged in her heart. Guilt about Ellen, guilt about her son, Stephen. But most of all a nagging fear that by trying to make things right she might tear apart the years of hard work. She would have to tread carefully, but it was far too late to confess to teenage crimes. Too many lives would be irrevocably broken apart, and any precious thread that might remain between her and Stephen would be gone forever. Ava dredged in her pockets and produced her phone. She scrolled down with numb fingers, reaching her folder of photos. Every picture she had managed to scrape from Stephen's social media sites, every photo she had begged from Paul, was there. Stephen had been told his mother didn't care about him, and she knew Paul had made her out to be a hard bitch, who cared only for her job.

When she recovered from the trauma of her teenage years, her counsellor had urged her to build bridges with her son. But Paul was having none of it, and resorted to threats that could have ruined her career. Although she never truly believed he would tell the police about Ellen and their drug-addled childhood, it was the final fence he needed to keep her out of Stephen's life. If someone told you long and hard enough what a crap mother you were, and that you didn't deserve a child, eventually you believed it. She sighed, flicking back to her emails, looking for the message that had ripped everything apart.

Although she was trudging up the hill in the darkness, instantly she was hundreds of miles away, about to start her night shift in LA.

* * *

'Dear Ava,
This is a tough thing to write, but Penny feels you need to be told. I'm dying. I expect you are wondering why the hell you should care? Obviously you don't, but it isn't all bad news – I will be leaving this earth a bit sooner than I ever thought. The doctors reckon I have two months at the most. Time for you to take on a few responsibilities. Much as I hate to tell you, Penny says our son will need you, and I want her to have some kind of support that doesn't come from the village, or her uncle. I'm sure you understand that, at least, as you are aware of her situation. Let

us know when you will be arriving. I suggest the
Birtleys' for your accommodation.
Paul'

'Fuck!' Perching on someone else's desk, Ava automatically
scrolled down to check the rest of her emails, before returning
to Paul's message. He had always written to her in this slightly
over-formal, stilted style. It was as though they had never shared
a bed, or a life, together. Just like that, her delicately balanced
world was being pulled apart.

He was wrong, she did care – about her son *and* her ex-husband.
It was just buried so deep that the love for them had gotten
entwined with other memories. Like barbed wire twisted round
a baby's hand.

From the control room she heard the clicking of keyboards,
and the repetitive murmur of voices as the emergency dispatchers
dealt efficiently with incoming 911 calls, their trained responses
smooth and calm. There was a buzz of chatter from the crowd
round the coffee machine, and through the open door she could
see an elderly cleaner in a blue overall pushing a mop round the
reception area.

But even the yells and crashes of the drunks in the cells couldn't
pierce the sudden mist that engulfed her mind. A male voice
came from miles away, but the hand on her backside was much
too close.

'Hey, Ava, much as I welcome your cute bum on my desk at
any time, I need to get this paperwork, so if you wouldn't mind,
honey…'

Fighting her way back to reality as the cop grinned before
snatching up the pile of printed notes and heading back to the
conference room, Ava walked over to her own neatly organised
desk. She grabbed her now lukewarm coffee and downed it in
one gulp. The Los Angeles sun slashed a golden knife blade

through the dirty blinds, picking out the empty takeaway cartons, piles of paperwork, blinking computers, and jumbled family photos that cluttered the other desks. Ava had one photograph, framed in white wood, of her with her parents at graduation. No boyfriends or kids watched her as she worked, or distracted her with 'I love you, please come home' phone calls. Usually she didn't mind; this was her and this was the life she had finally chosen. But today, she would have given a lot to get one of those phone calls. Occasionally, in unguarded moments, she would drift off to sleep imagining an email or text from Stephen that began, '*Dear Mum...*'

* * *

The sound of singing snapped her out of her memories. Soft, lilting and slightly disturbing, the voice reached out through the icy air. The track had widened and she was passing the old garage – 'Mick's Place', it had always been called. But now the sign was hanging by one nail, and the petrol pumps were surrounded by a tide of rusty vehicles in various stages of disintegration. The smell of fuel was still strong, and it mingled alarmingly with the smoke from a fire.

Ava paused, straining her eyes in the darkness, peering past the crackling flames. The fire, in an old oil drum, was bright and pure against the sullen winter evening. The warmth reached out to her. The soft chant continued, but whilst she was drawn by the brightness and promise of defrosting her numb hands, she was repelled by the words.

'From starlight, to flame-bright,
Who will be burning tonight?'

The song floated like smoke dancing on the cold air, and the crunch of boots on gravel stamped out the beat. A few moments later a guitar joined the song, its melancholy thrum adding to the menace of the words.

'*Burning to the death,*
Until a last dying breath,
Brings redemption to us all.'

The singer halted abruptly but carried on strumming his guitar. The fire crackled and spattered a handful of glittering sparks onto the dirty concrete of the yard.

'Oi! You… didn't you used to be Ava Cole?'

'I… oh, Christ, it's Rhodri, isn't it?' Close up, his mop of red hair was unmistakable, even if his shadowed, weather-beaten face and slumped shoulders were that of a much older man.

Rhodri stopped playing and set his guitar down. She could see that there were several small animals roasting on a spit over the flames. Or to be more exact they were being burned to charcoal.

'Your dinner's burning,' Ava told him, walking across to his side of the fire. The heat scorched her cheeks, and she stretched icy hands to the blaze.

He spluttered with laughter, 'That's not my dinner, love, that's just a few rabbits from number four. The kids got bored of them.'

'Right.' Apparently, Rhodri was a long way from the cheeky, freckle-faced boy she had known at school, or even the wayward flame-haired teenager who would sit playing his guitar next to Big Water. Always on the edge of Leo's group, he would smile vaguely at them, lost in his music, but good-naturedly taking requests for all the latest hits.

'They were still alive you know, when I skewered them. I like it when they turn to black, and then tomorrow they'll be just soft little flakes that blow in the wind.' His voice was low, husky, and his strongly accented words seemed to hang in the darkness. He could have been an actor on a darkened stage, revelling in the drama, his audience hanging on to every word.

Ava narrowed her eyes, studying his face by the light of the flickering orange flames. Clearly, Rhodri had taken something, and was flying high over the valleys tonight. Well, it wouldn't be the first time. They had all taken pills back in the day – hell, for

14

a while pills had meant everything – but Rhodri had been more than fond of a smoke. It used to make him mellow, not a murderer of small creatures, though.

'Don't try and freak me out, Rhodri, because it never worked. I don't give a shit if you roast the entire rabbit population of Aberdyth.'

'I suppose not, but it was always fun trying to play games with you. So why are you back? Because of Paul, I suppose. I heard he asked you to come back, but I never thought you would. Is it strange, being the angel of death riding in to kiss your ex goodbye before he drops down to the fires of hell? Why bother to bring Ava back, when she probably wants to kill you anyway, I told him. Nobody could fight like the two of you, could they?'

'I'm sure that went down well. I have never wanted to kill Paul, and I certainly haven't come back to argue with him. Bit of sympathy for a condemned man, Rhodri.'

'Paul knows I've got his back, and I don't give him all the shit the others do. They carry on with this "I'm sure you'll pull through" crap. Like Penny, she keeps chirruping on about miracle cancer patients, who just get better and nobody knows why. Well, he won't. I've seen it before and when you've got that death sentence you just have to deal with it in any way you can.'

Ava vaguely remembered that Rhodri had a close family member he had lost to cancer when they were at primary school. His aunt, maybe? She didn't want to probe what was obviously still a painful, bitter memory. He was entitled to his opinions. 'I'm back because of Stephen, not for Paul. He's got Penny,' she corrected.

Rhodri shrugged, reached down and grabbed a bottle of beer from a crate. 'You never cared about the kid all these years, so why now? You know, you sound like an American. That's crap, *cariad*. Your Welsh has all gone. Want a drink, love?'

She barely hesitated, lifting a beer quickly from the crate. 'Thanks. I always cared about Stephen, I was just screwed up and he was better off without me.'

'You left him in Aberdyth, love. How is that better? You should've taken him with you. Paul was pissed off when you went to America. He thought you'd come back.'

'I know.' She was fighting the painful coils of guilt that wormed their way through her chest. Rhodri have never been one to skirt around a subject. Why hadn't she taken her baby? Because at the time she was blinded by her feelings of inadequacy. At one point she had become sure she would kill her own child, checking him constantly night and day, fussing over formula milk and sterilising bottles over and over again until Paul yelled that she was a crazy cow.

'You seen Leo yet?' His glance was sly now.

'Yes.'

'You gonna fuck him while you're here?' Rhodri screwed up his eyes, peering at her in the firelight, his mouth wet with drink. He dragged a sleeve across his face, waiting for her answer.

Surprised, she lowered the bottle from her own lips. 'No. Not that it's any of your business, but Leo and I were over a long time before I married Paul. It's ancient history.'

He studied her face, eyes knowing, smirking like he knew something she didn't. 'Aw don't get mad, love, I remember the two of you when we were at school. Everyone knew you were Leo's girl, and he never looked at anyone else. Although Penny and Ellen wouldn't have said no, would they? Especially Ellen, she was always trying to get with him.'

It was a challenge, and she brushed it neatly aside, sidestepping his words. 'Is your dad still here?'

'Died a few years ago.' Rhodri waved an unsteady hand, allowing himself to be diverted. 'All this is mine now, love. Mine to burn to a crispy fucking cinder if I want to. You got any pills?'

Clearly Leo was the only one in Aberdyth who kept up with her life. On second thoughts, maybe Rhodri did know about her job, and that was a cutting little reminder of their shared past. 'I'm not a teenager any more, Rhodri.' Ava finished her beer and stood up. He started strumming his guitar again. His fingers were gentle and rhythmic on the strings, but he watched her with wild, haunted eyes. His 'musician look', she remembered suddenly.

'See you around.'

'*Nos da, Ava.*'

She hesitated at that, drawn into tasting the language again. The moment passed, and she forced herself to ignore it. It was over and done with. Any thread of pleasure at finding an unthreatening, familiar face had vanished, and she was now shivering. The yard, full of the skeletons of dead vehicles, and now this half-recognisable face from her childhood, stirred unwelcome memories. But the darkness of the road, broken only by a few lonely houses, welcomed her like an old friend, and she took a deep breath of the raw, freezing air. How many times had she and Ellen made this journey, giggling hysterically with the after-effects of illicit alcohol, sharing a cigarette, hand in hand? Rhodri's softly spoken words followed her, whispering on the cold night air.

'From starlight, to flame-bright,
Who will be burning tonight?'

Chapter 3

She's back. I can hardly believe it. I'm sure she will appreciate the treat I have in store for her. One last time, Ava Cole.

Of course, I was prepared for her to have changed. I knew she would be harder, stronger and less of the wayward, but malleable, teenager I remembered. She has no idea that I have been watching her for years, skimming neatly below the surface of her social media accounts, her work intranet, and even her personal emails. I have access to her life, and up to a point it has kept me fed and entertained. I know her so well, but I don't know her in the flesh anymore. I remember her taste, her touch, but the memories are dull, like faded flowers.

I tell myself this makes the rediscovery all the more exciting. I do like a challenge, so I just need to rearrange the board and we can start. Ava has no idea what I have planned. In fact, she doesn't really know me at all. Not like I know her...

The only thing that always annoyed me is that her conscience pricks her a little too much. She would never join me in the ultimate hell slide to the finish, when you can taste the fear, and feel the hot blood slick on your body. Something in her soul is different to mine and I don't like that, if I'm totally honest.

I always wanted Ava to admire me, to see me as more than an

equal, and for a while it was wonderful. When she went it was terrible. If I was being poetic, I'd say she ripped my heart out. But you know what? I don't think I have a heart, or I wouldn't have been able to play my games the way I do.

Even whilst I'm thinking about Ava, I'm carefully tending to the fire. My boots are soaking from walking up the hill and down to East Wood earlier, so I should probably put some newspaper inside to dry them out.

I remember Ava at eight years old, when her parents first moved from Florida to Wales. She had that dumb American accent then, and she seems to have got it back. That's too bad. She needs to keep her Welsh, or she's going to struggle out on the game board. I was in the same year as Ava at school. I let her share my desk and helped her with the language. I let her share my pencils too – as soon as I saw that she used to absent-mindedly suck the ends when she was thinking hard.

When she put one down, I would pick it up, as casually as I could, and slide it into my own mouth. I could taste her sweetness, and from then on I made up my mind to own her.

I used to wait at the gate, after I helped my mum get dressed and all that shit. Ava would come running down the hill, in those blue denim shorts and a tight T-shirt, black hair flying out in the breeze. Then she'd smile at me. It was a proper smile, from a proper person – not like one of these fucking losers who just bare their teeth. She was real. And then I lost her.

If I look out of the window, I can see nothing but darkness. But I know if I went out, I could stand peacefully in the icy air, under the moon. The village would be spread before me like a chaotic nightmare, but as I watched, the stars would come out and create perfect order. The dark squares of houses criss-crossed with pale squares of gardens are like squares on a board. I see games everywhere.

There is a box of dice on the side, and instead of making a coffee I select a couple and idly give them a roll. They clatter and click across the surface before coming to rest next to the piano. I peer down. A double six. Of course – it would be. Satisfied, I pack them carefully away, revelling in what is to come.

'*Ava Cole, ydych chi'n dod allan I chwarae heno?*'

'**Ava Cole, are you coming out to play tonight?**'

Chapter 4

'Are you going out to see Paul now?' Mrs Birtley poked a scowling face out of the living room, and for a moment Ava was engulfed in the sickly waft of her perfume. The TV was blaring a comedy theme tune, and she caught a glimpse of Mr Birtley ensconced on the overstuffed pink tweed sofa, sipping his cup of tea.

'I am. Can I have a key please, so I don't have to disturb you when I get back in? I think you must have forgotten to give me one earlier when I signed in.' Ava tried for a sincere smile, forcing her expression into a kind of frozen politeness.

'I don't think I can give you a key, Ava. Things have changed in Aberdyth since you left. You weren't exactly angels as teenagers, but this latest generation are far worse – they'd steal anything if I gave them half a chance.'

'That isn't a reason for not giving me a key though, is it? I mean, I'm not one of the village teenagers anymore.' She kept her smile light, but the prod was intended, and she could see Mrs Birtley's cheeks redden under her make-up.

'It's a matter of principle.' Her beady black eyes were almost hidden by the pudgy folds of skin that framed her jowly face. She looked like a furious pug dog. Her helmet of short grey hair stopped just below her ears, and a pink hair slide looked bizarrely out of place.

'Right, I understand. Apologies in advance for waking you up then.' Ava notched her expression down to frosty politeness, resisting the temptation to say more, and marched up the narrow flight of wooden stairs to grab a thick jumper. Penny and Paul's farm was a half-mile walk across the hill. She had expected hostility; she'd even thought that the Birtleys might refuse her booking when they realised who she was. Clearly their 'principles' allowed them to take her money though. They obviously needed it; she had noticed only one other guest at the little B&B – a nondescript, middle-aged man in hiking gear who was heading out as she arrived.

* * *

It took longer than she reckoned to get to the farm, partly because, despite the torch, she took a wrong turning. Memory failing, she had been mindlessly following the old sheep track, when it suddenly disappeared into a mass of dead weeds. The skeleton of a rusted lambing shelter lay sprawled in her path.

The pale beam of torchlight picked out the disintegrating wood and corrugated iron. She jumped back, the light jerking upwards into the icy blackness at her involuntary reaction. A wave of sickness hit her like a punch in the belly. It wasn't this one. It couldn't be this one.

The darkness had been warm then, and the heady scent of early summer clung to the hills as they carried the body along the track. Ellen's first resting place had not been East Wood, near the old oak, but down a boarded-up hole in a lambing pen. It was Huw's idea. He had said the strong smell of sheep would keep any official search dogs away.

Not that there would be any trouble with the police because Ava must write a note to Ellen's parents, Leo had said firmly, backing up his friend. She would write exactly what he said, and nobody would be any wiser. Ellen would be just another teenage runaway leaving the valleys for the diamond-strewn pavements of the city. Everyone left eventually.

Ava bit her lip, tears drenching her cheeks, the knot of guilt and frustration yanking tight in her stomach. Despite herself, the whispering was louder, her mind flooded with unwelcome memories.

* * *

'She's dead! She's not breathing!'

'Shit. Are you sure? I mean… Ellen!'

The voices came and went, urgent, alarmed and angry. It was a while before Ava, only half-aware that something had happened, pushed herself onto her knees. The high-pitched voices continued, raw with panic. The crown of her head was throbbing and the pain beat insistent waves through her body, suggesting someone had hit her. She used a tree branch to haul herself to her feet, and staggered towards her friends, vision blurred with drugs and night. Ellen was sprawled on her back in the mud and the leaves, her dark hair fanning out across the path. The group around her parted, turning towards Ava, their faces pale blurs, watchful and defensive.

Someone, it was hard to tell who in the darkness, the confusion, but she thought it might have been Rhodri, was pulling Ellen's top down over her chest. The snapshot of memory stayed with her, niggling away like bugs scratching her stomach from the inside. Rhodri was looking for a heartbeat, trying to see if Ellen was breathing, that must have been what he was doing. The sick realisation that Ellen's eyes were wide, but she wasn't seeing, made Ava forget everything else, and scream in horror. She shoved the others away, fumbling for a pulse, allowing only Penny near the body.

The other girl's face was wet with tears. 'She's gone, Ava, I already checked. She's not breathing.'

'So we do that mouth-to-mouth thing. For fuck's sake, Penny, come on!' Ava bent down and tried to seal her own lips over Ellen's cold mouth. She was shaking so much it was impossible to tell if any air went in. What else? Oh yes, tilt the head to open the airway. Her mind was unfogging. Penny, sniffing and sobbing, but taking her lead, was pushing her hands ineffectively on Ellen's chest.

And the boys? What were they doing? So much blackness. They were all a similar height and build, all wearing dark-coloured hoodies and jeans. Accusations were spinning around, and were two of the boys even coming to blows? Huw was shoving Paul, his voice low and threatening. She smelled cigarette smoke and screamed at them to call an ambulance several times. Did anyone move?

Eventually it was obvious that Ellen was not going to breathe again, and Penny collapsed sobbing in Ava's arms. The girls clung together, but Leo was talking low and hard to the others.

'What happened? What the fuck happened to her?' Ava finally gasped out the words, pain and terror ripping through her chest, making it hard to talk. 'Did you call an ambulance?'

It was Huw who detached himself from the shadowy group and explained. Ava had been 'out of it', he said, omitting any mention of a blow to her head, and Ellen had decided to do the zip line dare. She had washed down some pills with a couple of swigs of vodka, and seemed steady enough. But she had fallen from about halfway along and landed awkwardly. When they ran to her she wasn't moving. There was nothing anyone could do, but now they needed to make sure they didn't get blamed for her death. The police would say it was their fault, their game, and she was mixing alcohol and drugs! What would their families say? School? The paper would get hold of it too...

If they hid the body, Leo added, nobody would ever know.

* * *

Ava stood doubled over, fighting away the voices that scolded her, breathing slowly and deeply. It was over. She couldn't take it back, but she supposed, with her career choice, she had been doing her best to atone for her sins, as Mrs Birtley would have said. But if he discovered the truth, Stephen would never forgive her. Not just an appalling mother, but a coward who had helped bury her best friend too. It seemed an age before the sour taste of nausea and regret passed, and she was able to continue her journey. Her world narrowed to a line of yellow torch beam, whilst all around the hills were wrapped in suffocating blackness.

Cursing the extra jumper now, she arrived on the front porch breathing heavily from the last climb. Someone must have been watching out for her, because the door was flung open even as she raised her hand to knock.

The two women stared at one another, a whole world of shared history pulsing between them, before Penny gave a tight-lipped smile. 'Hallo, Ava.'

'Penny.' Ava smiled back, mechanically, awkwardly. This was going to be horrible and there was no way out. She was a coward not to have faced it long before this.

'Come in and take your boots off then. We'll go in there in a minute, but I wanted to talk to you first.' She indicated an oak door leading off the wide, immaculate, stone-flagged hallway, before fixing Ava with a hard, curious stare. 'I suppose you must have got some sleep this morning. Paul said your flight landed early. Did you manage to hire a car or did you get the bus?'

'Oh, I hired a car, because the bus didn't leave until the evening, and it was cheaper than a taxi. I need to drop it off in Cadrington tomorrow sometime. I remembered what the roads were like round here, and it only just made it up the hill to the Birtleys.' She was gabbling, words tumbling without meaning or thought, and she forced herself to shut up. The silence hung tense and sharp.

Clumsily, avoiding Penny's curious gaze, Ava tugged off her boots. She refrained from commenting on her movements of the day, and she certainly wasn't going to tell this woman how long it had taken her to cross the bridge back into Wales. Jetlag or no, there had been plenty to deal with as soon as she landed into Heathrow. She'd actually had to pull over, before she managed to gather enough courage to cross the bridge. All too easily, the dark panic she associated with crossing in the opposite direction, all those years ago, had come stealing back into her mind. But she'd been prepared for it, and that was the real reason for not taking a taxi from the airport. The last thing she needed was the driver thinking he'd picked up some lunatic.

Penny had always been a pretty, sharp-faced imp of a girl, popular and fun. Despite being in the same year at school, she was almost a whole year younger than the other members of the little Aberdyth gang. Physically, she often couldn't keep up with Ava and Ellen, but the boys let her hang around because she was cute and amusing. Once Ellen was gone, Penny had become a confidante and close friend. Whilst the boys avoided the subject, Penny and Ava would spend long hours talking about Ellen, about their terror that someone would find her grave, and about how much they missed her.

'How is he?' Ava asked hesitantly.

Penny shrugged. 'As well as you would expect. I think he's pretending it's not happening. The pain is bad at times, but we've got drugs to control it. When he's going through a good patch, you wouldn't even know he was ill, but other times he's like an old man just going through the motions. It's horribly cruel, when he's still so young. How could this happen?'

'I'm so sorry,' Ava said softly. She was going to be saying it a lot, but it was heartfelt this time.

'Before we do go in' – Penny raised a hand, too close to Ava's chest, but she didn't touch her – 'I've always wanted to ask, but it isn't something I can say by email, or even on the phone. I needed to see you for real. Ava, why did you never tell me you were going? You could have trusted me…'

'I couldn't tell you. I'm sorry, Penny. I couldn't tell anyone in case Paul tried to stop me. You know how he was. Once I got home to the States, it seemed better to make a clean break. Look, I know I fucked up, and I haven't just come back to try and pick up where I left off.'

The other woman nodded, her pale green eyes softening, 'Good. I know you wouldn't expect to anyway. You're too clever for that...'

Ava smiled properly, and surprisingly Penny leaned in for a clumsy hug.

'I'm about to lose my husband, so anything else really seems pretty insignificant. I don't want to fight with you, Ava. I loved you, you know, when we were kids, and I love Stephen like my own.'

Despite the hug, Ava noticed the warning, even as Penny looked up with bright eyes, and flushed cheeks. Her shiny blonde ponytail was draped over one slim shoulder, and she had clearly made an effort tonight, with lots of make-up and delicate silver earrings. Or maybe she was just a lot more glamorous than Ava.

'Thanks for understanding,' Ava said, still slightly shocked by the pace of the conversation, and the unexpected show of affection. 'You know, I can't think of anyone better to be Stephen's mum. I was a teenage fuck-up, but you always had everything totally together. I did see the wedding photos, and I was happy for you. My aunt sent them over. She sent photos of Stephen, too, but Paul said he didn't want to know me, so it seemed better to stay right out of your lives.' It was something she had repeated to herself over and over, covering the pain with a plaster of flabby lies. Later, she might tell Penny of Paul's threats, but this was not the time to slag off her husband. Perhaps Penny even knew, and had been happy to keep Ava away from her stepson? It was something Ava had agonised over for years, opting for the cowardly route of not untangling her former life, even if it meant she couldn't see her own son until he had grown up.

Penny was glowing, her icy manner softening slightly, and her expression animated. 'Stephen has been very happy with us. Paul said you felt he was better off in Aberdyth with a stable family, and you have your career of course…' An edge to her voice, that was quickly covered by a change of subject. 'Your aunt was always lovely to me, and I was sad when she moved away. Perhaps when you've rested, we can get together tomorrow? It would be just like old times.' The words, despite their warmth, were almost mechanical.

It was the last thing Ava wanted, but if an olive branch was being offered, she should take it. She forced herself to accept Penny's invitation. 'I'd really like that. I need to hear about your bakery business too. I missed you Pen, I really did.'

'Do you remember when we bunked off school and hitched to Cardiff that time?'

She did, and it was a rare untainted memory, so she seized it. 'You had that pink Lycra body suit, and plastic cowboy boots.'

'And you had sequins and stars on your face, and denim hot pants. Christ, we were lucky nobody took us for a pair of prossies!'

Ava smiled, but a little twist of sadness for that lost innocence caught in her chest. Pen, despite her sweetness, had always had a sense of fun, and had always been the one to suggest the wildest childhood adventures.

'Penny? Is she here then?' Paul was calling from behind the closed door, and the laughter died abruptly. His sentence ended in a cough, but she caught the name Stephen.

He was here too? Ava dug her nails into the palms of her hands, swallowed the lump that had suddenly risen in her throat, and Penny nodded encouragingly. 'God, please don't let him hate me…' Her ex-husband's bitterness she could cope with, but her son's… She squared her shoulders. Whatever he felt, or said, she deserved it. She had been a shit mum and a worse wife. Now it had come back to bite her.

The room was quiet and smelled of smoky log fires and furniture polish. She might never have been away. Paul was sitting at the wooden desk, behind a neat stack of paperwork. When she was a child, visiting for tea, his dad would be sitting in that exact same place, in that exact same position.

He didn't look like someone who had a death sentence hanging over him. The dark hair was as thick and curly as ever, despite whatever treatments he must have had. His brown eyes roved across her face. In jeans and a well-ironed check shirt, he looked the cliché of a gentleman farmer. A glass jug of water and a half-full glass stood within reach on a little iron table. Three collies were sprawled at his feet, and the Welsh weather had burned lines and hardness into his slightly round face. Just like his dad.

In fact, he was still very attractive, and a good match for slight, blonde Penny. But Ava was casting quick looks around the room, her stomach churning. There was someone missing from this unhappy family reunion.

'Where's Stephen?'

'Gone out with his girlfriend. Sorry, Ava, you know what teenagers are like… well, you don't actually, but he's old enough to make his own decisions now.' Paul didn't look sorry – he looked amused but his hand shook as he poured, then gulped another glass of water.

'Doesn't he want to see me?' It came out as a plea, and she cursed herself for showing weakness. Her brain was stupid and numb, which was a blessed relief, because she could tell the pain would come roaring back later. After the smooth way Penny seemed to have welcomed her back, she couldn't expect it all to be easy. After all, she hadn't been married to Pen.

'He does want to see you. He just needs to get used to the idea,' Penny said hastily from the corner of the room. 'Remember we always told him he could contact you when he was eighteen, if he wanted to, and I know he'll have been thinking about it.'

Ava looked round gratefully. The other woman was quickly folding clean washing from a plastic basket. A lock of gleaming blonde hair fell across her forehead, and she glanced up, and smiled when she caught Ava's eye on her. She still looked more like the girl who hitched to Cardiff for a night in the clubs, than someone who had been a farmer's wife for over ten years.

'You can sit down, Ava,' Paul said blandly, indicating a brown leather sofa next to the fire. 'What Penny means, of course, is that Stephen doesn't want any contact from you. He's happy here, and if this bloody cancer had never happened, we would never have dragged you over to cause trouble.'

Ava met his eyes, stormy and dark with anger now. It was as though she had never been away. Soon he would probably start telling her how everyone else managed to have a baby and look after it, so why did she have to be so weak? The dogs opened sleepy eyes, scenting conflict, but a word from Paul kept them under the desk.

'I don't mind them. I like dogs,' Ava said with an effort. She was stronger now, and this man would not bully her as he used to. The shouting and the cowering were in the past.

'I remember.'

'What are they called?'

'Amber, Rex and Tin.'

She further sank into the brown leather sofa, but forced herself to sit upright, knees together, shoulders squared. Silence, as the fire spat and hissed, one of the dogs snored, Penny sorted her washing and Paul stared at her, daring her to start an argument. He would always wait for her to make the first move, she remembered, and then leap on her with the solid fury of a fighting bull. Ava focused hard on the details of the familiar room. The good, solid oak furniture shone with polish, the floor tiles were clean and swept, and she noticed a dozen new horse brasses had been added to the gleaming collection over the fireplace. The place looked far better than when she had lived here. Housework had never been her thing, but then if Pen's business was going well, she supposed they might have a cleaner.

'I read about your baking – my aunt sent me a link to the

Guardian piece. It named you as one of the top Welsh entrepreneurs. You've done so well.'

Penny smiled. 'It was hard for a few years, but then it just took off for some reason. I suppose everyone likes Welsh cakes.'

Paul cleared his throat. 'The farm's doing well out of it too. We added another hundred ewes last year, and Pen wants to get some rare breeds for her meat sales.' His pride in his wife was evident, and Ava blinked back a few tears. Whatever she had triggered in Paul, she could detect no hint of discord between these two. How cruel that all this was about to be ripped apart. She was never normally this emotional about things – she needed to get a grip.

A few framed photographs showed the happy family over the years, and a larger picture in a silver frame was Paul and Penny on their wedding day. Ava squinted at the other pictures, recognising some she had been sent when her son was younger.

The silence was back, and Paul clearly felt enough had been said. He stroked the dogs, and watched her, anger back in check. She searched for another subject, but everything she thought of had the potential to inflame the situation or hark back to their shared but unwelcome past. Ava coughed and complimented them on the new slate in the hallway.

Paul said nothing, and Penny just smiled again, still folding the washing quickly and neatly. Just as Ava felt she might scream at the awkwardness of the situation, someone hammered on the front door.

'Are you expecting company tonight?' Penny raised her eyebrows at her husband.

He shook his head, without moving his eyes from Ava's face. 'Unless Stephen's lost his key again.'

Oh shit. Ava's heart started pounding, and she rubbed sweaty palms together. Her neck prickled and she felt light-headed. Suddenly the cosy, tidy room seemed far too hot. She heard Penny greeting someone, and then the outside door banged shut and the room was full of people.

'Hallo, mate, evening, Penny darling, you look gorgeous. Why are you all dressed up? Look who I found down the pub! I know you mentioned Ava was coming tonight, so I'd thought we'd all pop back and say hallo.' Leo was grinning at his friend. 'Ava. Nice to see you again.'

But Ava wasn't looking at either her ex-husband or her ex-boyfriend. She was staring at her son.

He was scowling, the blue eyes very like her own, but his features, and the dark messy hair were all his father's. Of course she knew what he looked like, but to have him in front of her after all these years in the flesh... she could hardly keep herself from crying out. All the emotions she had locked away were bubbling and boiling in her chest, and despite her good intentions she felt a tear trickle down one cheek.

'You look... well,' she managed, made stupid by the occasion. She cleared her throat, forcing herself to meet that scornful gaze.

'No thanks to you.' His voice was flat and sullen.

'You're actually his mum?'

Ava had hardly registered that Stephen had a girl with him, but now she turned to face her. Thin, black-haired, with unusual grey-green eyes and high cheekbones, she was also staring at Ava.

'She's not my mum, Bethan, I told you.'

The girl frowned at him, pursing her rosebud lips. She really was very pretty. Next to them both, Leo smiled, his face alight with mischief. The bastard.

Penny came back in with a tray of tea and a couple of bottles of beer. 'Help yourselves to drinks. Stephen, do you want to talk to Ava in the kitchen where it's a bit quieter?'

'I suppose.'

'Paul and I will have a catch-up in here. See you in a bit, Ava,' Leo said, winking at his friend.

Ava noted Paul's sudden malicious grin, and even in her confusion, equated it to the kind of look the boys used to exchange before they got up to some mischief at school. She pushed it aside and concentrated on her son, following him across the hall, noting his slender height, the square set of his shoulders. No longer a child, but a teenager who had finished school. He was taller than she was.

The kitchen was a warm cavern, with the same stone flags as the rest of the house, and arching oak beams meeting high in the roof. Ava stood, one hand braced on the table, waiting until Stephen stood facing her. His girlfriend (Bethan, was it?) sat carefully on a chair, her feet tucked up under her, long dark hair grazing the table top. She looked vaguely familiar, but Ava couldn't think why. It was the unusual eyes, and the mannerisms…

'All I ever wanted to ask you, was how you could just fuck off and leave me?' Stephen spat at her suddenly, his eyes blazing. 'I mean, I know it seems a bit sad, but it's all I want to know. When you've told me, you can piss off back to Los bloody Angeles.'

'Stephen!' Bethan said, reaching slender white fingers to touch his arm, but he waved her quiet protest away with a shaking hand.

Ava found she had to take a long breath before she could speak. 'I can't explain how it was, and I'm not making excuses, but I wasn't much older than you are now. Suddenly I had a baby, and I was married, and all I could think of was that I couldn't do any of it. I was failing at the most basic level. It became obvious that I needed to get out or I was going to have some kind of breakdown. I thought… I thought if that happened they would take you away and say I wasn't fit to have a child. That's how confused I was.'

'Your best friend ran away, didn't she?' Bethan put in, chewing a thumbnail thoughtfully. 'My dad told me about it. That must have been horrible. I said to Stephen it was no wonder you lost it a bit later. Anyone would, if something like that happened, and then they had a baby to look after as well.'

Ouch. Ava met her wide, innocent gaze, blocking any attempts to go down that beaten track. 'She did go, yes. I missed her terribly, and still do. But that was before I was married, and I'm not giving

33

you any excuses for what I did. I'm not saying anything I did was right, and I do know it is useless to say sorry now. I'm just trying to explain why I did it.'

Stephen's expression was still stony, and his hands were now clenched on the edge of the table, knuckles whitening. 'You never got back in touch. All these years. You know, I used to pretend Penny was my mum, until some bloody kid at school told everyone I'd been left by my real mum. How do you think that felt?'

Struggling to control her hammering heart, taking comfort in the fact that at least he was listening to her, Ava chose her words carefully. 'When I reached the States, I went back to my parents and at that point I did have a breakdown. Bethan is right, but I'll say again, I'm not here to make excuses, just give you facts. The breakdown was attributed in part to the trauma of Ellen's running away, but also to having PND. That's—'

'I know what that fucking is. Dad told me that was what was wrong with you. He's been good to you. He never slagged you off in front of me. Penny didn't either. The way they went on about you, it's like you never did anything wrong. Even Uncle Leo went on about you being this detective in Los Angeles and working on big cases.'

Uncle Leo. 'Stephen, your dad and I decided it was best that you made your own choice whether to see me, when you reached adulthood. I understand that you haven't wanted to get in contact, I really do, but please believe me when I say that I always wanted to be part of your life when I recovered.' She wanted to scream that Paul had given her no choice, but she forced the pain away. It would do no good to tell him the whole truth now, not when his eyes were dark with anger, and Paul was sitting in the next room.

'You left me as a baby. What sort of mum does that to her kid?'

Ava met his gaze, willing herself to keep her voice calm and steady. Now was probably not the best time to tell him about the

34

money she had saved for him. Everything she had earned, since she worked the bar at college, she had taken a piece out for her son. Over the years it had built into a very nice sum of money, that could be used for university, for travel, for setting up his own business... but now the time had come, and she was suddenly terribly afraid he would see it as blood money, a substitute for love and all that she was capable of.

'My dad always said you tried your best, you know, being pregnant so young.' Bethan broke the silence, sliding her hand across and stroking Stephen's arm again. She had very long, slender fingers, and dark red glossy nails.

With an effort, Ava dragged her gaze away from her son, and back to the girl. 'Sorry, Bethan, but do I know your dad?'

Stephen rolled his eyes, dragged a packet of cigarettes from his pocket, lit one and passed another to his girlfriend.

Bethan smiled. 'You were at school with my dad. His name is Huw Davis. We live down the road. Do you remember him?'

Huw's girlfriend had been pregnant the same time as Ava, but she had lived in Cadrington with her family, so they had limited contact. She remembered Huw boasting about his daughter, showing pictures on his phone of a tiny scrap, topped with a mop of black hair. Ava's mouth was dry, and a headache throbbing behind her eyes. 'I do... yes. Does he still live in Aberdyth then? I thought he went to live in Cadrington with your mother. I assumed everyone else had left too.' Christ, this was getting worse by the minute. Nobody stayed in the valleys if they could help it, but it seemed that everyone she really didn't want to ever see again was back here, waiting for her return. Ava remembered Paul comparing her with Catrin, Bethan's mother, asking why Ava couldn't cope as well as Huw's girlfriend...

'Yeah, I know.' Bethan lit her own cigarette and blew smoke across the table, her beautiful eyes narrowing. 'My mum left us, but he got a new girlfriend so he's happy enough. My brother's at uni in Glamorgan, well, he's really my half-brother, and I've got twin sisters who are six months old. Well, I suppose they're like half-sisters too, but Dad says he'll never marry Isabell.' Her chatter was strangely engaging, and she smiled at Ava, pleased at her reaction.

All these people, all these names that spun into a tangled web behind her eyes. It seemed ridiculous that she hadn't imagined the children would meet. But Huw's daughter, and her son... Ava pressed a hand to her forehead, just for a moment.

'Everything all right? Ava, did you want a beer?' Penny appeared at the doorway.

'No, I'm fine thanks,' Ava told her, swallowing hard. She really hoped she wasn't going to vomit right here in Penny's sparkling kitchen.

'We're going out,' Stephen said suddenly. 'Kai's having a party at his place.'

Penny was frowning at the cigarettes, and Ava sensed that had she not been there, her son and his girlfriend would have got a bollocking.

The teenagers slammed out of the house – Bethan smiling slightly apologetically, drifting along behind her boyfriend, and Stephen ignoring everyone. Ava made her own excuses.

'Sorry, Penny, I should probably go too. I hope I haven't made things worse, but at least he's heard it from me now,' she said carefully. A proper talk would have to come later, when there weren't so many people around. How was she going to give him the money? It had seemed like such a good idea, but now, faced with his anger... Certainly she could never tell her son about Paul's threats to expose Ellen's death because she would have to tell him the whole story. What a fucking mess, and how was she, the icy, rigidly controlled workaholic, getting into such an emotional flap?

'You're going so soon? Don't you want to have a proper chat with the boys?' Penny asked, her face unreadable.

The boys. 'No, I really must go. Jetlag catching up with me, I think.'

'Well, all right. Why don't you give me your phone number and we can arrange that catch-up? I never… well, Paul always said it was best we didn't contact you, so he never would give me your number, otherwise I might have tried to get back in contact sooner. But you knew where I was, didn't you? I suppose if you had wanted to speak to me, you would have called. But that's in the past, I've got so much to tell you now.' Penny's glass-green eyes were hopeful, but the smile was back to being a little sharp, her fingers nervously twisting her ponytail into little curls.

'Yes. Great idea, and thank you for… you know,' Ava snatched her phone out of her pocket, swapped details with Penny, and headed for the door. Again, could she tell Penny that part of her deal with Paul was never to contact Penny either? She could still remember his exact words. 'You fucked up, so make your own life and stay away from all of us. I'll give Stephen the choice when he's old enough, but don't expect miracles. That part of your life is over now, so piss off and waste someone else's time.'

Paul was calling for his wife now, asking for another drink, and she smiled apologetically at Ava before answering him, and disappearing into the living room.

Alone in the hall, Ava wanted to make a quick getaway. As she grabbed her coat the door swung open and Leo smiled out at her. His eyes had that familiar glitter of annoyance, and his mouth was stiff. 'Aren't you coming in to talk to us now, Ava? Paul's just having some more painkillers. He'll be fine after a few minutes. We need to catch up, and fifteen years is a long time. I suppose we could always play a quick game of "Spin the Bottle" to make you feel right at home.'

'Funny, aren't you?' Darting a quick glance towards the kitchen, she lowered her voice. 'Why would I want to come and have a little chat? Oh, yes, so you and Paul can take it in turns to try and wind me up. I don't think so, Leo. Grow up, the both of you.'

His expression changed and the naughtiness was back. 'That's a bit harsh. I thought we might talk about old times. I'm proud of how you turned your life around, but out of everyone, only you and me managed to get away. It proves something, doesn't it?'

'It doesn't prove anything. Fuck off, Leo.'

Ignoring her warning, he was coming closer. So close that she took a step back and came up hard against the wall. His breath was warm on her cheek, and she could smell the sourness of alcohol. One hand slid around her waist. 'I missed you, Ava.'

Horrified, Ava shoved him away and hissed back, 'And I think you must have turned stupid in your old age. Either that, or you really are still a sick bastard. Just fuck off and keep away from me, Leo!'

Leo shrugged, accepting her words, still amused, still smiling and swaying slightly from the drink. It was always like that. She argued, threw insults, and he stayed serene and got what he wanted. Well, not this time. Ava pulled on her coat, shouted goodbye and swung the iron latch on the front door. The icy air blasted in, and the darkness hid everything but her first few steps. She strode carelessly down the slippery path, sure-footed from instinct as fury drove her back out onto the hills.

Before she was quite out of earshot, his words floated after her. 'Be careful on the hill tonight, Ava, and remember to go left at the lambing pen…'

Chapter 5

Don't get me wrong, I like the kid. He's got guts, and that stubborn streak I admire. Of course, he's also got a look of Ava, which helps. He does his thing, and I do mine. Outwardly it seems like I'm doing a whole lot more, but I think I've mentioned that I'm pretty clever. I know how people tick, what they admire, and how nobody really looks that deep if they have something else to focus on.

He's just another piece on the game board. It wouldn't bother me if he had to be sacrificed at the roll of a dice. Honestly, it wouldn't.

Tonight I was up late, planning my moves, irritated to see the clock ticking onwards, killing my peace. I like the blackness of night. It excites me. Often I wonder if it is light or dark that you see when your time comes.

There are photographs up on my computer screen. This particular girl looks beautiful, and I'm sure she'll remember that night for the rest of her life. She has no idea the magic I worked later on, and the horrors I added. I imagine she'll never see the finished product, which in a way is a shame. I've turned something sick and twisted into an art form, simply by being cleverer than them all. Hollywood would welcome me with open arms if I let people know what I could do. But those people will never see that side of me.

A notification pops up on the screen, and I click to see more Instagram followers. My social media is perfection, so glossy and sexy, and fake. It's a distracting game to play, and out here in the harsh daylight people are easy to fool. Or perhaps not? Is it all a double bluff? The thought makes me sigh with pleasure.

How have I waited so long for Ava? I've been planning. It keeps me sane, and I did have one little leap across the board. I was right about Fate, and he stepped in, in a totally unexpected but totally deserving way. I landed right on the edge of a black square. The memory of his useless screams comfort me during the long hours of daylight. I watched him frantically trying to regain control, using everything he had to survive. But it was impossible, the odds were stacked against him, and when it was over I went to check, inhaling the luscious smells of blood and terror. I could almost taste it, but I couldn't linger long.

The road was lonely, but fuel spilling from his bike into the dry summer grass might cause a fire. Not that it mattered because he was gone, but I needed to be at home, waiting to hear the news. It was an accident, the diesel in the road that caused the bike to skid could have come from any tractor, any delivery lorry… or from a can in the back of my Land Rover.

I didn't enjoy that move, but when fate presents an opportunity I'd be a fool to turn it down. Still, it was never part of the game plan. My first ever kill was the same. It was rushed, and although better planned, I made mistakes. Naturally, at thirteen years old, I was a beginner, but everyone has to start somewhere. With the darkness still complete, my mind wanders back to that day…

I knew that morning before school that she had to die. It just came to me in a rush as I helped her wash and dress, chucked her shitty knickers in the bin, and made us both some breakfast. She mumbled something incoherent, and when the doctor telephoned to check on us, I was careful to say she seemed a bit better and had taken her tablets. I mentioned that I was going out with a friend after school so I wouldn't be back until about four. There was nobody else in the house that day.

Before I left the house, she had heaved herself onto the sofa, and was shouting for me to bring her cigarettes and a cup of tea. I knew she had a couple of bottles stashed under the sofa, but instead of emptying them as usual, I left everything as it was. Only the thought of freedom kept me going. I don't relish the memories of this kill. As she bled out, it was more a rush of relief so intense I nearly threw up, than any actual enjoyment. I was careful to leave the knife in her hand, and the note propped on the Welsh oak dresser.

When it was all over, I lingered in the kitchen for a full five minutes, savouring the peace I had created. Then I got to work.

Back in the present I close my game board with a sigh and walk carefully to the spotless bathroom. My footsteps are stealthy in the darkness, and the shadows leer and dance in doorways and on window ledges.

In some ways my whole life is just spent waiting for the next game, the next high. Killing is great, but the rush of playing the game is better than anything. No artificial high, no orgasm ever beats that feeling of my players moving to an unseen order, inching closer to their fates.

I flush the toilet, and head across to wash my hands. It has always been important to be very clean, I suppose a therapist might track the compulsion back to earlier childhood. I count the number of times I apply soap and lather up. After the sixth rinse, I am sated. The water gurgles away with a satisfying gasp, but there's a smear across the tap in the bathroom. Red. Is it blood? A tiny paper cut on my thumb trickles a rebellious streak of scarlet. My mind races again, scrabbling with the image, skittering back to my childhood and the day of that first kill…

As I stood in the kitchen after it was all over, staring out the

41

window, I noticed a smear of blood on an apple – spoiling the ripe, juicy perfection of the pile. There were green pears, and orange apricots too, carefully arranged in a white dish on the sunlit windowsill. The arrangement was a gift from a well-meaning, but deluded neighbour. The fruit seemed almost too bright, the colours too perfect, given what they had witnessed.

It was annoying, that smear, spoiling my view, spoiling my happiness. But whoever knew that blood could gush and spurt so far? I licked my finger thoughtfully and leant across the sink to remove the offending stain, inhaling a lungful of bleach as I did so. Cleaning had been easy – I was used to it, and had got stuck in. I'd given myself twenty minutes to finish, and the tick-tock of the yellow alarm clock had driven me on. When I was done, the house was looking like a normal home, as opposed to somewhere social services would have been called to in an instant. That's what I mean about taking time with appearances. People see what they want to see, and if you can help them along…

By the time the uniformed police officers arrived, I was sitting on the bottom step, teary-eyed and snotty. They fell for it, of course. It was the easiest thing to do. The alternative was to believe a thirteen-year-old was capable of murder. She always said I looked like butter wouldn't melt, with my charm and wide-eyed stare – well, in this case blood didn't stick either.

'Oeddet ti'n gwybod, Ava Cole?'

'Did you know, Ava Cole?'

42

Chapter 6

'Did it go well last night? I expect that boy of yours was pleased to see you?' Mrs Birtley was sitting at her little mahogany reception desk in the pink hallway as Ava passed.

Ignoring her questions, Ava zipped up her jacket, smiled and pointed to her earbuds. Luckily, like several women of her generation in the village, Mrs Birtley was not familiar with the latest technology, and clearly assumed Ava couldn't hear her. Ava was able to escape unscathed and un-interrogated into the icy air. Her friends all laughed at her fondness for country music, but alone on a run she could indulge unhindered. Thomas Rhett and Miranda Lambert filled her head as she warmed up.

The crisp beauty of the frosty hillside and the pain in her leg muscles as she ran up the steep, muddy inclines quickly drove everything else from her mind. Her lungs burned and her breath came in gasps. Despite the cold of the morning, she was soon wiping sweat from her face. The sky was spread above like a baby-blue sheet straight out of the wash, and even East Wood, down to her right, was cloaked in glittering, mystical beauty. The ugly, pebbledash houses of Aberdyth were given a sparkling makeover that turned the place into a fantasy wonderland. Forcing herself not to consider what lay beneath the frosty charade, Ava paused at the top of the hill, glancing at her watch. Twenty minutes for a 5km. Not bad, despite the jet lag and the hills.

Her phone vibrated, and she checked it out of habit. But it wasn't her friends back home, her mom, or even her on-off boyfriend who she hadn't checked in with yet.

'*Cofiwch fi*'

'**Remember me**'

'Oh fuck *off*, Leo!' she said out loud. She didn't doubt it was him. When the messages had first started coming she had been shocked, even scared, thinking that the horrors of her past had finally caught up with her. There had been no question the messages were related to Ellen. Only seven people knew about the carved letters on the oak trunk. Only seven people in the entire world knew exactly how much it would rattle her to get a message like that. It was more than a shadow across the sunny beach – the darkness she kept locked away had started to seep into her carefully constructed life.

Safe on her icy hilltop she allowed her mind to drift back to the first message. That had been a hell of a night shift, starting with Paul's email of course. Her regular partner, Pete, had noticed her lack of attention on their first shout.

* * *

Pete slammed the car door. 'Coffee and doughnuts?'

'Please. I'm going to stay out here for a bit. I just need some fresh air.'

'Fresh air down here? You sick? If you aren't feeling well, go home and sleep it off. You do realise you just ran a red light back there?'

'I'm fine. Three doughnuts and black with two sugars please!'

She could tell he wasn't fooled for an instant – with all the smog, fresh air in LA was a joke unless you were hiking in the hills. For a moment she was tempted to bail out and go home to an empty apartment. Darkness was sneaking in from the sea, the long black fingers of shadow triggering the familiar slash of neon lights slicing along the streets. Shouts and music mingled with the smell of fries and vomit and the hot air curled around her like a snake, oppressive and threatening.

As Pete shrugged and shambled off in search of food, Ava's phone pinged again. She dragged it out, stared at the screen, and instinctively found her hand on her gun holster.

No name in the sender box, and just two words:

Cofiwch fi?

Remember me?

* * *

Coming back from the farm last night, she'd taken a long time to get to sleep. In the end, she'd downed a couple of glasses of duty-free whisky. There was no ice at the B&B unless you counted the frozen trough outside the front door, so she drank it straight, with a dash of water from the tap. The comforting smoothness of the alcohol had knocked her out for a good eight hours. So now what? She had three weeks' leave to hang around Aberdyth, to get to know her son, and she supposed, to say goodbye to her ex-husband. To talk to Ellen's parents… and what could she really do but offer comfort again? She could never tell the truth about Ellen's death, but now she was an adult, it would be good to offer something more. Perhaps elaborate on Ellen's reasons for going, and make it sound like she was definitely heading off on a big adventure. That would give them hope that their daughter was somewhere, living her best life. But it would also be cruel to give them false hope. How did you make something right, when it was all wrong?

From this height she could see all the way to Big Water. Her gaze sharpened as she spotted figures scurrying like ants at the water's edge. The early sunlight caught flashes of metal or mirrors, and a few more trucks were pulling up next to a copse. Of course, that must be Leo's film crew. He'd mentioned they were filming for *Tough Love* up there.

After a few more calf stretches, she jogged slowly back down to the Birtleys', dodging a couple of flocks of sheep, seeing nobody else but a pair of hikers in the distance. She already missed the beach and her surfboard, the sweaty little gym where she did kickboxing a couple of times a week, and even her job. It was hell having to leave an open case, but her boss had been very understanding, and promised to keep her updated. Exercise always helped in times of stress. So here, with no gym, no sparring partners, and no icy waves, she would need to run off her emotions.

She had just jumped in the shower back at the B&B when her phone rang. Swearing, she leant out, across to the pink bath top and grabbed her mobile.

'Hallo, Ava. I hope you slept well. It's Penny… I just wondered if you'd like to come down to the pub later for some dinner?' Her voice was eager and girlish, but that hint of sharpness still played at the edges of her lilt.

Shit. It was not what she wanted to do but – 'Yes, Penny, that would be great. I… is Stephen around today?'

'Okay. If you get there for about five, we can have a few glasses of wine, and a good chat before the boys arrive. Stephen and Bethan are staying at Kai's house tonight, but they have promised to join us for a meal.'

'Kai?' queried Ava, trying unsuccessfully to reach the pink fluffy towel on the wash basin, whilst continuing her conversation.

'Oh, I forgot you probably wouldn't remember. He's Jesse's son. Of course, Jesse went off to stay with relations in Yorkshire after we left school, didn't he, and stayed up there when his girlfriend got pregnant, so you probably never met Kelly. They came back here eventually though – after you'd left. Did you hear Jesse was killed in a motorbike accident a few years ago? So it's

46

just Kelly and the boy now. Kai is a nice lad, and he works bloody hard. I think he wants to go to university, or take a year out travelling in Asia. Sounds great, I wish I'd gone travelling at his age, and got out of Aberdyth.'

'Oh, I'm sorry about Jesse… I didn't know,' Ava wondered if Penny was aware of the coolness of her words. Just another baby, just another friend gone. There were other ways out of Aberdyth. And Jesse was dead. Why had her aunt not told her? Why had Paul never mentioned it? 'When exactly did Jesse die, Pen?'

'I told you, about two years ago. It was in June, I think,' Penny chattered on, and Ava could hear sounds of washing up in the background. 'We did think of telling you, but Paul said you wouldn't want to be bothered with things from your old life, you know? Your aunt had moved away by then, and we hadn't heard from you in ages. Jesse, well, he always did ride crazy fast, didn't he? They said he lost control on the bend. You know that sharp corner before the speed limit sign – right before you come to the Aberdyth bridge?'

'Yes… yes, I remember it. Poor Jesse.'

'Yes, it was terrible for his parents. I've got some really exciting news about Stephen and Bethan though! We've known for a while now, but we wanted you to get settled in a bit before we told you.'

'Tell me she isn't pregnant,' Ava said warily.

There was a pause before Penny giggled. 'Of course not you dafty, something far better.'

'Are you going to tell me, then?'

'No, this is one I'm saving for when we're all together. See you later.'

'Okay, Pen, I'll see you later,' Ava said. Penny had always loved to be ahead on the gossip, and surely this must be something good, or she would have sounded worried. Maybe a surprise party or something, or one of the kids getting a new job. With a jolt she realised that very soon her son would be moving on, and she had no idea where he would be going. All her stalking on social media told her simply that he had a talent for photography, and a lot of friends. He would have dreams that she hadn't shared in, hopes and worries that she wasn't part of.

'You still there, Ava? See you in the pub, lovely.'

Ending her call, she finished her shower, ignored a load of messages from her friends in LA, and sat on her bed, wrapped in a towel. Fair-haired Jesse, with his rosy cheeks and snub nose, had been part of Leo's band of friends. Like Rhodri, he'd been a bit of an outsider. Also like Rhodri, he'd been part of the gang who were in East Wood the night her best friend died.

Forcing herself to breathe deeply, Ava knew what she had to do next. Ellen's house. It was still hers, even though she lay in the cold woodland down the hill.

The mirror on her wall caught her as she turned to chuck the phone back onto the table. The pink towel slid downwards, exposing the intricate ink work across her lower back. Although the flowers and sun (so innocent and pretty), stretched down to the curves at the top of her butt, she knew that underneath were two words. Leo had done it himself, and when she screamed with pain, he'd given her more pills. She remembered frantically shaking, scrabbling with sweaty fingers for the drugs he held out. The words on her back weren't inked either – they were twisted white scars etched into her skin with a sharp knife. At the time she had wanted the pain, wanted to be indelibly marked, scarred in a way she would never forget. It felt like the least she could do for Ellen. Leo had offered to do the job, and the others had watched.

It was a miracle she had managed to get out of Aberdyth at all. Horrified by her pregnancy and impending hasty marriage, her parents had moved back to Florida before Stephen was even born. Their bleak hilltop caravan park had finally gone bust, and they offered to take Ava with them. There was no need for her to marry Paul, they said, when she could return to America and have their help in raising the baby. When she refused, to her surprise, they went anyway. It left her with no ties, apart from those she subsequently created for herself. Ava often wondered what life would have been like if she had gone then, but she had been carried away by the idea of marrying Paul, raising her child, trying to prove she was an independent adult. To an outsider, it was laughable, the mistakes she had made. Except it wasn't funny at all. She had made so many wrong turns, and that, perhaps, was one of the reasons she was so good at dealing with the victims and perpetrators at work. Often the dealers were just kids who'd made bad choices, who were desperate to escape poverty, and who had been promised wealth and freedom. The real evil players were those who traded on those dreams.

Ava reached for her iPad, quickly checking emails, grasping for the return of her cool efficiency. Work always did this to her. She was like a machine, her boss often said. There was nothing new on the handful of cases she was personally connected with, and no progress on her current job. There was a suggestion from Pete, her partner, that she might have to send someone in undercover to crack that particular drugs ring.

Her own drug-taking had stopped when she discovered she was pregnant, so teenage-Ava couldn't have been all bad, she told herself. But those years had taken a vicious toll on her mental health, and being a young mum pushed her nearer the edge, until finally, she saw that the only thing to do was to run. When Stephen was nearly two years old, she had kissed him goodnight for last time, scrabbling to drag her backpack from the wardrobe. The devils that whispered in her ears told her to go, to go now or she might hurt her son. She had failed as a wife and mother, and they would be better off without her. Her son cried, and she soothed him back to sleep, driven by a teeth-chattering panic. Before Paul came back off the hills, she was gone, leaving nothing but a brief note. Paul's dad was in his study, and she sometimes wondered afterwards if he heard her go. Good riddance would have been his attitude, she knew.

If the drugs hadn't been so easily available throughout their early teens, she doubted any of them would have bothered. Aberdyth was a desolate village between two hills, and the nearest town was a bus ride away. Even then it was another ex-mining community, dragged down by lack of jobs, and lack of money.

Maybe she and her friends might have dabbled a little on rare nights out in the city, certainly they would have smoked and drunk. But to have pills handed out like bags of sweeties...

It was a joke really, she always thought, that so many of her current friends claimed to be in therapy for this and that, but her own monthly sessions really did keep her sane. Hell, after everything that had happened, she was allowed a little craziness, and in LA she fit right in.

She chucked her iPad back down on the bed. Combing out her long, wet hair, Ava blasted it with a dryer, and plaited it neatly out of her face. Her dark, shiny fringe was cut just above the arctic blue eyes and framed the determined face in the mirror. Her dad always said there was Native American blood in the family, and her darker skin colour, high cheekbones and full lips made her a dead ringer for her paternal grandmother. Maturity had added stubbornness to her square chin, and the year-round tan added warmth to her smile, but some darkness in her expression kept most people away – men included. Detective Ava Cole was tough, independent and athletic, and that was just how she liked it.

She yanked on her jeans and hill boots. The Birtleys were out and the house was quiet as she slipped out of the front door. A few battered trucks and a mud-plastered Land Rover decorated the track downhill. She turned the corner and marched briskly past the pub, ready to ignore anyone who challenged her. There was only a dog to watch her progress. It was a shabby, red-coated mongrel, and its half-hearted bark didn't bring anyone running.

Breathing fast, eyes down, Ava reached the garden gate, and stopped. Her throat was tight and her eyes stung. She needed to get a grip.

Ellen's place was the same as it always had been, up on the end of the row of houses, just above the wood. The garden, even in early spring, was well tended and neat. She smiled as she recognised the greenhouse, the garden gnome, and then pushed down the acidic swell of nausea as she also recognised the little wooden gate at the end of the vegetable patch. Ellen's shortcut to the woods. Jackie and Peter had always been stricter than the other village parents about curfew, and to their knowledge Ellen had always been home and in bed by a certain time. Unfortunately for them, but fortunately enough for her friends when they had to cover up her death, Ellen would often wait until her bedroom door was closed, slip out of the window, and run down behind the trees into the East Wood.

The front door opened, and Ava clenched her hands in her woollen gloves, willing herself to walk up the path, pinning a smile on her face.

'I knew you'd come. As soon as I heard that you were coming back, I knew you'd come down and see us.' Jackie Smith reached out her arms. Ellen's mum.

Her face was older than her fifty odd years, and her hair had gone white. But despite, or maybe because of, her lines and wrinkles, and her kind of grief-stricken serenity, Ava thought she was beautiful.

'I'm sorry I couldn't stay in touch,' she almost whispered, submitting to the warm, scented embrace.

'*Cariad*, we never expected you to. We knew why you went in the end. It wasn't having a baby that messed you up, it was Ellen's going, wasn't it?'

Ava studied Ellen's dad, Peter, carefully. He was bald now, which gave his dark eyes and beaky nose the look of a ferocious bird of prey. As always, she had been handed a cup of tea and some *bara brith* and settled down on the sofa. She could tell, just by looking around, that there would be no lodger, and the lights in Ellen's room were still for her.

After a bit of chat Ava carefully sidled around the subject. 'Do you think you'll stay here? I mean, my mum and dad keep on about you moving out to live on the Keys with them... I wasn't sure if that was just my dad being bossy as usual.'

Jackie and her husband exchanged glances, and she was the one who spoke. 'Actually, we are moving. Not to Florida, but to England. I must tell you, *cariad*, we decided this when we heard you were coming back. The thing that keeps us – it sounds so stupid when I say it aloud – but we never believed that Ellen ran away. To have kept silent all these years. She just wouldn't. Your parents agree that she would at least have contacted you, Ava. The two of you were like sisters. But the police never bothered to look too hard, did they, and we hoped for so many years she would just come back. Then, Jesse – you know he was killed in a motorbike accident?'

Ava nodded, heart pounding, and a trickle of sweat edging down her backbone and along her hairline.

'Jesse was a nice boy, and he always liked Ellen, didn't he?' Peter looked at Ava with Ellen's eyes. The almond shape, with long lashes, were almost too pretty for a man, but luckily the rest of his face was masculine enough. The eagle image persisted.

'Yes... What... what did Jesse say?'

'We were having a drink one night, and he brought the subject up himself. Actually, I tell you how it happened. He had been doing some course online, graphic design I think it was – wasn't it, Peter?'

Her husband nodded, and carried on carefully sipping his tea, quietly observing both Ava and his wife.

'Anyway, he had been offered a job in Glasgow, and we talked about leaving Aberdyth. I think I mentioned that we couldn't leave until we found out what had happened to Ellen, and he took it very badly. Said he had the same trouble, but he was going to put it right, and then we could all leave.'

Peter turned to his wife. 'And those were his exact words, weren't they, Jackie? We didn't know quite what to say to him after that, but of course we tried to question him when he had calmed down a little.'

She nodded, lips trembling a little. 'He said that… he said that he had proof of where Ellen was, but he needed to check something…'

'Wasn't it he needed to check with someone? I'm sure that's what he said,' Peter put in suddenly, his voice sharp.

His wife waved his comment away. 'Do you think so? Doesn't matter, anyway, because it never happened. Of course, after he said it we questioned him a bit more, but he left straight away, practically ran right out into the darkness. Peter went after him, but he headed down to East Wood, and disappeared. Perhaps he had been drinking before he came to see us, because he seemed very unsteady on his feet. All I can remember clearly is him rushing out, shouting that he needed to do something, or check with someone, but he would tell us tomorrow.'

'Did you speak to him later at all, or try his house?' Ava asked, annoyed that her voice came out husky. She cleared her throat and reached for her cup of tea, trying to calm her pounding heart. 'Did he mention what his "proof" was? Did he give any hint of where she was?'

'We weren't sure. There have been a lot of people trying to tell us things about Ellen over the years, but Jesse… We wondered if he really had found something, so naturally, yes, we telephoned him that night, and Peter even went over to his house. As soon as it was morning, we phoned again, but there was no answer. He was living with his cousins and his girlfriend, and they said he took his bike out as soon as it was light. I telephoned the police as well, after what Jesse said, but it is such an old case, and I had nothing to tell them other than a drunken boy's claim to know something. I can't blame them for not following up on it.'

Ava could hardly breathe, and her fingers were clenched so tightly around the china cup that her knuckles shone white. 'Then what happened?'

Jackie was shaking her head, eyes bright. 'Well, they didn't find him until the afternoon, but by then of course, it was too late. It's such a lonely road, and apparently there had been a diesel leak from another vehicle that made him skid. He was dead. It was a couple of years ago now. I went up to Glasgow, to speak to the people who offered him the job, and he'd already rented a flat...'

'You wondered if Ellen was in Glasgow, and that Jesse had found a trace of her?'

'Yes. But it was a dead end. Just like all the others. The only copper who took a bit of notice was one of the team who dealt with Ellen's disappearance. Sophie Miles. She's a Detective Inspector working with the Major Crime Team down at Cadrington now, and she was very interested, but eventually admitted there was nothing to pursue.'

'When we heard that you were coming home, we knew that it was our last chance. You saw her before she left, and she gave you that letter. It sounded so simple, that she was going to live a little, travel and meet new people, and we needn't worry, but the police were never convinced, and neither were we. There was no catalyst for it, was there, *cariad*?' Peter smiled benevolently at Ava, but his voice seemed to be echoing down a tunnel as she fought to get a grip on her emotions. This was far worse than she had imagined, far worse even, than the questions at the time. He continued, 'But I'm sure even you must have wondered if she really went, or if something else happened. Because she's never been in touch with you either, has she?'

'No,' Ava whispered. 'No, she hasn't been in touch.'

'We knew you would have told us if she had. Ellen loved you, so if she was in trouble, even if she couldn't tell us, it would have been you she turned to. So anyway, we have hired a private investigator. He's coming down from Cardiff to stay here for a while, and I hope you won't mind if he interviews you?'

Chapter 7

People have always judged me on my appearance. I don't blame them. I mean, we are all a bit fickle like that, aren't we? We say, 'She's all right, but what's she doing with that ugly fucker?' or we assume that if you are one of the beautiful people you can't have a brain, or maybe that you can't have beauty and brains. Luckily I am one of the beautiful people. Even at school the other kids would like to be around me, share bags of sweets with me, and tell me their secrets... Stupid, stupid, because with secrets comes the power to fuck people over.

My days are filled with activity, and whilst I go about my mean-ingless tasks, I consider my players. They are ready to go now, lined up neatly in their start positions. All I need to do is roll the dice.

There's no keeping secrets in this village, which is pretty funny when you consider what I do. Nobody looks beneath the surface, do they? By midday I'm sure everyone knows what Jackie and Peter have done. I make it my business to find things out. I was a bit shocked when I first heard, and then I wanted to laugh out loud. The presence of this pathetic private investigator merely adds another thrill to the mix. He arrives tomorrow and I really can't wait to meet him. He'll be staying at the Birtleys' with Ava. The irony of this makes me smile to myself.

My phone pings with a message, and without thinking I tap out a genial reply. I also take another phone out of a drawer, and quickly, while I think of it, send a message to someone else.

Cofiwch fi

Remember me

I wish I'd thought of this years ago, but in retrospect maybe now is when it all comes together. This was meant to happen, and I am in total control of the blood rush that will inevitably follow. I chuck the phone back with a dozen more I bought especially for this purpose.

I check my emails, logging quickly into my secret accounts, adding a few pictures to my regular forums. Of course, I always hide my true identity, using the latest software to cloak and mask my addresses, my names. In most cases, depending on the customer, I am neither male nor female – a nameless, faceless entity, but a powerful one. People rely on me to deliver what they crave. I have rich customers, young, old and male and female. They all share that same dangerous taste, and they all know I deliver for their delectation.

I knew it would be a while before I got some new pictures, so I've been stringing these out. She has long dark hair, and a full, curvy body. I went into town, hunting, with the venue and guests all arranged. Behind the screen I can do anything, as can my guests. The questions and requests all come at an alarming speed during my parties, and I enjoy the challenge of fulfilling them. This time, as we talked, I felt that throb of excitement. She was the one. My own body fizzed with energy, and suddenly I was back in a world of bright colours and endless possibilities. She would never have considered me a threat, because that would be laughable, so we chatted for long enough for me to know what I would do with her. It's important to know what they enjoy, and what will bring them to the edge of that hellslide. It is always a risk, but luckily, occasionally, there are others who are willing to take risks for me. They also have to hide their predilections from the world. I am lucky to have cultivated such contacts. I do it for the money and the thrill, they do it because they have to. It is their obsession, their sickening guilty pleasure, and I have them all hooked. When I play a game like that, every sticker-fingered invite is treasured, and every payment is made promptly.

I fed them fit to bursting with the pictures of her dusty bare legs, and pink painted toenails. It was business of course, but still worth it for the fun and the money. She was sprawled across the floor, brown eyes dull and glazed with defeat. The dark, glossy hair, that attracted me earlier that evening, was now greasy with sweat. I watched the blood pool, and dipped a fingertip into the gooey redness. It was pleasant on my tongue, but missing that special sweetness that comes with reality.

My clients believe what they see, because they want to, but for the two of us, in our little hotel room, it is all mirrors and smoke. I paid her well, but for me, she wasn't special. She asked for my number, and I gave her a fake card.

I would never contact her.

We both knew it.

I drift back to a type of reality, and open a drawer, considering the line of keys inside, neatly labelled. Nearly time to make my next move.

Mrs Birtley has always been too polite to say what she really thinks of me, so she was happy to let me in for a chat. She's a boring, jumped-up bitch, but as she scurried off to get the cake, it was simple to snag the spare keys off her rack. I copied them, and slipped them back the next day when I delivered that history book she wanted. I always try to plan ahead for the big games.

Now Ava occupies one of the rooms and the private investigator hired by the poor, deluded Smiths will soon be snug in the same building. It's time to start playing. I should feel a little sadness that this is the last time, but instead I am overwhelmed with excitement. I need to keep up appearances, so I give my face a quick wash to get rid of that sheen of sweat, drying it with a soft towel. See what this does to me?

There are voices outside, so before anyone else can disturb me, I lean down to the cupboard, and take out the board. Drawing a long breath, I shake the two dice in my right fist, pause to kiss my bunched fingers, and release the dotted cubes.

They fall with a clatter, soothing my thundering heart, as they have so many times before. A double six. Of course, it would be. I pick up Ava's piece, caressing the wooden curves as though it was her flesh, and move her out onto the board.

'*Wyt ti'n barod, Ava Cole?*'

'**Are you ready, Ava Cole?**'

Chapter 8

When Ava walked into the pub later that evening, she stopped conversations and drew stares. The chatter resumed almost immediately, but she could feel many eyes upon her. It was like being the new kid at school, but far worse. Ellen was everywhere – laughing at the bar, downing shots at that corner table, sneaking out to the toilets with a bag of pills… Everything and nothing had changed. She was an hour late, missing out on Penny's invitation to chat before the others arrived.

'What are you drinking, love?' Rhodri was beaming from a large table set for eight. He was sitting next to her ex-husband, who stared down into his pint, ignoring her. His square face was set and sullen, a good-looking playground bully who had never grown up. Penny, her blonde hair a shimmer of silk tonight, was on his right, and Leo was draped casually over the bench seat on the other side of the table, glass in hand.

'Hi, Ava. You're really late. Is everything okay?' Penny seemed genuinely concerned, but Leo had that annoying smirk that said he was up to mischief.

'I said to Pen just now, that you'd probably be late. Some things never change, do they?'

Rhodri laughed, and even Paul cracked a smile. They watched

her like a pack of wolves, bound by their secrets, scenting that she might cause trouble. She was back to being the outsider from America, a face that didn't fit.

'I'm fine, thanks. Just had to answer a few emails from home. I share an apartment with some friends, and they wanted to catch up.' She spoke without thinking, but noticed something change in their faces. Was it relief? Hell, what were they expecting her to do?

'Must be hard not having your own place,' Leo said. 'Sounds a bit like student accommodation. I hated sharing when I was at uni.'

Fuck, it really was like a school reunion. Bubbles of hysteria rose in her throat, and she took a quick breath, trying to control the slamming of her heart. 'I'll get a round. What does everyone want?' Ava said, crossing the sticky carpet, and slamming her money on the bar with unnecessary force. Could it get any worse? She decided it probably could. After all, Stephen was missing, and if they were going for a full reunion, Huw and Jesse should have been present too. Except Jesse was out of it now – released from whatever torment he had been going through. And surely he must have struggled, as she had, with the memories.

She ordered the drinks and waited whilst the sour-faced bloke behind the bar made a big show of loading up the tray. Jesse had been a nice kid, obsessed with his football and his movies. Why would he rock the boat? He'd been right there at the scene of the crime, hunkered down there in the woods, black hood pulled down over his thin face. Rhodri had been right next to him when they started the game, the firelight making ghostly patterns on the ground as he offered round the grubby cloth bag. He had been as obsessed as anyone with their game. 'True Lies' was an extension of the old favourite, 'Spin the Bottle', and they had pushed it to the limit. That night, it had been Ellen's name picked out of the scrunched pile of paper slips in the bag.

Then Leo's as 'The Liar', and finally Ava, who had to discern the truth to save her friend from paying a forfeit. It had been her fault. Whatever she told herself, it had been her choice, her answer that made Ellen do that dare. She could still hear Leo's mocking voice, even after all these years…

* * *

'You're wrong, Ava. Now you know what has to happen.'

She felt his breath hot on her cheek, fingers on her chin, turning her face towards him, and his lips on hers for a brief, hard kiss. Just for a second she tried to pull away, but the grip tightened painfully.

'Leo, I don't want any more tonight.'

A girl's voice floated down through the oak wood, calling her name, and Ava struggled again.

'She's coming now, Ava, and just remember, this is your fault. "True Lies" is for real.' Huw was leaning over her too, his face livid and twisted in the flames, voice thickening with excitement.

'Ellen, down here! We're by the picnic tables… Ellen…' Ava's own voice was shaky, and someone pinched her arm hard. Her brain was fuddled by the drugs, and she knew something bad was going to happen. The blackness was coming in waves now. It was a familiar feeling. Desperately, she dragged at Leo's arm, but he pushed her down onto the mud and the leaves. He was gentle now, hands lingering on her body. Her eyes were still open, and she strained to see, to speak again…

Ellen appeared now, picking her way carefully along the grassy path. She raised one arm, grabbing a low branch to help her up the slope. Her long hair was caught up in a high ponytail, and one wrist was covered with multi-coloured layers of plaited friendship bracelets, 'Sorry I'm late… Oh, did you start without me? Shit, that's half the vodka gone already, you greedy pigs.'

Ava raised herself on one elbow. 'Ellen, I'm sorry—'

Before she could say anything else, the chemicals pumping

around her bloodstream overwhelmed her, Ava closed her eyes, rolling heavily onto the leaf-strewn ground.

* * *

Ava slid onto the bench seat, trying to stay in the present, smiling at Penny, carefully avoiding Leo's arrogant blue stare.

'Isn't it lovely to have Ava back for a while?' Penny raised her glass in a determined toast. 'It's going to be so lovely catching up on all your news, Ava.'

Rhodri was already merry, and he lifted his own glass, his hand shaking slightly. '*Iechyd da!*' There was sheen of sweat on his pale face, and his eyes glittered.

It was farcical, but nobody argued with Penny, who chattered on, beaming at them all, turning the whole evening into a charming social gathering. She had always had cheerleader tendencies, Ava remembered. Blonde ponytail swinging, she was the first to stick her hand up in class. She even turned up every Saturday to cheer on the local football team.

Her Uncle Alf was the coach, so at least she got to sit in the car when the weather was bad. Ava and Ellen had waged a term-long campaign until the coach grudgingly accepted the two girls could actually play better than some of the boys, and let them come to matches as part of his 'B' team.

Leo was still watching Ava, studying her face with an intensity that made her shiver. Whatever they had done, whatever they had meant to each other, it was dead and finished. She would make sure it stayed that way. Her finger flicked across her phone screen, and she glanced down, quickly tapping out a reply to her on-off boyfriend, Joe, reassuring him she was fine. Joe, like the others before him, was fun, and their relationship was only picked up when they both had time. They surfed, drank and had great sex but that was it. There was no deeper connection. He was an out-of-work actor from Chicago, hoping for his big break, attending auditions with thousands of other hopefuls, and coming away each time a little more broken, but very little wiser. Everyone had a dream, but when were you supposed to stop chasing rainbows? In LA you could be searching for your whole life, and still wind up under the pier in Santa Monica.

'So your boss didn't mind you taking time off work then, Ava?' Paul eventually entered the conversation, grudgingly, and heavily prompted by his wife.

Ava saw how his big, scrubbed hand was marked with the scars of cannulas, veins raised like worms, as he put his pint glass back down on the table, and how his rugged, handsome face was set, jaw rigid. He had never hit her, but abuse wasn't always physical – she knew that to her cost. She felt something then, a sudden rush of pity that she knew he wouldn't want. 'No. He's a good boss.' All the questions she wanted to ask about Paul's treatment, his death, would have to wait. A crowded pub was not the place to discuss something so personal.

'Are you working on any big cases at the moment?' Rhodri asked.

Ava shook her head and took a long drink. 'Just tying up a few bits and pieces. I couldn't tell you anything even if I was, unfortunately.'

'Shame. I love those true crime documentaries on TV. I'm pretty good at guessing who's guilty.' Rhodri was smiling at her now, scratching his red curls thoughtfully.

'Really? Actually I like baking programmes. I've seen Penny's website. It looks amazing!' Ava injected just the right amount of enthusiasm into her voice, neatly swinging the subject back to them. She was genuinely impressed with her old friend's business acumen, so it wasn't hard. The pub doors banged and Ava jumped nervously, looking quickly over her shoulder for her son.

'She has done well. She's even won some awards!' Paul was smiling fondly at his wife, and Ava was pleased to see the genuine affection between them. 'Although she won't mind me sharing that it was me that taught her how to use her computer properly. I even built her website for her.'

Penny was laughing, sat right in the middle of the boys, her cheeks flushed pink with all the praise. 'It isn't just Welsh cakes, it's Welsh honey, and vegetable boxes, and the meat. Not to mention the craft items. Online is the way to go nowadays. Mrs Birtley still keeps asking when I'm going to stop messing around on my computer and open a proper shop in the village. It's weird, because I've got Miss Addley from number seventeen as a supplier for those gorgeous hand-knitted quilts, and she's been selling them on Etsy for ages, yet Mrs B, who must be ten years younger, can't even switch a computer on!'

There was laughter, real laughter, for the first time. The tension dropped a notch, and the smiles were more than just bared teeth and stiff lips.

'Stephen should be over soon,' Penny said, glancing at her watch, and then quickly at Leo and Paul. 'He and Bethan were just finishing their packing.'

'Packing?' Ava queried.

'Shall we tell her now?' Leo asked, without moving his gaze from Ava's face.

'Yes, come on. Penny wouldn't tell me the big news earlier, and I've been waiting in anticipation ever since.' Fuck, that sounded sarcastic, and she caught Paul's glare. She fidgeted with her phone again, trying to push down the instinctive reaction at the mention of her son's name – the unwelcome burst of agitation that set fiery bugs crawling in her stomach, and made her throat tight. It couldn't be worse than last night.

Rhodri leaned forward now. He smelled of beer and stale sweat, his red hair was matted, and his eyes were still too bright. 'Stephen and Bethan are taking part in Leo's show.'

'In *Tough Love*?' She wasn't sure what to think. It certainly wasn't the dramatic reveal she had been expecting. 'Why would they want to do that?'

Leo was grinning lazily at her. 'I think Bethan wants to be famous, and Stephen likes a challenge.'

'Don't you think it's exciting?' Penny asked, leaning forward eagerly. 'It's such an opportunity for both of them. After all, Leo started out as a reality show contestant, didn't you, lovely?'

'True. *Made in Wales*. It makes me cringe now. All I had to do was play to the game and pull the girls. It wasn't hard.' He grinned as his friends booed. 'Seriously, it is a great chance to make things happen, and they're both smart kids. Good-looking too. We only ever have good-looking people on the show.'

'You don't. That girl, Frannie, in your last series was an ugly cow!' Paul told him, smiling.

'Okay, we mostly have good-looking people. She worked well because she argued with everyone on the whole show. But generally beautiful people work best on camera! But if you work it the right way, it can be a stepping stone to other things. I reckon Stephen and Bethan are smart enough to have worked that out. They won't get on with the fame-hungry mob I've got lined up, but it will make great TV.' Leo slid his phone out of his pocket. 'Sorry, got to take this call.'

As Leo headed off outside, Ava sipped her drink, and tried to absorb the new information. Did it really matter? Not really. It just meant that her childhood friends were all still bound together, all doing each other favours, tied by their past, but seemingly unaffected by what had happened. Rhodri, of course seemed set on the most destructive path, but he might have done that anyway. And Jesse?

'Come on, we need to eat. Ava, what are you having?' Penny pushed the menu over, and pointed out a few dishes. 'The curry is great… or the lamb, or fish and chips?'

The drink was blurring the edges of her anxiety. 'Yeah. Curry would be fine, thanks. Shall I get some more drinks in?'

They nodded, and Leo grinned over his pint glass, 'You can still pack them away, Ava. We'll all have hangovers tomorrow morning at this rate.'

She smiled sweetly at him. 'Shall I get you a Coke instead? With a stripy straw in?' It slipped out before she could stop herself. An old shared joke, from a time when she loved to tease him. She bit her lip, furious at her mistake.

'Of course.' Amusement made his eyes gleam, and the white teeth showed under the curve of his full upper lip. Yes, still a good-looking bastard. And she wasn't going to let him get to her.

Coming back with another full tray, she found Stephen and Bethan wedged uncomfortably at her end of the table. Her son scowled at her when she congratulated them on their selection for *Tough Love*, but Bethan beamed. She was wearing a tight black wool top, and ripped jeans. Her hair cascaded wildly across her pale little face.

'I'm so excited. I can't wait to start. Dad is more excited than I am. He keeps trying to give me advice on how to get across the hills faster, and where to land after the zip line. I mean, there is only one place to land isn't there? Right in Big Water!'

'Is Huw happy you're doing the show then?' Ava was surprised. She had no say as a parent of course, but surely Huw must have some reservations about his daughter going on such an outrageous show. Although it was billed as a test of survival, a love story set in the Welsh hills, and various other tenuous claims, contestants were always fame hungry, and happy to get viewers' votes in any way they could.

'Oh yes! He's always been really supportive of my career. He drives me to modelling auditions and all that. He wants me to be famous like Leo. I will do it too…' Her face was bright with promise, and watching her, even Stephen's expression had lightened as she spoke.

Ava couldn't think of anything to say to this – being famous sounded like hell to her. She smiled tightly and took another slug of her drink. Who would want strangers watching every move you took, obsessing about what you ate, and who you were sleeping with? Plus, when you screwed up, it was front page news.

The spirits burned her throat on the way down and she choked a bit. Rhodri reached over and thumped her back. 'Cough it up, love, and then have some more.'

Ava turned awkwardly to her son. 'What are you thinking of doing after the show? Are you thinking of uni?' It was so hard to be natural and unemotional around him, when all she wanted to do was stare, to drink him in, to know every last thing about his life. She fought to keep her expression neutral, her voice cool.

Stephen met her eyes with an indifference that matched his mother's and gave a barely civil shrug, 'Maybe. I haven't decided. Kai's going travelling. I might go too…'

'You said you wanted to do media studies at Cardiff, didn't you?' Bethan said, grey-green eyes wide, her little mouth pursed.

He glared at her, and Ava searched for another subject. Her son was sitting so close she could have reached out and touched him. All the things she had wanted to say had skittered away, leaving her mind as empty and blank as a fresh sheet of paper.

'Isn't it fantastic? Let's have a toast to Stephen and Bethan's success in *Tough Love*.' Penny raised her glass again, and the others muttered and raised their own.

'I'm really sorry about Jesse,' Ava said to the group as the food arrived, steaming hot on rough white dishes. 'When Pen told me earlier, I was so shocked. I had no idea.' It was a tester, or some stray thread of instinct that made her speak, and the reaction was… interesting, Ava thought, forking up the tiniest bit of fragrant curry. There was enough on her plate to feed the whole table.

The pause in clattering cutlery and clinking glasses was sharp and shocked.

'It was such a horrible thing to happen, but he always did go too fast,' Penny sighed sadly. 'Kai and Kelly have made the best of it, though, and they've still got the house at least. The council tried to throw them out, the bastards, but they won the appeal. The local papers got involved and everything.' She was neatly unwrapping her paper napkin, and smiling at the young lad who dumped her plate of food on the table.

'I don't think you saw Kai as a baby did you, Ava? I forget what happened before you left and what was afterwards sometimes. It was so long ago,' Paul muttered without making eye contact.

There was a moment of silence as everyone around the table registered the barb. Stephen was watching his mother with narrowed eyes, waiting for her response. Ava opened her mouth but was saved by an apparently oblivious Leo.

'He was a good rider, and he knew that road like his own garden. The police reckoned it was his error at first, and they said that maybe some animal ran across the road and he swerved to avoid it. Later, they said it was a diesel spill that made him lose control.' Leo was digging into a vast forkful of flaky fish and mushy peas.

'No room for error on that corner,' Rhodri added, watching Ava as she picked at her chicken madras. 'Not hungry, love?'

'No, I mean, I am. I was just thinking about Jesse.'

'Well, don't,' Penny told her. 'It was a while ago now, and accidents do happen, don't they?'

The atmosphere was electric suddenly, and even Bethan narrowed her eyes at the adults, clearly picking up the tensions.

'Yes,' Ava agreed. 'They do. Excuse me for a moment. Are the toilets still in the same place?'

'Straight past the bar and down to your right. There's a new block too. Pub's gone up in the world,' Leo told her with a grin.

She locked herself in a cubicle and pressed her hot forehead to the coldness of the stone wall. After a long while the nausea and dizziness passed, and she was able to breathe properly again. The toilet block smelled of piss and disinfectant, and the floor was wet and sticky beneath her boots. But it was preferable to sitting with her old friends, her ex-husband, her son…

It was like being locked in a tiny box with her worst nightmares.

How could they all be so blasé about Ellen? Talk about the cliché of the elephant in the room – Ellen's presence was more like a fucking great mammoth. Her name wasn't mentioned, of course, but even Penny crassly saying how nice it was to get everyone back together, just showed how far they seemed to have come. Of course, it was such a long time ago they probably thought they were safe.

Word would have got around that Ellen's parents were going to move, and what about the PI? Nobody had mentioned him yet, but she was certain they knew, were waiting for her to bring it up in conversation. Waiting, Ava thought bitterly, to see what she was going to do. They were a pack, and she was an outsider. Their faces were just too set, eyes too bright and the laughter forced and loud. In some ways they were right, everyone had to move on. But she couldn't shake her own feeling of needing to clear her conscience.

She took a deep breath, controlling the dizziness with an effort. Once the room had steadied she headed back out past the bar, pausing for a moment to observe the group. They were deep in conversation. Stephen was pointing his fork at his dad, laughing. He was a good-looking boy, and when he smiled, she could see a trace of her own features. Or was it just wishful thinking?

Ava shrugged the thought away and sat down.

'Here you go, Paul just got you another drink.' Penny pushed a glass towards Ava, and topped up her own from a bottle of wine that now stood on the table.

Still picking at her food, mindful of Leo's body wedged close to hers on the bench seat, and her son glaring at her from across the table, Ava carried on drinking.

Chapter 9

I saw her naked last night. It was delicious and disturbing. It's such a long time since I have touched her bare skin. I'm surprised how easy it was to slip the drug into her drink, but I suppose the awkwardness of the situation put her off guard. I've done this so many times before. Usually I'm there when they wake up, and to be honest, I prefer them to know what's happening. It's more exciting. This was a bit different, and just a tiny taster of what I have planned.

Now, I'm alone in my room, reliving the thrill of last night, hugging my arms around me, and almost shivering with excitement. Will she know something happened to her, after she crept into her hard bed, or will she just dismiss it as a hangover? Will she sense where my fingers trailed across her body? My invisible prints would cover every inch of her skin. I noted a couple of new scars, the way her hips have thickened slightly with age, but she's in great physical shape, with long lean muscles, and high, firm breasts. She is still my Ava.

I could have done more, God knows, I could have done a lot more, but the last game must be played slowly and carefully, so I can savour each new move.

My visit was timed to the second, and whilst I played, I made myself constantly aware of the tick-tock of the clock on her bedside table. It took a while to get what I needed, but I am a bit of an expert at my craft, and whilst I hate to give credit, I did learn from a master.

The knife is new each time, and of course it had to be pristine and unsullied for Ava – anything else would be sacrilege. I cut very slowly, relishing the dots of scarlet springing up as the blade slid across her pale skin. I may have even panted a little as the blood became a red thread, its presence startling and out of place against the homely setting of the Birtleys' best bedroom.

Before I could stop myself, I knelt by the side of the bed, lowered my head and licked the wound. The sweet, metallic taste is always so sensual, but with Ava it was more. She was like nectar on my tongue. She is special. I was part of her, and just for a moment, I held her in my mouth. Her breathing got a little faster, almost like she recognised I was there, and I waited until she quietened again, almost holding my own breath.

Tick-tock, and I couldn't do any more that night. She is supposed to wonder, but not to know. Not yet.

Petulantly, like a child cheated out of a bag of sweets, I left my parting gift next to the obnoxious yellow bedside lamp and slipped stealthily back across the room. Two minutes, and I paused at the foot of the bed, relented, and allowed myself a final treat…

Leaning down, I felt her warm breath on my cheek, and my lips found hers. A gentle, chaste kiss, but I fought the urge to tear at her lips like a ravenous animal.

A last look and I was back at the door. The house was shadowed, quiet, and I let myself out, and walked home. The freezing air was nothing to me, and elation warmed my blood. I hurried back, eager to move my player along to the next square.

The hill is always an effort, but I paused at the halfway point to admire the shadows, the dips of blackness where the evil things dwell, and the eerie moonlight that turns the Big Water into crumpled paper.

Now, with a few stolen moments alone, I can relive my night, before I face the world of normality. My game face is back on, and I'm ready for our next meeting.

'*Wnaethoch chi gysgu'n dda neithiwr, Ava Cole?*'

'**Did you sleep well last night, Ava Cole?**'

Chapter 10

Ava woke late, her sleep-bugged eyes struggling to focus on the clock next to her bed. How the hell was it past nine? Even with jetlag kicking in, she was never up this late. She groaned, pushing down nausea, her limbs heavy and a grinding headache pushing at the base of her skull.

Surely she hadn't drunk that much last night, but the memories were blurred, and there was a strange gap after she left the pub. A gap that lasted until a few seconds ago. She was too confused for fear, but alarm sent electric shocks spinning across her painful head. She remembered this feeling, or something like it. It was almost as if...

She blinked hard and reached for the glass of water on the bedside table. As her eyes focused, her hand froze, fingers outstretched but motionless. Among the random personal objects she had unpacked, was something new. A plaited cotton band, made up of three colours; purple, blue and gold. The band was faded, and slightly crumpled, but Ava knew it immediately. The laughter was loud in her head, the sun hot on her face...

* * *

73

'Make me one now!' Ellen threw the bag of cotton at Ava. 'Please. It can be a special one.'

'You've already got loads of friendship bracelets.' Ava laughed at her best friend's intense expression.

'This one would be the most special because you will have made it. All these' – she indicated her skinny wrists, which were loaded with cheap bracelets – leather, metal and fabric – 'were bought from the market. Please, Ava. Look, purple, blue and gold, like the football shirts Coach Thomas is totally going to let us have!'

'Okay, I'll do it. But he is not going to let us play in the match next weekend.'

'He is!' Ellen was triumphant. 'Penny said she'd have a word after school on Wednesday if he was in a good mood, and then he phoned my mum last night to say we're playing. He's picked Huw as Captain too, so that's another hot boy to look at.'

'Bloody hell. And Coach Thomas is not a "hot boy", he's all grown-up. You haven't got a chance there.' Ava deftly twisted the cotton, entwining the colours quickly, and knotting the ends. She was absorbed in her task, head bent, long dark hair hiding her face. 'I wonder how Pen managed that. She should be here soon. She said her uncle had a few jobs for her, but then she'd be down.'

'Great.' But Ellen's voice was slightly dismissive.

Ava looked up sharply. 'What?'

'Oh, nothing. Does she always have to come with us? I love Pen, you know I do, but she can be so happy about everything, like all the time. I mean, is she ever in a bad mood?'

'Not everyone's a grumpy cow like you. I thought you liked her?'

'I told you, I do, it's just that she always seems to be tagging along.'

Ava peered at her friend. 'Or could it be that you're pissed she got off with Jesse last week? We all just had too much to drink. He prefers you.'

'No! Of course not…'

Ava shrugged. 'Whatever.'

'Look, Leo's coming up the hill with Jesse and Rhodri,' Ellen said suddenly.

'I'm nearly done. Come on, let's go!'

'Don't you want to see them? Leo fancies you, and okay you're right, Jesse is hot too.' Ellen smiled, stretching her legs out in the warm grass. 'Pleeeease.'

Both girls' feet were bare, and for a moment they leant back in the sunlight, admiring twenty carefully painted pink nails wriggling among the greenery. The blue sky overhead stretched across the hills into infinity, and the air was sweet with the scents of summer.

'Only for a minute,' Ava relented, her stomach churning as the boys saw them and waved. Of course, Ellen had no idea what Ava had been up to last night, or who with…

* * *

Ava touched the faded friendship bracelet, just her fingertips brushing the threads. Tears blurred her vision, and although her brain seemed to rattle when she swung her legs over, the fear was breaking through. Had she picked it up somewhere last night? Had someone given it to her?

She stumbled towards the bathroom, crashing clumsily into the door, as though she was still drunk. Of course she did occasionally get hammered, but not often. And she never drank whilst she was on a case. Collapsing onto the toilet, head in hands, she tried to force her brain to respond, searching frantically for any memories. The dinner, the pub, and the door closing behind her as people called their goodbyes. The air outside had been icy enough to make her gasp. Had she been holding on to someone's arm?

The nausea passed, but realising her left leg was stinging,

itching even, Ava leant down, puzzled by the long livid scratch. What the fuck had she been doing last night?

Now Mrs Birtley was rapping smartly on the door. 'Ava? Are you all right? There is a man here to see you. I've asked him to wait downstairs.'

'What? To see me?' The pink bathroom was spinning slowly again, a vanilla-scented nightmare that prodded at Ava's unsettled stomach.

'Ava!'

She gathered herself, flushed the toilet and hung on to the sink for dear life. 'I'm fine, Mrs Birtley. Who... who did you say was here to see me?'

Ava could hear the note of malicious excitement in the older woman's voice. 'He's a Mr Jennington, and he says he's the private investigator Jackie and Peter hired. Apparently you agreed to speak with him yesterday. He's a lovely man, and we've already had a chat, so no hurry for you to get yourself down, if you've been having a lie-in.'

Fuck, the Smiths and their investigations – she'd totally forgotten. But had she really said today? 'I'll be right down... Tell him... I just need to get dressed, please Mrs Birtley.'

As soon as the footsteps tapped away, Ava heaved into the pink toilet, throat burning with bile, coughing and groaning.

Twenty minutes later she was showered and dressed, pale but controlled, and ready to face Mr Jennington. She hadn't even formulated a proper plan, beyond trying to persuade Ellen's parents that their daughter really had run away. Was this a sign she could do more? Short of telling the truth, which after all these years she had no right to do, it was hard to see what else could happen. But her mind was still foggy, and her steps were too careful. What had happened last night?

He was younger than she expected, and immaculately dressed in yellow cords and a bottle green jumper. A tweed jacket hung over one of the chairs and a leather satchel was open on the wooden floor. PIs were a bit of a wildcard. She'd worked with good ones, and shit ones. There were a lot of ex-cons and a lot of ex-cops. It didn't always make for a great mix on a case. Fingers crossed Ellen's parents hadn't hired a lemon. Or maybe fingers crossed they had?

'Miss Cole, thank you for agreeing to meet me.' He rose from his chair, to shake hands. 'I'm Alex Jennington. I understand you're with the LAPD?'

His face was thin and pale, grey eyes small, like hard pebbles. Although he smiled, there was no warmth in his tone or expression. He had a slightly upper-class English accent. Shiny shoes, too.

Ava sighed. 'No problem. I'm not sure if I actually fixed a time, but as you're here… Like I said to Ellen's parents, I'm not sure how I can help. Everything I know was said at the time. Sorry, I was meeting up with old friends last night, and we had a few too many. I feel like death this morning.' She returned his smile with a cold one of her own.

'Well… oh, thank you, Mrs Birtley.' This, as the landlady carefully laid a flowered plastic tray loaded with cups, teapot and a plate of biscuits onto the small table.

Ava was desperate for a coffee, and the smell of the biscuits and tea made her want to gag again. She forced the sickness down and hastily poured herself a glass of water from the pitcher on the sideboard. 'You were saying, Mr Jennington?' Out the corner of her eye, she could see Mrs Birtley lurking just outside the door, fussing around with a curtain drape.

'Call me Alex, please. If we could just run through a few questions, Detective… I assume you have no objections to me recording our conversation?'

She shook her head, coolly meeting his gaze over her water glass. '"Ava" is fine.'

'Good. I apologise in advance if any of my questions upset you.' He flicked a button and recorded the date and time.

'It's not my favourite subject, but I would be very happy if Mr and Mrs Smith were able to find closure on Ellen's disappearance. Therefore, I am happy to help you with your enquiries.' The brain fog was still there, dulling her intelligence, making her movements clumsy and uncoordinated. When she sat down, she nearly missed the chair. Something about being back in Aberdyth was interfering with her usually sharp brain. That, and the fact she was still half-pissed.

Alex looked hard at her, but didn't comment on her pathetic state. 'Good. Now in the weeks preceding Ellen's disappearance, did she seem to have any worries? Any major arguments with parents, or trouble at school that she might have confided in you, but not shared with her parents?' He was taking notes as well, pen poised to record her answer.

'None. Well, nothing that would lead to her running away.' Ava thought quickly, trying to remember what she had said all those years ago. Deny everything, tell them nothing, Huw had ordered. In their terror and grief, the girls had obeyed him, and she assumed the boys had come to their own arrangement too. 'We had a strong friendship group, with the usual occasional boyfriends.'

'Any special activities that you all shared out of school – clubs and sports?'

'Ellen and I loved sport, and the three of us – Penny was the only other girl living up this way at the time – spent most of our time together.' She made her eye contact steady, inviting confidences. Her hands were laced firmly around the water glass, in an effort to remain casual and keep her sweaty palms from shaking. But surely any odd behaviour could be explained away by the subject of the interview? She would be slightly tense at having to relive painful memories anyway. She just needed to make sure Alex Jennington had no idea how painful they were.

'Boyfriends? I know Ellen was seeing Jesse, wasn't she? Anyone else you were aware of? Perhaps she had her eye on someone she hadn't mentioned to her parents, but she might have told you about?'

'I really can't remember who was seeing who, but I do know Leo and I were an item. You're right, Jesse was very keen on Ellen, and maybe Paul and Penny, or sometimes Ellen and Rhodri if she'd had a row with Jesse... It was all fairly amicable, and never anything serious. Hell, we were young, experimenting with first kisses and all that. It was pretty innocent stuff.' She stared him down. After seeing Jackie and Peter, she had panicked all the way back to the Birtleys' that the PI would discover the truth. She dragged her thoughts together. 'Even when we left the village school and took the bus to Cadrington for secondary school, we retained our strong friendships. It was always "the Aberdyth kids" all lumped together. We liked it that way.'

'When Ellen vanished, would you say she and Jesse were still a couple?'

'Yes... I mean, it wasn't serious or anything. We were fifteen, you know what teenagers are like! It was Ellen's sixteenth the week before, actually.' Ava watched his cool expression, listened to the smooth, emotionless voice and allowed herself to wonder what he had been like at fifteen. She often played this game during interviews. It gave her an insight into the perp's mind without them knowing. But in this particular interview, it was she who was on the wrong side of the law. The nausea rose again and she reached for her water.

'Had she argued with anyone of your group in particular?'

'No. Not really. I mean we all argued occasionally. She had a right row with Huw at football, because she thought he had her playing the wrong position. He was team captain most of the time. And another with me because I forgot our kit. Nothing serious.'

The interview continued. He was methodical, and occasionally asked her to repeat herself, or asked the same question in a slightly different way. She kept ahead of him at every stage, checking her voice, her posture, her facial expression. This needed to be real, despite her current state. He was very interested in the relationship between Ellen and Jesse. Perhaps this way would be better, shifting blame onto someone who could never defend themselves. But someone who had left a girlfriend and a child. The part of her that shrank from the truth applauded this idea.

'And you last saw her after school that Friday evening?'

Ava made herself answer that one promptly and as convincingly as she could. 'Yes. She said she might come out later, but had stuff to do, so she might just see me tomorrow. Ellen gave me the letter, and I never saw her again.'

'You were the last person of your group to see her?'

'I believe so, yes. The others saw her at school, but then we usually split up for various sports clubs. Often we would meet up later in the evening, but it wasn't unusual for one or more of us to be missing. I know Jackie said previously that Ellen seemed fine, did her music practice, and spent an hour on the computer before she went to bed.'

'Finally, Ava, what do you think happened to Ellen? I think we have agreed that she would surely have made contact if she was still alive. It would be very unusual for a runaway like Ellen, with a stable background and no apparent reason for going, not to get back in touch, or even return home after all this time. Her note telling her parents she was bored and off to have a proper life, simply isn't enough. It makes one wonder what she was covering up...' His voice trailed off with the faintest hint of a question, and he closed his notebook, but kept the recorder running.

For years she had thought of what she would have liked to say, what she felt would give Jackie and Peter peace and closure. 'Of course, it has always been at the back of my mind. I was surprised, and hurt that she never contacted me, never confided in me. And I can't tell you the number of times I wished I had looked inside the damn letter, instead of stuffing it in my school bag, and forgetting about it until the next day…'

She could see the scrawled words as they had been when she wrote them, with Leo and Huw arguing about the content of the letter, and Paul adding that they should send a text from her phone to her mum, instead of writing. He was overruled, and Ava, with shaking hands helping to mask her own handwriting and focus on Ellen's, continued to form the sentences.

Mum and Dad,
It is really hard to do this, because I love you both so much,
but I need to get away. I feel like there is so much I need to
do and see, and I need to be away from Aberdyth. It's closing
in on me. I know you don't even want me to go to uni because
it's too much of an adventure, which is why I'm going like this.
Love you forever,
E xx

'You were just a child, and if there was nothing to suggest urgency when Ellen gave it to you, it is perfectly reasonable.'

'We often gave each other silly notes, and we always just put the initial of the sender on the back, and the recipient on front.' Ellen had had very distinctive writing, and Ava had always been able to copy her extravagant, looped letters easily enough.

'Your thoughts?' The man prodded softly.

She met his gaze, wide-eyed and calm. 'As we got older, we occasionally hitchhiked into Cardiff, or even just to Cadrington if the bus wasn't running. It seems a ridiculous thing to do now – three girls alone on the roads at night. We would go to a couple of clubs where the doorman didn't look too closely at IDs, and go dancing. Penny and I would get tired, but Ellen could dance all night. So, I have two theories. Firstly, I think Ellen may have met someone on one of those nights out. Someone she didn't mention for whatever reason, to either Penny or me. Perhaps he was older, or… I don't know. More than any of us, she was impatient to grow up, impatient for new experiences and excitement. She may have run away with, or to someone. Secondly, she might have had a bit of a row with Jesse, and planned to scare him by running away for a bit. Their relationship was very on and off. She was a drama queen and would have loved to cause a bit of a stir. Ellen may have tried hitchhiking on her own and run into trouble.'

Alex was shaking his head slowly. 'The police never found anyone linked to Ellen from the clubs, did they?'

'No, as I said before I went through everything with the police at the time. Every detail I could remember, I shared with them. Jesse was grilled about his relationship with her, but he didn't know any more than I did. Obviously there was no body, and no leads. I know Jackie and Peter think that the police didn't bother to look for Ellen, because she was just another runaway, but from what I remember, and obviously what I know now, I think they were very thorough. Eventually they had to close the case, simply because there was nothing to go on.'

'Quite. I agree, this certainly isn't a case of police incompetence, but you and I know that Ellen's case is unusual, for the reasons we have mentioned previously. Ava, do you think it's possible that Jesse could have killed Ellen? I appreciate this is difficult because you are so involved in this.' Alex wasn't writing now, he was drawing doodles – neat little gridded boxes over and over again.

He would have been a complete idiot not to try this line, especially after all the crumbs she had tossed during their conversation, and the Smiths' insistence that Jesse had been going to tell them something important about Ellen.

She pretended to think about this, but something just wouldn't let her go down that path. 'No. Jesse wouldn't have killed her. I agree his death may well have been suicide, and he certainly indicated to the Smiths that he knew something. But I just can't see it.'

'Even if he found out what she had planned, and intercepted her on her way out of Aberdyth?'

'Possible, but unlikely. Jesse was with us in the woods, drinking vodka and smoking until past midnight. Yes, all this was relayed to the police as well. Ellen's parents know none of us, including Ellen, were angels. We were normal teenagers. I can't see why, if Jesse did kill Ellen, he would suddenly feel the need to confess. Or if he did kill her, then where is the body?'

'Yes. And of course, if she was killed in a lovers' tiff in her home village, or surrounding countryside, then surely we might have a body by now? You know how many bodies are discovered by walkers and their dogs, or farmers ploughing fields...' He looked slightly dubious at this. 'Although I admit the terrain is pretty wild around here, and the odds would probably be against this.'

'Exactly.' Ava's mouth felt stiff, her limbs wooden. She moistened her lips and forced herself to smile at him, but Ellen's face was everywhere, as though the photographs hung around the room were not of animals and flowers, but of her best friend.

'Well, I think that's it. Thank you for your time. I have obviously made extensive enquiries and done a lot of research since the Smiths asked me to take on the case, so this really is just confirming my theories, and seeing if anything new comes up.'

'Oh. I got the impression that you were just beginning your investigation. Just out of interest, when did Peter and Jackie hire you?'

Alex frowned, glancing through his phone. 'A little over two weeks ago. Why?'

'No reason, really.' As soon as they heard that she was coming back. 'So, if you are coming to the end of your investigation, have you drawn any conclusions?' Ava sipped her water, feeling slightly better as it was obvious the interrogation was over, her stomach settling.

'A few. I'll be staying here for a couple of days, interviewing and tying up loose ends. I can tell from talking to you that we certainly agree on one aspect of the case, possibly the most important.'

She almost held her breath, but forced herself to take another sip of water, gulping down her fears, 'Which is?'

'Ellen Smith is dead, and probably has been for a number of years.'

Chapter 11

She's not perfect. Her face is too hard, and she lacks that special quality I require. The best of a bad bunch, as my mum used to say. I watched them all arriving last night, on that stupid great silver coach, the cameras capturing every grimace and giggle. As they filed into the tent I made quick assessments – the way they carried themselves, looks, height and probable fitness. She was at the back, giggling with her boyfriend, her dark hair plaited and hanging down over her shoulder blades.

It was harder because Ava is back, and I find myself comparing every girl to her, wanting a player whose life is worthy of being saved by Detective Ava Cole. But time is short, and my game has already begun.

I throw the dice and they spin across my keyboard and land on her photograph. Two and five. Her own place in the game will be limited, but she has a few squares of freedom. Will she fight for more?

The idea makes my heart beat faster. I imagine her struggling against the drug, fighting me off as she slowly regains consciousness, and the pleasure is intense.

A quick look online confirms that four people are locked in a bidding war over one of my films. Following my usual routine,

I showed a five-second snippet to entice them, and a couple of stills from near the end of the night, and then the bidding commenced.

I shut down the computer now, and leave my study. I must be quick, because I have an appointment with Alex Jennington, the private investigator. He was so polite and colourless on the phone, that I could tell I would enjoy pitting my wits against his. But what to tell him? Not the truth, but I do need him and Ellen's stupid parents out of the way.

They could ruin everything at any point, and I need to clear the way for my players. Perhaps Jesse should take the fall. I've always kept that in my back pocket, so to speak, since his death. Everyone knew Jesse and Ellen were an item. I'm quite sure her parents would not like to know they were having sex, or that I have some film hidden away of them doing just that. I could use it if I had to.

Jesse was an idiot, and he deserved to die. In fact, I think he wanted to. He came whining up from the Smiths' house, half-drunk, and told me how he needed to come clean before he left. How he couldn't leave without telling Ellen's parents the truth, and how it had been playing on his mind for so long. None of us talked about it after Ava left, but Jesse was a drip, and whilst I appreciate the other troubles he went through during his early teens, I managed to get over things, and he should have done too. He had no idea that I also knew about his slightly random relationship with Rhodri as well. I know what happened between them in the wood the night Ellen died, and he knew I was watching. It was unexpectedly exciting, and helped to confuse the players further.

I steered the conversation to a conclusion, promising to help, agreeing that we should face the others and make them see sense. Blah, blah, blah… I never would have gone along with it, of course, but I figured he'd sober up, see sense and get lost in Scotland with his girl and kid before long. End of story.

But then he started rambling on about something else that had been bothering him, and before long he was threatening to reveal another element of our childhood. Well, that certainly wasn't going to happen. Ellen was one thing, and manageable because I had a contingency plan – this was entirely another.

Before he had got halfway through his rant I knew he needed to die.

Chapter 12

When Alex Jennington had finished up, he informed Ava he would be going to interview Paul, Penny and Huw, and thanked her very nicely again for her help. Guiltily, knowing she had been lying through her teeth once again, Ava hauled her kit on and went for another freezing run. Although she had been over the questions about Ellen in her head, trying to remember what she had said to the police all those years ago, she still had a niggling feeling of unease. It was a toxic mix of guilt and frustration.

Why the hell hadn't they just come clean years ago? A load of stupid kids playing in the woods. One decision that would last forever. But the longer it went on, the more years that passed, the easier it seemed to just keep quiet. The time to speak up would have been on the night it happened. Ava remembered the bitter arguments that had ensued, and through it all the horror of Ellen's lifeless body. She could blame Huw for bullying them into keeping quiet, or Paul for threatening her later on, or even Leo for helping to plan Ellen's 'disappearance'. But deep in her heart, she knew she should have spoken up, been the one to call the police, the ambulance, gone against her friends.

Added to this was her hangover, which resolutely refused to disappear. The bracelet sat in the locked suitcase in her room. Her mind and body still felt at odds with each other. Had someone given it to her before she got back from the pub? Maybe she had picked it up somewhere… Where had she been after all that alcohol? The thought of being out of control made her gut clench with fear.

There was still a jagged tear of nothingness in her memory. There was one last clear picture she forced out. It was of her walking, slightly unsteadily home, tripping on the icy road, steadying herself on someone's arm. Who had been with her? She had a vague memory of laughing as she reached the door of the B&B, of turning to speak to… Shit, was it Leo?

Another wave of panic hit her as she jogged slowly down an incline, running shoes thudding dully on the dirt track, limbs still leaden and uncooperative. She was used to being alone, to being an independent woman, and she was always careful. Always street smart, and in control, whether she was at work, or out on the beach with friends. Despite the weakness for liquor, she never lost her edge. Until now…

The run was slow, almost unsteady, and even another hot shower afterwards didn't clear the sick, dizzy feeling. She took a pad and pen, and curled up in bed, scribbling a timeline, trying to work out what had happened, the other hand idly tapping out responses to emails as she did so. The mind fog refused to lift, and she cancelled her planned lunch with Penny.

Penny thought it was just jetlag, but added with a touch of malice, 'You were drinking a lot last night too, Ava. You should take care of yourself. Go and have a quiet afternoon, and an early night and we'll see you ready for filming tomorrow.'

'Thanks, Pen. Um… Penny, did anyone walk back with me last night?' Ava chose her words carefully, licking dry lips and pulling the thick blanket around her.

She caught the gurgle of laughter in her friend's voice. 'Don't you remember? This is just like the old days. You were a bit drunk and Leo offered to take you back to the Birtleys'. You staggered off arm in arm like a little old married couple. Ava?'

Ava hit the 'end call' button with a vicious thumb. Something had gone on last night, and somebody was playing games with her.

Leo's phone went straight to voicemail, but after cursing him she supposed there must be a lot going on with his production team, as they started the filming tomorrow. She left a sharp message, asking him to call her. Bracing herself, she also rang Stephen, hoping that she could speak to him on the pretext of wishing him luck for *Tough Love*. The phone was switched off.

Frustrated, she slid out of her cosy nest on the bed and she unpacked the supplies she had brought from home. Her phone buzzed whilst she was toasting a cinnamon bagel and making a steaming cup of coffee. Of course, she could have gone down to the local shop and stocked up, but the bagels were from Vons and the coffee from Traders – just little reminders of home to keep her grounded. The Birtleys' accommodation might be lacking a modern touch on the decor, but the room's essential plastic table of toaster, cutlery, mugs and cafetière were much appreciated.

She curled back onto her bed and scrolled down through the anonymous text messages. Who the hell was trying to mess with her mind? Rhodri had mentioned at their very first meeting that she had lost her Welsh, or something to that effect. He had seemed pretty narked about it. Could he be playing games?

Shit. This was getting really fucking stupid. Ava tried calling the number, as she had so many times before, but the phone was switched off. There was no way of tracing the number, although she had tried after that very first message. Whoever was sending these was being very careful. Probably switching off and removing the SIM card as soon as the message had been sent. Each number was different. Burn phones were impossible to trace without resources. Ava had no way of tracking where these had been purchased, checking CCTV or delivery addresses, or any of her usual avenues of inquiry. She was cursing herself for not having looked into it more when she was still at home.

Ava tried Leo again, but he still wasn't answering. She now had Penny and Rhodri's numbers, but she didn't feel like either of them would be any help. Pen was probably the most likely, but Ava hesitated to confide in her former friend. Penny had enough going on with Paul, without Ava freaking her out with random threats.

Idly, she pulled up Penny's website again. It was cleverly done, with a professional gloss that was easy to navigate. Penny herself posed on the homepage with a plate of Welsh cakes in her hands. Clearly Paul's talents extended to more than just farming. The two of them were so right for one another, as she and Paul had been so toxic.

She flicked through her emails again, trying to distract herself from her current situation, turning on the light as the early darkness swept through the valley. Her social media accounts bored her, and she didn't bother to update them half the time anyway. Things must be bad if she was scrolling through Facebook trying to occupy her mind. Distracted, she almost missed it. Her profile picture had changed, from a sunny beach photo with a gang of friends to…

'Fucking hell!' Ava was shaking. The picture quality was good, even though the light was not. It must have been taken on an iPhone. She lay naked on the Birtleys' bed, hair fanned out, eyes closed, hips twisted slightly to protect her modesty. Her breathing quickened, heart pounding viciously at her ribcage. Someone had been in her room last night, and they hadn't just left a gift.

The privacy settings had been changed on all her social media profiles, and the same vile picture appeared on all of them. Ava closed down all the accounts, quickly snapping screenshots of the profile, checking the recent postings before she did so. Nothing else had been changed, and the pictures had only been posted an hour ago. A few people had commented with a '?' and there were also some salacious comments from strangers. Her inbox had a couple of concerned messages from friends, but that was it.

Now what? She hugged her arms around her body. She was shivering, violated. There was no question someone had spiked her drink, probably with some kind of Rohypnol, sneaked into her room and photographed her whilst she was unconscious. With Ellen's bracelet and the text messages, it was pretty obvious that one of her former friends was warning her off. Ava scrolled down her contacts page, thumb lingering over a couple of numbers, deciding against them, frowning with indecision.

The obvious thing would be to go to the police. A crime had been committed, someone was threatening her. But this would lead to Ellen. There was no way she could go through a police investigation without explaining the history, and the significance of the bracelet. Ava bit her lip, running a shaking hand through her hair. She hadn't come back to confess the truth about Ellen's death, but everything seemed to be pushing her towards that particular precipice.

Alex Jennington rang at about five o'clock to confirm a couple of details. He was staying the night at the B&B, but explained he had another meeting in Cadrington later in the evening and wouldn't be back until around eleven. He had seemed very interested in Rhodri, and pressed hard on whether Rhodri and Ellen were ever in a relationship, or even if Rhodri 'had a crush on her but it wasn't reciprocated'. That was a surprising train of thought, but she had to put it to one side as a flood of text messages came in. Each text had three lines of the familiar wording.

'*Cofiwch fi*'

'**Remember me**'

She tried ringing the number immediately, but the phone was switched off as usual. She sent a text back.

'*Fuck off, Leo*'

But the text wasn't delivered.

He had walked her back, therefore, she told herself, it was most likely Leo who had spiked her drink. It was a logical, if sickening, assumption. He'd been in here, watched her, photographed her and left her Ellen's bracelet. Or were all her friends playing the same game? Perhaps, like a well-organised tag team, they had conspired against her from the very beginning. It was a sickening thought, to be up against a gang of people who had once been your friends.

Finally, as evening dragged into night, she locked her bedroom door, and wedged the table underneath the handle. She was still shaking, and despite herself, she looked again at the photographs. His hands had been on her body, stripping off her oversized T-shirt and socks, arranging her limbs. For what? To warn her off, or just because he could? Remembering the cut on her leg, she leant down and ran a gentle finger across the scab. Had she somehow fought him off, and didn't remember? Perhaps that was when she cut her leg... It didn't make sense.

In one photograph she was on her front, her tattoo clearly visible over her scars. At first she thought it was just another pervy shot of her bum, but the picture was carefully framed around her lower back. Another not-so-subtle message?

A couple of glasses of whisky later and she was down to the dregs of the bottle. She could just imagine what the locals would say if she popped down to the new Tesco Express in Empire Road tomorrow and filled her basket with bottles. She wished she hadn't sent the car back now. Perhaps someone would lend her a vehicle. Penny and Paul seemed to have plenty to choose from. She remembered the smooth, floodlit sweep of gravel, edged with a few Land Rovers and other agricultural vehicles from her first visit back to the farm. It was new since she had lived there, and more in keeping with a fancy mansion than a place full of sheep.

The darkness was oppressive, and the lights in her room were not bright enough. Ava checked the time and began scrolling through her contact list again. She would not sleep and give him another chance to find her vulnerable.

'Hi Mom.'

'Ava! How are you, honey? How are Stephen and Paul?' Her

mom was always full of high energy and non-stop chatter, but she was also pretty smart. 'Did you manage to talk to Stephen properly yet?'

'Sort of. Yeah, they're both okay. Stephen is just about speaking to me, and Paul is coping as well as you would expect. It's… tough. I want to say so much to Stephen, but I don't want to freak him out. You and Dad all right?'

'Busy with the park. Retirement isn't really retirement for your dad, is it? Have you been up to Four Winds for a poke around? I heard it was empty. Shame, for such a nice area, that there is nobody to take on a caravan park.'

'I haven't been up there yet. Mom, did you know Jackie had hired a private investigator to find out what happened to Ellen?'

She could hear a sharp intake of breath on the line, and imagined her mom fiddling with her blonde curls, the way she did when something bothered her, twisting the ends round and round with thin fingers a bit like Penny did. 'No, honey, I had no idea. I do know they want to get out of Aberdyth, and they wanted to tie up loose ends, but I didn't realise they'd hired someone. Have you spoken to him?'

'This morning. I can't add anything else to what was already said, but I hope the Smiths get what they need.' Ava heard the slight tremor in her own voice and swallowed hard.

'Is anything else bothering you? Apart from the obvious of course. Is Leo filming his TV show at the moment? He was on another magazine cover when I went to the shop this morning – one of those gossip and glitz titles so I didn't buy it. Must be very strange being that famous, but I always said he was a good-looking boy.'

'Everything is fine. Leo is filming his show as a matter of fact. He's offered Stephen and his girlfriend a chance to be in it. They start tomorrow, and I'm going to watch.' She was gabbling, and out of breath. 'Anyway, I just thought I'd check in, and let you know that everything was fine.'

'Okay, honey, if you say so, but ring anytime if you want a chat. I know this is very difficult for you. Stay strong, Ava. Remember, once this is over, you can get back to LA and your job. To where you belong.'

'I know. Bye, Mom.'

Ava ran through a few more calls, chatting to friends, listening to a rundown of the night from her work partner, Pete, who had just finished his shift. It killed a couple of hours. She sat up upright, still, propped on pillows, draped in blankets, but at some point she must have dozed off.

It was just a small noise.

Her eyes flicked open, cold fingers grasping for her weapon. Ava sat very still. Was that a scraping outside her door? Just a slight footstep maybe, but... She slid off the bed, automatically reaching for a weapon that wasn't there. The noise came again. A quick scrape, as though someone was using a tool to try and lever the door.

'Who's out there? Leo?' she snapped out, furious to find that she was shaking again.

A few moments later and the door handle moved downwards. Grabbing her phone in one hand, and the lamp in her other, Ava kicked the table out of the way. She stood well to one side and booted the door.

The door slammed open with a bang, and she flung herself at her assailant. But her hands met air and darkness, and her feet met a warm solid body. Clicking the light switch in the hallway she saw a perturbed tabby cat looking up at her. It didn't seem offended she had nearly stamped on its head, and walked purposefully into her room.

'Ava? Is everything okay?' It was Alex, the private investigator, fumbling into a brown velour dressing gown, clutching a spray deodorant in one hand.

'I... yes, thank you. Bloody cat was scratching at my door, and I thought...' She regained her breath, thankful that she was still wearing jogging bottoms and a white fleece, rather than more conventional nightwear.

'Oh. Well, that's all right then. As long as you are all right.' Alex's thin body was enveloped in the flapping dressing gown and blue pyjama bottoms that almost covered his long pale feet. He was looking at the floor now, a flush of pink touching his cheeks.

Reluctantly, Ava pushed her door wider. 'Thanks for coming to the rescue. The Birtleys probably wouldn't notice if I was murdered on the premises. Look, I've got some whisky in my room – there's not much left, but would you like a glass?'

He smiled thinly, and she thought he would refuse, but, 'That would be most welcome. Thank you.'

It was a bit awkward, being in such close proximity, but she poured them both a drink (a small one as her supplies dwindled to nothing), and perched on the bed, whilst he sat in the over-stuffed pink armchair.

'So how did your interviews go?'

'At Cadrington, or in general?'

She shrugged. 'Either. All of them. You said you only planned to stay a couple of days, so I'm thinking you probably have it all wrapped up by now.'

His lips twisted into a glimmer of a smile, and the lines around his grey eyes wrinkled briefly. 'You realise I can't tell you anything, of course, Detective Cole.'

Ava answered the smile with a genuine one of her own. 'I know. I suppose I settled on my theory years ago. There is always something about a cold case, though, especially one you are personally involved in. I still expect to get a phone call or email or something from Ellen, even though I have accepted it can't happen.'

'I'm sorry. Ava, can I ask why you were so worried about the cat in the hallway? Were you expecting someone, or were you worried by anything?'

She glared at him. 'I didn't know it was a bloody cat, or clearly I wouldn't have reacted like that. And no, I wasn't expecting anyone. It was a turn of phrase.'

'As you say…' He downed the last of his whisky, and rose from the chair. 'I'm staying until Wednesday, just a few things to summarise for my report, so I hope I'll see you again before I leave. As I said, I can't tell you too much, but, well, there aren't any surprises in my notes. I truly believe that the Smiths will be able to leave Aberdyth with the information I do have, but it isn't by any means conclusive.'

She understood what he was trying to say. 'Of course. I think they will be happy with any closure they can get, and if they feel it comes from an official source, it will be enough for them. The filming starts on *Tough Love* tomorrow, so I'll go down and a have a look.'

'Your son is going to be one of the contestants, I believe?'

'No secrets in this village, are there? Yes, he and his girlfriend have been invited along.'

'Ava, before I say goodnight, can I just ask you something?'

'Of course.'

'How well did you know Alf Thomas?'

She had to think for moment, then spoke with genuine puzzlement. 'Penny's uncle? He was a really nice bloke. He used to coach the football team. Ellen and I were the only girls in the team and he let us play in matches.'

His expression said that he already knew this. 'And he now lives in Kingsmead Residential Home?'

'Yes. It's that big old place behind the bungalows, at the bottom of the hill. I believe the land used for the new development used to be the garden. You can see it from the pub. I haven't spoken directly to Penny about it, because there hasn't been time, but I think he was diagnosed with MS quite a few years back. He lived with them at the farm for a while, until his condition advanced, and he needed round-the-clock care. Why are you interested?'

Alex shook his head. 'Background, that's all. Now two other names for you; Andrew Menzies, and Sara Blackmore. Ring any bells?'

Ava frowned. 'Mr Menzies was the old headmaster at our primary school. Nice old man, but strict as hell. The boys adored him because he let them play rugby every afternoon. He was very traditional, keen on clean hands at lunchtime, and shiny shoes, that kind of thing. Sorry, Sara Blackmore I can't recall.'

'No matter. I'm just trying to build up an accurate picture of Ellen's childhood, the key figures, the places she went, that kind of thing. Miss Blackmore is a librarian who worked on the mobile library that used to visit Aberdyth.'

She nodded. 'I do remember her now. She had short black hair and she never smiled. Oh shit, and she was the one who kept writing to the local papers about the bad behaviour of teenagers in the villages. Ellen and I loved reading, but she almost seemed to actively discourage us from borrowing anything. What connection does she have to Ellen's disappearance though?'

'None, as far as I'm aware. I'm just checking off names, building that picture. Thank you, that is very helpful. Now are you sure there isn't anything else I can help with, Ava? Look, your intruder seems to have made himself at home.' He pointed to where the cat was curled at the foot of her bed, purring loudly.

She hesitated for a second, wondering whether to confide, but shrinking from showing him the photographs, of leading a trail to Ellen's grave before she was ready. She smiled at him. 'No, I'm fine thank you.' She was pretty sure he knew she was lying.

Chapter 13

Big Water was shimmering in the early morning sun, glittering rays bouncing off the water, dancing back up the hills and across the distant icy rooftops of Aberdyth. Ava had decided to run down, as nobody had offered her a lift and she didn't feel like asking. It was only about five miles, and it helped lift her mood slightly.

There were fewer people than Ava had expected. The film crew were drinking from flasks of coffee, two trailers boasted catering and toilets, and a mobile office Portakabin sat underneath a winter-blasted oak tree.

'Ava, over here!' Penny said, waving excitedly. In her red scarf and woollen hat, with her blonde hair just peeking out around her face, she could have been twelve again. Only the lines around her eyes, and a slight hardness in her pointed face spoke of life experience that was the unwanted gift of ageing. 'Are you feeling better today?'

'Yes, I'm fine. Sorry about yesterday. As you say, just a combination of hangover and jetlag. I slept most of yesterday.' Ava scowled as Leo approached. As soon as she got him alone, she was going to interrogate him, the smug bastard. The photographs burned in her brain, and she was still jumping at every shadow after a crap night of staring at the bedroom door.

Penny gave her a quick hug. 'I'm so glad. I was worried about you!'

'She worries about everyone. I think she even tried to pack Stephen's case for him yesterday.' Paul had emerged from one of the trailers and slid a possessive arm around his wife's shoulders.

'I didn't!' Penny smacked him on the arm, but she was laughing.

'He didn't need it anyway. Look, they have to wear those coloured shirts and headbands. Stephen and Bethan are near the back.' Paul pointed to the nervous group of contestants. He was moving slowly today, as though in pain. His manner seemed to have softened slightly towards her, but Ava knew he would never take her into his confidence. That was okay too – she had hurt him and abandoned him. She had never expected anything more than a type of armed neutrality from their relationship.

Today, she had other things on her mind.

Leo waved at them, and ran over briefly. 'We're all set, so if you want to grab a drink from catering, you can watch them come down the zip line. We've got a couple of drones set up overhead, and of course cameras on the raft in the water, so you can watch on the monitors when they get out of sight.' Without waiting for an answer, he winked at them and ran back to his crew.

Ava, Paul and Penny drifted towards the coffee, and were soon clutching plastic cups. The coffee was about as good as it was back in the precinct at home, Ava thought wryly, sipping black goo, and reaching for the pink packets of sugar.

Penny slipped an arm through hers, beaming up at her. 'Isn't this great? Stephen is going to be part of *Tough Love*! I can't wait to watch him on TV when the show airs.'

Ava nodded; her tongue seemed to be glued to the roof of her mouth. She gave up on the sugar and chucked the coffee onto the icy ground. If she was completely honest, she didn't want Stephen competing in a reality show. She wanted to talk to him, get to know him, try to explain a bit more maybe. The money she had saved for him was stashed away in a separate account – it could wait until she figured out how to give it to him.

A man with a loud hailer instructed the contestants to start walking up the hill. There were fourteen of them. As always, they had been carefully chosen to appeal to different viewers, so there was a mix of body shapes, ethnic backgrounds, and fiery personalities. Ava lived in LA, she had dated actors, hell, she lived with one, and she knew that bland personalities were not welcome in reality shows.

There was some good-natured competition in the run up the hill, with a couple of the muscular boys already drawing ahead, seemingly forgetting their girlfriends. That would not look good when the public came to vote in the final. Leo was busy giving some spiel in front of the camera, in his blue *Tough Love* polo shirt. His confident, cheeky persona, the messed-up black hair and dark-blue eyes had gotten him a worldwide fan base. Ava told herself she found it sickening. A few specially selected journalists were chatting with the crew, and there were photographers dotted along the trail up the hillside. In this initial scrum for the lead, every tiny blunder, every cross word or expression would be recorded. Later, the cameras would be fewer and further between challenges, giving more chance for the contestants to relax.

One girl was already having a tantrum because her lover had left her behind. After every sob, and every flick of her long blonde hair, she peeked up to find out if the cameras were still on her. Her shirt was straining to contain her large breasts, and her fake tan had turned her an unnatural deep mahogany colour.

Ava snorted in amusement and disdain, but her eyes flicked between Leo and her son. Stephen and Bethan were in the middle of the pack, running easily side-by-side. They would have a massive advantage, being brought up in these hills. Although everyone knew *Tough Love* wasn't just about physical fitness, it was a huge part of the game.

As the first runners disappeared over the crest of the hill and into the flash of winter sunlight, Leo finished his chat and walked back over. He was crackling with energy, enthusiasm, and could have matched Penny with excitement. This was part of his appeal, Ava supposed. He was never bored, always got into the heart of the game… and the hearts of his viewers. It had made him a millionaire several times over, according to the press.

'If you watch up by that red flag on the next hill… That's where they get on the zip line. Long way down, isn't it?' Leo smiled at Ava. 'Are you feeling all right today? Sorry, I saw you tried to call but I was up to my ears with all the paperwork. Was it something important?'

A block of ice, that had nothing to do with the coldness of the day, lodged itself deep in her stomach. 'No, it wasn't that important, but I do need to talk to you later, Leo. If you've got time of course,' she added, trying to keep the anger out of her voice.

'Sure. Give me about an hour to get everyone swimming in the lake, and then I will have recorded all my bits for today. We can have lunch by the lake. It's a bit cold but there'll be some soup from the catering van.' He was unconcerned, big blue eyes wide and guileless. He moved closer. 'You look gorgeous in fitness gear; you always did have a sexy bum.'

Before Ava could retaliate, Penny stepped forward. 'Leave Ava alone, Leo. Lunch sounds lovely, though.' She beamed at them both, but her husband frowned at her. 'Oh, sorry, I mean it would be, but we need to go to a doctor's appointment at two. Paul, don't you think we might be able to just stop for lunch?'

Paul was staring at the hilltop, his eyes narrowed in the white light, face drawn and old. There was a row of beaded sweat on his forehead. 'No. Sorry, but we need to get back…' His voice was distant, almost faltering over the words.

Penny looked over, her face changing, eyes brightening, 'Of course, love.' She kissed his cheek, taking his arm in hers.

'See you later! Stephen's up there now. I just need to pop over to the office,' Leo said, resting his hand briefly on his friend's shoulder. He ran off, shouting instructions to a couple of crew members. They gave him the thumbs-up and resumed their tinkering with a couple of huge cameras.

Penny pointed at a large group of people in a cordoned-off area near the gate. 'See the boy near the front, with blonde hair and the red top? That's Kai, Jesse's son, oh and the boys to his right are Emlyn and Joshua. They're village boys too, but I don't know their parents well – they come from the estate down the hill.'

Ava studied the tall, slim Kai in his red Nike hoodie. He was leaning against the gate, looking at his mobile phone. Even allowing for the distance between them, he looked nothing like his dad. How much of his past had Jesse shared with his son? The unwelcome thought made her shiver. Did Kai know anything about Ellen's death, or her own disappearance? But if he did know, he clearly hadn't shared the truth with Stephen or Bethan. Their questions that first night at the farm had been focused on her failures as a mother. Bethan had mentioned Ellen in passing, she recalled, but without any avid curiosity.

'Bloody stupid, this whole idea,' Paul said suddenly, breathing heavily. The familiar stubborn expression had returned to his square face, and he scowled at Ava as though it was her fault. Everything, from the broken washing machine to the fact Stephen was born by emergency C-section, instead of naturally, had always been her fault.

'It's made Leo a lot of money,' Penny said mildly.

Ava got the impression it wasn't the first time they had argued about this. Herself? She supposed she admired her son for jumping in feet first. He had made no effort to contact her before the show, although Penny assured Ava that he now had her mobile number. She had hesitated to call him, but now wished she had just bloody done it. A reality show would never be her bag, but it was a tried and tested way of launching a career, so she should probably support him. 'Does Bethan really want to be a model?'

'Oh, she does! She was the one who suggested going on the show, but I don't think Stephen minds. Bethan fancies some of that cash prize, I suppose, as well as being famous for five minutes. Apparently she wants to study media or something at university, and then go into television presenting,' Penny said.

'Really? She seemed so quiet… not really the type.' Ava was surprised.

'She's Huw's daughter all right. A madam when she feels like it. But then Stephen's got an attitude on him sometimes. Just like his dad.' Penny softened the words with a wink and smile, and her husband grudgingly smiled back.

'What does Stephen want to do for a career?' Ava asked quickly. He seemed so far removed from her life, and now instead of getting to know him, she was watching him head off into the hills. She wondered how much her coming home had influenced his decision to do the show, or if it was his way of distracting himself from his dad's diagnosis. The horror of losing Paul, the man who had brought him up, must be fresh in his mind, especially as Paul's illness progressed.

'He's not sure. He's very lazy at school, but last I heard he was talking about photography and media studies. That might have been just to please Bethan though. She wants to go to Cardiff to study. I'm not sure if he really has his heart set on travelling with Kai, and Bethan certainly doesn't want him to go away,' Penny told her.

Watching the film crew working efficiently together, shouting directions, laughing and swapping jokes, made Ava long for her own team. People she could trust, and talk to with no ulterior motive, no exhausting history to be constantly bypassed. Another plastic cup of coffee, and a rubbery croissant, whiled away the time. She studied the hills, the dots that were the contestants, the drones circling overhead, and the long zip line that led onto a distant platform in the middle of Big Water.

Paul, who was standing next to Ava, suddenly turned and looked hard at her. 'You all right, Ava? You look… a bit pale? I was saying to Penny you look like you haven't slept well.' He smiled with his mouth, but his eyes remained cold. Was there a trace of amusement in the unexpectedly solicitous words?

Ava shivered. 'Fine thanks. I need to get back and have a shower soon. I probably stink after that run, and my hands are frozen.' It was hard to get a handle on Paul at the moment, and any judgement or suspicion was clouded by the fact that this was someone living out a death sentence. And the clock was ticking.

He nodded slowly and turned back to the hill, where Stephen could now be seen jostling with his fellow contestants.

Ava studied his averted profile for a moment, and then smiled at Penny, who was watching them both anxiously, clearly worried Paul would say the wrong thing. If Leo took the pictures, maybe Paul knew about them? Hell, maybe the whole group were in on it, turning against her – always the outsider coming back to stir up trouble. She could dismiss her fears as paranoia, but she was still on the other side of the fence, and their laughter, their little glances, spoke a different language.

The weather was changing. That glittering fairyland of frost and icicles was now dampened by huge grey clouds rolling in from the west. Ava shivered, stamping numb feet as the sunlight disappeared, leaving the valley gloomy and dank.

The first contestant on the zip line was a blond boy, and he made a competent descent, followed by two girls, who were equally quick, their long hair fanning out behind them as they screamed their way down to the landing platform. The row boats were tied to the raft in the middle of Big Water, and after unclipping their harness, the contestants had to row halfway to the opposite bank, before reaching another platform, putting on wetsuits and swimming the final five hundred metres to the bank.

Stephen, black hair tousled in the wind, was soon gaining on his competition, but Bethan was stuck at the top of the zip line, apparently scared to take her turn. The monitors next to them showed the girl, apparently gathering all her courage for the steep descent into Big Water. Finally, after coaxing and a few tears, she completed the challenge, hopping neatly into her rowboat, and speeding across the gloom to the next challenge.

'She was faking that,' Penny said suddenly. 'I don't think she was scared at all.'

Ava grinned. 'But she did know that all the cameras would be on her if she made a fuss. You know, I think she might be going to have a good career in the media...'

Finally, with all the contestants safely down the zip line for the first time, Leo approached Ava. 'What was it you wanted to see me about? Come on, we'll grab some lunch... Unless you want to come over to my house tonight and I'll cook you dinner?'

She stamped frozen feet and frowned at him. 'I'm not fussed about lunch, and I certainly don't want to have dinner with you.' She gave the crew a quick glance, but they were all out of earshot, jostling good-naturedly as they loaded up plates at the catering Portakabin.

'Fine. What then?' Leo's eyes narrowed, and his other hand fidgeted with his phone.

'The other night, after we had dinner at the pub – did you walk me back to the Birtleys'?'

He laughed. 'Are you embarrassed? You were a bit pissed, darling, but I was a total gent and escorted you back to the door.'

His expression was so like the teasing, confident Leo of old, she fought an urge to hit him. 'And then you went home? You didn't come in at all?'

'No! Come on, Ava, we might have had a little kiss for old times' sake...' He stopped, laughing again at her expression. 'We didn't, okay? I didn't touch you, except to stop you falling head-long into the drainage pit by the side of the road.'

Ava stared at him, anger rising again. She had been so sure... Of course, he could easily be lying. Never mind Bethan, Leo was also an excellent actor. She opened her mouth to ask him about the photos, but then closed it again. He would deny it and she would have to show him the pictures, making herself vulnerable. He would exclaim with horror, and she would kick him in the balls. Appealing though that was, she forced herself to stay calm, focused. The only way to handle this was by outwitting him.

His expression softened to concern, and his voice was gentle. 'Ava, why are you so bothered? Has something frightened you?'

'What? Why would think that, Leo?'

'You have that look. It's the one I remember from when we dated, and you would say that everything was fine, but it actually wasn't… I saw it a lot after Stephen was born, and you weren't fine at all.'

'No.'

'So tell me.'

Ava shook her head; she needed all her secrets safe, whilst she decided what to do. 'It's just the situation, you know, with Paul, and Stephen… plus I had an interview with Alex, the PI. He's a smart man, Leo, and he's pushing hard for answers. There are a lot of things that don't make sense.'

Someone was calling Leo from the office, waving a bit of paper. Leo paused, then turned quickly back to Ava. 'I know you're not telling me everything. Someone or something else is bothering you. You've got my number now, use it any time. Sorry, I've got to go…'

'Leo, just one last thing?'

'Yes?'

'Will you talk to the PI? About Ellen?'

He smiled, but she could tell it was one of his camera-smiles that he slipped into with the ease of a professional performer. 'Of course. I would like her parents to be at peace, and I would like them to leave Aberdyth.' The words were as smooth as his expression, reminding her why he was so good at his job, why he had risen to fame in the first place. He was a game-player, risking the odds to take the prize.

Ava watched as he ran swiftly towards the office, taking the paper, surrounded immediately by several others from his team. There were sharp questions, and someone was snapping orders into a phone. Far above East Wood, a drone circled, a speck in the clear air.

Penny had wandered over. 'Sorry, but we need to go now. I didn't want to say in front of Paul, but I said to that PI I'd speak to him later, before I take Paul to his appointment. I don't want Paul upset. You've been interviewed, haven't you? What was he like?'

'Nothing to worry about. He's just about wrapped it up anyway. He told me that there was nothing new. Ellen is gone, and her parents need to accept it,' Ava said. She reached out and touched Penny's arm. 'He seems like a nice bloke, and at least this way Jackie and Peter can get out of Aberdyth feeling like they've done their best for Ellen.'

Penny sighed. 'It just brings it all back, you know. I still wonder what she'd be like, what she'd have done with her life… I miss her so much.'

Ava tried to smile. 'I reckon she'd either be prime minister or in jail. Ellen Smith would never have settled for anything less.'

Penny leant in for another hug, promising to call later, after she'd seen Alex. Paul, watching from the Land Rover, didn't even wave. As they pulled away, sleet began to fall, drawing a curtain of ice across Big Water, and making the film crew curse at the lack of visibility. The drones were landed quickly on the bank and rushed to shelter.

Ava stood, almost enjoying the change in the weather, the pain of icy bullets on her face, her hands bare and numb, running shoes soaking up the cold. Ellen was back again, a slender phantom called by her former best friends. If Ava strained her eyes, she could see her running down the hill, dark hair flying. Then the image was gone, as the wind gusted the sleet into whirling eddies, and Ava was left alone in the storm.

'I miss her so much.'

Chapter 14

I had to use every skill I've ever learned to pull that off. But I've got her. One last time, so it is right, I suppose, that this should be the most testing game I've ever played.

It's been difficult in the past, but never quite like this. My blood is burning through my veins, my heart thudding so hard and fast that it beats not only in my chest, but also in my head. I've never felt so alive. Or so in control.

Her hair is long and silky, and her face is softened by sleep. An artificial sleep. I almost had to change my plans at the last minute, but as usual fate stepped in to lend a hand and helped me push that blonde bitch off the hill. The support crews, and the idiots wielding cameras effectively looked the other way whilst I completed my work. She fell with a scream and a satisfying crunch, and the medics were soon crawling over her like orange-suited locusts. Even better, she never saw me, so she'll tell everyone that she was pushed by one of her competitors.

It was then that I snagged my player, drawing her in with the care and skill of a fisherman reeling in his catch. She was pleased to see me, never suspecting that I might be a danger. It was right at the very last minute that I had trouble. She spotted the needle and started to struggle. But once I jabbed through her pale skin, the drug acted very quickly, and she slumped over the rocks. I don't usually use needles, but this needed to be very quick, and there was a chance she would have decided to abide by the rules of her own stupid game, and not take anything else I offered her.

Ava has deleted her social media profiles. I didn't expect that. I thought she might go down the proper channels and we could play some more. I could bring them up again of course, and I may do that tomorrow, but in the meantime, I have more photographs to take. I strip the girl off, quickly and methodically, folding her clothes neatly in a corner. I've had this place prepared for a few weeks now, and the only thing that bothers me is the weather. It really is unseasonably cold, and I'd hate her to die before I'm ready.

She photographs well, and I move the lights around a bit, taking twenty or thirty quick shots. I'll edit them later, before I start to distribute them. Perhaps I'll wait a little longer, stringing it out so that my opponent's nerves are raw and stretched.

I suppose many people would expect me to be weak after what happened to me, but instead I have an inner resilience that I have earned. When I was younger, my mum would whine on about me not being strong enough, tall enough, working hard enough. But I am, and I never play with opponents who might beat me. Always know your own strengths.

That was another one of Mum's pathetic sayings. Shame the bitch didn't act on her own advice. But then, thinking back, I really don't think she had any strengths. Is it possible to be born as prey or predator?

In the beginning I was prey, but I soon learned to how to become the predator. Nature versus nurture maybe…

The girl stirs a little, and one arm twitches, but I know from the dosage I gave her that she has at least four hours until consciousness returns. Even then she will be dizzy, struggling, and that is when I will break her. I shouldn't really, there are a good few squares on the board before I need her again, but oh,

110

I've missed this feeling. If the pictures are any good I might make some money out of her too, instead of just laying a trail for Ava to follow.

Today will be fun, pitting my wits against various players, including a rather late and unexpected entry from that stupid private investigator. What are Ellen's parents thinking? You can't just neatly tie up every loose end before you escape from the valleys, even if one of those frayed and trailing ends is your own daughter. The Smiths' candlelit ceremony ten years after Ellen went missing, attended by most of the village and a local reporter, was highly amusing. I was there with the others, looking sad and solemn, and Ellen was lying in her cold bed just down the hill. If I could have, I would have wet myself laughing.

He rang the house last night again, and I apologised for having to go out. I know Ava has spoken to him. I don't really need another player, but if he's any good it will add an extra buzz to my game. Of course, if he's too good, I'll have to kill him as well. That's how people are to me. If they don't feature in my games, and I don't want to fuck them or kill them, they don't exist. But this man seems to have pushed in. An illegal start, you might say.

The girl at my feet stirs again, flexing a bare shoulder. Mildly exciting, but nothing like seeing Ava naked. Before I leave, I unpack the supplies, and kneel to run a gentle finger across the bare skin, before licking my fingertip thoughtfully. No, she is an imposter – she tastes of nothing.

The dice are in my pocket, and on impulse I roll them across the rocky floor. They spin and dance in a stray patch of lighter shadow, before settling in the darkness, near the wall. I will leave her a torch, and take the big light with me. I want her terrified, disorientated and controllable. Squinting, I see a two and a six.

'Chwaraewch gyda fi heddiw, Ava Cole?'
'**Play with me today, Ava Cole?**'

Chapter 15

Feeling like a loser, Ava ate a pre-packed salad from the local store, alone in her room, half-wishing she had accepted Penny's dinner invitation. The claustrophobic, sickly scented B&B was already starting to annoy her. She slept surprisingly well, despite staying fully clothed, clutching an empty bottle, and the cat, which had appeared again that evening.

Her mom called to check she was okay, and to see how she was getting on with her son. Ava explained that she wouldn't see him for a fortnight now, because of the show. She could sense the disappointment, and it mirrored her own. As she'd sat on the plane from LAX, killing time by catching up with her work report, she had allowed herself to daydream a little about her son. In her imagination she had hoped they would talk things through, that perhaps she would have been able to make him see how much she regretted leaving him. But now he was locked in a camp on the hills, with a camera crew filming his every move.

Returning from her morning run, with much better spirits after a night without disturbances, she thundered quickly up the stairs. The hallway was deserted, but Ava stopped dead at her door. Her heart, already pounding after the run, was beating like she was in the final stages of a marathon, and she pressed a shaking hand to the wall to steady herself. What the hell was going on? Hanging from the round wooden door handle was a hair band. It was small, and easily missed, but surely she would have noticed if it was there earlier. The nausea and dizziness from yesterday returned with a vengeance.

She caught her breath, the dried sweat from her run itching her face and hairline. As before the hand that reached for the object was shaky, her fingertips scraping the door handle as she slid it off, and into her palm.

It was Ellen's. Even without the friendship bracelet from yesterday, she would have known. It was slightly grubby, a silver elastic with two neon pink beads. Ellen had been just as sporty as Ava, but she always had a cute girly edge that her best friend lacked. Ellen's shorts would be pink, Ava's black. Both girls had long hair, but whilst Ava's would be a loose shaggy mane, or pulled back into a careless knot, Ellen would spend hours experimenting with the latest styles. Once, to her parents' horror, she had stolen a packet of hair dye from the local Co-o, and turned her locks bright red.

Someone was messing with her head. Leo had been so adamant, but it was hard to tell when he was lying – always had been. Surely Paul wouldn't be able to wind her up like this? He seemed fine one minute, hardly able to walk the next, but she supposed he could be exaggerating his condition… Really? Hardly able to believe the direction her thoughts were taking, Ava frowned down the still empty hallway. Rhodri, the troublemaker, was more than capable, but again to what end? Perhaps they were all in on it, she thought again, ganging up to warn her off. Perhaps Penny's friendliness was all air and froth. Ava pocketed the hair band, and reluctantly headed back downstairs.

'Is everything all right, Ava?' Mr Birtley trotted in from the lounge, clutching a large mug of tea. His sludge green eyes, round puffy cheeks and flabby lips gave him an anxious, frog-like appearance. 'I'm afraid Mrs Birtley isn't here at the moment, but I can get you anything you need.'

Ava studied him for a moment. As children, they had always considered him a little odd, with his stutter and his stooped gait. The police had interviewed him as a suspect when Ellen disappeared, and the village had swooped on his oddities as proof of possible guilt. Ava liked to think that even if she hadn't known the truth, that she would never have entertained the thought that Mr Birtley was in any way responsible, and she and Penny had felt guilty his name was dragged through the mud. She smiled now. 'Actually, I was just wondering... has anyone visited whilst I've been staying here? Maybe this morning after I went out for a run, or late in the evenings at all?'

His murky eyes widened, and his tongue flicked out to moisten cracked lips. 'No. Well, only that Mr Jennington. Did you mean someone looking for you?'

'I mean anyone at all. Anyone local who might have popped in for a cup of tea, or deliveries maybe?'

'I don't think so.' He pottered behind the desk and produced a calendar decorated with flowers and hearts. 'If you don't mind waiting, I can just check for you. Is everything all right?' His voice was querulous and his hands on the calendar shook.

Ava remembered from her childhood that Mr Birtley was terrified of his wife, and life in general. It wouldn't do any harm to shake him a bit and see what happened. 'I think someone may have left something in my room.'

'Well, Mrs Birtley would have gone in to run the Hoover round a bit and...'

Ava watched him and said mildly, 'I did say that wouldn't be necessary. Certainly not every day. Have any of the neighbours called in?'

His eyes were darting now. 'No... the delivery man came with a package, oh and the lady from wholesale dropped some bakery products off yesterday afternoon. Sylvia popped over for a cup of tea the day before you came... Penny came up to drop off some of her new business cards. Oh, Rhodri from the garage came up to lend us a history book. That's it, I'm afraid. What… what was it that was left in your room?'

'Thank you. I had no idea Rhodri was into history. Please do feel free to let Mrs Birtley know of my concerns,' Ava told him, ignoring his question.

He persisted. 'Yes, Rhodri said his dad left him quite a collection from car boot sales, and some of the books are quite valuable. They are mostly Welsh history, and Mrs Birtley loves all that kind of thing.' He smiled fondly, before returning to his usual anxious expression. 'Silly lad will probably spend any money he gets on drugs. Was… was anything taken from your room? Because if so…'

'Nothing was taken, but something has been left,' Ava told him.

'Oh… oh dear. Well, best ask Mrs Birtley when she gets back, Ava, because I really don't think I can help…'

She left him dithering in the rose-scented hallway, his pale face a picture of unease. It was enough. Enough to know that, although guests might be thin on the ground, the B&B had various legitimate visitors on a daily basis. It would be hard for someone local to get in without a grilling from the lady of the house, but not impossible.

Struck by one last thought, Ava called back down the hallway. 'Mr Birtley?'

He was still there, still teetering between the comfort of the lounge and the emptiness of the kitchen. 'Yes, Ava?'

'Does Mrs Birtley have a time when she goes out every day? When she goes shopping or visiting?'

'Well, I suppose she does go shopping, usually in the morning…'

There was more, so Ava waited, tugging impatiently at her sweaty running vest. A hot shower was calling.

The man cleared his throat loudly. 'And she takes afternoon tea to her parents every day at three.'

Come again? 'I'm sorry, Mr Birtley, I'm a bit confused. I thought your wife's parents were dead?'

He peered at her through the banisters, slightly defiant. 'They are. She goes down to the church to see them. I'll certainly mention your um… worries when I see her again. Have a good day.'

Ava was still digesting this information as Mr Birtley, quick as a lizard escaping under a rock, made a dart for the lounge and shut the door firmly behind him. Interview over.

After a shower Ava called Rhodri. The phone rang and rang, but she remembered the Rhodri of old, and his hatred of early rising. Tough shit, this was getting worrying. The whole situation with Paul, Penny and Stephen, not to mention Leo, was hard enough without someone digging up Ellen. Alex may or may not be satisfied with his discoveries, but after their conversation she was fairly sure he could be steered in the direction of a runaway, even if the runaway had wound up dead. But someone was trying to warn her off, and she had surely given no indication that she was here to cause trouble. Perhaps it was simply her presence in the village that was unsettling the perp.

Eventually someone answered. 'Fuck off, I'm sleeping.'

'It's Ava. I'm coming over, Rhodri, so get some clothes on.'

'What? Who the…'

She heard him sigh down the phone line, before he disconnected the call.

* * *

The wind was bitter, and the sullen skies held a promise of more snow. She'd forgotten that some years it was June before the valleys got properly warm, and the hills were coated with vivid green instead of snow. In high summer, it was beautiful, wild and lonely. The rest of the year this place was desolate and freezing. More fool Leo for trying to film in this weather.

The dirty, pebbledash bungalow next to the garage looked derelict, but Ava whacked on the door with her knuckles anyway. There was no answer. She peered into the grimy windows but could only see signs of chaotic living between the grimy net curtains. Wading through piles of rusting vehicle parts, and two un-emptied bins, she made it to the back door.

The garden was concreted over, and a high wooden fence sheltered three more padlocked sheds, plus the now familiar spread of exhausts, tyres, doors. There was a stained, cracked toilet bowl, and a sink in a similar state. Both items had a thin straggle of dead brown weeds growing out of them. Creative gardening perhaps, she wondered, slightly amused, but mostly repulsed.

'Rhodri!' Her voice echoed around the yard. Frustrated, she gave the back door a shove, and it flew open.

Fine, if that was how he wanted it. She marched into the house. The back door led straight into the kitchen. The stench of dirty dishes, mingled with the sound of a groaning, churning washing machine, and the smell of cigarette smoke.

Ava followed her nose, trying not to gag, and found an open bedroom door.

'Go away, Ava,' Rhodri told her.

He was sitting up in bed, not troubling to hide his naked body with the crumpled sheets. The guitar lay next to him, and a full ashtray perched on the pillow. A couple of boxes of leather-bound books were stacked at the foot of his bed. The rusty bedside table held various drug paraphernalia, and she quickly averted her eyes. What you didn't see, didn't count. Sometimes it worked, and sometimes not, but she needed Rhodri on side at the moment.

'Glad to see you're conscious, and doing your washing. Listen, we need to talk. Something weird happened yesterday and today…'

As she had hoped, a glimmer of intelligence appeared in his brown eyes, and for a moment her childhood friend was back.

He frowned. 'What, like weirder than Paul dying, you coming back, and your freakin' son taking part in Leo's show? Fuck me, girl, you couldn't make that up. It's like *Happy Families* gone wrong.'

'Yeah, I know. Has that PI spoken to you yet?'

'That wanker!' Rhodri snorted with laughter. 'He leaves me polite messages on my voicemail. He's not rude enough to come barging in here like you. How did you get in anyway?'

'You left your back door unlocked.'

Rhodri shrugged, skinny shoulders hunched now. His red hair was the usual mess of mats and tangles, but the sheen of drugs was gone from his eyes for the moment. 'So what's the problem?'

'Did Leo walk back with me from the pub, when we all had dinner?'

He stared at her. 'Is that a trick question, Detective? You know he did. You were a bit pissed, and he said he would take you back to the Birtleys' before he went home. Don't tell me you fucked him, and now you're regretting it.' Rhodri shook his shaggy head, a smile flickering at the corners of his mouth, admiration in his expression. 'Ava, you haven't changed as much as I thought!'

'Can you keep your mind off sex for a moment? Someone has been in my room at the Birtleys', and not someone I invited in. The first night we went down the pub, and again this morning when I went out for a run.'

'Like broken in?' His amusement died, and his brow furrowed.

'No. The door wasn't damaged and the Birtleys never said they'd had a break-in. The first night, I know I was a bit pissed so I can't be sure it wasn't there when I got back, but there was something left on the table next to the bed...' She hesitated. 'In fact, I think someone spiked my drink.'

'What the fuck?'

'I know. This morning, something was just left on my door handle. I found it when I got back after my run. Look...' She displayed the objects in the palm of her hand.

Rhodri leaned in, the covers sliding further. 'Bloody hell!' He recoiled as though she'd held a poisonous snake in her hand, 'That bracelet thing... that was Ellen's, wasn't it?'

'Yes. And the hair band was hers too.'

His breath was coming in gasps now, and his chest was heaving.

He scrabbled on the table and dragged a grubby blue inhaler from the pile. After a puff, his breathing gradually calmed, but his skinny white hands still held the sheets in a death grip. 'What are you saying? That one of us left this to freak you out?'

'I thought your asthma went away? Okay, none of my business. Yes, I am saying that. Ellen was wearing this the night she died. I don't know if she was still wearing it when they took her to the woods two years later. Was it you who left these?'

He put a hand to his forehead, knocking at his skull with a clenched fist, 'No! Fuck, Ava, I wouldn't have kept anything like that. I might wind you up, but that... that would be fucking sick. That's disrespecting the dead.'

Ava tucked her feet under her, studying his face. It was probably best not to mention that Huw, Leo and Paul moving Ellen's body two years after they first buried her was pretty disrespectful too.

Rhodri was reaching tentatively for the bracelet and hair band now. He stroked them both with a gentle finger, turning them over in his hand. Eventually he looked up. 'Sorry, Ava, I know she had that bracelet thing on the night she... the night she died, but the other one, I'm not sure. I think she even had her hair down, all loose around her shoulders.' He frowned again.

'They would both have rotted underground, so I'm thinking they were taken the night she died,' Ava said, slowly turning the possibilities over in her mind. Her phone buzzed with a message, and she flicked across the screen. Penny wanting to meet up later, and her mom wanting another chat. It was bizarre to think of her normal life in the States continuing without her. She had three weeks' leave from work, and so far she'd sent only brief messages to her friends, her sometime-boyfriend and her parents. It was like Aberdyth was sealed in a bubble – but her coming seemed to be changing that.

Rhodri was turning the objects over in his hands, gently, as though they were still Ellen's. 'Have you asked Leo?'

'Not about the objects, no.'

'Paul?'

She shrugged, much in the same way he had done earlier. It was not dismissive, more an acknowledgement of the sadness and legacy they all carried. An acceptance of wrongdoing.

They sat in silence for a moment, Rhodri still staring at Ellen's possessions, his lashes lowered, mouth set.

'Who do you think might have left these for me?'

'Christ knows. I mean... well, Jesse's dead isn't he? Paul, the bloke's dying, and I really don't think he'd have the time for games with you. Huw's a wanker, and you know I've always thought... Never mind.'

'What about Huw?'

He met her eyes, then quickly looked away. 'You must have thought about him. He had a temper, and he always has. Forget it, *cariad*.'

'No. What do you mean?'

Rhodri seemed to be choosing his words carefully. 'We made our choice, and he made it clear at the time that his family would've killed us if we went against him – and they would, wouldn't they? I'm just saying that if I had that night again I would have sided with you and Penny, and been up for going to the police. Anyway, that's over now.' He looked up, mouth set in a familiar stubborn line, and then he quickly changed the subject. 'If you're looking for a game-player then I'd look at Leo because...'

'Leo does have time for games with me,' Ava finished his sentence. She was still thinking about Huw. It was almost as if Rhodri was about to tell her something, but she knew from experience that if pushed, he would never tell. In childhood, he had been the secret-keeper, the one they all trusted. Again, she shrank from discussing the photographs. It was too painful, made her too vulnerable. She brushed her hair back from her face with an impatient hand and looked up to see Rhodri grinning. 'What?'

'Like I said. You haven't changed so much after all. I was wrong, that first time you came to see me. *Ydych chi'n meddwl ei fod Leo yn wneud hyn?*'

Ava stared back at him, silently accepting the challenge. He had spoken slowly, clearly, inviting her in. The pain was sharp in her heart, making her fingers tingle. '*Efallai...*' The single word tasted odd, but it was still there, right at the back of her consciousness. She made a decision. 'Rhodri, there is something else... Someone took photographs of me whilst I was asleep.'

'You really are freaking me out now, girl.'

'They took photographs of me and posted them as profile pictures on Twitter, Facebook and Instagram. I've deleted all my social media accounts, but whoever is trying to fuck with me – and I do know it's one of you, okay, not you personally, but one of the old gang – whoever it is, they are going to regret it.'

Rhodri nodded slowly, reaching for his guitar. 'I hear you, *cariad*. I'm assuming these are not the type of photographs you want shown around.'

'Correct.' She didn't offer, and was surprised and relieved when he didn't ask. They sat in silence for a moment.

'If you need me, I'm here, Ava. But I don't know who would do any of that, or mess with Ellen's stuff. It's... it's too much after all this time. But if you get worried, or anything else happens, call me. Just not at fucking seven-in-the-morning, you evil bitch!'

Ava smiled through the stupid tears that were now unexpectedly snail-trailing down her cheeks. 'Do you know who I last spoke Welsh to?'

He moved then, covering her hands with his. His nails were yellow, and his palms were calloused and veined with motor oil, but his touch was as gentle as any Ellen would have given. 'I miss her too. After all this time, I miss her so much, and I regret so much. But you, you got away and you're successful. Don't lose that. Whatever is going on at the moment, don't give up on what you have or you'll be stuck here like the rest of us. I wonder sometimes if fate is kind of making it up to Ellen. Jesse, Paul,

121

me, Huw – the dead, the dying and those of us leading generally shit lives. Only you, Penny and Leo seem to have done all right.'

'Deep, Rhodri.'

'True, *cariad*. Here, you'd better take these back. Keep them safe for Ellen. Ava, you know I'd be the last person to say so, but you might want to go to the police, with this.'

'And dig up Ellen? Because that's what would happen, wouldn't it? I don't know, Rhodri, I really don't. I didn't come back to rake up the past. It would hurt too many people, ruin lives, ruin careers… Imagine what the press would make of Leo's involvement, or mine for that matter. It can't happen. I've paid my respects to Ellen, and I've talked to her parents, but she needs to stay buried.' She got up to leave, dodging piles of rubbish, heading for the back door.

As she inched past the overflowing bins she heard the strumming, and Rhodri's husky, smoker's voice.

'One night was all it took,
The memory scars my soul, and your words play on my mind,
And your words play on my mind…'

Ava thrust the bracelet and hair band deep into her coat pocket and set her face to the wind. The pub was shut, and the sign swung in the wind, creaking like a character in a ghost story. A couple of kids were playing ball against the graffitied war memorial. They scowled as she went past, and she scowled back. She paused at the end of the road, undecided. To her left, the road ran down to the new development, and to her right, the old primary school stood, boarded up and crumbling. Rusting wire fencing was decorated with icicles that tinkled merrily in the wind. The roof was half frost, half straggling brown weeds, and the chimney had clearly been lost in another winter storm.

For a moment she saw them all as they had been; a big gang would have been playing kiss chase in the sunshine, probably with Ellen in the lead, and Huw losing interest and kicking a ball high into the school garden. Leo would have been plotting with Paul and Jesse, sneaking glances at herself and Penny, who might have been playing ring-a-roses in the playground, hands linked, hair fanning out, spinning, faster and faster. Their faces were bright with promise, and their innocence made her heart fill, and her throat swell. What had happened to those children?

'Hey, Ava! I thought it was you.'

Ava dragged herself from her unwelcome thoughts. She could have walked past him in a crowded street and never recognised him. But here, in this setting, she could just about make out the former captain of the football team, the big, square-shouldered golden boy, who had tussled with Leo over the girls. Now his hair was prematurely thinning, and greasy strands covered his forehead. His face was lined and desperate, and the smile revealed yellowing teeth. A paunch had replaced the muscular torso, and his clothes were dirty. Huw Davis, father of pretty Bethan.

'Hallo, Huw.' She turned the objects over in her pocket, caressing the band with a gentle finger, trying not to show how shocked she was by his appearance. He was thirty-one and could have been taken for a man a dozen years older. 'How are you?'

'Oh, you know, fine... I'm going to watch the filming today. Leo said they already got some good footage of Bethan on the zip line for the second circuit. Apparently, she let go halfway down, and the crew freaked out and started shouting for medics!' He chuckled indulgently. 'I told them she would have been doing it to get noticed. She's not stupid, my girl.'

'Right.' Letting go of a zip line of that height, or any zip line come to that, just to get on camera seemed very stupid to Ava, but hell, what did she know. 'I'm heading over that way myself if you want to give me a lift. I was going to ask Penny, but she won't be back from the hospital yet. She said Paul had an appointment.' She was searching his face for emotion, feeling her own heart twist and a fist in her stomach at the thought of another zip line accident, another girl who had fallen. Yet Huw seemed quite happy for his daughter to be doing just what Ellen had done before her death.

For a moment he said nothing, a flash of wariness turning his face from light to dark. He swung a plastic carrier bag, in one hand. 'Sure. As long as you don't mind the Land Rover.'

Ava shook her head, and they walked in an uneasy silence down the hill to the vehicle. She hadn't had any intention of returning to the film set that day, but it was a good chance to have a little chat with Huw. Although she couldn't help comparing him with the dynamic teenager she remembered, she supposed she also looked very different in her thirties. You just didn't really notice when you saw yourself in the mirror each day. Weirdly, Huw and Leo were exactly the same age, sharing a July birthday, but their lives from that point had clearly been very different.

Ava waited whilst Huw opened his front door and dumped the bag inside, yelling to someone that he would see them later. She caught the sound of young children wailing, and a woman's voice shouted something that sounded like, 'Whatever, you fucking stupid bastard.' Interesting that Huw seemed to have moved on, away from his family. As a child he'd lived in a crowded but pristine van, on the other side of the village. Perhaps the house was for his kids, or the girlfriend. It didn't seem like a good question to ask right away, and she didn't want to piss him off until she had to.

'So, do you like living in Los Angeles then?' Huw made a big show of grinding the gears and hauling the wheel as they backed out into the high street. Changing up, and avoiding potholes, they soon left the village, and bumped down the frozen track towards Big Water. His jaw was set, and every so often he ran a hand across his thinning hair with a quick, nervous motion.

'Yes. Leo said you teach down the valley at St Merlon's... Wow. I never would have thought of you as a teacher, Huw. You were such a rebel. And you've got kids now too... Bethan's turned out beautiful, she looks like a model,' Ava prodded, exploiting his pride in his daughter. She shifted in her seat, and he almost cringed away from her.

'Well, you know... people change. Got myself a house and everything now, and that's down to bloody hard graft.'

'They do change. How's the family? Your uncle still around?'

'Yes, the old git's still breathing. My cousins are still in the village, and a few more half-brothers and sisters that you wouldn't know about. The traveller site has been almost killed off, but my da's just about hanging on to his old van.'

'That's a shame about the site.' Ava remembered some good times hanging around with Huw's extended family. It was a whole different lifestyle to the one she was used to as a child, and the boys had been encouraged to be violent, the girls to keep the home clean. She turned to him again. 'You know there's a private investigator asking questions about Ellen's death?'

Huw clenched his hands on the wheel and drove straight through a large hole. 'I heard.'

'So? Will you speak to him? He said he's going tomorrow, but I know you were on the list of people for him to interview.'

Navigating an open five-bar gate set between a line of pine trees, he drove across the field to the little group of lorries and other 4x4s, yanked the handbrake on and turned to face her. His eyes were darting, frantic even. 'No. It has nothing to do with me anymore. Ellen's death was a tragic accident. Okay, we shouldn't have covered it up, but we were scared kids, for Christ's sake. And who's to say her parents weren't better off thinking she'd run away, and has been living quite happily all this time?'

So that was it. Ava opened her mouth to speak, but he put a large, rough hand on her arm.

'Don't rock the boat, Ava. Your coming here has stirred things up. None of us want the past to come and bite our arses, so just let it go.'

'Why would you think I've come back to drag up Ellen's death? I've come to see Paul and Stephen, not to reopen old wounds.' She was genuinely shocked that he would think that, and debated whether to show him the bracelet and hair band, confronting him. But she didn't trust Huw. Even the new version of Huw, this ageing, angry man who seemed to shrink away from her, was dangerous.

The force of his reaction shocked her. In some ways, he hadn't changed at all. He leant right over to the passenger seat, reached up and cupped her chin in cruel fingers and spoke slowly, viciously. 'You think I believe you? I mean, for fuck's sake, Ava, you're a copper now, aren't you? I expect you could rig it so you got off with a little slap on the wrist, but you'd destroy the rest of us... I mean it, you fucking try anything and I'll get my family round to the Birtleys—'

She jerked her head away. 'Don't touch me, Huw, especially not like that, and I wouldn't drag anything up. I just told you! Look, it's like you said, it was an accident. Yes, we were pretty wild teenagers, but Ellen's death was one of those awful things, and we made the wrong choice. I repeat, I haven't come to tell the world what really happened. It didn't even occur to me.'

Huw was still ranting. 'Don't you think it's better this way? If you told them their darling daughter took drugs and shagged me and Jesse every weekend for months, they would be devastated. How do you think they'll feel? What's the cost just for you to clear your conscience?' His voice softened. 'Let them keep the image they have of her.'

Ava felt it then, in between her pain and Huw's fear – Ellen was with them. Her brown eyes were bright as they had been that night, her ponytail swinging, and her full lips curved into a naughty smile. Was she wrong? But in her pocket her fingers brushed soft cotton and elastic. And Rhodri had suggested she go to the police... She really hoped it wasn't Huw who had been in her room that night. The thought of his hands on her naked body was stomach-churningly awful. She took a deep breath, trying one last time to penetrate Huw's single-minded fury. 'I agree with you. I haven't come to stir up trouble. You need to believe that. And, Huw?'

He turned to her, sullen and still spoiling for a fight. How was this man a teacher? 'What is it?'

'Don't ever threaten me again,' she told him.

'Hello, you two! Just catching up, are you?' Leo banged on the bonnet and smiled at Ava, but his eyes locked onto Huw's.

'Yes. Just catching up,' Ava told him, jumping out of the Land Rover and slamming the door behind her. 'How's filming going?'

Leo's sparkle faded slightly. 'We had a slight incident and four of the girls ran off into the woods further up. They've been gone since the camp dinner last night. It does happen – they are all desperate for airtime and the more drama the better, but we've sent the crew out to find them.'

Huw stamped round from the driver's side. 'Is Bethan one of the girls who ran off?'

'Yes. Sorry, Huw, but like I said they all go a bit crazy when we set them loose. This particular group were arguing with some of the boys, including Stephen, and the general gist is they thought they could make it to the next camp on their own. Great footage, of course, and the viewers will love the fact the girls have struck out on their own, but they do know they shouldn't have done that.'

Ava bit her lip. 'I take it they haven't turned up yet?'

'Well, not yet. They are only around two hours late. But if they went off course a bit, and are probably coming at it from the other direction... Well, the hills are steep, and there is a good chance of getting lost in that wooded valley. They'll be a bit cold and hungry, but that's what the game is all about.' Leo didn't seem quite as confident as he could be, and flashed another loaded glance at Huw.

Surprisingly, for a concerned parent, Huw was smiling as he lit a cigarette. 'I figured as soon as you mentioned it that it would be Bethan. Told you before, Leo, my girl knows how to play it. She'll turn up later and put it on for the cameras about how she was lost on the hills, then she'll make up with Stephen and the viewers will love it. She'll get more votes and go all the way.'

'Aren't you worried at all?' Ava felt her voice rise incredulously.

'No offence, Ava, but you haven't really been a parent, have you? I know teenagers, and I know Bethan, and probably Stephen too, far better than you do.'

Ava glared at him, but she couldn't deny it.

'Huw, do you want to grab a drink or something, and then we'll go up to the next camp and watch the filming later. You know where everything is.' Leo smiled at his friend.

'Yeah. See you later, Ava.' Huw gave Ava another unfriendly look and marched off towards the warmth and the catering Portakabin.

Ava's phone began to ring, and she glanced at the number before mouthing to Leo that she needed to take this. He nodded, moved away and took out his own phone.

'Hallo?'

'Ava. Can you talk?' Jack Marsden, her immediate superior in LAPD did not ever ring for social chitchat. He had two passions – policing and surfing, and no time for anything else. Ava both liked and respected him.

'Yes. Is there a problem? I'm on leave until next—'

He cut her off. 'It isn't about your leave. Have you had any trouble in Wales, since you arrived?'

'Trouble?' Shit, how could he possibly know? All she'd given him were the basics – terminally ill ex-husband and estranged teenage son. 'No. I'm just catching up with everyone. My ex-husband is pretty sick of course, but he's managing at the moment. What do you mean?'

'I got an email, with a link to some photos. The email came from your work account, but I'm guessing you didn't send it?'

Ava swallowed, moistening her lips. *Some photographs.* 'No, I didn't send you anything.'

'Someone has hacked your account, Ava. They...' Jack, who never had any problems saying anything, was clearly struggling for words. 'Look, Ava, there's no easy way to tell you this, but the photos were of you. They are on a website. I've got straight onto it and they'll be taken down as soon as I can get it actioned, I promise you.'

Chapter 16

He's such a colourless man, Alex Jennington. I've been dodging him for the last day or so, but after his chat with Ava, I supposed it would be better to gauge how much he had discovered. He sat neatly in the kitchen, asking his stupid questions, whilst I made him a coffee, and told him a bit about Aberdyth. The house doesn't look much from the front, but the view from my windows is magnificent, daunting and awe-inspiring. I could almost see him wincing at the rural setting he'd been forced to work in for the last couple of days. I can imagine him living in a spotless flat in the city, and that alone makes me want to despise him. But I can also see that he is quite close to getting a sort of inverted version of the truth, after all his digging.

It's so useful that Jesse is dead, because dead men can't defend themselves. Alex – he told me to drop the 'Mr Jennington' – was impressed by my memory. I hear myself speak, and my mind drifts back to the night Ellen died. She had no idea what was coming. She was so sure of herself, so confident and cosseted. If anything went wrong she could run back to Mummy and Daddy. I wanted her to see that some things are so bad that you can't run to anyone. My players gave her exactly what she deserved, and I enjoyed every moment. It was thrilling, and worth all the pathetic mess afterwards.

I'd just decided that he didn't know anything that might ruin my game, and had been happily led right away from the truth by my little confidences, when the atmosphere changed. Right at the end of our conversation, Alex threw me with a few casual questions, and he was so near the mark, I nearly dropped the mugs I was taking to the sink. How typical that the stupid Smiths have accidentally hired someone with a brain, and someone who has discovered a well-hidden secret that doesn't have anything to do with Ellen's death. Not really anyway…

Aberdyth is full of secrets and lies. They simmer just below the surface of the gossip, never quite rising to the top in a scum of bubbles, as they should. It scares people, how much I know, and they are always so pleased and eager to be my friend. Many things lie beneath the surface, as I know full well from my activity on the dark web. We skate along, safe in our own little bubbles, but deep inside, underneath that cosy exterior, the evil is rising.

It won't take Alex long to piece things together now, and then everything will be destroyed. I am not ready, and this wasn't part of my plan. Only I can reveal these things and he will ruin everything. I can feel hatred bubbling in my chest, and when I bade him goodbye, I made sure to take his number. Next time we meet I will have to kill him. I will not have players behaving like this. He pushed his way in, and now he will find out the hard way that you either win or lose in my games. I take a long, calming breath, returning to my computer. I know Ava is pleased with her gifts. It has shaken her, I can tell, but she is alert and ready for the next roll of my dice.

'*Chwaraewch ymlaen, Ava Cole.*'

'**Play on, Ava Cole.**'

Chapter 17

The frozen field, the iced, white hills all swung slowly around her head, and Ava grabbed the Land Rover bonnet to steady herself. Her nails scraped metal, her head spun and she was breathing fast. Her boss was still talking, but she wasn't taking it in. His voice seemed to be coming from miles away. Nausea was rising in her stomach, and her legs were shaky. 'Fucking hell, Jack, what kind of website? On second thoughts, don't tell me. I'll take a look and ring you back. Send me the link.'

She heard his slow intake of breath and pictured him leaning against the grimy wall of the precinct in the glaring LA sunshine, shirt sleeves rolled up, cigarette in his other hand. 'Sure you want to see them?'

'Just do it.'

'Okay. Ring me straight back.'

Leo was laughing at someone on his phone, but still watching Ava. She half-imagined she caught a flash of concern, but dismissed it instantly as more of the kind of look a predator gives before it kills its prey. Too bad. Someone was messing with her, and if it was Leo she'd fucking kill him.

With trembling fingers Ava logged in to her email account and hit the link from Jack. The signal was crappy out here in the wilds, and the site took ages to load, whilst Ava did that pointless thing of waving her phone around, marching up and down the field, trying to get a better reception.

'If you need to use the internet we've got a booster box set up in the office,' Leo said, having finished his call. 'What's up?'

The site still hadn't loaded. Jack would be ringing back if she didn't call him first. He was that sort of boss. 'Yes, I need to get onto a website. Quickly.' Furious, she felt a hot wetness behind her eyes, her throat tightening. It probably wasn't as bad as she was imagining.

It was worse. She got Leo to give her the code for the internet access, and then booted him out of his own office for privacy. Surprisingly, he went, touching her arm briefly in a way that might even have supposed to be comforting. Confused, she slammed the door shut, and sat down with her phone.

The site was called 'For My Eyes Only'. How original. It was a smutty, black and pink layout filled with adverts for escorts and sex toys. It was a busy site though, with a visits counter clicking up to two thousand visitors in the last hour. Most of the photographs were grainy, indistinct, and the subjects were all female. The link led her directly to a forum called 'Last Night Nude'. Ava nearly vomited all over Leo's very tidy desk. Both her hands were clenched on her phone, and her mind was whirling, detaching from the horror of the situation. This was far worse than the profile picture collage on her now deleted social media accounts. Here, there were five photographs of her lying in bed at the Birtleys' B&B. She was naked, dark hair spread across the pillow, eyes closed, but her limbs had been arranged into various vaguely pornographic attitudes for the shots. The shot of her lower back and bum was at the top, again the tattoo clearly visible in this black-and-white version, but with no trace of what lay beneath it. It must be a warning.

Ava couldn't stop shaking and clung on to the side of the chair as another wave of nausea hit. The room spun, and she was dimly aware of Leo knocking on the door.

Okay, calm down, she told herself, remembering for the first time in years all those breathing exercises her therapist had given her. She needed to get herself into work mode, that was it. She could view this as a case, and distance herself from the fact some sick fucker, most likely one of her childhood friends, had drugged her, undressed her, touched her and…

Leo was calling her name, hammering on the door now. Well, he was top of the list of suspects so she might as well start with him. At that moment her phone rang – Jack calling back. That was good, it would force her back to normality. She couldn't show weakness in front of her boss.

'Hi, Jack. Yeah, I got it. No, I've got no idea – well, actually I might have a bit of an idea. I think someone is trying to warn me off. It's a cold case from my childhood down here.'

'Have you told the local police?' A sharper note crept into his voice. 'I'm assuming you didn't give permission for these photographs to be taken?'

'Of course not!'

'Right, well the local police should be your next stop. Ava, I'm sorry to ask this, but were you assaulted at all?'

'No.' She remembered the cut on her leg. 'Not like that anyway. Look, Jack, there are a few things I need to sort out. This is a bit more complicated than it seems. Can I give you a call later?'

Her boss agreed and added he would have it taken down within the hour. 'Ava, whatever is going on, I can help, okay? Don't try to handle this by yourself, and for Christ's sake get the police over there involved. I'll get this filth taken down first though.'

That was a big promise, given the scope of the dark web, but whatever. Jack was no tech whizz, but their team included Zack, who had worked on various high-profile cases involving the dark web. The last one had been a child trafficking, and the perpetrators had been tracked via their online presence. She remembered Zack saying something about Tor software not being infallible. Even when users thought they had covered every base, concealing movements and identities, there would be other hackers, working on the other side, who could find the faintest of shadowed identities. She had no idea what he was talking about, but then Cyber Crimes guys and girls always seemed to talk in code. It didn't matter, because they got shit done, and caught the bad guys simply by superior brain power.

The hammering was increasing. 'Ava, let me in! What the fuck is going on?'

She opened the door so quickly he almost fell through, and then she slammed it shut again, blocking out the curious faces, and amused expressions of the film crew.

Leo handed her a Styrofoam cup of coffee and she downed the hot liquid, scalding her tongue, keeping her phone screen shielded from him. He appeared genuinely worried, but what if it was him? From what she knew of their childhood relationship, it would be just his style to play games like this.

'Leo, I need to ask you something, and I need you to tell me the fucking truth, all right? This isn't a game, this is grown-up crap.'

He did that innocent face thing, and came and sat next to her, their knees touching.

She moved slightly away, suddenly unsure how to begin. *Think work, Ava.* 'Two weeks before I came back, I got some weird text messages, all from different numbers, all untraceable. Now I'm back, there have been a bunch of odd things going on... Leo, before I show you this, I want you to tell me straight up. When we all had dinner at the pub, did you spike my drink? Because I wasn't just drunk that night, Leo, I was drugged.'

'Ava? Are you sure? Of course not. Why would I do that? Come on, I just walked you back to the B&B. I was only taking the piss when I said I'd kissed you. It was just a bit of banter!' The glint was back in his blue eyes, concern or amusement flickering across his face. 'You and I always had a spark, didn't we, babe? But come on, Ava, you know I wouldn't do anything unless you wanted me to.' He was serious again now, leaning into her space, searching out her gaze.

'I don't know that actually, but I do know that after that night out, I went back to the Birtleys', and someone snuck into my room and took these...' She spun the screen round so he could see the pictures, watching his face closely.

There was anger, but something else that could have been fear... then it was gone and the smooth mask was back, 'Christ, Ava, who would do this? I can't believe you thought it was me. How did you find out? This was... you poor baby.' He caught himself.

Baby, babe, sweetheart, he used to call her all of those things when they were dating. Back in the wild days. It grated on her nerves, 'I'm not a baby, Leo, but I am more than pissed off that one of you lot would do this. Because it was obviously one of my so-called friends. This is assault, and I will be speaking to the police. Somebody has hacked my social media accounts too, and my work email account was used to send the link to this site.' She would keep the rest to herself and see what happened. Somehow she didn't want to tell Leo about Ellen's bracelet just yet. Let him wonder...

'So how did you find out?'

'I got sent a link from my boss. Somebody sent these to my boss, for fuck's sake, so if you are warning me off talking about Ellen, then message received loud and clear – okay? I also got another weird text message, from another new number. Huw just made a big thing out of how he thought I was here to tell the truth about Ellen, so maybe I should put out an announcement. I have no intention of dragging up the past, beyond paying my respects to Ellen's parents. Are you lot so fucking stupid that you think I don't have anything to lose?'

He touched her then, but gently, just a brief hand on her arm, and his eyes met hers. 'Ava, I would never do this to you. When I heard you were coming back, I hoped we could be friends. You know, tidy up the past in a way we couldn't back then. Sure, I couldn't resist teasing you a bit, and you are more gorgeous than ever, so don't blame me for trying my luck the other night. But you turned me down.'

'What about the others? Anyone particularly upset I was coming back?' she probed. 'The thing is, Leo, I will go to the police about this, although I haven't worked out what the hell I'm going to tell them yet. Whoever did this, if they are trying to stop me bringing up Ellen, has totally screwed up. So, who really hates me at the moment?'

'Nobody hates you… I mean Huw and Rhodri were a bit wary that you might stir up trouble, but they wouldn't do something like this. They're good blokes, and since we lost Jesse they've become closer. You know Jesse was always Rhodri's best mate, wasn't he? It hit Rhodri really hard when Jesse died, and I don't think he's ever come out of it. But Huw has been great with him.'

Quite. All the boys sticking together. But there was something in Leo's tone, and the way the words were framed, that made her take note. 'What are you not telling me?'

He shook his head. 'It isn't important, and it doesn't have anything to do with this.'

'Don't you think I should be the judge of that?' Ava clicked off the website, but the pictures danced around her brain, blurring the edges of her hard-won sanity. She stood up, leaning down to adjust the jeans around her walking boots. Her nails raked skin and she winced, leaning down.

'What are you doing?'

She carefully rolled up her jeans, exposing her calves. 'The night I was drugged, I also picked up this scratch. I thought maybe I went through some brambles next to the Birtleys' gate, perhaps I had been drunker than I thought. But now…'

He looked bewildered. 'So? I mean, how would you do that in your bedroom?'

'Exactly. Someone must have cut me deliberately.' Sighing, Ava

136

dragged the site up again and examined the photographs. It was slightly easier this time. She forced herself to look at them as a detective viewing a crime scene, and reminded herself that Ava Cole was a bloody good detective.

Leo looked, then glanced away. His phone rang, but he ignored it. 'Why though?'

'Look, it's my left leg, and in the photos I don't have a cut. This was done after they were taken.'

'Who would do that?'

'I don't know, Leo. I've only just arrived back, remember, and I've been assaulted in my room. Now suddenly, instead of catching up with my son, I'm trying to work out who attacked me while I slept. Not only broke my skin, but touched me, took photographs of me and put them up on some revenge porn site. Nice welcome back, don't you think?'

She glanced at him, but his face was shuttered, eyes sombre. Who the hell knew what went on in Leo's head? According to the media, whatever it was had made him a millionaire. What else had it made him?

There were no other clues from the pictures. No shadows, just enough light from the lamp to get goodish photos from what must have been a fairly top-of-the-range smartphone. No reflections in the mirror or window. One last thing, she moved her fingers and zoomed into the bedside table. Nothing. The cut and the bracelet had been left after the photos had been taken. The question was, why? To warn her off still seemed to be the most likely, and it seemed fair to assume the same person or people was also responsible for the text messages, and they had started before she even got to Wales. Huw and Rhodri?

Huw had certainly seemed very angry, but he hadn't been in the pub that night. Leo had been at the pub that night, and with their tangled history he was definitely capable. Paul obviously hated her, but that was understandable, he had his own problems to worry about. Her ex-husband had a massive ego though, and

137

always had done. Perhaps this wasn't about Ellen, but about getting revenge on a wife who ran away? Rhodri had been genuinely moved by the objects, and sad and regretful about Ellen. Jesse was dead. Jesse, who according to Ellen's parents, had been about to tell them what really happened to their daughter…

'Did you think that private investigator was any good?' Leo asked suddenly, breaking into her thoughts.

'Yes. I hope you're not going to suggest the photos were down to him.'

Leo's lips curved, dimples showing. 'No. I'm just saying a few people might have wondered what you were saying to him. I've spoken to him myself, and I would say he's not stupid, and quite capable of working it out for himself, even without our help.'

'You would? I'd probably agree with you, but from what he said he seems to be leaving it as an unsolved missing person. I won't just ignore this bullying, Leo. This is extreme, and I feel totally sick just thinking about what happened that night.'

Leo came closer, his hands on her arms. 'Ava, darling, I love that you are still a crusader, and hell, you do it for a job now, and I agree someone has gone way too far but this is one battle you need to leave behind.'

'What do you mean?' She didn't move away.

He frowned. 'I'm worried about you. Now I've seen those pictures and you've told me about the messages, I'll do some digging of my own. Nobody will hurt you, Ava, but what are you going to tell the police about all this? Somehow, you need to think of a way to report the photographs while leaving Ellen out of it.'

'I honestly don't know if I can!' Ava pulled away from him and ran her hands through her hair, pulling her fingers through the strands as though she could yank away memories. 'It's the perfect motive. You think I'm going to, what, lie to the police like I did back then? I am the bloody police now. What's the worst that will happen if I do tell the truth? Yes, it will devastate the

Smiths, but they have pretty much already decided that Ellen is dead. They're right – if she was alive, she would have called them, so they've been mourning for years anyway. Will it kill our careers? Especially yours, being in the public eye, and mine being in law enforcement… Stephen hates me now, and if he finds out the truth about Ellen, I'm quite sure he'll hate me even more.'

Leo leaned against the wall of the office, watching her rant. 'But you are going to do it?' It was hardly a question.

'The alternative is not going to the police, letting this sick perp have it all their own way. My boss has seen the photographs, and there's no way he's going to let it go. At the end of the day, it was an accident for fuck's sake, Leo, and we were stupid kids. It was just an accident, and her parents want to move on.' As she said the words, arguing against herself, there was hot panic, fear of ruining her life again, but also a twinge of something that could have been relief. It might ruin her, but now she was backed into a corner and the choice wasn't hers to make anymore. If whoever had done this was warning her off, they had achieved the exact opposite. She looked back at Leo.

He was too close. His breath was warm on her cheek, and he hesitated for a bare second. 'It wasn't an accident.'

For the second time in an hour the little office spun, and Ava wondered how many more shocks she could take today, but somewhere at the back of her mind was a thought. Was this what she had suspected all along?

Leo pulled out a packet of cigarettes, and without thinking she grabbed one herself, her hand shaking. His voice seemed to come from miles away, tinny and faint, and she forced herself to concentrate. Everything had slowed, was muffled – her heartbeat, the hum of the heater, the double ping of her phone as a message arrived.

'You were never supposed to know, but you need to understand why this can never come out, and why you can't tell the police. Ellen was murdered. This was never an accident. That night in the woods, someone killed Ellen and, I'm fairly sure, sexually assaulted her.'

'What?' She took a drag of her cigarette and nearly threw up as the smoke hit the back of her throat.

'Sit down. It isn't cut and dried, and before you start hitting me, it wasn't me. I would say that anyway, but you'll have to trust me on this. I didn't kill Ellen, or hurt her, and I don't know who did.'

'But then… how do you know she was murdered? She fell from the zip line after I got the answer wrong in that stupid "True Lies" game. That was her punishment for me not being able to tell if you were lying.' It had haunted her forever. But that was their insane game. There was a series of physical dares that the loser had to complete, from the zip line high in the oak trees, to the box in the ground you were shut in for five long minutes. It was stupid, but it was kid stuff. Kids testing their strengths and exploring each other's weaknesses. Shame they were all high on drugs at the time, but that gave it an extra edge.

'Leo? Fucking talk to me!'

He sighed, tapping ash into a plate on the desk. 'When you passed out, I laid you on the ground. You always were a lightweight with those pills. We all had dark hoodies on, didn't we, so there was nothing distinctive about anyone once it got late. I don't expect you really remember properly, do you? She checked you, had a couple of pills, and some booze, then she did the zip line. She… came back and sat with us. We had the music, the fire and the vodka. I went back to check on you next…'

'How kind.' The sarcasm was automatic. Her memory of the pain in her head faltered. She had assumed someone had hit her, knocking her unconscious, but what if it had just been the drugs taking effect?

'We were just sitting around talking, zoning out. I think Ellen had a row with Rhodri at one point, but then she was off snogging Huw, and Paul was watching. You remember how it used to turn him on, watching someone else?'

Ava did, and she had discussed it with Penny and Ellen, but the two other girls seemed to enjoy the attention. Uneasily, she remembered how, off their heads with booze, her two best friends had often been persuaded to put on a show for the boys, snogging and touching each other. The first time it happened, she had felt sick, shouted at the boys to stop encouraging them, and at the girls for doing it. But Pen had called her a prude, and Paul told her to get lost unless she wanted to join in. Furious, she had gone home early. She wasn't a prude in any way, but the sight of the boys watching, like a pack of wolves lusting after prey, freaked her out. After that, when they started she either left, or turned her back.

Leo was still talking. '… That night, it was easy to lose track of everyone, in the dark. I dozed off a bit too, even though the music was pretty loud.'

'I'm sure you did, Leo. How convenient. So what happened then?' Ava was struggling to adjust her mental picture of the night. All these years… 'How did she…?' She couldn't say it, and was still breathing fast, heart pounding.

'I could hear them all laughing before I went to sleep. Ellen too, I think, and I swear I didn't think anything of it. I must have been out for a good half an hour, we reckoned later. She never screamed, or someone would have heard her.'

'But the music was loud,' Ava commented. 'And the fire pit was always full of dried leaves and that made a noise if you were sat near it.'

'I shouted that I needed a piss, but they didn't hear. Don't forget I'd taken a lot of drugs too. Everything was a bit like a dream world, you know how it was, Ava. I was there, peeing in the woods, you were asleep under the tree, and then I sort of noticed that something was happening behind me.' Leo paused, as though dragging the painful memory back.

'Get on with it.' Ava clenched sweaty fists, biting her lip.

'Someone was yelling that Ellen was dead. I thought they were still laughing and, you know, joking around. Rhodri and Jesse brought her to the space near the fire and laid her on the ground. They were holding her between them, like some broken ragdoll, and Paul made some joke about her having had a threesome with them and said what had they done to her.'

'Rhodri and Jesse were carrying her?'

'Yeah… but they said they thought they heard her call out a bit further up the wood, and went to see if she was all right.'

'They didn't see anyone with her?' Ava snapped. Shit, this changed everything, and made it about a hundred times worse that they had never called the police. If Ellen was assaulted and murdered it didn't necessarily mean it was one of her friends involved. They could have covered up for some random sicko wandering the hills… But the police had interviewed everyone, she remembered. Had they missed something, all those years ago? It might have been just another teenage mispo case to them, but there had been uniformed officers in the village for weeks. She had been terrified they would uncover something, unable to sleep or eat because of her guilt at Ellen's death, and unable to grieve properly because she had a role to act out. 'Go on, Leo. Are you sure nobody saw anyone else in the woods that night?'

'No, but they said she was lying on the ground, and they could tell she was dead. Huw came back then. He said he'd just been having a piss too.'

'The weak bladder thing must have been catching. Christ, I can't take this in. What else, Leo? What else do you know?'

He was fidgeting with his phone, turning it over and over in his hands. 'There is something else. She had definitely been assaulted. Her knickers were missing and her clothes were all undone, and pulled around. She had bruising around her neck, and it was all purple and black in the firelight. We panicked afterwards, and made a pact not to tell you. Huw… well, Huw got really mad, violent, and he threatened all of us. You know what he was like when he got scared… Don't you see? We were

142

all there, but not together. Who would have believed that I didn't do it? In a way we were all responsible. It got totally out of control that night. I mean we quite often had sex, didn't we?'

'You didn't think maybe Huw did it, and that's why he was so keen on keeping everyone quiet? And having consensual sex is one thing, rape is another, and you know it. That's what you are trying to say, isn't it? That one of you raped Ellen and then killed her. Who was it, Leo?' Her voice was hard now. Another thought occurred to her. 'Penny must have known what happened. All these years and she never said anything. What the hell was she doing whilst Ellen was dying?'

'I don't remember. She was off in the trees with Paul to start with. Wait, no, she was crying and hugging Ellen's body afterwards. She was yelling at Paul and Huw, hitting them in the chest with her fists.'

'Big of her.' Penny's betrayal was worse, far worse than any of the others, even Leo. She had known, but she'd never said a word. Why? Ava supposed she knew the answer to that one. If the boys had threatened her, she would have gone along with it, and then secrets like that were impossible to tell after a certain time. Especially if you were married to someone who just might have committed rape and murder. Hell, she thought she was sitting on a few big secrets herself, but this... God, this was nuclear. 'You bloody stupid idiots. Someone committed a violent crime and you covered it up, to what... protect each other? It doesn't make sense. Who raped Ellen?'

His eyes dropped, and he flashed a look from under his lashes. 'Jesse?'

'Bloody convenient that, isn't it, seeing as Jesse is dead. Why would it be Jesse anyway? Ellen was already his girlfriend. I know, remember, I was her best friend.' Tears were starting. 'I was her best friend, and I was out cold when she needed me. Who was it really?'

'I told you. I think it was Jesse.'

'And Jesse had an attack of conscience and decided to tell Jackie and Peter? Then he crashed his motorbike. How very convenient.'

'Ava! You can't think… If you really want to know, Jesse had been weird for a while. He never got over Ellen, and he split up with some girlfriend in Cardiff, came home to Aberdyth to lick his wounds. He was so down, and drinking a lot, but he seemed to get better when he met Kelly. Then Kai was born and they were going to move out of Aberdyth. He nearly did it, Ava. He nearly got away.'

'I'm not being self-righteous, because I accept I am just as much to blame for covering up Ellen's death as the rest of you, but if I had known the truth, nothing would have stopped me from going to the police. Nothing.'

Leo stood up, stretching, glancing at his watch. 'That's why we agreed not to tell you. We just wanted it to go away, and for a good few years, it has. Whoever did it, isn't exactly a serial killer, are they? I think one of the boys probably just got a bit heavy-handed. Perhaps she had a fight with Jesse, and he wanted to make it up… She always was a drama queen, and she used to push his buttons.'

Ava shook her head slowly, unable to believe what she was hearing. She was tempted to hit him now, right on his perfect jawbone. That would make a fun bruise for his make-up artist to cover up. 'I can't believe Penny would go along with it. Did you threaten her?'

'Huw did. He didn't hit her or anything… Okay, a little bit maybe. Penny was going to go along with it because she was so bloody scared that Paul might have been involved. He and Ellen didn't get along so well, did they? So, what are you going to do now you know? I don't want you to get hurt, Ava.'

'Huw hit your friend and you let him? And why would I get hurt? Is that a threat?' She scowled at him.

'No, don't be stupid. That's one of the reasons I never told you. That and guilt. I should have looked out for Ellen too. She was killed metres from where we were, and I never heard a thing, and never did a thing to help her. So yes, guilt is a massive part of staying silent.'

'And it must have now occurred to you that whoever did kill Ellen, is now trying to get at me? The fact that you say her knickers were missing suggests another trophy. I hope they appear next, because I will take them straight to the police. Whoever is trying to get at me, whoever left these trophies.... Trying to threaten me with Ellen's things does not suggest fear, remorse or anything else of that nature. It suggests gloating and bullying.'

They sat in silence for a moment, before Leo's phone rang again. He glanced doubtfully at her, and answered. Only a short conversation, but he hung up looking slightly pale.

'Was that about the missing girls?' Ava had caught the gist. With this new information, the fact that there were also girls missing in the area did not add up to anything good. She was trying to push away images of Ellen struggling on the ground, screaming for help, maybe, and herself under a bloody tree. Who was she really angry at – herself or Leo?

'Yes. They haven't found them yet. But, hell, I mean look at this map...' He stood, clearly glad at the chance to dodge the subject of Ellen, and pointed at a large scale map of Big Water and the surrounding hills. 'This area in red, that's where we always run *Tough Love*. The camps are these blue triangles. Seven camps, for seven days of the competition. The show airs once a week, so that's seven weeks of entertainment, plus the voting, which is the day after the actual show.'

Ava looked, noting the vast hills, and the wooded valley between, criss-crossed with camps. She quickly calculated the scale. It was a big old area to get around. 'I suppose you have a rescue team, in case anyone gets into trouble?'

'Of course. One of the contestants had a fall on the hill the day after we started, and the medics were there within half an hour. She said that she thought Bethan or Cerys pushed her actually, but there is always a lot of catfighting between the girls, so we didn't really take too much notice. It works well when we do the edits, you get your most hated contestants trending on social media and you're made. We have cameras all over the place, and the drone team take shots from the air, obviously. But as you so rightly pointed out, it is a big area, and there are places we can't get to.'

'So would it be possible to make it out of the red hatched zone, and leave the film set area completely?'

'No. The rules are strict. If you leave the area, you are automatically disqualified. Plus, we have a temporary boundary fence that surrounds the entire place, with wire that triggers an alarm if anyone tries to get out. This is as safe as it can be, Ava, given the nature of the show.'

'Are you worried about Bethan and the others?'

He met her gaze. 'I would say no, but after what you've told me, I'm going to be honest and say yes, I am. I can't see how it could possibly be connected with what's been happening to you, but something is going on. If you're affected, who's to say they might not take me down as well?'

'Depends who really killed Ellen, doesn't it? If you do know, and it wasn't Jesse, you must tell me, Leo.'

'I… Look, Ava, it's true, I don't know.' He met her eyes reluctantly. 'Huw said it was Jesse.'

'And Huw is always right?' She sighed, but in her mind Ellen's bright gaze sharpened into Bethan's, and both girls lay still on the ground. Another time, another girl missing. Fear stabbed needles into her stomach, and something like panic rose in her throat, but the words came out calmly enough. 'You need to find these girls, Leo. Get your team in for a briefing and tell them there may be trouble. I need to speak to Huw again.'

'I will get them in, yes, but they are already looking, and I'm not going to tell them anything else. If I do, something will get out to the media, and it will get blown out of all proportion. I could lose everything.'

'And if someone is playing nasty games, you could lose a life,' Ava snapped. 'You might even need police backup, and I'm not just talking about Ellen and my own experience. I assume the nearest is still Mythran Fields?'

'No, it's Cadrington now… Do you really think it might come to that?'

'I do. I'll have to tell the police about Ellen now, too. But you must have known that when you told me she had been murdered.'

He nodded slowly, eyes fixed on her face, saying nothing. Had he also unknowingly been waiting for this moment?

'Are you ready for this, Leo? The press will have an absolute feast over your involvement, in fact over all of us. And then there's the kids… Our families. Fuck, my parents only just about forgave me for running away without Stephen when they saw what state I was in. Now we're all adults, and there is so much to lose.'

'Unless we run with the accident story?' Leo ran a slightly unsteady hand through his hair, and then glanced at his watch.

'Don't be so bloody stupid, Leo. You've just told me Ellen was murdered. This is huge, and we screwed up.' Ava snagged another cigarette. To hell with her health.

'Are you ready to lose your job?' he needled back. 'And if the police reopen Ellen's case, how ready are you to see one of your childhood friends go to jail? What if it was Paul, and I'm not saying it was, but what will Penny and Stephen say if he is convicted of Ellen's death? They'll never forgive you, especially the way things are now.'

She swung away from him, restless now, the adrenalin pumping through her veins, demanding action. Fifteen years too late. 'Did it not occur to any of you fuckwits that it might not be one of us who killed Ellen? In the panic and the scrabbling to avoid blame, did it really never cross anyone's mind that if she wandered off alone, she could have met anybody?'

He scowled, anger flitting across his face, eyes darkening, the way they always did when he got mad about something, 'No. I can honestly say it never came up. Come on, Ava, this is Aberdyth. Who would be just "wandering around" in the woods, hoping on the off chance to find a girl? The nearest road doesn't lead to anywhere but the farms.' But she could see he was jolted.

'Okay, fair enough, but it could have been planned. Lots of people knew we spent a lot of time in the woods. By keeping quiet we might have let some sexual predator go on to offend again.'

Leo moved suddenly, holding her elbows, pulling her closer. His eyes were glittering, and the bones in his face sharply accentuated. He always looked sexy when he was angry, and she knew on the original show that made him famous he had been known as a hothead, a playboy picking fights over the girls. But it seemed that was what people wanted. 'If you think you need to do this, go ahead, but don't blame me if after this, people really are out to hurt you.'

Ava pulled away, still facing him, eyes locked, annoyed to find she was slightly breathless. 'Thanks for the warning, but I can take care of myself.'

* * *

Outside, Huw was talking to some of the crew, and Leo, avoiding his eyes, quickly found some rough footage of Bethan for him to watch back. Ava watched them both, biding her time, pretending to drink her disgusting coffee. This changed everything, and the nausea was rising, her stomach twisting at the horror. One of them had not only killed Ellen, whether deliberately or not, but also sexually assaulted her. It was devastating that she hadn't known at the time. Frustration made her long for the gym and her punch bag, to sweat off what might have been, and what was to come.

Either she went with the theory that there was someone else in the woods that night, maybe hidden, watching them, and maybe not for the first time… or she accepted that one of her friends was a murderer. There was no way around it. Logically, given their history, it was probable that whoever did it had, as Leo put it, simply gone too far. Ellen had been an expert wind-up merchant, and emotions could run high when drink and drugs were involved. But murder… She struggled to get her head around it. And now she needed to tear her life apart again, to tell everyone how they had betrayed Ellen, ruthlessly disposing of her body, keeping a hideous secret all these years. She hoped Leo had a good PR team.

'See my girl, Ava? She's going to be a star,' Huw told her, jabbing a dirty finger at the screen, bringing her back to the present. 'Told her she didn't need any of that plastic surgery nonsense. She's got the whole package and it's natural. Not like some of these girls, they look like bloody blow-up dolls!' He gave a harsh bark of laughter.

Ava rubbed her eyes, trying to ignore the headache that was throbbing into life at the base of her neck. Bethan was certainly far more animated on film than she had been in the kitchen with Stephen, or even in the pub. She was wearing a lot of make-up, and had tied her long dark hair back with a red bandana. Underneath the *Tough Love* polo shirt, she wore a tight red bra top, and the shirt was unbuttoned to show more than a hint of cleavage. Despite the weather, tiny denim shorts, thick socks and chunky hiking boots completed the picture.

As Leo flicked through the footage, and Huw made more 'proud dad' comments, Ava watched the girl's interaction with her fellow contestants. She wasn't popular, picking fights, flirting with the other boys, whilst still being overtly physical with Stephen. Stephen didn't feature in many of her scenes. Again, this seemed totally out of character from what she had seen of the girl.

Her son was in the background, seemingly relaxed, laughing with the other male contestants, ignoring his girlfriend's behaviour to a certain extent. Bethan was pretty much unrecognisable, so different was her behaviour to that of the pert, quiet girl Ava had met in Penny's kitchen.

Stephen looked so much like his dad, with those cheekbones and the blue eyes. When he smiled, that sparkle lit up his face, and the dimple showed on his chin. A wave of emotion hit her smack in the breast, and she turned away. Her son. Despite her fucked-up attempt at motherhood, he had turned out good. She supposed she should thank Penny and Paul for that. But they had both betrayed her, had both known the truth about Ellen. Huw was still watching the film footage, and members of the crew were milling around. She made a quick decision.

'Leo, I need to go back now. Can I borrow a vehicle?'

He gave her a quick, unreadable look. 'Sure, take my truck. Just leave it outside the Birtleys' and put the keys under the wheel. I'll get a lift back with Huw. Ava?' There was relief on his face, but he couldn't possibly know she had a cosy chat with Huw planned for tonight, and if his family were at home, so much the better.

She caught the keys and turned to leave. 'What?'

'Take care.' His face was serious, but Huw, who had also looked up, was scowling again.

'Nice to see you again, Huw.' Ava smiled at him. 'I'm sure we'll catch up soon.'

He nodded, no more than a rough jerk of his head, and turned back to the screens, staring fixedly at his daughter.

Chapter 18

I've left another gift for Ava Cole to find.

She's moving fast after a couple of double sixes. It is almost as if she has never been away, she is so much part of the hills, the village. I see her face everywhere.

The girl is locked away, and I've finished my work with her. She is temporarily stuck on her square of the board, and she will only move forward in the game if Ava manages to find her. We loved games as kids, and the games got wilder as we got older. I see no reason to stop playing, as an adult.

The drugs were a good way to push people into losing their inhibitions. I learned this from a master, and of course from personal experience.

The night Ellen died, I was there, watching, enjoying the fun. Funny that I wasn't actually instrumental in her killing, although as I supplied the drugs for the party, I suppose you could say I helped to escalate the proceedings, and the confusion. I'd been saying for a while that it turned me on to watch that kind of stuff on the internet, even showed a couple of the friends my favourites. I wanted them to wonder about me, and I wanted to see how much power I really had.

It was good that Ellen was gone. If she hadn't died that night,

I'd probably have found another way to get rid of her. She was too close to Ava and she was in the way. Luckily my girl made her own decisions.

The filming has delivered a golden opportunity and provides a perfect backdrop for my own game. There are so many people coming and going, not to mention the press occasionally hanging around, that nobody notices if I disappear for an hour or so.

In a case under the spare room bed is a loose floorboard, and in a classic adventure story cliché this is where I hide my trophies. Now, I jemmy the board, lifting out my trinkets, surveying them with appreciation and a certain amount of pride. There are two missing, of course – the gifts I left for Ava – but I have plenty more. My mind drifts for a moment to another stash, more trophies, but I push that one away. That suitcase is not for me to bring out. Not yet anyway.

Everything is ruthlessly planned, and timed. I enjoyed last night. I relished the moment when blood spurted into the cold air, steaming as it hit the icy grass, and I felt a thrill deep in my bones when I outwitted the film crew, the blundering security team, and the silly alarms on their boundary fence. I'm tired now, so I grab a handful of medication to get me through the day. My bedroom window is vast and square. I can look out onto my sugar-coated kingdom and know that I have achieved all I needed to. If it wasn't for the restlessness that lies beneath, the stirring in my blood that creates such a craving, I think I would be at peace with the past. But I am a gamer, and peace is never an option. My calling is to keep on playing. I am special. I was always told that, and whereas before I knew it was lies and pain, now I know it to be true. Everyone knows it, and I feel truly famous. A silly tune from childhood rolls around in my head:

'*Os ewch i lawr i Llyn Fawr heddiw, Ava Cole, fe welwch chi syndod mawr...*'

'**If you go down to Big Water today, Ava Cole, you'll find a big surprise...**'

Chapter 19

Ava rolled over, rubbing sleep from her eyes, groaning as the sun hit her face. She needed to get out for a run, clear her head after that cheap wine. What a stupid thing to do. Her gaze landed on the door, noting that the chest of drawers was still pushed up against it, wedging it shut. The window was still locked with a double length of twisted wire.

Fine, it was all still fine. Hopefully those ridiculous girls would turn up today, if they hadn't already. As for Ellen... Ava was still struggling to rearrange her memories. Ellen hadn't died in an accident, she had been murdered. It changed everything, and Ava's past was shattered once again, reforming slowly, in jagged puzzle pieces. Her overwhelming emotion was frustration. If only she had known, if only she had gone to the police at the time...

But she hadn't, she had gone along with their story, had missed signs of bruising on Ellen's neck, which Leo claimed were definitely there. She had missed, in her grief and confusion, any signs that her friend had been assaulted. Or had she? If she had looked deeper, taken a moment to think, could she have prodded the others into confessing a crime had been committed? Her therapist had told her that sometimes people rearranged the past to suit themselves, to prevent pain, to remove blame... Had she truly known on some level that Ellen's death was not an accident?

The thought was like a blow to the head. She could have helped catch Ellen's murderer, instead she had likely helped them get away with it. Cold cases were unpredictable at the best of times, but now she meant to help in every way she could on this one. Perhaps this was why she had been brought back? Even if she lost the job she loved, and she desperately hoped it wouldn't come to that, maybe this was the price she had to pay.

Ava thought of Penny's slightly panicked message on her phone yesterday evening when she got back from the *Tough Love* filming. She had said that Paul was rude and aggressive to Alex when he visited, and had finally thrown him off the farm, and told him to stop sticking his nose in where it didn't belong. As he was staying at the B&B, Penny wanted Ava to talk to him, to smooth things over, and reiterate how ill Paul was.

But she hadn't seen Alex last night. After everything Leo had told her, she didn't want to speak to anyone until she'd contacted the police. So she had grabbed a quick bite to eat at the pub before retreating to her room with a bottle of wine. A preliminary call to the police at Cadrington had resulted in a desk sergeant taking details of the photographs and promising someone would be over for a talk. She hadn't been sure about ringing the local police station, but she needed to make initial contact that night before her courage failed her, and it was hardly a 999 call. Once she had reported the pictures, she would try to locate that PC who had worked on Ellen's case – now apparently DI Sophie Miles. The Smiths had mentioned she had been very interested in Jesse's death too.

She had to talk to Alex today – mainly to try to discover if he had uncovered anything else, but also to apologise. Oh, fuck, and she needed to call her mom, her boss, and see Ellen's parents. That was going to be horrific, but she couldn't wait for them to hear the news from the police. Last night, she had already prepared a preliminary report for whoever took charge of Ellen's case, detailing everything she could remember. She spared nobody, including herself, and it was a raw, stripped-to-the-bones honest account of what happened, finishing with various possible theories as to the perp's identity.

Ava swung her legs out of bed, grabbing her phone as it buzzed with a message. Seeing it was in Welsh, she froze, once again summoning her childhood language with difficulty;

'*If you come down to Big Water today, Ava Cole, you'll find a big surprise...*'

Was that right? She was very rusty, but she was sure that was right. Please God, this didn't have anything to do with the girls from *Tough Love*. Quickly she tried to ring the unfamiliar number, but as before, the line was dead.

She yanked on her running gear from the pile on the floor, fingers fumbling with her laces. It would take a good half an hour to run down to Big Water, it was maybe four miles from the village. But who to call? Huw had a Land Rover, but would he lend it? Yeah right. Rhodri didn't appear to have any transport, despite living at the garage. She phoned Penny, but there was no answer at the farm. They were probably out lugging hay around the hills for the sheep.

Ava was out the door before Leo answered her call.

'Ava? Are you all right?' His voice was sharp. 'Have the police got back to you?'

She had sent him a courtesy text last night after her call to Cadrington. 'I'm fine. Are you at home?'

Leo's vast modern house, perched just above the village, with huge windows overlooking the valley, popped into her mind. Could he see as far as Big Water from there?

'No. I stayed the night at one of the camps in the end. We found two of the girls. They just went off course. They're a bit cold and hungry, but they're fine. We got some great footage. Bethan and Cerys are still missing. The papers are all over it already, so some bastard has leaked the story.'

'I'm thrilled for you. Did they say where Bethan and the other girl, Cerys, are?'

She heard the sigh in his voice. 'They had a row and went and split up. Every series, I forget how much they all hate each other. Helen is still saying Cerys or Bethan pushed her off the hill and she's winding up Stephen.'

'Is he okay?' Ava asked quickly.

'Of course. I have a team on site offering counselling and help to the contestants whilst they are being filmed. It's bloody hard trying to keep them from sneaking in phones and leaking things onto social media, though.'

'It's your show, Leo, you should be used to it. Anyway, I need your help. Have you been down to Big Water this morning?'

'No chance, we're right on the other side, over near Caban Valley.'

'Shit. I got another weird text that told me to go to Big Water. I'll have to run... Leo, you haven't mentioned anything to the others about me going to the police, have you?'

'No. We agreed not to. Give me some credit.'

'Right. I need to go then.'

'Ava! Don't go by yourself. Look, I can meet you there if you take old man Birtley's truck,' Leo suggested.

'He's got a truck?'

'In the outbuildings. It still runs and he takes it into town every week to get prescriptions and stuff. Just tell him it's an emergency. I'm sure you can drive it.'

'So am I.' She ended the call and went in search of Mr Birtley.

*　*　*

The truck was an old black affair and seemed to be held together by mud and rust, but it bumped, sure-footed, out of the village and along the track to Big Water.

Ava yanked the wheel, ground through the gears, and stamped

156

on the brake pedal, slowing to a crawl as she navigated around the last few potholes. Coming out of the woods, and the heady smell of frosted pine, the five-bar gate to Big Water was shut and looped round with a padlocked chain. Fuck, she should have thought of that. After a second of chewing her thumbnail in frustration she abandoned the truck and vaulted over the gate, phone in hand.

The stillness of the cold morning, combined with vastness of the grey water, was eerie. A few delicate rays of sunshine hardly warmed the frosted grass, and the clouds were already rolling in from the west.

She didn't see it at first, instead taking her time to search around the field and Portakabins, her shoes crunching in the iced grass. An engine roared in the gloom, making her jump, stomach clenching. She turned to see Leo bumping down the hill to her left in a Land Rover packed with men in orange tabards. She scanned the silent Portakabins again, noting the locks still in place, the lack of fresh tyre marks.

There were signs of vehicles, footprints, and a stack of wooden crates covered in a green tarpaulin, but these were all frozen solid. The cluster of trees at the very bottom of the hill, where the land rose steeply upwards in a series of uneven steps, might be worth a look. It was the only other cover this side of Big Water. It would take ages to search the banks, but hopefully Leo's search team could help out with that. Or perhaps she had translated the Welsh into something quite different, and it actually said 'Go to the pub' or something.

She scanned the still water, heart jerking painfully as a bird flew down from the clouds and landed with a splash and a squawk. The zip line was still in place, ready for the grand finale but something was wrong. Her eyes followed it back up towards the starting point on the hill. Fuck.

Ava gripped her phone, her hand once again going automatically to a gun holster that wasn't there, reaching for a weapon.

Someone was hanging on the wire, but they seemed to have got stuck halfway. The body swayed gently, as tension was picked up then released in the light breeze, and the odd sunbeam illuminated, and then cast a dark shadow, on the waters beneath.

Ava shouted, squinting into brightness, but the person on the wire made no attempt to shout back, or wave at her, merely bobbing in the breeze, legs swinging.

Leo must have seen it too and had already dispatched a few members of his security crew, their bright orange tabards now dotting the icy whiteness of the bank. They were pointing and shouting instructions, but he headed straight for Ava.

'What the hell is going on? Who is that up there?'

'I don't know, Leo. Can we get out there in that boat?'

'Well… yes, but it would be easier just to reel them in. We've got a safety mechanism if anyone gets stuck, and it will just wind the handle back up to the top of the hill. They might need medical help… unless it's Bethan and Cerys pulling some stunt. I can't see in this light.' He was squinting at the figure on the zip line. 'Looks like a man though…'

One of the security crew panted up to them, his medical bag on his back. 'It isn't one of the contestants, or any of our lot. But, whoever it is, well…' The man wiped beads of sweat from his brow. He was still breathing deeply. 'It's a man and as far as we can make out he's dead. Better get the police in, Leo.'

'Fucking hell!' Leo hauled his phone out. 'This is just great. We've still got another five days' filming to go. They'll shut us down, and the insurance people will go ballistic.'

'Leo, I hate to point out the obvious, but if this is a murder scene, you're going to have far more problems than just a delay in filming,' Ava snapped at him. 'Aren't you worried it might be someone we know?'

The expression on his face said that hadn't occurred to him.

'Let me call the police.' Ava was glad to feel her professional self kicking in. 'We need to get out in that boat and have a look at the victim close up. Nobody is to contaminate the scene. Don't move anything, or wind your zip line, and don't start telling anyone else, or you will have the press here before the police. Get someone to open the gate to this field. The bloody thing is padlocked.'

Leo, looking mutinous, muttered that the keys should be in the production office, and hurried off across the field. This time Ava called 999, giving her location quickly. She added that they would need an ambulance, but that they had medics as part of the film production team already on scene. Wincing slightly, she also informed the man on the other end of the line that she was a detective with LAPD and finished the call by giving as much detail as possible about the body.

'I know this is a bit out of order, but if DI Sophie Miles does attend, I have a few things to tell her that are definitely relevant.' Ava tried to quit panicking. 'No, I don't know who the victim is. We can only see from a distance, but we're going out in the boat now.'

'You ready?' It was one of the crew, standing on the bank, ready to launch the boat. 'Is Leo coming?'

'No. He's gone to unlock the gate for the police and ambulance.'

'Don't reckon there'll be much the paramedics can do for that poor bloke,' the other man said, shivering in his wax jacket. He pulled the collar higher, his face pale.

The inflatable cut a swathe of white froth through the grey water, splashing freezing droplets onto the occupants. As they got closer, Ava was able to make out the features, and her heart began to thump so hard it actually hurt her ribcage. The face was grey and frozen, but it was unmistakable.

'Here, I've got some binoculars if you want to take a closer look? He's up pretty high, and it's going to be hard seeing anything from this angle.' One of the crew thrust them into her numb hands.

The binoculars confirmed what she already knew. The body

hanging pathetically, strung out for all to see, was the private investigator who had been so sure he had cracked Ellen's case. Alex Jennington had assured her that there was nothing new in his investigation, hadn't he? So what had he discovered last night that had deserved this? She remembered Pen's message. Paul had thrown him off the farm about four o'clock, and she hadn't bumped into Alex at the B&B later or when she'd popped down to the shop for supplies. Where had he gone then?

They were still out in the boat when the police 4x4s bounced over the icy ruts towards Big Water. Ava was still studying the victim, trying hard to be objective. There was a straight cut to his jugular. He must have bled out before he was hoisted onto the zip line, because although his clothing was stained, it wasn't the dramatic amount she would have expected from an arterial spray. The wire was clean. His white hands were roped firmly to the handles of the pulley, and his head lolled in a grotesque fashion.

He appeared to be fully clothed, but without a jacket, boots or socks. Did the murderer remove them, or had he been killed inside, and moved down here? His grey eyes were wide open, and his long skinny feet were bare. Shoving emotion away, she slammed a fist against the hard rubber side of the boat. 'Fuck! How could this have happened?'

She said it more to stop herself throwing up than to get an answer, and the two men in the boat with her looked fairly green themselves.

'Do you know who it is?' one of them asked.

'Yes. His name is Alex Jennington, and he is, or was, a private investigator.' Ava studied their faces as she spoke. 'He's only been in the village a couple of days, and I believe he was leaving tomorrow.'

'Oh, him. He was down on set the other day. Talking to Leo, I think. They had a bit of a row about something. Leo's a right grumpy git when we've got a job on – everything has to be perfect,' the other man volunteered. 'The police are here, so do you want to go back now?'

Ava nodded, her mind whirring, hands clenched on the rope handles on the side of the boat as they powered back to the shore. So Alex had discovered the truth about Ellen, and somebody had taken care that he didn't get a chance to pass on his discovery. It seemed logical. It also seemed ironic, that today was the day she would be speaking to the police about Ellen herself.

Back on dry land, Ava introduced herself to the police contingent. There were two uniformed cops, and she was unimpressed.

'We've put out an alert for the Major Crime Team, and they'll send a DI out, but that'll take a while. Are you the person who made the 999 call?'

'Yes. The victim is Alex Jennington, a private investigator. He was staying at the same B&B as me,' Ava said, her gaze still fixed on the body.

'Okay, if you wouldn't mind coming over here with me, I'll take a statement whilst we wait for backup.' The elder of the two was courteous, but his eyes were red and tired. Both eyed Ava warily. It was clear that they were slightly overwhelmed by the scene.

Glancing across the field, she could see Leo being interviewed by the other officer.

Half an hour later more vehicles struggled through the gate, and the ambulance crew trudged off with another uniformed officer, presumably to pronounce that life was extremely extinct. Another team started to cordon off the crime scene.

Ava, sitting in the police car, watched with a surreal feeling. This couldn't be happening. A tall woman in grey trousers and a red jacket was clearly receiving a briefing. The officer pointed at Ava, and the woman swung round to stare at her.

Ava left the warmth of her seat and walked over, ducking back under the cordon.

'You must be Ava Cole. I'm DI Sophie Miles. I believe you found the body?'

The DI was probably over six foot, and she carried it well. Her face was gaunt, and her grey hair spiked out from under a red ski hat. Her eyes, frank and expressive, were dark green, and she didn't smile. Her words rattled out like machine-gun fire.

Ava found herself stumbling over her own words, and when Leo came over, urging everyone to help themselves to coffee, she grabbed a cup and wrapped her frozen hands around it. It was a bit tricky, introducing herself as probably both a suspect and a colleague, but the DI took it well, her expression neither accepting nor showing any coldness.

Her team still seemed slightly wary of Ava, watching her like curious cats as the introductions were made, but they were quickly dispatched onto the lake, and up the hill to where the zip line started. The uniformed officers had moved on to interviewing some of Leo's crew.

DI Miles took a few quick notes from the officer with Ava, and nodded at her again, before striding off to confer with the paramedics. The zip line, with its grisly cargo, had been slowly winched back up the hill.

It felt extremely odd to be on the other side of the fence, observing a crime scene through the eyes of a witness, and Ava was glad when Leo finally came over to sit with her.

'What do you think then?' Leo asked. His face was pale and he looked exhausted.

'About Alex? No idea, but it obviously leads back to what we were saying the other day.' She sighed. 'I'm going to get DI Miles' number and see if I can speak to her later, or tomorrow, about all the other stuff. I only gave uniform a basic witness statement so far, mainly about my drink being spiked, the photographs, and their connection to an old case. I've not even mentioned Ellen's name to them yet. Any news on Bethan and Cerys?'

'No. I thought… I really thought for a moment that the body was going to be one of them. This is going to create a bit of drama at the camp, when they get to hear what's happened,' Leo said. He was turning his phone over and over in his hands, biting his lip. 'My PR team are going to put out a statement. I know you don't want to hear it, and I am sorry that the PI has been murdered, but I need to focus on the production. I've got a lot riding on this, and I need to get my side across before I start getting investors pulling out.'

Ava nodded. She couldn't blame him for putting his business first. Her mind was spinning with suspects, but she didn't have the energy to start a discussion with Leo. She still needed to ring Jack too, her mom probably, and oh God, she'd need to try and see Jackie and Peter before the additional news broke. Her limbs were weak and she closed her eyes for a second, blotting out the activity, blotting out Ellen's screams for help that she had never heard. Deep inside, she also felt stirrings of panic. That fluttering tightness in her chest that could build and build until she couldn't breathe, and her hands were left curled like claws, desperate to hang on to something.

She hadn't had panic attacks for years – not since she had left Wales and spent three years recovering with her parents in Florida. The therapy had been tough at first, and progress slow, but gradually she had made her way out of the darkness. The first time she managed to drive herself to the local store had been a major triumph. She forced herself to remember the triumph, the return of a tiny glow of confidence she had felt at the achievement.

There were other achievements, but she could list them later, each one was emblazoned on her memory to help combat the bad times, and, she supposed, to atone for the way she had treated Ellen and Stephen.

They sat in silence for a long while, watching the police working. It was thorough and methodical, and for Ava so familiar and yet strange. Leo was smoking one cigarette after another.

A temporary command centre was soon established in Leo's office. She felt herself relaxing slightly, despite the fact that the really bad stuff was yet to come. It would be okay, and she could do this. She could finally untangle the past and leave it behind. For Ellen and for herself. And now for Alex too…

A muscular blond man, with a ruddy wind-blasted complexion strode up to them. 'I know you've given a statement already, Miss Cole, but I just have a couple more questions. I'm DS Dave Sharon, and I work directly with DI Miles.'

'I would say nice to meet you. Call me Ava. Would it be possible to leave a number for DI Miles to give me a call a bit later? Or I can ring her?'

He studied her quizzically. 'You can say anything to me that you would say to the DI, Ava, and as you know it's all confidential. Shall we go back into this office? It'll be warmer.'

'Sorry, yes I know. It's just that I think I have information on another case she worked on previously that may be relevant to this one.' Ava shot a last look at Leo as he snagged another coffee off the table. The big hot water tank was steaming gently in the icy air, and someone had left a tin of biscuits.

DS Sharon shrugged. 'No worries. Here's her card and one of mine. You're with the LAPD, one of the boys was saying?'

'That's right. Do you mind if I call my boss back home? As I mentioned, there has been some other stuff happening that could be connected, and as well as the text messages sent to me, he was sent an email.'

'Yes, go ahead,' the man told her, dumping his iPad on the table, and carefully moving Leo's neat piles of paperwork. 'And that was Leo Evans wasn't it? I've seen the show. It's very interesting, almost a psychological experiment really. One of the PCs has already taken a preliminary statement from him, but we'll need more of course.'

Ava's phone rang, and she sighed with relief when she saw it was Jack. She looked quickly at DS Sharon for permission and he nodded, pale-blue eyes sharp with interest, his fingers busy logging the information so far. 'Listen, Jack, things have escalated here, and I've got a body. I'm with the police now.'

'Who is it?' His voice was sharp with interest, and there was no trace of sleepiness, despite the time difference.

'Some private investigator hired to find a local girl who went missing fifteen years ago.' She hoped her voice sounded natural, but he picked her up immediately.

'Around the time you left Wales?'

Her boss retained pretty much everything anyone ever told him, which was both a blessing and a curse, for a cop. 'A couple of years before, actually. I'll… I'll tell you about that later. As I said, I'm with the local police now, and I really wanted to know if you found anything on whoever put those pictures up?'

She heard clicking, then rustling. Jack was a paperwork-not-gadget type of guy.

'Firstly, pictures are down, but of course we have the screen-shots. Secondly, no. The website is owned by a company called Blue Dreams, based in Chicago. We checked, and they are a legit supplier of porn, sex toys, chatlines, and crap like that. But the guy I spoke to denies any knowledge of this particular site, and says they play by the rules. Of course, he would say that.'

'Or whoever runs the site just uses them as a front to seem more legitimate?'

'Right, but that wouldn't be unusual for a dodgy site like this, would it? We're still digging on the bloke who posted the photos. He calls himself BoyNextDoor – you know what it's like trying to track down these people. It really depends whether whoever took the photos is the same person who actually posted them, or whether the photographer took them, sold them on, and then crawled back under their rock.'

Ava considered this for a moment. 'No, I think someone who went to those lengths would want to gloat. They'd want to be part of the victim's… my… humiliation. I got another weird text this morning, saying that I should go to the lake to find this poor vic.'

DS Sharon was watching her intently, and Ava wrapped up

her call. 'Thanks, Jack. I've got to go, but let me know if you get anything won't you? Oh, for reference the lead on the case over here is DI Sophie Miles. I've got a bunch of contact details for the team, so I'll send them over for you to liaise.'

'Sure, got that. Call me later anyway and tell me the full story. I can tell there's a lot more on this. And Ava... be careful. Don't get any more involved than you have to.'

He always had been a perceptive bastard, she thought, almost amused. Then her gaze went out the window, settled on Alex's body, slowly making its way up to the top of the hill, and she quit smiling in an instant. 'Always, Boss.'

Chapter 20

That was fun. It was so much fun I almost forgot to visit the girl. She surprised me a bit today – clearly she has a feisty side, and being with me has brought out a better side of her character. Suffering is good for some people. Luckily, I prepared for a cold snap, but the weather is showing no sign of lifting. How disappointing if she dies before Ava has a chance to save her.

Honestly, the number of ridiculous mistakes people keep making, it truly makes my mind spin. If I didn't love Ava, I would have killed her for spilling any secrets to the law. As it is, she is doing well, and the game is taking some pretty interesting twists. Ellen's death has always been fairly low on my list of secrets, anyway, and I have a number of options prepared for the police. Unlike certain other people, for years I have been sure that at some point Ellen's body would be discovered. Therefore, I laid down plans to cover this eventuality. I have adjusted the board to reflect my players. Only one has been retired so far, which means the others have everything to play for.

Alex Jennington was an easy kill. I didn't bother with any games – not when I have the girl locked away, and Ava so close. It was quick, and he was still half-asleep. I think he was rather excited by the idea of his new source, and I assured him I had thought long and hard about divulging this key bit of information.

I can't be sure he wasn't recording our initial call, and where that might be stored, so I kept it fairly vague and semi-formal. It wasn't until I met him in the darkness by the old primary school that I was able to ascertain he had put all the facts together. He still didn't know who had killed Ellen, but he did know about something else. It would have pissed Ellen off, to know this isn't just all about her. She always was a selfish bitch. Beautiful, but a bitch.

It made my skin prickle with anger as Alex Jennington described his plans to gather more evidence. His rather colourless voice was lit up with excitement and interest. There was pity, too, and that burned my soul. Pity is one of the most disgusting of human emotions. It is one of the reasons I have arranged things as I have.

It was just too bad he had stumbled on this particular secret in the course of his investigation. I had hoped he might get distracted elsewhere. All he really needed to do was find out enough to tell the Smiths their daughter was probably dead, and it might have been Jesse who killed her. End of story. The police were never going to waste time on a 'maybe' cold case, and the parents could depart knowing that the reason their daughter never contacted them was because she was probably dead. Jesse was dead, so there was no line of investigation.

Neat and safe. But no, Alex Jennington had to come sniffing around me and my doings, and Ava has taken this whole photography thing and blown it out of proportion. Surely she knows on some level that it was me in her room? Perhaps her intelligence is slipping... That would be bad news for the girl.

I picked him up in my Land Rover and drove down to my kill site. I offered him a drink from my flask as we wandered down to the Big Water and talked about the things that had happened to me. We wandered right up to the high point, near the cluster of bent and twisted trees. Their bleached limbs were pale and ghostly in the darkness. The zip line was all set up for *Tough Love* of course, and this was the start point. I needed him close to the line, ready for the next stage of my plan. No point in lugging a dead body around if you don't need to. I checked his body carefully for recording devices, and took the SIM card out of his phone as he bled out. He thought I was going to show him a grave site, and of course he was right, he just didn't realise it was his own.

'Wnaethoch chi fwynhau hynny, Ava Cole?'

'**Did you enjoy that, Ava Cole?**'

Chapter 21

'Penny, can we meet up for dinner?'

'Of course, lovely. I heard about you finding the body! Poor Alex, such an awful thing to happen. He seemed such a nice man, and I feel so bad Paul threw him off the farm. It makes me feel sick to think of him being murdered.' She sounded shaky, and despite the usual chitchat she seemed to be trying too hard, pretending everything would be all right, as usual.

'I don't know, but the police are looking into it. It is awful, but we just need to stay calm and tell the truth.' Ava tried to stem the flow of anxious chatter, at the same time wondering if Penny would mention Ellen. It was obvious the two cases were connected, even without the other stuff that had been going on.

'The truth about Ellen, you mean? Ah, I see. Leo told me you knew.' Her voice had an edge of ice, now.

Typical – Leo hadn't been able to resist spreading the news. 'We won't talk about it on the phone, Penny, we can talk properly later. This is for the best though, I'm sure it is.'

Silence, and then she bounced back with the sweetness that had always been such a part of her character. 'Do you want me to cook, and you can come here? Paul is in bed at the moment, and his meds have knocked him right out, but if he feels better later, I'll drive him over to the respite centre for a few hours. It will be easier to talk if it's just us anyway. Does eight-thirty suit you?'

Ava bit her lip, shoulders sagging with relief. At least she wouldn't have to face Paul at the same time. Grilling Penny would be far easier. 'Thanks, Pen, that would be great. Oh, just one thing. The police have taken Alex's iPad. They looked through his notes and think he went out to meet someone last night, before he was murdered. Any idea who he might have been seeing? Did he catch up with Huw yesterday? I mean, after he saw you and Paul?'

Silence, and Ava pictured Penny tapping her lip with her forefinger, the way she always did at school when she was thinking hard. Eventually she said, reluctantly, 'I'm not sure. I do know Huw was supposed to meet him earlier but then changed his mind. Huw is always a difficult one, and he was so worried you were going to bring up the whole thing with Ellen. I know you and he haven't ever really gotten along that well, but he isn't a bad person.'

'Have you spoken to him today?'

'No, I did ring him after we heard about Alex, but Isabell, that's his girlfriend, said he'd gone into town to the builder's yard. Is Bethan still missing?'

'Yes. He... he didn't seem that concerned the other day. He just said she was playing for the cameras. What do you think?'

'He is very ambitious for her. But he adores her, idolises her even, so I would imagine underneath he is pretty worried. Oh God, Ava, I just can't believe this. That poor man. Who could have done this?'

'The police will be interviewing everyone later today. I asked if they would just abandon filming, but they are going to hang on to the contestants for a bit. After all, they are all suspects now. I bet that's a drama none of them ever dreamt of.' Ava sighed. 'Stephen's fine. I haven't been allowed to speak to him yet, and I expect he's worried sick about Bethan, but he's okay. Leo was

171

talking to another officer about Bethan, and I imagine they'll put another DI onto it. DI Miles will have enough to do, trying to sort out Alex's murder.'

'I'm so glad Stephen is all right. I'm sort of reassured we have all these police around us now too. It makes me feel a bit safer, with all this stuff going on. I did ring Leo last night, just to check if he was okay, but there was no answer on his landline or mobile. I expect he was down at the camp.'

'He said he was. Okay, thanks Pen, see you later.'

Ava stretched aching limbs, dropped her phone and laptop on the bed, and let out a long breath. There would be time later to ask Penny exactly why she had kept the true circumstances of Ellen's death a secret all these years. She would get her talking over a home-cooked dinner and the bottle of wine she would buy from the store on her way over. Suddenly, exhaustion was beating waves around her head, but she had just fifteen minutes before DI Miles turned up for a chat.

She had given DS Sharon the bare bones yesterday, but there had been a lot going on, and when DI Miles rang late last night suggesting an informal chat away from the chaos, Ava had agreed eagerly. Ava told her the whole story would take a couple of hours, and she was willing to come down to the station if someone would pick her up, but the DI vetoed this, saying she would bring one of her team to take notes.

It was still a struggle, but she was part of the law enforcement team now, not a scared teenager who made a stupid mistake. She had managed to speak to her boss, giving him an outline, reiterating she had believed Ellen's death to be an accident. He had given no indication of what might happen next, but she had been reassured by his usual unruffled demeanour. There was an element of surprise, and a few times he had asked her to go back over what had happened that night, but his main point, and she did agree with this, seemed to be that none of the other kids had suspected another person might be in the woods that night. The more Ava thought about this, the more she felt forced to conclude they knew which of them did kill Ellen. All of them knew, and they were protecting each other for different reasons.

There was no answer from the Smiths' telephone, and her mom and dad were out and not answering their mobiles. Bloody typical.

A sudden thought struck her... Perhaps it wasn't one person, or all of them, but two of them. Paul and Huw? Paul and Leo?

Her mind drifted back to the night of Ellen's death, and once again she began ticking off her list of suspects. Leo, Huw, Paul, Rhodri and Jesse had all been in the wood with herself and Penny that night, making up the whole gang. Sometimes there would be another girl or two tagging along, if the boys brought one, but that night there had just been the eight of them. She tried now, with this new evidence, to force herself to remember any fresh details, anything the others had done or said, that might implicate them.

Ellen had been late arriving, but that was nothing new. She would have taken her time making herself look gorgeous, choosing the right top, brushing out her long dark hair.

Tears were prickling at the back of Ava's eyes, and her throat was tight and sore. Ellen's flowery scent filled the room, and she could almost feel the warmth of her hand on her arm, see the laughter in her eyes. She was always challenging Ava, always daring her to go higher, run faster, aim for the stars. Ellen, like Bethan, had wanted to be a model, an actress, to be on the covers of magazines.

Ava's gut, something she used a lot in her job, told her that Jesse wasn't responsible for the rape or murder. He was weak, and had followed Ellen around like a little dog. Sure, she had flirted with the others, thrown scenes to get attention, but he had remained constant with his affections. The other boys' faces flashed past her eyes, laughing and young as they had been all those years ago. Was it the same person who had been in her room, touched her naked body, hacked her accounts, or were there several perps, years apart, committing crimes for different reasons, but tied to the same secret in the woods? Alex had been a bit too close to the truth, and he had been silenced. That part she did believe. She had been warned, but she would not keep quiet. Not this time.

A car drew up outside, and Ava peered out of the condensation-streaked windows of her room. Time to face up to Ellen's death. With no hesitation this time, she bent and unlocked her case, removing Ellen's bracelet and hair band, and popping them in her pocket. She ran downstairs, pulling on her thick coat and gloves as she did so. It had taken half an hour in the pink bath last night to stop the shivering.

'Can I get you some tea and biscuits?' Mrs Birtley was hovering in the hallway, pulling at the sleeves of her purple cardigan. 'I didn't get a chance to say, earlier, but I heard you found poor Alex's body, Ava? We had the police here yesterday morning whilst you were still down at Big Water. They went through his room and took things away. It feels wrong. The man's barely cold and they're poking around his things.'

'Yes, I did find him. Well, me and a few other people. Mrs Birtley, there will probably be someone coming to look in Alex's room again today, can you just make sure you keep it locked until then please? And obviously, I'm sure they mentioned – don't clean it all, will you?'

'Of course not. I'm not daft, Ava. It's such a terrible thing to happen, and all after you've only just got back. It seems like, and don't take this the wrong way, but there has been nothing but trouble since you came back to the village, and you've barely been here a week. Whatever will happen next?' Mrs Birtley clicked her tongue, passing a yellow duster over her desk. Her podgy, pale face was alight with excitement, despite her reproving words. The Hoover was propped, ready for action, in a corner.

The DI stood with a colleague, surveying the scene, her mouth pursed, but her eyes glinted with something that could have been amusement.

Ava turned to the senior officer. 'Actually, I think we need to go for a bit of drive, if that works for you?'

'Of course.' The other woman smiled now, understanding and amusement flickering across her thin face. 'Get in the car. This is DS Harper. He'll be recording our conversation so I can refer back to my notes later.'

Ava nodded. She would never have come out to meet a suspect on a case without backup either. There was also the plain fact that, for better or worse, every tiny detail needed to be documented. The police knew that anything missed would be picked over in court, and any doubts could cost a case. Everything went into the DL, or Decision Log, at home in the States, and she guessed it was probably pretty much the same over here.

They drove, at Ava's direction, out of the village, and up as far as the hairpin bend where Jesse had met his death. There was a lay-by leading off to the hills, and nothing but a few sheep to disturb them. The sky was still leaden with snow, sullen clouds pulsing their way across the very tops of the bare hills.

'DI Miles, I'll just tell you what I know, and then we can try and work out what is significant and what isn't. Sorry, I realise I'm way out of my zone here, and a suspect to boot.'

'Okay, Detective, you said it and not me. Go ahead, and hit me with the info. And for Christ's sake call me Sophie, it makes me feel younger.'

'Sure. It's Ava, and just stop me if I'm talking too fast. It's kind of a bad habit.' Ava smiled at her, grateful for the brisk manner, and responding in kind. She went quickly through the timeline, starting with Ellen's death, working her way up to the current situation. It took an hour, and by the time she was finished, she was exhausted, but strangely relaxed. The terror at having to reveal the secret, a secret that would affect so many people, ruin so many relationships, and surely alter the course of her own life, had vanished. The floating feeling, the fact that her body felt weightless, yet pinned to the seat, was not uncomfortable. It was done. Maybe this was why people went to religious confession, to get rid of their worst secrets. Most people probably didn't have murder on their conscience. 'The last thing is, and I realise it may not be possible, but I want to be there when the news of Ellen's murder and burial in the woods, gets broken to her parents.'

Ava watched out the corner of her eye as, unobtrusive in the back seat, the DS scribbled notes, scrolled down on his iPad to check details, and tapped details into his phone. He half-smiled as he looked up and caught her looking.

Sophie Miles smiled coolly showing very white, even teeth. Throughout the story, she had maintained an impartial, emotionless stance, occasionally prodding for further memories, but she must surely be shocked. 'You're right, it won't be possible. I can't let you become involved at all, but there is nothing to stop you ringing them before I send someone round. Which will be as soon as we finish our conversation.'

'It's okay. My fault, I should have done it years ago.'

'You should.' The ice in her voice was noticeable, and Ava felt herself rebuked.

'You worked the original mispo case, didn't you?'

'I did. Ellen Smith's case was one of the first I worked on, and it's one that has stayed with me, so now, to find that – as I feared – there is far more to it than a teenage runaway... Let's just say I wish one of you had come forward a long time ago. You know, of course, that the likelihood of us managing to get a viable suspect, let alone a prosecution, on this, is negligible.'

'Understood.' She couldn't say anything else. No excuses, no promises.

For the first time, warmth coloured the other woman's voice, and she returned to the facts. 'And the rest, well, that is a lot to process. Let me just double check a few details. You were fifteen when Ellen was assaulted, or raped, and then murdered. You thought it was an accident, but recently discovered it wasn't. You had a baby two years later, and went on to marry Paul Jones. You were the only one that night who didn't realise what really happened to Ellen. And after you left Wales you didn't have any more than sporadic contact with anyone else who was involved?'

Ava shook her head. 'No. In fact none at all, until my aunt – she lived in Cadrington for a while – began sending emails with news of Stephen. Eventually, Paul and I would email each other a couple of times a year, just with brief updates. That was it. He… he asked me to stay away from Stephen until he was eighteen. I agreed this was for the best.' She knew she could have told the truth about Paul's threats, but a strange remnant of loyalty remained. Or was it guilt? Paul would die soon, and he had been a good dad from what she could see. Let it rest. For now.

'And whilst you were still in Wales, how did you as a group handle Ellen's disappearance? It must have put a strain on relationships…' She turned the heater up, pulling her ski jacket tighter around her shoulders. 'This bloody weather. You'd think I would be used to it after all these years.'

'It did. We were so bloody scared. Of course, now I see that the others were far more so than me, knowing Ellen didn't die in an accident. Leo and I fought a lot anyway. He was going to uni, I wasn't sure what the hell I was going to do. Penny and Paul broke up. She started to see some boy who worked in the factories at Cadrington.' Ava remembered the needless arguments, the fretting about the police investigation, all mixed with the usual teenage stresses of exams and parental relationships.

It was to spite Leo, and because they were both lonely and afraid, that she had slept with Paul. Their stuttering relationship had infuriated Leo, and Rhodri had expressed surprise at the pairing. As Paul went off to do work experience on another farm she saw less of him, but they continued to refer to each other as boyfriend and girlfriend. One night, meeting Leo off the coach from Cardiff, where he had been to a university interview, they had slept together one last time.

That fatal mistake had resulted in her pregnancy. There could be no chance Paul was the father, as she'd had her period right before her night with Leo, then had felt so guilty she'd dodged Paul for the next month, telling him she needed time to sort her head out. With Leo leaving Aberdyth, and Paul and his family offering a home she had felt there was no choice but to lie. Where Leo was wild, not likely to settle down, and would have been horrified (she felt) at the prospect of a child, Paul was delighted. He'd proposed, and his dad talked couldn't stop talking about another generation for the farm.

It was a huge mistake, and yet another secret simmering under the surface. Now as a teenager, Stephen looked just like his dad. His dark-blue eyes and bone structure were all Leo's, yet at no time had anyone pointed it out. At least to her knowledge. Had Paul or Penny guessed?

'Are you all right, Ava?' Sophie's voice pierced her thoughts, skewering the sadness that now threatened to overwhelm her.

'I think it's just reliving the past. There so many memories I have tried to bury. Oh, not about Ellen,' she said quickly. 'More about screwing up motherhood.'

'Your son is taking part in *Tough Love*, you said?'

'Yeah. I arrived, and he disappeared off to the camp in the hills,' Ava said, trying to smile.

For the first time, she detected a real warmth in Sophie's expression. 'If it's any consolation, my teenage daughters won't speak to me at all at the moment.' It was almost like she had been reserving judgement on Ava.

'Are you from round here originally?' Exhausted, Ava felt the need for some small talk, and a quick breather before she delved back into the past, dragging her memories out like a line of blood-stained washing flapping in the breeze.

Sophie took out a packet of chewing gum and offered some to Ava. 'My parents moved out to Wales when I was twelve. It was a bit of a culture shock, but I was used to moving around. My father was in the RAF, and he moved into training.'

'The Mach Loop?' Ava ventured.

'Yes. I'm surprised you remember that.'

'One of the guys I share a house with is crazy on RAF stuff, and military aircraft in general. There is a forum where you can watch all the low-level flight training videos between Dolgellau and Machynlleth. I'll admit, when he showed me, it was kind of weird. I spent years trying to forget Wales, and suddenly I'm sharing a home with a guy who keeps trying to remind me of the place.' Ava smiled, and took her time unwrapping the gum, twisting the silver paper into a ball as she thought. 'You know, after that night everyone was terrified. It was the opposite of huddling together. We hardly spoke to each other except to argue. I think everyone put it down to the fact that we were so shocked by Ellen's disappearance. Can I ask you something?'

'You can, but if it's about the case, I may not be able to answer.'

'When you investigated Ellen's disappearance, did you have any potential perps? Any real leads?'

Sophie looked away, apparently studying the bleak landscape out the window. When she looked back she shrugged. 'There were a couple, but nothing I can share at this stage.'

'Fair enough.' Ava was thinking that she could look up the press reports from the time, and perhaps as Sophie got to know her, prove she was trustworthy.

'It was one of those cases that doesn't ever really go away. It's like having something stuck in your back teeth, and all the niggling in the world can't shift it.' Sophie smiled thinly. 'I always did think there was more to Ellen's disappearance than just a teenager running away.'

'I don't remember you.'

'It was a long time ago, wasn't it? We probably didn't even

179

meet. I was busy doing all the legwork with a couple of other uniforms.' She glanced back at her notes, ignoring her phone, which was buzzing. 'Going back to Ellen's body. You say she was originally buried on Paul's farm? Can I ask who suggested that?'

'Huw. He said that if the police did suspect anything else other than a runaway, they might get search dogs out. He said he'd seen a movie where a body was hidden under a cattle shed to put the dogs off the scent. We had a picnic blanket that we'd hidden in the woods. We used it for our Friday night parties. It was easy for the boys to wrap Ellen's body in that and transport it across the field to the sheep pen below Paul's farm. Once she was wrapped up, they seemed to find it easier. I tried to pretend it wasn't Ellen inside at all…' She wiped tears crossly from her face.

The DI shoved a tissue in her direction. 'But the body was moved. Why was that?'

'It was. That was just before I left. I suppose you could say it was the final stressor that drove me to run. There was a lot of new housing going up on land between Aberdyth and Cadrington, and one of the developers approached Paul's dad about the farm. His mum had passed away a few years before, so it was just Paul and his dad. Anyway, the outline of the proposed development went as far as the local planning department, and Paul showed us all. Fifteen hundred houses right across the old sheep pen where Ellen was buried.' Exhausted, Ava yawned. 'Sorry.'

Sophie turned the car heater down. 'Who suggested the move?'

'It was Leo and Paul really. Paul was desperate, because of course it was his land, and Leo was always his best friend. He would back him in anything. Huw and Jesse agreed in the end, and Penny and I weren't given any option to vote.'

'Jesse is the boy who died in the road accident?'

'Yes. Here actually.' Ava indicated the road in front of them.

'I'll get the files on the accident. So Ellen's body was moved to East Wood?'

'Yes. I wasn't supposed to be there, but I sneaked out. Stephen

180

was sleeping, and Paul's dad was just across the landing anyway. I… I just couldn't think about anything but seeing Ellen. It sounds mad, but I'd almost convinced myself that maybe it wasn't her, that maybe she really had run away.'

Sophie flicked her a sidelong glance and made another note.

'I know, but my mental state by then, was just this side of sanity.' Ava hesitated for a moment, and then added, 'Leo was pressuring me to leave Paul and get back with him. We were just teenagers, far too young to be married with a baby.'

'I understand. You don't have to explain your reasons for running away. We all know that the human mind is an incredibly strong tool, but it has limits. You had reached yours. Getting back to Ellen, did you actually see them move the body?'

'Yes. I don't remember whether she had the hair band and bracelet on though. I would imagine whoever took them did it when she died. The fabric doesn't look degraded enough to have been stored in the ground for a few years.' Ava put the objects on the palm of her hand and offered them to Sophie.

The other woman took them gently, holding them up to the light. 'Trophies, then?'

'That's what I concluded,' Ava said.

'And yet they were given to you. Interesting. I'll be in touch. Naturally you realise this makes it difficult for any of your evidence to be admissible, just because of your involvement. Can I keep these for a while?' Sophie was frowning again. 'In essence we have a mispo cold case, and this new mispo with the two girls from the film set, both connected to you. It doesn't look good. But you know that.'

'Of course, and I do realise that this is a weird situation. At the moment, I am most concerned for Bethan and the other girl. It seems perfectly clear to me that they were taken as an escalation of the warnings left for me. I will call you as soon as I have any contact from the perp, because, as you say, this is a game to them.'

'But are these connections with you warnings, or are they just to lure you into going along with whatever they are planning? I agree it seems very possible you were supposed to be scared into silence… but if the original suspect killed Ellen, and left her for your friends to find, or one of your friends killed Ellen and has now taken these other girls, either way the outlook doesn't look good. You say the messages started before you even left LA?'

'Yes, I noted the dates and times, and I gave them to DS Sharon yesterday.' Ava frowned. 'I did wonder why I should be warned off before I even returned to Aberdyth, but it would have been common knowledge that Paul was terminally ill, and he and Penny would have mentioned I had been invited to come back. Word would have got round very quickly.'

'It could be just the fact you are now with the police that rattled the suspect, but I would say it goes deeper. This has the hallmarks of a control freak. They like to keep us jumping, and they are arrogant enough to assume we will keep following them. It's a challenge, to keep stringing you along. These objects left, the photographs posted online, the message sending you down to Big Water this morning to find the body… it's almost like—'

'A treasure hunt, with Bethan as the prize? Shit, I hope not.' Ava rubbed her forehead, feeling a niggling soreness lurking behind her temples. She hadn't had migraines for years.

'Did you tell anyone apart from Leo about the photographs, and the fact you felt it was going to be necessary to come clean about Ellen's death?'

'No. Since I've been back, I've spoken to everyone who was in the woods that night, apart from Jesse of course, and I would say most of them were fairly convinced that I was coming back to, as you say, come clean. I tried to make it clear I wasn't, until now.'

Sophie gave her one of those hard looks, and Ava felt like a kid kept back after recess. Just like that she'd made her decision and torn their lives apart, after stressing that was exactly what she wasn't going to do. 'You know, the photographs are nothing compared to the fact that Ellen was murdered, that these girls are now missing, the fact that history seems to be repeating itself.' A chill, that had nothing to do with the weather, swept over her body, and the ice settled in her chest, because she couldn't ignore the timing. This was about her, and nothing was going to stop her from finding those girls and bringing them home. The windscreen was patterned with condensation, and Ava was surprised to see Ellen's face outside, dark hair flying in the wind, eyes serious for once, her pretty mouth set in a worried frown.

Sophie nodded briskly, banishing the ghosts of the past. 'Right. You have all my numbers, and we've already got the search and rescue teams out looking for Bethan. Can you send me copies of any more texts? Keep your phone on all the time in case the suspect tries to contact you again. If you remember anything else at all, either about the more recent issues, or about the night Ellen was killed, ring me straight away.'

Perceptive and smart, Ava thought. This woman was a winner, no mistake. 'I'll update you as soon as anything comes in. Oh, and Jack, my boss, is emailing over the file connected to the photographs. Here, I've got one of his cards, so you can get him direct if you need to.' She met Sophie's cool eyes. 'Just let me call him first.'

'I'll drop you back at the B&B. You get anything else, you contact me direct. I've got a colleague, DI Hevis, coming down to take over the mispo case. He's a top bloke, so Bethan will be in safe hands, but I'll remain in overall charge.' She scowled briefly. 'Which as you know just means I get all the flak from the DCI, but make no mistake, my top priority is getting these teenagers home alive. Stay safe, Ava, and don't do anything stupid, will you?'

Chapter 22

The afternoon was filled with savage snow flurries, and Ava could easily imagine the trouble the teams down by Big Water were having, trying to salvage any crime scene evidence.

'Ava, you're very good at your job, and I'll fight your corner, but depending on what happens with the Welsh cops, there will have to be an investigation over here too.' Jack took a breath down the phone, and she could hear the flick of a lighter, seabirds screaming and the background crash and hiss of waves on the beach. 'It's a fucking shame you didn't come clean about it on the night it happened though.'

She wanted to scream that she knew that, and yes, she had made mistake after mistake, but now was the time to make things right. Ava forced herself to respond coolly, calmly. 'I'm aware of that, and thank you for your understanding.'

He rang off, clearly pissed with her, and rightly so. Fucking hell, it had begun already. Next thing would probably be a procession of her childhood friends coming up the road to lynch her. Ava reminded herself she was a fighter, and just now nothing in the future mattered as much as bringing those girls home safe.

She had trudged down to Ellen's parents' bungalow as soon as Sophie dropped her off, and nearly cried with frustration when she found they were out for the day. Mrs Dressin, who lived next door, told her they were visiting an estate agent in Cadrington, and had only left half an hour ago.

Oh, Christ, could she really do this by phone? By the time the Smiths got back, half the Cadrington force, including Sophie herself, would be waiting for them.

Ava tapped out the mobile phone number Jackie had given her on her visit the other day. It went straight to answer phone. What could she do? Short of driving into Cadrington and stalking around the estate agents herself... She rang one more time, holding her breath, praying that Jackie would answer. She didn't, 'Hi Jackie. There's something I've been meaning to tell you about Ellen. Please call me as soon as you get this, and... I'm so, so sorry.'

That was it. It was all she could do – the ultimate anti-climax of years of secrecy and guilt, and the ultimate betrayal of trust. Ellen was everywhere suddenly, as though by exposing her secrets, Ava had released a genie from a bottle. She only had to sit and relax her mind for a moment and the memories flooded back. This was the bend in the road where she had been sick, and Ellen had held her hair back, that field was where they had played football, endlessly arguing about who was in goal. That was the tree they had scrawled their initials on. Even the local store still had sweets laid out on display, just as they had been when she and Ellen each stole a handful of dolly mixtures...

Ava sat cross-legged on her bed, iPad open and a neat pile of notepads and pens beside her. Sophie would investigate officially, and Ava had no doubt she would do everything in her power. But, she, Ava would also work the mispo case. This was what Ellen had wanted, she realised suddenly, admitting once again to herself that she had failed last time. This time would be different.

Making a rough timeline, from when Leo said the girls first went missing, she worked up to Alex's murder. Every text message she had ever been sent by the perp was dissected yet again. She must have missed something. If Alex had found a lead, then so could she. Remembering the names he had been querying, she quickly Googled Andrew Menzies, her old primary school headmaster.

There were a few relevant entries, and she flicked open a new note on her iPad, noting dates. Andrew Menzies had moved away from Aberdyth six years ago, when the school closed. He had moved to Glamorgan, taking on another headship, and successful turning around a 'special measures' school. The last entry was from a local paper, announcing his retirement, praising his dedication to education.

Well, he was unlikely to have nipped back to Aberdyth to kidnap a couple of girls. But what had Alex seen that she didn't? Or was he really just ticking off background names from Ellen's childhood?

Sara Blackmore was more promising. She was active on social media, and many of her postings were dark musings about life and death. Ava studied her Facebook profile, where she listed herself as a writer, previously librarian. No partner, no children, no pets. Her location was listed as simply 'Wales'.

Her messages pinged, and she tapped the icon. Jack sent an email updating her on the photographs. When they resized them they could see a blurred image in the mirror on the wardrobe door;

'… You wouldn't be able to see it without magnification, and it's impossible to tell what sex, or any details, but medium height, medium build with hat or hood pulled down over their hair. Probably describes half of Wales. I've got a bit of time off over the next couple of days, so I'll keep digging.'

Ava went back to Miss Blackmore, cutting through swathes of information, before she scored a hit. Sara Blackmore lived on a farm in Machnagden, which was a hamlet about ten miles away. There was nothing to suggest any links to either Ellen, or Bethan and Cerys. Ava sighed, glanced at her watch, and realised she needed to get a move on.

Struggling through the snow on the way to Paul's farmhouse, Ava wished she'd thought to bring the truck. But part of her relished the fight, the swirl of icy elements dancing all around, half-blinding her, stinging her face. It gave her a chance to think, before she spoke to Penny.

'Ava! You'll never guess what happened...' Penny was speaking even before Ava crossed the threshold. 'The police came round after I spoke to you, and started asking us all about Ellen. Paul is furious all over again. When they left he went mad.' Penny pulled a face. 'I drove him over to the respite centre for a few hours, and he seemed a bit calmer when I left, but I'm honestly terrified by all this. First a murder, then girls missing. What the hell is going on?'

'Oh, Pen, I'm sorry I didn't get a chance to warn you,' Ava lied quickly, 'but I had to tell the police everything, what with Bethan and Cerys missing. I did explain to them about Paul and his situation, but what else could I do?'

Penny was stirring a pot on the stove, licking the spoon and adding various herbs. She had her back to Ava as she spoke. 'You could have told me you were going to confess about Ellen! At least I could have been prepared, warned everyone that it was coming...'

'There wasn't time! Surely you can all see that getting those girls home safe is the only thing that matters.'

'I would have just liked to know, that's all. This is such a big thing, and I don't know what Stephen will make of it, especially with Paul the way he is at the moment. It just seems like everything is crashing down around us, and now this.' She flicked a bright glance at Ava, who watched her in silence. Penny reached in her apron pocket for a tissue and blew her nose loudly, wiping her eyes. 'It's just the shock, isn't it? Nearly ready. Paul isn't eating much at the moment, so I'll do him a bit of toast when I bring him home. You must be furious I never told you the truth about Ellen.'

It was said casually, but the tissue was still out, and Penny's pretty face was pale and drawn with worry. Ava shrugged. 'Hurt that you felt you couldn't trust me, more than anything. What did the boys threaten you with?'

Her lashes came down, hooding her eyes. 'How do you know about that?'

'Leo told me everything. Once he told me Ellen was murdered, he had to tell me why you lied to me.' Ava tore off a piece of garlic bread and popped it in her mouth, waiting.

But Penny didn't take the bait. 'It was terrible when the police started talking. To find that they knew everything – I thought Paul was going to have a heart attack or something. I mean, I wanted so much to tell you that night, to tell you afterwards, but I was too scared. The longer it went on, the harder it became, and then of course you got pregnant, and there was never a good moment to say anything. I am truly sorry about that, Ava.'

'It's okay, Pen, it really is. I understand. The boys can be very persuasive, and I'm sure you were terrified. I know how it is. When I ran away, after I began to feel better, to make some kind of life, I wanted desperately to call you, to try to explain…' She smiled at the other woman. Too many lies, too many years gone past, and now this, this ripping of lives. Ava reminded herself that she had been pushed into confessing to the police. It wasn't just the cryptic messages, the trophies taken from Ellen's body, or Leo's devastating body blow about the murder, it was Alex's murder, and the two missing girls. Who was doing this?

Penny was talking again, her voice warming into naturalness. 'I mean you of all people, you know how hard it was putting everything behind us. I just couldn't stop thinking about Ellen after they went. You know those silly little habits she had, how she laughed like a man, and when she dyed her hair. I wish so much it had never happened, but ,Ava, you know I agree with you. I would have had it out in the open years ago. I did mention it to Paul and Leo once…' Her bright gaze faltered, and she busied herself with checking crisp baked potatoes that were on a steaming tray on top of the cooker.

Ava poured herself and Penny a glass of wine. 'What did Paul and Leo say?'

'Paul got very angry, and Leo was just laughing at me. He said I always was a goody-two-shoes. Isn't that a vile thing to say? I pointed out he had more to lose than any of us, and that shut him up.' She smiled with satisfaction at this minor remembered victory, and Ava raised her glass in a toast. 'Paul went on about it for days afterwards though. I never brought it up again. I pushed it to the back of my mind. It was always so busy round here, with my baking business taking off, Stephen to look after, and doing the accounts for the farm…'

'That smells great. Thanks so much for cooking, especially after such a shit day.' Ava took the proffered plate, and added a slab of golden butter, watching it ooze across the potato. 'Have you got any salt?'

'Here. I still think I should have done more, when Ellen was killed, and again I'm so sorry I never told you, but Paul and the others were so… Well, we were kids weren't we, and I was terrified by what I'd seen, scared that it might happen to me. We've known them all our lives, to think they were capable of that was enough to make me go along with what they said. And after, well, I think I started to believe it really was just a horrible mistake. A one-off. But now this as well. I'm scared, Ava, I really am. Someone has taken our girls, haven't they?' Penny took a slug of wine, and her fingernails scraped the glass as she set it down unsteadily on the countertop. Her eyes, usually so carefully made up, were red rimmed, and the bright lights of the kitchen picked out worry lines scratched around her eyes.

'I know. Pen, I hate to ask, but I'm sure you can see that it might help with the enquiry, and the police will ask you this, if they haven't already…'

Penny said nothing, but her shoulders drooped as she leant against the counter.

'Have you had any more thoughts on who actually murdered

189

Ellen? Anything, even if it's just a fragment of memory, would help. I've tried so hard, but all I can see is her on the ground. I hear voices, and they are angry, scared, but I can't pick out an individual.' Ava shovelled a massive mouthful of beef stew and baked potato into her mouth and waited. God, she was hungry.

Penny sat down on the other stool, starting to slice her own carrots into neat segments, frowning as she did so. 'I've thought and thought, but we'd taken those pills, and the vodka, and all I can remember is the darkness. I was kissing Paul, and after that everyone was laughing by the fire. The fire went out, and Ellen was there. She was laughing too, and she did her dare...' Penny took another gulp of wine. Her hands were shaking, food abandoned.

'There was music, and it was so dark, and the fire made shadows across the tree trunks... Paul was winding me up about something. I don't remember seeing Jesse or Rhodri, but Leo was next to the fire for a while. Then suddenly Jesse was yelling, and Rhodri was carrying Ellen out of the darkness. Her hand was hanging down. I was pulling someone to come and help, Paul I think, and shouting at him. Her clothes were all torn, and her skirt pushed up the way Rhodri held her, so I could see she had no knickers on. It was awful!' Penny gave a sob, putting down her cutlery and draining her wine glass. 'It still gets me, even after all this time. I tried to shove the boys out the way, but someone else, I think it might have been Leo, pushed me so hard I fell down against a tree. I must have hit my head because I had a massive lump on the back when I got home that night. I think I blacked out.'

'Leo pushed you?' Ava tried to slot this in with Leo's version of events and failed.

'I think it must have been him, because I remember the smell of his aftershave. You know that strong peppery one he used to pinch from his older brother?'

Ava did know. But that meant if Penny was telling the truth,

Leo and Paul never left the circle around the fire, and it put them in the clear. Or were they all still covering for each other?

'Pen, did you notice when Ellen left the group? Was she gone a long time?'

'I don't know. I suppose it could have been anything up to an hour really...'

'Was Leo there all the time? I mean, did he wander off with Ellen at all?'

Penny put a hand on Ava's arm, her mouth twisting, tears trickling like raindrops down her pink cheeks, 'I don't know. You were the only one who wasn't part of it, because you were out of it. Everyone else was down in the hollow round the fire, with the music and the bottles.'

'It's okay. So it could have been Leo?'

She shrugged, 'It could have been any of them. It could even have been Paul, if my memory is wrong! That was another reason I was so scared.'

'If you had to guess?'

'Oh God, Ava, I honestly don't know. Of course, I don't really think it was Paul or I wouldn't have married him. Jesse had no reason to... to assault Ellen, did he? I mean, he was her boyfriend – but they did row that evening. I don't like Huw, and I never have done, but only because he was an arrogant asshole at school, and he hasn't really changed much. That doesn't make him a killer. I thought afterwards that perhaps... perhaps it wasn't one of us. That maybe Ellen met someone else in the woods that night. But it made me feel sick to think we might have covered up for a stranger, so I pushed it away.'

'Do you remember the mobile library that used to come to Aberdyth?'

'What does that have to do with Ellen's murder? I... Oh yes, I do. The woman that drove it was a right bitch, wasn't she? Sara something.'

'Blackmore. Sara Blackmore.'

'That's right. Why?'

'No reason really, just thinking of people we might have known who, by that token, might have harmed Ellen.'

'Not the librarian! She was a woman.' Penny's eyes were wide, and shocked.

Ava shrugged, not pointing out the obvious – that women could be perps, be sexual predators, as well as men.

'There were always a lot of visitors to the Birtleys that time of year, and to the caravan site. Do you really think it might be someone else who killed Ellen?' Relief and hope coloured her voice.

'I don't know, but just now, for me, the only reason to look at Ellen's case is to see if we can get any leads on Bethan and Cerys.'

Penny's phone rang, and she snatched it up, frowning. 'Hallo?' She listened for a while, and then spoke quickly. 'No, I've got nothing to say at all.'

Ava opened her mouth to speak, but Penny was tapping out another number, which clearly wasn't answered. At last she turned back to face Ava. 'That was the local paper wanting a comment, so I just wanted to check they hadn't been on to Paul and upset him again. My business number is on my website,' she added in response to Ava's enquiring look.

'Did they want you to comment on the cold case, or on Bethan and Cerys?'

'He asked about Bethan because he'd heard my son was dating her,' Penny said slowly.

Ava made no comment, ignoring the 'my son', and moving on. 'You need to get that business number diverted to an answering service for a while, maybe.'

'Maybe.'

'Did you do the website yourself? I've looked at it a few times now, and the photographs look like a professional job.'

Penny glowed with the praise. 'Oh, no, I had help with the

website from Paul. I'm no good at technical stuff and he's clever with things like that. And Leo did the photographs for me. He has all the lighting, and expensive cameras, and he did a course at uni along with his media studies degree.'

Ava noted this, but again moved the conversation along quickly. 'So you can box this stuff fresh and send it anywhere in the world?'

'Pretty much. I mean some of the goods are frozen and have to be couriered in special packaging, but the cakes are easy. I have customers in America, Australia, China. Lots of people who have moved away from Wales and want a taste of the real authentic food, or others who have relatives or ancestors from here – they all feel like there's a link.' Clearly pleased at Ava's interest, and relieved at the change of subject, Penny was gabbling, slightly breathless. She topped up Ava's wine again.

'I think it's amazing, Pen. You're so clever!' For a moment she was afraid she had gone over the top, but the other woman was smiling.

'Well, so are you. I mean, you're a detective!'

Ava laughed. 'So now we know how wonderful we both are, let's finish that wine.'

'Oh, I can't have any more. I need to pick Paul up at ten.'

Ava took a deep breath. They might as well clear the air completely. 'Penny, Paul always loved you. Our stupid little fling was just that. He would never have married me if I hadn't got pregnant. You know what his dad was like about having an heir to the farm. He was the most old-fashioned person and Paul always did what he said.'

After a few minutes of awkward silence, Penny covered Ava's hand with her own. 'I know. He's told me himself. He loves Stephen to bits, and he always has. He's as proud of him as Huw is of Bethan. Oh God, Ava, I hope the police find that poor darling girl safe.'

Ava winced. 'I'm sure they are going to do everything they can.'

Penny nodded, blowing her nose briefly before returning to their past. 'But, Ava, lovely, we were all still trying to deal with what happened to Ellen, and with all the booze and pills, we were lucky nothing else went wrong. Stephen was, and is, a blessing, and I love him to bits. I've never wanted kids of my own, and Paul already had one of his own, so it was perfect. A weird way for everything to end up, but it has worked for all of us, hasn't it?'

Ava supposed it had. Right up until the point she exploded their secret.

'I just need to grab a coat and then I'll drop you back before I go and get Paul, shall I?'

'Thanks, Pen.'

The Land Rover made easy work of the snow-covered hill, grinding along in low ratio, as Penny competently swung the vehicle into the B&B driveway.

They sat for a moment in the darkness, the headlights picking out the snowfall, monotonous and hypnotic.

'Actually, Ava, there is one other thing I want to tell you.'

'Sure.'

'I didn't tell the police, so this will be up to you if you want to pass it on, or maybe take a look yourself.'

'Go on,' Ava said softly.

Penny rubbed her face like a child, as though trying to clear unwelcome memories. 'When Leo was at uni, we went up a few times for a party weekend.'

Ava waited, shivering in the passenger seat.

'We all went out this one time, just like we normally did, but the boys were wild. They were taking more than usual, and it just turned out crazy.'

'That's it?'

'Yes. It's just... Leo pulled, and he was boasting about it to the others. He had photos on his phone, of other girls too. When I asked he just said it was another pissed student, who regretted giving it out. He said… he said that there were too many girls and mostly they were gagging for it.'

'He said that?'

'Yes, and the others laughed, then Paul sort of seemed to remember I was there, and he tried to pretend he didn't agree with Leo.'

'Thanks, Penny. That's very interesting.'

'See you tomorrow, lovely.'

Back indoors, defrosting, Ava headed up to her room, flicked on her iPad and checked her emails. Lots from work, a couple from DI Sophie Miles, one with a file attached… It took a while to work through them all.

Her phone rang as she was busy tapping out an answer to her boss.

'Penny? Everything all right?'

'Yes, I'm just on my way to the respite centre. Don't worry, this is hands-free. I suppose because we've been bringing up the past, and you and the police were asking about Ellen… There was a bit more I didn't tell you. About the weekend at uni…'

'Go on.'

There was the sound of a horn blaring, and Ava took the phone from her ear wincing. 'Penny? Are you all right?'

'Sorry, it was some idiot on the wrong side of the road. Probably one of Leo's film crew – the car's just turned up his driveway. Loonies. Anyway, I don't want to get him in trouble if it isn't him, but…'

'Penny, get to the point. If you remember something important, you need to tell me.'

'Okay, so that weekend in Cardiff, it was me, Paul, Huw and Rhodri. Jesse was away on some delivery job. Like I said, we went out to some clubs, did the usual nights out. But something happened whilst we were there, not just what I said before. I read in the paper that there was a girl on campus who was raped. I'm not saying there's a connection, I'm just saying, we were there.

Me and Paul were together, but the others all went off with different girls, and we know something happened to Ellen before she died…'

Shit. 'Thanks, Pen, that's really helpful.' Ava ended the call and started searching the internet. Sure enough, a few of the local papers seemed to have got hold of the story. The girl was an English student, and she reported the rape after a night out with friends. The stories got shorter as Ava tracked the follow-up articles, but the gist seemed to be that the girl dropped the charges, and the stories suggested quite strongly that she had been drunk, possibly even lied about what had happened. But they had been there, almost the whole gang. Ava reached for her phone again.

Chapter 23

The board is open in front of me, as the long hours of darkness stretch ahead. The police interviewed me today, and we talked about Alex Jennington's sad demise. So amusing. DI Sophie Miles is clearly an intelligent woman, although her looks let her down. I've never liked women with short hair. None of my customers would consider her special enough.

Who would have thought that Ava would react so well to the supposed truth about Ellen's death? I fed her bits and pieces, and she scurried along the trail. I can see why she is good at her job. When she asks questions her voice is clear and soft, and her turquoise eyes hold yours. Her dark hair is still long, but the fringe frames her face now, making her seem gentler, more vulnerable than she actually is. Experience has shaped her, moulded her, just as it did me, and now we are both older, the games are even better.

Ava spilling her guts has produced a few challenges, I admit, but nothing I can't handle. The trouble today is that I haven't been able to visit the girl. I don't want her to die yet, not after all the trouble I went to getting hold of her. Ava must have incentive to carry on with the game, and this is the only sure way to get her to play. Her instinct is always to save people, and in adult life seemingly to lock up the bad boys and girls. I'm sure she now knows that there is no definite line between good and bad. It is not her place to judge the outer shell of others.

Everyone in the village is gossiping about the murder. The older generation love it, and I was careful to bump into Mrs B at the store and give her my version of events. After what Ava has said, it won't take the police long to work out Jesse wasn't the one who murdered Ellen. This isn't a total disaster, and naturally much police time and effort seems to be going on trying to find Bethan and Cerys. There is another DI working on that case, and I hoped he might be less perceptive than his colleague. Unfortunately, he is just as shrewd. They can't find her yet. The key to my success is going to be keeping them all busy, using switch and bait, so they are distracted by the promise of finding a living victim, as opposed to just seeking out the killer of a corpse. It won't be long before they find a sweet little reward along the trail. That will make them think they are so terribly clever.

She's a lovely girl really, now she's adjusted to being with me. Not that we didn't know each other before. It's just that she has never seen this side of me. It takes a bit of getting used to, I suppose.

There is a white tent up over Ellen's grave site, and lots of white-suited people staggering around East Wood. Big cordons and blue-and-white police tape are keeping out the local press. It won't be long before the nationals figure out that this is a great story. It doesn't bother me, because the more of them that know, the better really. I do want a big audience for my finale. I want to go out in a hellslide of trumpets, thunder and lightning and applause. The applause will come afterwards, but I hope I will just catch the faintest whisper of it, and of the gratitude.

The dice clatter and roll for each separate player, and I move them methodically around the board. It's peaceful, and exciting at the same time. Tomorrow I will send Ava another clue, and if she gets it, she'll be ahead of all the other pieces on the board. My fingers hesitate on a spare player. This one is green wood, like her green eyes. Inspector Miles joins the game. I hope she won't feature much, but she'll add to the thrill of the chase.

I had a long chat with Mr B yesterday. It is so important to take time to lay the foundations of lies. He has always been a fan, and he understands what I am going through. He never really liked Ellen though... Ellen was a bad judge of character. She adored Coach Thomas because he was good-looking and let her on the football team, yet she disliked Mr Birtley because he was short, balding and stuttered a bit when he got excited. So superficial, and fickle to judge everyone like that. If someone tells you that you are special, they always have an agenda. I didn't realise this to begin with, but I soon got wise to the facts of life.

Anyway, Mr B was on tea duty, so I carried the tray for him, all the way down to the graveyard. Mrs Birtley's parents have been dead for several years. I believe they died within months of each other. She is so devoted to their memory, so agitated if anyone questions that devotion, that I sometimes wonder if, like me, she is hiding something. Anyway, every day she makes up a polished silver tea tray with cups, teapot and slice of cake on flower-patterned plates. Apparently, the china tea set was a wedding present, all those decades ago. It is pretty, so very, very pretty, that I was tempted to drop a brittle china cup to see how it sounded shattering on the road. But I didn't. I chatted away to Mr B, and set the tray gently down by the grave. I helped him clear away the fading flowers and arrange some new ones, and then, I left him sitting forlornly on the cold bench. He'll have to wait there until she gets back from her WI meeting.

The headstones make me shiver. What will mine look like, and will anyone come to lay flowers by my decaying bones? Most importantly, will I be able to watch from my position in the heavens? Will I be able to look down, or will there be nothing? The thought of nothing terrifies me, but I comfort myself and imagine it might be peaceful. It might even be like flying, that safe position above everyone. No touching, no shouting, no pain, just a soaring feeling of light and love deep in my chest.

I had my next errand of mercy to carry out, and I slipped a knife into my bag. After that I will have to head back down to the film set. That's where the action is going to be.

'Cwrdd a fi wrth y tân, Ava Cole.'

'Meet me by the fire, Ava Cole.'

Chapter 24

Ava woke to her phone buzzing, and she fumbled, bleary-eyed for the device, knocking her glass of water onto the floor as she did so.

'Ava! I've been trying to get hold of you for ages.'

'Leo, it's only just gone five. I don't normally go running until six. What do you want?'

'Good news and bad news. Cerys has been found!'

'Thank fuck for that. Is she okay?' Ava's heart was pounding so hard it seemed to shake her whole body, thumping out a drumbeat in her head. She could barely breathe. Please let Bethan be alive too…

'She was with the group that went missing. When they split, she and Bethan heard Helen fall, but she swears they had nothing to do with it. It did unnerve her though. She wanted to go on to the next camp, but Bethan told her they should wait a bit longer. Anyway, they argued and the stupid girl went off into the wood on her own. But the interesting thing is someone followed her. Cerys says she was assaulted, her hands and feet bound, she was gagged, and then she was dumped in the crevice in the woods, where she was eventually found. She swears this was some of the other contestants, but she doesn't know all their names. The woods are dense in that area, and there are some rocky crevices in the middle.'

'And she thinks it was someone from *Tough Love*?'

'She is convinced that one of the other girls must have got their boyfriend to do it. She reckons there were at least two of them tying her up – one male and one female.'

'What do you think? The search teams must have covered the whole area. Why didn't they find her before this?'

'Come on, Ava, you know yourself what the countryside is like around here, and the weather has been shit,' Leo said. 'If we are able to go ahead she should get lots of votes. My team are with her now, trying to find out exactly who was involved, and I'm sure the police will be keen to talk to all the contestants again.'

But Ava had heard enough about Cerys. It seemed unlikely, given the events of the past week, that the girl had been attacked by her competitors, but certainly possible. Sophie and her team could deal with that. It was enough that she was safe. After the first wave of relief, Ava was bracing herself for the bad news. 'And Bethan?'

His voice was sober now. 'The police have found Bethan's boots. One of the search teams found them under a bush next to Big Water. Apparently, they were laid together neatly, laced up, with her socks stuffed inside. Next to them were Alex Jennington's socks and shoes, again laid out very neatly. The other search team is over at East Wood digging up Ellen's body. Ava?'

Ava tried not to retch, and the hot surge of guilt that had made her check her phone practically all night mixed with bile. The Smiths had never called back, and the police would now have told them before she had a chance to confess.

She tried to process the information Leo was giving out, even as another incoming call made her phone vibrate. It was Sophie Miles. She would ring her back. Presumably she was only ringing with the same stuff that Leo was currently imparting, and she still needed to grill Leo.

'Ava? Did you hear what I said?' Leo's voice was agitated now, and so far away from his usual lazy, amused tones. 'She might have gone into Big Water and drowned, or, been drowned by whoever killed that PI. They say they're going to send divers into the lake later today. My insurance guy is going ballistic, and the press are in a frenzy of excitement. It's even trending on Twitter.'

Was there a note of pride underlying his words, even though he was undoubtedly stressed? Ava stored the thought away. He didn't seem bothered by the fact Ellen's body was being removed from its woodland grave, or that her parents would now get another hit of betrayal when they found out who was involved in her death. 'Yeah, I'm still here. Look, I've got things to ask, so can we meet?'

'Yes, can you come up here?'

'Come to your house? I'm not sure that's a great idea. Aren't the press staking you out already?'

'They are mostly down at the production offices, and here I have electric gates to keep them out. Just drive at them, and they mostly hop out of the way. Wear a hat or something if you don't want to be in the papers tomorrow. Do you want me to come and get you?'

'No, I'll take Mr Birtley's truck again. He said I could borrow it any time.'

She dragged on her coat and gloves, listening to Sophie's message as she trudged down to the shed where the truck was kept. It was an update on Bethan, the same news Leo had just told her, with the additional plea to let her know the instant any other cryptic messages arrived on her phone.

* * *

Leo's house was set just above Aberdyth. It was a new-build, all glass, chrome and right angles. There were a few photographers camped out by Leo's gate, but she pulled her baseball cap right down over her eyes, and drove straight past, blanking them. She yanked the truck to a halt inside Leo's compound. The stone walls were high enough for privacy, and she caught a glimpse of a snow-covered infinity pool, and perfectly edged flower beds with tall frosted plants, before she approached the front door.

A housekeeper showed her in, frowning slightly at Ava's snowy, muddy boots. Leo was waiting in his living room, hair still wet from the shower, barefoot, in jeans and a white T-shirt. It was a large house, giving the appearance of an industrial loft, but instead of being cold, it was warm and smelled slightly of wood and polish. The view across the hills and valley was breathtaking, and Ava stood for a second, in her socks, soaking up the underfloor heating, admiring the beauty and the wildness.

'Told you electric gates are the answer.' Leo moved across to the sofas, and dumped a tray of coffee and pastries on the table next to her. 'Sit down. So what do you think of the house?'

Ava looked around at the immaculate white walls, the spot-lights, huge TV and black leather sofas. There was a smart kitchen at one end, with glossy white and chrome fittings, and the floor was dark, Welsh slate. Framed photographs of Leo at various stages of his career covered one wall, and black-and-white pictures of the valleys covered another. The only sign of any personal touches was the stack of books on the kitchen counter, next to a bowl of shiny green apples, and a monopoly set on a shelf.

'I think it suits you perfectly. You always were the cleanest, tidiest teenager I knew.'

Leo grinned. 'It didn't take long to get permission to demolish my nana's old place and build this. My dream house. I designed most of it. Of course, I've got a flat in Cardiff, and a place in Shoreditch for when I'm working properly, but this is my bolthole.'

Ava sipped her hot coffee and snagged a pastry. 'Don't tell me you made these?'

'No. My housekeeper likes cooking, so she quite often leaves me stuff.'

'Great. Leo, have you spoken to Huw today? He must be in bits by now. This does suggest Bethan is not just fooling around for the cameras. Do you normally have this much trouble with your cast?'

Leo glanced away, brow creasing, quickly checking his phone. 'They can be difficult, and yes we have had minor accidents, but never this much trouble. I tried Huw last night, and then when the search team told me about the boots. Apparently, he took the Land Rover out last night, and he's not back yet. He told his missus he was going into town.'

'Cadrington?'

'I suppose so.'

'Right. And what do you think? Is it possible Huw is involved in all of this, right down to harming his own daughter?'

Leo's eyes opened wide. 'Fuck no! Huw loves Bethan. I mean, Christ, he idolises that kid. You saw how he was on the set. He keeps all her videos, photos, runs her modelling website. He's obsessed. The other kids don't get a look in.'

'Do you not find that slightly weird?'

'No. Well... that's just how some parents are, isn't it?'

'I wouldn't know. Did the police ask if you thought Ellen's case was connected to this one?'

'Yes.' He sat next to her, still smiling, still charming, but with a hint of ice in his voice. 'I told them the absolute truth about what happened the night Ellen died, and I also told them everything I know about Bethan's disappearance.'

She held his gaze. 'And did you?'

'Think whatever you want to think, Ava Cole. You seem to have forgotten I can take care of myself. I have made a living out of taking chances. Even this incident with Bethan and the murder can be turned around. I admit I feel slightly sick when I think of my team kicking back, being paid with nothing to do, but I can turn this media invasion to my advantage. Great PR for the next series.'

Ava stared at him. 'That is twisted. What about Bethan? What about Alex?'

He waved her protest away. 'No it isn't, I'm just using things to my advantage. Remember when we used to play "True Lies" as kids and I was always winning? That's because I know how to play the game.'

'So who really killed Ellen?' she snapped.

Leo rolled his eyes in mock frustration. 'I don't know. If I had to guess before all this blew up again, I really would have said it was Jesse. Now, I suppose, and I do hate to say this, Huw has been the most stressed about you coming back. He hates the police, so you being one of them made him sure you were going to stir up trouble. And so you have! He wouldn't hurt Bethan though, so don't let that thought cross your mind.'

'So are you saying Huw raped and killed Ellen?'

'No. I'm saying that he might have done. Remember we don't know she was raped. I said it looked like she had been sexually assaulted, because of the way her clothing was torn and missing, but we were prepared to believe the worst that night. I can't be sure. Are you recording this, Ava?' He was grinning at her again, and before she could speak, he slid a hand around her shoulders, moving round to her neck. 'I don't know how these things work for cops, but I assume you would be hiding things under your clothes. Maybe I should ask you to take your clothes off?'

'Oh, fuck off, Leo. This is not a game. People are dying!' Ava poured more coffee, gulping the hot restorative liquid, feeling warmth and energy flowing through her body. She couldn't afford to be tired, or go off point. Someone was out to get her, and they were doing very well at outsmarting everyone so far. Not to mention Bethan's life was on the line.

'I'm aware of that, and I'm aware that there is nothing I can do to help them. Oh, and Ava, you're wrong. Do you want a cigarette?'

'No. What am I wrong about?'

'About me, for a start. I am not involved in the murder of that nice Alex Jennington, and I am not involved in Bethan's disappearance. From everything I know and that you have told me, this is a game, and whoever is playing against you... well, I'd say you need to be careful.'

'Are you threatening me?'

'No, I'm just giving you some friendly advice. I won't let anyone hurt you, Ava.' Leo blew smoke away from her, blue eyes fixed on her face.

'Thanks, I feel totally reassured now.' Ava's phone buzzed. She stood up and moved away from Leo. 'Hi Jack.'

'Ava, I've just got some more background for you. Can you talk?'

'Not right now, so just tell me. There's been a development here too. One of the missing girls has been found. She is fine, but her hands and legs were bound, and she was gagged. She swears the other contestants must have done it, but it seems far too much of a coincidence. The other girl, Bethan, is still missing – they just found her boots by a reservoir.'

'Shit.'

'Yeah.'

'Okay, so firstly, I have been trying to trace the person who put those photographs up, and the IP address bounces around all over the place. I looked at your childhood friend Leo, and with his contacts and finances it would be pretty easy for him to be responsible for any of this.' He took a breath and waited.

Ava didn't hesitate, despite the fact she was beginning to think Leo might be telling the truth. He was an easy target for a set-up, but she would need proof of innocence before she struck him off the list, 'Agreed.'

'Nothing that the local police won't be able to find on that university rape – there is very little about that as the charges were dropped.'

Ava waited a moment, but he clearly wasn't going to mention

anything about Ellen, or that her job was hanging in the balance. It didn't matter, anyway, she told herself. Nothing mattered but finding Bethan alive. 'Fine, thanks, Boss. Sophie Miles is a smart woman, although some of her team seem a bit wary of any outside involvement. Thanks for doing all this, I know how stretched we are at the moment.'

'No problem. I was curious, so I've been digging in my spare time. Keep me updated.'

'Will do.' She ended the call and turned to Leo. 'Thanks for the coffee. I need to go now.'

'And who are you going to interrogate next, Detective?' Leo stubbed out his cigarette. He grabbed another pastry, sinking his teeth into the flaky centre and ripping it apart.

She scowled at him. 'You seem to forget I have no jurisdiction over here, not to mention being personally involved, so I won't be interrogating anyone. I'm going to see if Huw's girlfriend will talk to me, then I might come back and piss you off some more.'

'Sure, anytime. It's not like I have anything to do at the moment.'

He leant over and handed her a key. Surprised, she turned it over in her hand, letting it rest on her palm. 'What's this for?'

'I said I wouldn't let anyone hurt you, Ava. Someone already did whilst you have been staying at the B&B. If you want to move in here, have a base in Aberdyth where you are safe, it's all yours.' His face was serious, with no trace of mockery.

'Thanks.' She was thrown a little off balance by the unexpected gesture. 'I'll think about it.'

'Do. Keep it for now, and if you want to use it, do. I have plenty of spare bedrooms.' The smile was back now, and the mischief danced in his eyes.

Ava said no more but finished her coffee and headed out into the cold. Her boots crunched on the white gravel as she stomped over to her truck, and the phone buzzed again. Fumbling with numb fingers she missed the call, cursing as she noted the

unknown number. She slid into the driver's seat and checked –
one voicemail.

Starting the engine, Ava listened. The words were robotic, eerie
and an echo rang out in the background. It could have been
anyone, male or female. Having heard similar calls before, she
could tell someone was using a voice distorter, but that didn't
stop the words sending chilly fear spiders scuttling across her
shoulders.

'You had a little cat called Boots, didn't you, Ava? He ran away.
He might even have run all the way to Big Water and drowned. I
hope not. I'm sure you remember that, but do you remember me?'

Almost before she had time to process the message, her phone
rang again. Hand shaking, she answered quickly.

'Ava? It's Jack, I've had another link to more photographs.
Same person posting them, but the pics aren't of you. It's a girl,
maybe late teens, dark hair… Sound anything like your mispo?'

'Fuck, yes. What…' Ava cleared her throat, trying to take a
hold of her whirling thoughts, trying to focus. 'Is she hurt?'

'A few cuts, again impossible to say if they were added during
editing, and she looks to be unconscious, but nothing obvious.
The thing is, she doesn't look like she's in a room anywhere. She
looks like she's in some sort of cave. We can see stone floor, rocky
walls, and some camping equipment. Didn't you say she was a
contestant in that reality show?'

'Yes. A cave. These hills are full of them, but of course they
aren't all marked. Thanks, Jack. Did you send them to Sophie?'

'Yeah, just before I called you. Pretty big clues this perp is
throwing out now, aren't they?' A siren drowned his voice for a
moment, as he added something else.

'Sorry, Jack, I missed that.' Ava was staring at her snow-covered
windscreen, noting the light but steady fall of white flakes that
would hinder any rescue teams trying to search the hills.

'I said you must be getting pretty near the end game now. Be
careful.'

'Will do.' She hit the call end and replayed the message one more time. She'd forgotten to tell Jack about it. Quickly, Ava sent it to both Jack and Sophie, and then she sat for a long moment, shivering in the cab. Jack was right, but what the hell was the end game for this person?

Chapter 25

I wish I could have seen Ava's face when she received my latest message. Such a clever bit of kit I got off the internet. I wasn't sure at first, because it seemed more like a child's toy. But now I realise if I can talk to Ava as my other self, it adds another dimension to the game. She needs to get a move on, because the girl is becoming weaker. The photographs I took the day after I took her off the hill were sent to Ava's boss. It is important to ensure she knows I have complete control.

DI Miles is a constant irritation, and I'm wondering if I'm going to have to kill her too. She is pretending to like Ava, I can tell, and the two are forming an alliance. The thought of them giggling in corners reminds me of Ellen. She often said when we were all much younger that she would marry Jesse. How funny that she should have been so wrong. Now they are both dead – star-crossed lovers indeed. How romantic and revolting in equal parts.

My mind keeps flipping back to DI Miles, and Detective Cole; they are both outsiders, but Ava belongs to me.

I am equal to their attempts at interrogation, simply because I have the knowledge that could break the case. In the meantime, I roll the dice quickly, moving my players feverishly around the board. The end is coming, and I feel a fizz of excitement touched with regret. Am I really so scared of dying? I've thought about it so many times, but now it is a reality, and the unarguable way to finish things, I find myself still… a little afraid.

There was another girl missing on the hills, and one night, after I checked my own captive, I passed her, wandering around, confused and swearing to herself. It did occur to me to put her out of her misery, but I'm not a greedy person. She was not part of the game, so I let her stumble off, crying a little, her footsteps tentative and unsure.

It seems right that I now have so many of the things I craved as a child – money, and a position, even fame of a sort. I will leave a legacy, and it is something nobody could ever imagine. It will be my gift to everyone who has suffered like I did, and when I die, everyone will remember me.

'*Byddwch yn colli fi, Ava Cole?*'
'**Will you miss me, Ava Cole?**'

Chapter 26

Skipping any thoughts of dropping in at Huw's house, Ava drove straight back to the Birtleys'. As she bumped back into the potholed yard, there was another vehicle parked outside the stone building. Ava parked quickly and joined Sophie in her car.

The DI was curt and got straight down to business. 'Just to reiterate, obviously you can't, officially, be anywhere near this investigation, but we're running out of time. I listened to the voicemail, and Jack sent over the photos. They are definitely of Bethan and as he mentioned, definitely underground, but Christ knows where.'

'I assume the search team have been all over the area where Cerys was found?' Ava queried.

Sophie gave her a cold look. 'The weather has beaten us a couple of times, but yes, of course.'

'Sorry, I didn't mean to—'

The other woman interrupted her. 'We've got bodies mapping the area at the moment, and the PULSAR Team are on their way with extra equipment and dogs. I'm getting more men and extra funding after the last briefing because the DCI has declared a Critical Incident. We will find her, and find the bastard doing all this. Anything else come in?' She paused for breath, turning the car heater on to combat the bitter cold outside.

'None. I keep checking my phone.' Ava waved at Mr Birtley as he scuttled down the path to pick up his mail from the little wooden box at the gate. He half-heartedly raised a hand, slipped in the snow a little, and then continued his errand with his gaze fixed firmly on the ground. 'Do you think Cerys is telling the truth about being attacked by the other contestants?'

Sophie shrugged. 'It's possible, but equally it's possible that this was arranged by the suspect as a diversion tactic, or as part of their game. Either way, although she has been interviewed, she insisted on staying at the camp. The medics have given her the all clear...'

'What about the voicemail on my phone?'

'We can't get the voice any clearer, and of course the phone was untraceable. I've got divers searching the reservoir, but after this I'll call them off. We have to assume that these pictures are meant to show us Bethan is still alive, and the game is still on, not that she's at the bottom of the lake. It's also a big old stretch of water, and I don't have bodies to waste at this moment in time.'

Ava yawned. 'I need coffee. I've been up since five. That store has a machine, not great, but better than going back to the Birtleys' and having Mrs B trying to get all the gossip. I'm sure you agree it would be better if we aren't seen together as much as possible.'

Sophie nodded curtly. 'Agreed. My boss would be going crazy if he knew that I was talking to you like this, but you have a way in, and I don't. I'll use any leverage I can get if it saves a girl's life.'

'Your DCI is right though – how do you know I didn't kill Ellen, and came back to wreak havoc on Aberdyth?'

The other woman studied her, green eyes narrowing, and she gave that harsh blast of laughter. 'I've been working a long time, Detective Cole, and let's just say I don't think you killed Ellen. Alex Jennington? Maybe, but you aren't top of my hit list. Believe me, you'd know all about it, if you were.' Her expression was grim.

Ava grinned. 'Fair enough. I'll go back and see if I can get anything else out of Leo later. You said on the phone you wanted me to go and see Rhodri?'

'Yes. When we spoke yesterday you mentioned he seemed upset when you showed him Ellen's hairband and bracelet. You might be able to build on that. I don't want to pull anyone in for questioning just yet. DI Hevis agrees, and he's working day and bloody night on this one. The way I see it, the suspect needs to think they are way ahead of us, and hopefully we just need to give them a bit more rope… I'll wait here in the car, and you see if you can get anything sensible out of Rhodri.'

Ava sighed. 'Depends how much he's taken. It's funny isn't it, it was such a joke at the time, the pills, and the effects, but now the effects have spread way beyond teenage amusement.'

'Do you remember who first gave you drugs? What did you take?' Sophie asked, tapping her fingers lightly on the steering wheel. Her phone buzzed and she quickly checked the screen.

'I honestly don't remember. If I had to guess it would be Paul, because he or Leo used to have them in little plastic sandwich bags. We would laugh at them, and call them our dealers, but they would never say where they came from. It wasn't an issue. They just appeared like bags of candy, and we discovered that this type of candy made us lose our inhibitions, fly to the stars and spin around in the darkness.'

'So some type of drug that would induce hallucinations? Ecstasy?'

'There was a sedative too – perhaps some diazepam derivative? Blue pills and white ones with a flower stamped in the middle. It made you feel limp like a ragdoll, and then you passed out. Even Rohypnol, I suppose, would have a similar effect. Penny hated that one. She would never take it, and I was always the first to pass out. It's terrifying, looking back now, to see what we were doing. Our silly dare game, "True Lies", stopped being about heights, and pushing ourselves physically, and became more about mental cruelty. There was the one where you were buried in a box for five minutes, and then, fuck I wish I could remember who thought of this one, but it was hanging, semi-strangulation.'

'So your games became more about hurting each other, making each other afraid?'

'Yes.'

'And who were you most afraid of, Ava?'

She could see his face, laughing down at her as he shut the box, the moment of darkness, the smell of soil, and the thump as he shovelled earth on top. 'Buried Alive' was Huw's favourite dare. 'Huw enjoyed the cruelty, and was, and still seems to be, sexist, arrogant, and angry. He was always angry, and always one to say his family would "get us" if we crossed him.'

'Was he angry with Ellen?'

'With all of us sometimes. He fought Leo and Rhodri more than once. I mean proper fighting, not just a few punches. Leo had to have stitches in his forehead. But we were all wild and out of control. I hate myself for not being strong enough to stop it.'

'You blame yourself for Ellen's death?'

'Of course. Wouldn't you?'

'I would, but I would also remind myself that I didn't kill her.'

Ava shook her head. 'But I did. I was there, and I should have stopped them.'

Sophie looked at her for a moment. 'Let's get that coffee, and then see what you can get out of Rhodri.'

*   *   *

The shop was crowded, mostly with elderly people doing the morning shop. Their baskets were crammed with brightly coloured boxes of soup and bags of bread. Talk was of the unexpected snow, the murder, and Bethan's disappearance. A young woman with straggly highlighted hair was trying to calm two fractious toddlers, and everyone seemed to be trying to help her.

Finally she burst into tears and fled, rattling the buggy over the road to the row of bungalows beyond.

A chorus of sympathetic chatter streamed out of the open door after her. Ava caught the gist. This was Huw's girlfriend, Isabell. Bethan had mentioned her that first night. What had she said? That Huw wouldn't marry her or something. She hadn't seemed to particularly like or dislike her pseudo stepmother. It had been a passing comment about her mother leaving Huw. Interesting though. Ava made a mental note to ask Rhodri what happened to Bethan's mother.

Clutching their paper coffee cups, Ava and Sophie brought the shop to a standstill. Whispers were hostile and glances sharp. She could guess what they were saying: that Ava Cole had come back, and brought nothing but trouble.

'I spoke to her yesterday, Huw's girlfriend. Nice girl, and very concerned about Bethan. More concerned than Huw, it seems…' Sophie gulped her coffee, and headed for the safety of the car. 'See you in a bit, and good luck.'

Ava walked back up the road, as far as the turning, and then began to climb around the rubbish piled around Rhodri's house. The metal bin was scorched black from another recent fire, and a plastic box of electrical wires was propped on the bonnet of a grubby white Audi. It took a while to get to the front door, and as she had expected, he didn't answer.

Sighing, she called his mobile again. No answer. The way around the back took her longer than last time, and she swore as she sliced her thumb on the skeleton of a rusty wheelbarrow. It occurred to her that Rhodri was literally barricading himself in. She peered in at the grimy windows as she navigated a heap of water troughs and farm gates. Nobody in the living room.

The back door was still unlocked, and she slid inside. A cat was mewing somewhere, and the stench was worse than before. Whatever happened, before she left the valley, she needed to get Rhodri some help, she thought grimly. Her phone rang, but she ignored it, focusing on the chill that wasn't just the cold outside seeping into the flimsy bungalow. The quiet, the stillness, was all wrong to Ava, who was a veteran of hundreds of crime scenes. Something was very wrong. She slowed her breathing, long deep breaths, moving lightly on the balls of her feet, reaching for the hundredth time for a gun that wasn't there. The beep of voicemail made her jump.

'Rhodri? It's me, Ava?'

She pushed her way over piles of clean laundry stacked on a narrow hall table. The house was cold. The bedroom door was shut, and she knocked gently, before pushing it open.

Rhodri was lying on his bed, sprawled on his back. One arm was flung away from him, the other was livid red and purple, and sported a tourniquet, and a syringe.

'Fuck! Rhodri? Rhodri, can you hear me?'

He was still warm, and bending to his face, she could feel the faintest of breaths touch her cheek. His chest heaved, then stopped for a while, before his rib cage heaved again. Ava grabbed her mobile.

'Sophie, I need the medics, and get in here now. It looks like an overdose.' It would be quicker for Sophie to get her team up here, than go to all the trouble of phoning 999.

'On my way. Is he breathing?'

'Yes, but unconscious. Don't worry, I haven't moved him.' Careful not to disturb anything, Ava kept a watch on Rhodri's breathing as she waited for help to arrive.

The thin, sunken face was pale, lips slightly blue, and his messy red hair was greasy and tangled. His head was turned slightly to one side, and traces of vomit streaked his yellow pillowcase. How had it come to this? Had Ellen's death set them all on their current paths, or would they have become who they were without the tragedy?

She glanced quickly around the room. It was impossible to tell if anyone else had been in here with all this clutter. It was a good fifteen minutes before her phoned buzzed with a text, and Sophie started hammering on the front door, calling her name. Hastily she began to clear a way to open the door, chucking random objects to the sides of the hallway. It didn't take long before she was yanking at the rusty locks, and swinging the door as wide as she could. The paramedics were closely followed by Sophie Miles, and DS Sharon.

'Any sign this wasn't an overdose?' Sophie muttered to Ava, who shook her head.

With the DS present, Ava kept her distance, unable to believe she was yet again first on scene, and the patient was potentially another murder victim.

Ava moved into another room, remembering she still needed to check her voicemail message. She was almost afraid to look, but it was just a message from Penny. Her heart rate was beginning to notch down a little. Rhodri's guitar sat on the torn and grubby sofa in the living room, and she had to stop herself from trailing a gentle finger over it as she passed. Emotion stabbed her hard in the chest, but frustration wasn't far off. The perp must know if they kept killing suspects the list would eventually close in on themselves, so perhaps this was a genuine suicide attempt. No obvious note though. She peeped into the bathroom, and wished she hadn't.

The stinking, claustrophobic house was crowded, and she stepped outside, anxious not to get in the way of the teams working in there. Perched on a discarded car bonnet, Ava listened to Penny's shrill, slightly sharp voice.

'Ava, lovely, I hope you're all right. Have you heard anything about Bethan? I know I shouldn't ask, but Huw is going out of his mind with worry, so I just thought if you had heard anything unofficial that the police know more than they'll tell us… He's finally realised that his girl isn't just playing for the cameras. They won't let me talk to Stephen either, they've just locked all the contestants in the camp while they investigate. He must be going crazy. Even bloody Leo only said he was "okay", not that I could talk to him or anything. If you want to meet up later, let me know. Paul has a hospital appointment, and I'm going to be up at Kingsmead Residential Home until about four, visiting Uncle Alf, but any time after. Bye, lovely.'

Ava sat in the cold and fiddled with her phone. She hit Jack's number but his phone was switched off. Mentally she tried to work out the time difference and concluded he might actually be catching some sleep. She left a message, trying to inject a business-like tone into her voice. 'Hi, Boss, just keeping you in the loop. I've got an OD on one of the suspects. The medics are with him now, and hopefully they got to him in time. He's a known drug user, but as we know, it would be pretty easy for this to be down to the perp. My gut says it isn't a genuine suicide attempt. Catch up soon.'

Rhodri was leaving the house now, swaddled up on a stretcher, an IV line replacing the tourniquet and syringe. His face was still and white, as though he was already dead.

Ava felt her stomach lurch, as he was bundled into the ambulance, and a flash of fear made her speak more sharply than she intended. 'How's he looking?'

Sophie came up behind her, dusted her leather jacket off, pulled down her ski hat, and shrugged. 'Okay for now. Obs are good, considering. Looks like he took a lot, but you got there in time. You sure you didn't mention to anyone that you were visiting him today? Just a passing comment?'

'No. You only suggested it this morning. So, any thoughts?'

'Same as you probably. If he was going to OD, why wait until now? You get home and the body count rises. On the other side of the coin, I looked into Jesse's RTA, and it seems the investigating officer wasn't happy with the verdict. There wasn't enough evidence to prove anything, but the diesel on the road was a convenient way to get a bike to skid out. The fact that lorries and tractors use that road all the time meant that it was impossible to prove it was a deliberate sabotage act. Jesse had been drinking, and he was over the limit, which wasn't helpful. That would have been a contributory factor to any incident, of course.'

'Did they interview anyone?'

'Yes. Jesse's parents, Ellen's parents, and his friends. That would be Huw, Rhodri, Leo, Paul and Penny. The usual suspects, but in this case, the same names that keep cropping up. The Family Liaison Officer noted that Jesse's dad seemed to be angrier that his son had stirred things up about Ellen, than at the fact he was dead.' Sophie was looking sideways at Ava. 'Any perceptive or enlightening thoughts, Detective?'

'Rhodri ran a garage. He had the knowledge, and I suppose all the others might have known. Leo had a bike once. I stole it when I ran away.' Ava sighed, trying to dredge up anything that would be of more help. The DS was watching her, taking notes now and again. God, she really needed to come up with something useful, something that would lead to the killer.

She turned back to Sophie. 'Back to Jesse though… He was always so in love with Ellen, but she used to tease him. She was a flirt. She'd flirt with anyone, the boys at school, older men when we were out. Hell, she even tried to chat up Coach Thomas at football practice. But she did eventually start seeing Jesse on a regular basis.'

'But if Jesse knew what happened, I don't understand what he needed to check? He could have just told the Smiths there and then.'

Something was niggling at Ava's brain, but she couldn't quite pin it down. She needed to talk to Jackie and Peter again. What had they said about Jesse checking, before he told them? Something jarred, but eventually she shook her head. 'I don't know. I'll leave you to get on and let you know if I get any more messages or genius ideas. Oh, one last thing. Are the *Tough Love* contestants allowed contact with the outside world? I really need to talk to my son.' She was so used to Stephen being at the back of her mind in everything she did, but the fact that he was so close, but she was unable to contact him was driving her crazy. Penny was right, too; he must be freaked by Bethan's disappearance.

'We kept them corralled for forty-eight hours whilst we questioned them about Jennington's murder, and again when we found the girl. Apart from that, I believe it is in their contracts that they have to stay put and get on with the game. No contact with families and friends and no internet access.'

Ava nodded. It had been worth a try. She would get on to Leo and ask him about Stephen. 'I'll get on then.'

'Thanks, Ava.' The DI turned away and was quickly absorbed in conversation with her team.

Wearily threading her way through a few curious bystanders, and two men in jeans and inappropriate jackets who were clearly reporters, Ava made her way back to the B&B. The snow was still light and steady, sugar-coating Aberdyth as it dusted the ambulance tracks with ice.

Mrs Birtley was behind her desk, but for once she ignored Ava, pursing her lips and turning deliberately to lift some paperwork from a drawer. Ava's door was still locked, and everything appeared untouched. Tugging off her boots, she pulled the elastic out of her hair, letting it fall heavily across her shoulders, breathing deeply. God, she was so tired. Out of habit, she checked her phone. Her mom wanted her to call back and discuss Ellen. No surprises there. She imagined that Jackie and Peter had been straight on the phone to her parents to blast their eardrums off.

Then there was a text from her boyfriend. '*I don't like to do this by text, but you have a lot going on. It feels weird that you are actually a mom, and I never knew...*' Great. She scanned down the lines. It was a brief break-up note. He had picked up a role in a biggish movie. It was being filmed in Chicago, of all places, and he would be away for at least four months. They had only ever been casual, but at this moment in time, she felt a pang of regret.

Wearily, she flicked her iPad on, and starting at the top of her list, she began to search. The police would be doing the same thing, of course, but if she could just use her insider knowledge, she might be able to snag a tiny detail they might not.

Leo's latest press and social media was all about the new show. There was a bitchy piece in a showbiz magazine that was interesting. According to the journalist, his last couple of projects didn't do so well, and he had borrowed a lot for this new series of *Tough Love*. So, Leo would be desperate for this series to hit high in the ratings. The viewing figures quoted were mind boggling, even for a short film that Leo had apparently funded, which promptly bombed. Millions tuned in for *Tough Love*, but Leo clearly enjoyed the high life. Fast cars, flying first class, owning four homes…

Leo had a home in the Hills in LA. That was… well, it was explainable, because he clearly spent some time there working on another show, but he'd never mentioned that one to her. Why?

She continued, interested to see Huw had won a teaching award a few months back. There was nothing on Rhodri. Penny's company was doing well with her export business. Solid profits for the last few years. Slightly surprising, given the state of the market and small business in general, but nothing to suggest anything underhand. Penny would be the last person to launder money, or not pay her tax returns. Ava returned to her searches, checking entries against Companies House. There was nothing illegal, but she was shaken to see Paul was listed as the majority shareholder. Almost everything was in his name. Fingers shaking, she tapped out more searches. The house was only in his name, not jointly owned. Did Penny know? She seemed so business-like, but what had she said? That Paul and Leo did her website, and photographs for her. She had laughed that she was rubbish at things like that. Why would Paul have everything in his name? Especially now, given he was facing a death sentence.

Ava frowned, rubbing her forehead, feeling a headache gathering force. She got up, rubbing her sore neck, rummaging for the pills. For years she had been plagued with migraines, and once she felt one lurking, the only thing to do was zap them with pills.

* * *

She had meant to just lie down for a bit, sleep off the headache, and try to see everything more clearly. Sometimes she had solved cases in that queer, crystal clear moment between sleeping and waking, but today, exhaustion overtook her, and she slept.

The ringing of her phone woke her. It was dark, and she blinked in bewilderment for a few seconds.

'Ava! Thank God. I've been trying to get hold of you... I nearly rang the police.'

'Calm down, Penny. What's happened?'

She heard Penny give a stifled sob. 'Huw said he would get Paul from hospital. It's a long drive to keep doing. Leo was helping out, but now he's tied up with the filming and the police investigation. They took him down to Cadrington for questioning. Did you know? I stayed a bit longer with Uncle Alf, and when I got back I thought they would be home.'

'Go on.'

'They weren't answering their phones, so I drove down there. I'm just outside A&E now. The day unit is shut but I found one of the nurses on her way out, and she said Huw was an hour late to collect Paul, and they'd only just left. She was cross, because she needed to close the unit, but Paul told her he didn't have any other transport and would have to wait for Huw. Why would he say that? They've been planning something, the stupid boys, I know it. Then bloody Huw rang, and he said that he was taking Paul for a "long drive to nowhere". Like some stupid cowboy. He loves those old Westerns... He said to tell you that he knows you know where Bethan is, and if we want Paul to be okay, you need to tell him.'

'What the fuck?' Ava was still dozy, fighting back to reality. 'Look, I don't know where she is, but the perp seems to have taken some pictures of her in a cave. They emailed the link to my boss in LA. We don't know where she is, though, apart from the fact she is obviously underground.'

'Oh!' It was a little cry of fear followed by another stifled sob, and Ava felt her own gut clench painfully.

'Sorry, Pen, but I wanted you to know. Can you think where she might be? The search teams are struggling with this shit weather, and with the temperature dropping, we need to find her. Regarding Huw, does he not think that if the police had the faintest idea where she might be they would be there by now?'

'I don't know! He'd been drinking, and I could hear Paul in the background laughing all crazy-like as he does when he's been drinking… He isn't supposed to have alcohol with his medication. Oh, Ava, he said if I told the police he and Paul would just go up into the hills and keep on driving. And why would Bethan be in a cave? I don't understand, and I'm not sure I can cope with much more. We had to fill out some legal paperwork about Paul's treatment today, and it makes it so much for real. He's dying, Ava! What am I going to do?'

'I'll ring him… Or I can ring Huw?'

'No. He said you need to meet him at the old outward bound centre – you know, Johnson's. He said you need to tell him where Bethan is and then he'll bring Paul home. I'm going to start driving back now, but it'll take me a good hour at this time of night. Oh, the evil bastard, Ava – why is he doing this?'

'Penny, you need to calm down, and drive safely. We'll sort it out, okay? It sounds like Paul is all right at the moment. Look, drive carefully because this weather is a bitch, and I'll go out to Johnson's. I'm also going to tell the police.'

'You can't, Ava – he said not to!'

'Penny, has it occurred to you that Huw could be behind all this? He might be the one who killed Ellen, who killed Alex, and…' She'd almost been going to add Rhodri, but if Huw was driving around in the hills with Paul most of the afternoon, pissed and angry, he was unlikely to have been injecting a lethal dose into Rhodri's veins a few hours ago. 'What time did Huw pick up Paul?'

'Um… I don't know! He said he was over in Cadrington picking up a part for the Land Rover, and it would be easy for him to get Paul. He's done it before, so I didn't think anything of it…'

'Okay. I'll take Mr B's truck and get over there.'

'Ring me when you get there, lovely. Thank you, and I'm so sorry.' She was calmer now, but subdued, and tears clearly weren't far away.

'It's fine, we'll sort it.'

After a moment's deliberation, Ava called the police. 'Sophie, I have another situation…' She quickly updated the other woman.

'It's not a good idea for you to go, Ava. Let us handle it. You're too involved.'

'I need to go. I don't know what those two idiots are planning, but Penny is going mad with worry.'

'I don't know why he should think we know anything more about Bethan. There is no news, other than the photographs at the moment. Someone is playing games again.'

'I'm going, Sophie, but meet me at the outward bound centre. It's derelict now apparently, and Huw said that's where they are.'

'I really don't think you should be anywhere near this, Ava.'

'I hear you. Oh, Sophie, did you find Alex's phone? Was it on his body?'

Silence, then Sophie spoke again. 'No. Nor in his room. Unfortunately, I think our suspect must have whipped it. Hang on a minute.'

Ava waited, hearing car doors slam, and quick urgent voices.

'All right. Johnson's did you say? I'm over in Coenheath at the moment, but I'll bring some bodies down. Actually, I've still got a vehicle and team down at the *Tough Love* camp, so I'll send them up too. They'll take longer and they will have to go the other way, but I'd rather have some backup. We'll be coming from the north, so any specific directions?'

'I hardly remember myself, but I just Googled it...' Ava gave her the postcode. 'It was always hard to find, probably why it went bust in the end – a bit like my parents' caravan park. It's a track a few miles north of where Jesse had his bike accident. Right at the top of the hill. We can meet by the end of the track in' – she checked her watch – 'half an hour?'

'Yes. And Ava?'

'I know, I know, don't go in by myself. I'll wait at the end of the track.'

'Right, and if anyone asks, I told you to keep yourself right out of it, okay?'

'Understood,' Ava said grimly. She was already fumbling for her boots. She was out the door in minutes, but got distracted by a text. Almost afraid to look, she made herself squint at the screen. Stephen's name came up, and she scrolled down, confused. He hadn't even given her his number, she'd had to ask Penny for it. And surely the contestants weren't allowed to contact anyone on the outside.

'You fucked up being a mum, so, Detective, why don't you try and do what you're supposed to and find my girlfriend.'

The very first text she had received from her son. She supposed it was progress of a sort.

Chapter 27

I make myself a coffee with the fancy machine I bought a few months ago. I enjoy having money. It gives me power. Inheriting the family business was something that I never considered. You don't, as a kid. You just imagine everything will stay the same, and then of course you hope like hell it won't.

I had to be quick, that night with Ellen, but it worked out for the best. In fact, I was really just a bystander, hiding in the shadows. It was dark and crazy, and I knew she was in for a bad time, but it didn't occur to me just how bad. It reminds me of fairy tales and that web of darkness that runs underneath the frosting and the fantasy. Who was in the wood that night?

For a crazy moment I wondered if I had blacked out and somehow killed her myself. But I knew the moment I saw him. He was edgy and not in the usual way. There wasn't any blood or anything like that, but I just knew. It made sense. That didn't stop me bringing up Ellen whenever one of the others started to annoy me, because you see, they weren't sure either. Only two of us knew for sure who raped and killed Ellen – just him and me.

The drugs were blamed for memory gaps, and the panic afterwards. Once you have concealed a crime, it isn't easy to confess, especially when you are worried, deep down, that you might be responsible. So you're grateful to your friends for standing by you, for protecting you from the law, from your parents.

But your tight little group splinters, and the secret becomes heavier and heavier. You blame each other, you try to run, and maybe you even succeed. Detective Ava Cole, I'm looking at you when I say this. Finally it occurs to you that perhaps you helped to cover up a crime you didn't do, and that your best mates didn't do… Perhaps you helped to cover up a bigger crime, with far-reaching consequences. But perhaps you really aren't meant to come to that conclusion because you would ruin everything.

My computer screen is covered in photographs, and I settle down to edit the best, ready for use. I'm good at what I do, and I get respect for that. It has never occurred to me to run away.

'Dal ati, Ava Cole.'

'**Keep on trucking, Ava Cole.**'

Chapter 28

The lights of the truck cut a slash of whiteness through the darkness of the road, as Ava drove carefully out of Aberdyth, past Leo's driveway, and onward. The wipers whined as they beat away the snow that clouded her vision. Her phone rang as she approached the bridge and seeing it was Penny, she answered quickly. 'I'm nearly there, Pen, where are you?'

'I'm stuck behind a massive truck. There's been an accident, and I'm going to be another hour at least! Oh God, Ava, do be careful. Have you rung the police?'

'Yes. They are going to meet me up there. I know you are worried, but we need their help. I'll be there first though, so I'll see if I can talk Huw down. I'll ring you as soon as I have any news, and drive carefully, won't you? It won't do any good you having an accident either.'

'Oh thank you, lovely, you are so kind. I'll keep my fingers crossed. If anything has happened to Paul...'

'It won't. I'm sure Huw is just trying to scare us, the fucking idiot. He always did like to think he was the big man.' Ava rang off, and changed gear up the steep hill. She was nearly at the top, going slowly, scanning the tracks either side for an entrance. Surely there was a pine forest before the turning... The snowfall intensified and she could see nothing but blinding whiteness. Distracted, she was only half-aware as another vehicle came at her head on. Fast.

It was on her side of the road, driving far too quickly to avoid, and she instinctively hit her hand down hard on the horn. The two vehicles were head to head when she swung the wheel sharply to her left. There was a crashing rending of metal at the near miss, and the vehicles scraped bonnet to bonnet before Ava felt a jolt, and her truck was bumping off the road down a bank. It slid to the level ground, and the engine whined in protest.

In those few moments, the other vehicle was still on the road, facing her, blinding her with their headlights. Nobody got out, and nobody rushed to see if she was okay. There was an eerie, icy silence and the half-imagined stretch of lonely white hills rising into the darkness, cloaked and softened by the snow.

Ava made a quick decision, straightened the wheel, let the brake off, and carried on driving. There were no fences as far as she could remember, and she bumped along the tussocky grass and little drifts alongside the road. The bank back up to the road was too high for her to consider, but this was a deliberate attempt to get her off the road, or worse, and she was damned if she was going to stick around and let them finish what they had begun.

As the terrain got worse, with bigger ruts and frosted holes, she would have stopped, but for the sheer terror and determination not to be caught. Sophie was right, it was a trap, and she didn't doubt that Huw was behind the wheel of the Land Rover chasing her. She remembered the first few letters of his registration plate. The other vehicle had descended off the road, too, now, and was pursuing her. Slowly at first, but inching up behind until the metal screeched as the vehicles met, and Ava shot forward in her seat at the impact. It was a treacherous race. She had no idea what was coming and relied entirely on the tunnel vision of her headlights. It was so many years since she'd driven in the hills, so many years since she'd driven anything but an automatic, that the constant gear changes, the hauling of the wheel made her arm muscles scream in protest, and a whiplash pain gave her neck an electric shock of agony all the way around to her jawbone, every time she turned her head to the right.

Sweat was pouring down her neck, her heart was pounding like she'd been running, and her back ached from constantly fighting to stay in control of her machine. For several miles they continued the reckless chase. Despite the cold, Ava's hands were slipping on the wheel, and she tasted blood from a cut lip. The snow was easing, and it was possible to see beyond a torrent of icy drifts – the headlights showing more terrain and giving her more time to think. The snowy hillside rose in big tufted ridges, and she edged over rocks, and swung around a tree copse.

Risking a moment's lapse of concentration, glancing down quickly for her phone, she saw the crash had jolted it onto the floor, where it rattled tantalisingly out of reach. Ava was beginning to think she might make it, as the bank between her and the road lowered considerably, when suddenly beneath her the headlights showed another river. It was all rushing, gushing and frothing white bubbles, edged with ice, and she plunged into it thumping the brake pedal uselessly. Mercifully the engine was still running, and the water reached only halfway up the side doors. But the truck kept moving forward, and she kept her foot hard on the accelerator hardly daring to hope she might make it. It was coming out of the river that her luck ran out. The gentle shingle rise was fine, but there was some kind of rocky outcrop, hidden under the snow, that caught on the undercarriage, and with an ominous grinding sound, the vehicle ground to a halt. The low chassis of the old truck, never designed for off-roading, had obviously caught on something.

Shit! She bent down, grabbed her phone and leapt down. She was off like a hare towards the road, but with no cover the other vehicle, having navigated the river with ease, quickly caught up, pulling alongside. Her boots crunched through the snow, her head was down, arms pumping, but it was too late. Strong arms reached out and grabbed her, and she heard the sound of familiar laughter.

'Paul?' She was blinking, inhaling alcohol fumes, shoving his arms away.

'That was so much fun, Ava. I had no idea you were such a good driver.' Her ex-husband was beaming at her. His face in the torchlight was pale and sweaty, but his eyes glittered.

'We only meant to frighten you into stopping. Having you playing chase games with us was just like the old days, wasn't it, Paul?' Huw, also sweaty, unshaven, and wearing just a shirt, was at the wheel.

Having pulled her roughly into the Land Rover, Paul pushed her back against the seat, beaming as though he was thoroughly pleased to see her, and he hadn't just nearly killed her. In her pocket she kept one hand firmly clenched on her phone. Huw was already back on the accelerator, and he spun the vehicle into a skid, letting out a catcall like some stupid teenager in his first car.

Ava hung on to the door handle, wondering if she could jump out. But from what she could see there was no cover. They would run her down in an instant. Surely the police must be coming soon... She must keep them busy until that happened.

Whatever they intended though, she needed to be careful, put them off guard. Both of them had such a low opinion of her, they might feel they were totally in control. She would use this. But they would expect her to be angry, and she allowed her genuine fear to break through, voice straining, as though holding back tears. 'You stupid, fucking idiots! What the hell are you playing at? Penny is going out of her mind with worry. Where have you been, Huw? The police are treating you as a number one suspect, and this isn't helping to find Bethan. They are taking everyone in for questioning, and avoiding them like this just makes you seem guilty!'

Huw took one hand off the wheel, leant over, and slapped her across the face before she could even have time to dodge. 'Don't you even mention my girl. Someone has got her, I do know that, and you're going to have a little chat with us and tell us who.' He yanked the vehicle to a halt now. The headlights picked up nothing but the endless fall of snow, engulfing them, cocooning them together on the hillside. He killed the engine, and they sat, breathing heavily.

'What are you even talking about, Huw? How would I know?'

'I got a call today telling me that the police know where she is, and if they do, then you do too. They know someone is holding her, but they won't move until tomorrow, because they need a warrant.'

'But...' Ava's mind was spinning, and she ran her fingers gently across the buttons of her phone, 'That's bollocks. Whoever called you, Huw, was trying to wind you up. If the police know where she is, they will be on their way to get her. Huw, have you seen the photographs?' She tried to take him off at a tangent, steering him back to reality. Was he really crazy enough to be behind this, to harm his own daughter?

'What photographs?'

'You had those missed calls from that policewoman earlier,' Paul pointed out.

Ava looked him in the eye. 'Someone has taken photographs of Bethan and emailed them to the police. She's underground, in a cave somewhere. Before you ask, I don't know where, but why don't you stop this madness, and get back to finding your daughter?'

For a long moment she thought he was taking in what she had said, that it was going to be all right. It wasn't. 'She's alive then... That's what the phone call said. Why should I believe you about the photographs? That could be bullshit. And you still know where she is.' He was sulky now, yet still glittering danger- ously. The drink had slowed his brain to such an extent that logical thinking was clearly impossible. 'My beautiful little girl, and you know where she is.'

'Of course I fucking don't. Didn't it occur to you that the call might be a prank? Didn't you think to ring the police yourself and check? Ring them now – go on!'

'He can't ring them, can he? Because like you say, they probably reckon he did it. Killed Ellen, and that stupid PI, took his own daughter… And the reason they think all that is because of you, you stupid bitch. I rang them and they wouldn't tell me anything either. Keeping their stupid information to themselves. A woman in charge is never a good thing,' Paul told her, viciously.

'Look, you need to understand, I don't know any more than you do about Bethan. She's in a cave and we need to find her. Surely that is the most important thing, especially in this weather.' Ava inched her fingers along the key pad and tried hard to dial 999. It was practically impossible. She pressed another couple of random buttons. 'As for Ellen, if you had told me the whole story years ago…'

'If we had told you the whole story, you would have gone straight to the police,' Huw said grimly. 'And screwed things up, like you have done now. Everything was fine until you came back.'

'Right, well, I'm not going anywhere now, suppose you tell me. Who did kill Ellen? You might as well tell me, because it will all come out in the end.' Unable to believe their single-minded stupidity on the subject of Bethan, Ava tried a snap change of subject. Sophie Miles and her team would be at the outward bound centre by now, wondering, waiting, then becoming alarmed.

The men exchanged glances, and Ava caught the amusement flash between them. More than amusement, a tangible evil. How had she ever been married to this man? She wriggled slightly away from Huw, and he pulled out a packet of cigarettes. Lighting one, he put it in Paul's mouth and then lit his too. Paul now had a firm grasp on Ava's other arm.

'How stupid do you think we are? It was dark that night. Lots of drugs and alcohol going around. Far as I remember, Ellen went off into the woods with Leo. I reckon Leo must have ripped her knickers off and killed her. What do you think, Paul?' Huw waved his cigarette within inches of Ava's cheek, and she flinched.

Paul blew out a lungful of smoke right into his ex-wife's face. He was choking with laughter. 'Naw, I'm sure Ellen was off under that bush with Rhodri. She was such a slag. In fact, I'm certain that we were just talking by the fire, weren't we? Then when Rhodri dragged her body back we tried to resuscitate her. Ava woke up and came running down, far too late to do anything. You were crying with Penny, all over Ellen's poor dead body. Women!'

'You do know Rhodri took an overdose this afternoon,' Ava told them, hoping to jolt either man out of their complacency.

Paul shook his head, but his eyes were glittering. 'So what? It was going to happen. I suppose he was just saving it for when we were all back together. Is he dead then?'

'Your concern is overwhelming. No, he isn't dead.' Neither man seemed especially surprised at the news of Rhodri, but then he was a known addict.

'Actually, Ava, I do remember something else,' Huw added thoughtfully, and Paul glanced sharply at his friend. 'That night Ellen died, I think I might have heard her call out. I walked through the woods in the general direction, and found Rhodri and Jesse.'

'What do you mean?'

'They were together, if you get my meaning. You're not the brightest, Ava, and I reckon you must have shagged your boss to get where you are, but use your imagination. So, I say Ellen found out Jesse put it about both ways, and she threatened to tell everyone his dirty little secret. So he tried to prove he was a man really, and roughed her up a bit.'

They were clearly throwing out names at random, trying to

hurt her, covering for themselves maybe? Ava was digging her nails into her palms. Actually, she had known about Rhodri and Jesse. She and Ellen had argued about it, and Penny took Ava's side, saying there was no reason to out them, and if Jesse still liked Ellen too, perhaps he would need to make a choice. It had been a shock, but the girls had agreed in the end to keep quiet, and then Jesse had seemed to be making more effort with Ellen.

Huw and Paul were silent, staring at her, wolves with their prey, waiting for her answer. Ava knew she shouldn't antagonise them, but she couldn't help herself. 'Because that makes you a real man, does it? I don't believe Jesse did it, and you wouldn't know the truth if it came up and smacked you in the balls.'

Paul pushed his friend back, and turned to Ava. 'Always did have a big mouth, didn't you? If you think Jesse didn't do it, perhaps you should be more careful. You might be speaking to a murderer, for all you know. We could easily kill you out here on the hill and bury your dead body like we did Ellen's.'

'The police know exactly where I am, and who I'm with. Don't be stupid, Paul. Do you really think it will help Stephen if you kill me?' She spat back in his face, pushing his arm away.

'Anyway, enough of this shit. Ava, you going to tell us where Bethan is?' Huw was close again and she could smell the drink on his breath.

'I don't know.'

Huw looked uncertainly at Paul, who nodded. 'I think she's telling the truth. We should have thought it might be a prank call, really. But it's been fun hurting you, Ava. I was so glad when you ran away, you know. You always were a pathetic, whining cow. If you hadn't got pregnant, I would never have had to marry you. Even that was only because my bloody dad would have disinherited me if I didn't. The only good thing you did was leave me a son. He's a good lad, Stephen. He'll have the farm when I'm gone.' The pride in his slurred voice was obvious. Whatever he had done, he had been a good dad to her son.

Ava tried to breathe normally. She didn't tell him she had figured all this out years ago, and Leo had tried so hard to persuade Ava not to stay with Paul. She obviously didn't share the knowledge that Stephen was Leo's son. If Paul hadn't figured out what was staring him in the face, given his condition, why would she be the one to break it to him? What an idiot she had been, ricocheting from one boy to the next, fighting with all of them, struggling to come to terms with Ellen's death. Only Penny had really understood, but she had also lied.

As the silence stretched into minutes, for one awful moment she thought Paul had realised the truth about Stephen, and was just toying with her, but he clearly hadn't. She took a deep breath, and said firmly, 'So you might as well let me go. Thanks for a fun night out, but I have to check in with my boss. I'm late already, and given the situation over here, he's probably on the phone to the inspector you despise so much, asking where the hell I am. She'll be coming with a response team soon, and I'm sure you don't want to be arrested.'

Ava sensed indecision. After the thrill of the chase, the excitement of the prey being captured, the men seemed at a loss. She could imagine the prank call coming in, after they had been drinking beer, the instant decision that the police where hiding something, and everyone was conspiring against them. The drunken agreement to snare Ava, without much thought or planning, would have come easily from either man.

'Penny wouldn't call the police. She hates them as much as we do,' Paul said.

'I called them, you idiots! Penny's that worried about you though, she would have agreed to anything. She loves you, much as I find that extremely hard to believe at this moment in time.'

Paul hesitated some more, and looked at Huw, who shrugged. 'Might as well go home then. I'll drop you off, Paul. You let me know if you hear any more about my daughter, won't you?'

Bewildered at this sudden change of heart, Ava didn't see the blow coming until she sprawled head first out of the door, plunging into the icy ground. Beside her the engine revved, horn sounded and the Land Rover drove off in a slipstream of diesel fumes.

The darkness closed around her, and her head ached. She spat snow and grit from her mouth, and wiped her face. Fucking great. Minus degrees, and she was stuck in the hills with no coat. At least the snow had stopped. She peered at her phone and the low battery icon flashed, once, twice. Ava called Sophie, but the signal was so bad she couldn't even hear if she had picked up. Without thinking, she rang Leo.

'Ava?'

'Leo, I need your help. I'm somewhere north of Aberdyth, maybe near the old outward bound centre. Past the bridge where Jesse died. I'm going to try and get back to the road… I tried to call DI Miles, but her phone signal is too weak… Leo?'

The bleep cut her off and her own phone died. Total blackness, as the clouds rolled over the hills. The ground was hard, icy, and packed on top with this new fall of snow. She thought hard, trying to get her bearings, but the run had zig-zagged her off course, and the men had driven her even further away from the road. Although she peered intently into the night, it was impossible to tell which way the road was now. Literally, impossible.

Sophie Miles was going to be, quite rightly, furious with her, and she hadn't even gotten any useful information out of two stupid drunk men. She stood very still, listening. Somewhere to the west she could hear water. The river. Ava began to stumble towards it. Had Leo known where she meant? Would he even bother to come and get her? Perhaps he would call the police and get through to Sophie. She peered into the night, once or twice yelling, watching intently for the blue lights of Sophie's team. Paul and Huw had tried to implicate Leo in Ellen's death, but if they were all in it together, this could be part of the game.

The river sounds were getting closer, and she tried to walk faster, but ended up falling. Her face was raw with cold, and her hands and feet completely numb. Slow and steady was best. She was shaking violently now, her teeth chattering so hard it actually hurt, jaw rigid, trying to absorb the spasms. Icy gusts of wind streamed down from the surrounding hills, notching up the arctic conditions.

She tried to distract herself from the very really possibility of dying of hypothermia on the hills, by going over the case, piece by piece. As she considered Jesse, that blinding moment of clarity that had eluded her earlier sliced into her brain. Hadn't Peter told her Jesse might have said he needed to 'check with someone' instead of 'check something'? What if he had gone to, say it was Huw, and told him he wanted to come clean. Perhaps Huw had some evidence, or Jesse just wanted another person on side before he took the leap... It fit, and she made a note to call Peter as soon as she could. Assuming she didn't freeze to death out on the hill tonight, and assuming Peter would actually talk to her. Sliding down a muddy gulley, and into another icy puddle, she suddenly saw headlights. The road! But it wasn't the road. The truck was still sitting on the bank, lights shining across the grass and rock, back end wedged on the shingle.

Energised at the possibility of warmth and shelter, she scrambled eagerly into the driver's seat. The keys were still in there, but when she started the engine the vehicle gave a grinding noise, and died. The road must be somewhere just to the east. She could get out and walk, or she could sit in the relative shelter of the truck. But she couldn't stay there all night...

Pocketing the keys and zipping her fleece firmly around her throat she jumped out of the cab. Headlights pierced the darkness as another vehicle slowed to her right. Her first leap of relief that Leo had come, was dampened by the thought that Paul and Huw might have come back to make sure she stayed out all night.

'Ava! Where the fuck are you?'

It was Leo, and she ran, forcing numb, clumsy legs towards the road. 'I'm here!'

The car reversed a little, and swung around, so its headlights blinded her. A dark figure leapt down the bank towards her.

'It's all right, Ava, I've got you. Look, I've even got brandy in the car, just like a proper mountain rescue team.' Leo helped her gently into the passenger seat. 'Here, drink this from the bottle, I don't mind. I've got a coat in the back, you can put that round you.' He turned the engine back on, and the heating up to max, whilst she shivered.

'What the hell happened?'

She drank the brandy, gasping as it burned her throat. 'Someone set Huw and Paul up to scare me. Whoever it is playing games…'

'I see.' He looked distant, face shuttered and cold. 'Did they hurt you?'

'No! I need to call the police. Oh God, and poor Penny. My bloody phone is dead. Can I use yours?'

'Sure.'

She quickly dialled Sophie's number from memory and gave her a rundown of the evening's events. Then she held the phone away from her ear and pulled a face as the full force of the inspector's rage flowed over her. Leo was grinning.

'I can't believe I let you even think of coming up here by yourself. Not only that but I've wasted time and resources on a total non-event. My boss is going to bollock me at the briefing tomorrow. You're bloody lucky to be alive. From this moment I need you to let me handle things, and stop putting yourself at risk. You are too involved and too vulnerable. Ring me later when you've warmed up, and tell me everything that was said. I'll have someone waiting at Huw Davis's house for when the fucker gets back from joyriding. We'll bring him in and see what he has to say for himself.'

Ava, still shaking violently in icy spasms, agreed, and rang Penny. Omitting the worst of their behaviour, she simply told her that Paul was fine, and she believed they were both on their way home.

Penny was only half an hour out of Aberdyth, and wanted to see her, and although Ava felt a twinge of guilt she explained that she had got lost on the hills trying to follow the men, and was now suffering from a mild dose of hypothermia. 'I just need a hot bath and some dry clothes before I even think about anything else.'

'Okay. I would love to say come over here, but, well…'

'I know. It's fine, Pen, just get yourself home and text me when he gets back, okay?'

'Ava, I don't understand why they would do this… It's like something they would have done as teenagers! If Paul isn't careful he'll miss his meds again, and you said he'd been drinking as well…' Penny was close to tears again, and the frustration in her voice was clear.

'I don't know, Pen, but like I said, Paul didn't seem bothered, and I'm sure they'll creep back in and Paul will be really apologetic. And if you're worried about anything, just call the police.'

'On my own husband? You've lived in America for too long, Ava,' Penny snapped suddenly.

'I actually meant Huw really, and I was thinking of your safety, Pen. I don't give a damn about Huw.' Or Paul, she added silently.

'I'm sorry, lovely, so sorry. It's just been a horrible day, that's all. I'll let you know when he gets back.'

'Fine.'

'And Ava? You don't have to be afraid of Paul, you know. He would never hurt you.'

'After tonight, Pen, I might hurt him though, so let's just leave it at that, shall we?'

'Okay.' She sounded sulky and there was the sound of a car hooting before she killed the call.

Leo leaned over and removed his phone from her shaking fingers. 'Right, that's everyone's lives sorted out. Now, Detective, come and get warm before you die of hypothermia.'

She managed a weak grin, despite the fact she felt a lump in her throat and her eyes filled with tears. It must be the cold, she told herself firmly. Another surge of panic gripped her chest, as she thought of Bethan, naked in her cave. If they didn't find her soon she would surely be dead, if the cold hadn't already killed her. 'Leo, the perp sent some photos of Bethan. She's in a cave. They're the same sort of photographs, same website, as the ones of me were on.' Her words seemed to be coming out wrong, slurred, and garbled like she had been drinking herself.

'She's underground?' Leo's voice was hard. 'Ava, babe, this is one sick bastard,' he added. 'Right, I haven't got a tow rope, so I'll come back tomorrow for the Birtleys' truck. Fucking idiots, they could have killed you.'

'Doubt it. They were pissed, and pathetic, not murderous. They told me you probably k… k… killed E… Ellen, by the way.' Her teeth were still chattering, body aching with the force of her shivering.

'Do you believe them?'

'No, as it happens I don't. But I do think you know something else about Ellen's death. You need to share that.'

He shrugged. 'It isn't anything important. The poor girl is dead, and we covered it up. All this stuff that's going on… I think it might be Huw. I know what I said earlier, but you just told me he tried to drop me in it. That's not part of the pact. He's been going off the rails for years, pushing his wife around, pushing his girlfriend around. You're right, the way he idolises Bethan – it's not normal. I actually offered her a part in the show because Stephen told me she's desperate to get out of Aberdyth. She thinks she might be able to do what I did and build a career out of a reality show. I reckon she also sees it as a way of escaping Huw's stranglehold. Don't look like that – he isn't doing anything to her or I'd have called the police myself. He's just obsessed. It must be suffocating for Bethan.'

'And now she has got away.'

'Yes.' His voice was flat, and his hand gentle on her shoulder. 'Ava, why don't you stay with me tonight?'

Chapter 29

I was eight when it started. My uncle had moved in with us, my dad had moved out. Mum had already started her enthusiastic scramble into alcoholism. She embarked on her wine-drenched journey with relief, almost as soon as Dad's car pulled away from the house. Anyway, she never gave a shit about me, and when Uncle Alf started taking me 'out to play' she barely looked up from her bottle.

It took a few months, and as I grew older, wiser, I recognised that it was that classic cliché of grooming.

He bought me new clothes – he bought me the princess dresses I craved, and gave me the brightly coloured sweets. He sat me on his knee to watch movies. Later he would show me his photography studio that he'd rigged up out the back, converting one of the run-down, rusty sheds behind the bungalow into a state-of-the-art facility.

I did what I was told under the bright lights, trying not to blink at the flash of the camera. I knew it was wrong – the way he looked at me, even before he started asking me to 'model'. The vague sense of unease, the sick feeling in my stomach when he touched me became full-blown terror when he started making me undress for his 'films'.

'You're special. People love you, and this will make the boys happy. You want them to be happy, don't you? Because the boys will pay lots of money for these photos and films, and I'll buy you more new dresses. Now just slip that dress over your shoulder and pull up the hem a bit more...'

On the outside, I managed to go to school, to play with my friends, to eat and drink, and occasionally sleep. Inside, the sick terror was replaced over time with a familiar, dull ache. My body was down below, under the heat and the lights, but I was soaring overhead, flying up, safe and untouched.

I found out later, that he used to drug me at first, just until he was sure I was obedient. By that time, he was taking me out on 'trips into town'. He had business contacts in Cardiff, and we'd go up on the Friday evening, spend the weekend, and then come back late Sunday night.

He always had a lot of money for a part-time slacker who 'did something in IT', and I wanted so badly for someone to question it, to question me. But it never happened. Hell, Uncle Alf was a nice bloke, tall, burly and bearded, with a deep reassuring voice, and big rough hands. He even found time to coach the local football team, and he was on the Parish Council. Nobody would ever have suspected he led a double life as a paedophile.

Occasionally he would head down to his studio without me, and sometimes he took my friends. They would come back for tea, he'd give them a glass of squash, and they'd become all dreamy and cooperative. I'd sneak down after them and watch. I'm not sure why. I didn't dare interfere, but I felt in some part of me that, if I was watching, I was looking out for them.

His business expanded, and I learned more. In Cardiff, we had secret meetings in grubby hotels. I learned that there are men and women who pay huge amounts of money for photographs and films of children, and Uncle Alf would introduce me as his special 'golden girl'. Those present at these meetings would look at me with the same predatory hunger as he did. The sickness swirled, but I headed up to my safe place on the ceiling.

Hard copies of photographs or DVDs would be exchanged in sanitary white envelopes, but as time went on, and more opportunities presented themselves, I could see that very soon much of the actual trading was done online. The internet quickly became an integral part of the business growth. I watched, did what I was told, and waited.

'*Byddwch yn amyneddgar, Ava Cole, dwi bron wedi gorffen.*'

'**Be patient, Ava Cole, I've nearly finished.**'

Chapter 30

Ava knew she should have just said no, she should have just asked Leo to drop her back at the pink, dust-free B&B. But she felt safe in the car with him, alone in the darkness. The aftermath of the adrenalin from the chase and the hypothermia made her body weak and defenceless. Plus, her heart was insisting he was telling the truth. Joe's casual dump-by-text and Sophie's fury at her screw-up, all made her head spin. Ava sank back against the seat and closed her eyes.

Leo leant over and pulled her coat tighter around her shoulders, and the smell of him conjured memories that stung and blurred. She kept her eyes shut, and his hand touched her cheek, his finger rough but gentle, and his breath was warm on her face. Before she consciously made a decision, his lips were on hers, just briefly. As the car moved off, she opened her eyes, watching the shadowy giants of the snowy hills blurring into the night sky. They drove in silence. The connection between them had always been violent, electric and passionate, but this was different.

She really shouldn't – a memory of Rhodri asking coarsely if she was going to fuck Leo, and her scathing reply. But Rhodri was in hospital, and that was another childhood friend possibly lost. Penny, who might have offered comfort, would be scolding her errant husband. There were no strangers at the gates tonight, no intruders into the luxury compound, and she slid out of the car, hugging both coats around her, still shivering. Leo's house was warm and he flicked a few lights on, stopping to kiss her once more at the bottom of the stairs.

'Ava, are you sure? I do have spare rooms you know… You've had a shit night, and you might regret this in the morning.'

It was so unlike the Leo she thought she knew, and the boy remembered, that she found herself drawing back and looking at him as though he was a stranger. She laughed. 'You're right, I will regret this, but let's do it anyway.'

His room was clutter-free and the huge bed lay in front of more of the glass picture windows. Just now the darkness was peaceful, lulling her senses, but she knew if she was alone it would become oppressive, terrifying, and the nightmares would return. She returned his kisses, sliding his T-shirt over his head. It was familiar and new all at once, and she allowed herself to sink into the moment.

* * *

Her phone woke her, and she raised her head, confused. Leo was watching her from the other pillow. He smiled. 'It's okay. I put it on charge after you went to sleep last night.'

'You… Right. Thanks.' She felt like an awkward teenager again, but somehow without the bleary-headed feeling she had always associated with sex with Leo. It was, she suddenly remembered, because she'd always been drunk or drugged when she'd slept with him before. This was real, and she felt… happy, almost cleansed. Who knew that sex could be good for you?

'You answer the phone, I'll get coffee.' Leo grinned at her, and slid out of bed, padding naked towards his bedroom door.

The phone had gone to voicemail, and Ava squinted at the clock. It was just after six, and darkness still blanketed the world outside. A few snowflakes were already blowing past the window, making the security lights flick on and off. She shivered and drew the covers closer, listening to her messages.

One was from Penny, apologising for being a bit shitty last night. Paul had returned home, drunk but safe, and Huw had driven off without a word of explanation. She would call later. The next was from Sophie, not apologising, but requesting a call back as soon as possible. The last was from a number she didn't recognise.

'You bitch, Ava Cole. You fucking bitch! You always had it in for Huw, didn't you? He told me you thought you were so clever, you and your friends, but he was always better than you. You'd better get him home, and you watch your back, bitch, because we're coming for you.'

Nice. Ava didn't know the voice, but assumed it might be Huw's girlfriend, Isabell, who according to Bethan, Huw would never marry. So had Huw not come home on purpose, or more likely he had arrived back and been taken straight in for questioning.

Leo came back with coffee, and Ava again marvelled at how easy it would be to slip back into a relationship with him. Then she got a hold of herself. It was just sex. She had been in need of comfort, and Leo had just rescued her. She had been vulnerable…

'Problems?'

'No more than normal. I need to ring Sophie, and Pen says Paul came home pissed but unharmed, and Huw is either AWOL or down the station cooling off.'

'He's been arrested?'

'Don't know, but if Sophie caught up with him, she might have directed some of that fire-eating fury towards him.'

Leo grinned. 'I've only met her twice and she terrified me when she started asking questions. Plus, that police station at Cadrington stinks like the gents' toilets, and the interview room feels like a prison cell. She's a bit like you, actually, the DI. You both have that look. Maybe it's a copper thing.'

'Thanks. Oh and thanks for… you know.'

'I do know. It was a pleasure. Still is. Look, you don't have to stay at the B&B and with everything that's been happening, you would be safer here with me. You don't have to look so freaked out – it isn't flattering! I don't mean you have to sleep with me. You can have your own room. It would be easier for you while you're in Aberdyth…'

'Thanks, I'll think about it… What about you? Will you be staying down here, even if the police have shut down filming until Bethan is found?'

'I have to. As soon as we get clearance I need to finish the show. I… I need the money from this one.' He took a sip of coffee, not looking at her. 'I made some unwise investments and overstretched myself. This series has to be a hit. The Inspector did say I can carry on, but we need to scale things down to one area, and get extra security. I know it sounds awful, but we have a really tight schedule, and if we fuck this up, it could ruin me.'

'I see.' She wasn't sure what else to say. She had discovered Leo's financial issues for herself, and now he was confiding in her. Did that make him more innocent, or less? 'I'm sorry.'

He smiled, finding her eyes. 'Not your fault, and I'll get out of it. It's all part of the game, and I like to live on the edge.' He paused. 'Ava, tell me about when you left.'

She looked up quickly, warily. 'What do you want to know?'

'I don't blame you for going, okay? All right, let's go further back. To when I was heading off to uni, and we were all in such a mess. Now Stephen is a teenager it's been obvious to me for a while that he is my son. My boy. That night we had together… It was then, wasn't it?'

Ava nodded slowly. 'I can't really explain, but I panicked. Then you kept going away, you were getting ready to start a new life and get your degree… When I found out I was pregnant, Paul and I had made up, and he guessed I was pregnant because I was so sick. My parents made it clear they wanted nothing to do with me if I stayed in Aberdyth, but it seemed so easy... Paul's dad was so happy, and Paul was talking about "his son" to everyone. I wasn't the only pregnant teenager around. I looked at what Paul could offer, stability and the farm, and I saw that if I told either of you that there was a possibility that you might or might not be the father, I would ruin my baby's life.'

Leo shook his head, blue eyes brilliant. 'You wouldn't have done.'

'Leo, you can't say that! We were young and selfish. You probably wouldn't have gone to uni, or taken part in that show, or be where you are now, if I'd thrown myself and the baby at you.' Her voice was bitter. So many mistakes, so many choices.

'Everyone makes mistakes.' Leo laughed softly. 'What a bloody awful cliché that is. I just mean... Actually, I don't know what I mean, except that you did what you felt was right, and thought of the baby. Now he's grown perhaps you can form a different relationship with him.' He watched her carefully. 'When you feel the time is right, I think he should know that I am his father.'

'It seems so weird that I came here to do just that, you know, to see Stephen, to answer his questions, and get ready for Paul dying, and now that's been pushed right to the back of my mind. Is that awful?' Ava sighed, drained by the revelations, and almost dizzy with relief at Leo's reaction. In her mind, she had built him up to be a monster, but now here they were, grown-up discussing their son. It felt right. Problematic of course, but right.

'Of course not. Stephen will be fine. He's got both our brains and my looks.' Leo grinned at her, and then his face became sombre. 'And as for Paul, I don't think anyone will believe it until it actually happens. He's so young. I never thought of anyone our age getting cancer, but I do realise how naive that is.'

'I know. I sort of feel the same, like it isn't really happening. I mean, he looks ill sometimes, but Penny hasn't really discussed the illness with me, and of course Paul wouldn't dream of it. Look, I should really call Sophie and see if she has anything on Huw, and then get out of your way.'

He shrugged. 'I told you, you're no trouble. She won't tell you about Huw, surely?'

Ava set her cup down carefully on the wooden tray, and wriggled over onto her front, phone already in her hand. 'She will. Not anything case-related, but I just want to know if he's being questioned or actually charged with an offence.'

Leo laughed. 'You always used to do that, lying like that to do your homework, or if you were listening to music…'

She smiled at him, brushing her long hair out of her eyes. 'But now I've grown up.'

'You're still beautiful to me, Ava. I don't care how old you are. You're still the same person, just a better version of what you were.'

Ava felt her cheeks burn, and she shrugged off the compliment. 'That wasn't quite what I meant by growing up, but never mind.' This time it was she who voluntarily returned to their past. 'I'm sorry for the way I left, Leo. You were right, I should never have married Paul. Hell, I should never have had a fling with him just because you pissed me off.'

'But there was Stephen.'

'Yes.' She didn't speak for a long moment, and he touched her cheek again.

'Like I said, I've known for ages he's mine, Ava. You know I always suspected, but now he's grown, he's just like me. Other people mention it too, but Paul never has. Perhaps he sees the resemblance, or perhaps he just doesn't want to see it. For years I told myself I wouldn't have been up to the job anyway, but then, Paul's my mate, how could I tell him his son was actually mine? He's so damn proud of everything that boy does. I couldn't do it to him.'

'I never thought of us as parents,' Ava said softly. 'I always kept him at the back of my mind. Ever since I left high school and got my first job, I've been saving money for him. I just don't know how to tell him. Before I left, I kissed him for the last time… his skin was so soft and sweet, and he smelled of… well of *him*. It broke my heart, but my head was a mess. I can't explain it, but it became more and more like there was this invisible curtain, or fog between us. Eventually, he would cry, and I would sit staring at the wall, unable to respond. Then I'd snap out of it, and become terrified that he was hurt or in pain. He was just being a normal baby, and as Paul kept pointing out, everyone else was coping. He was a good parent though, or I would never have left Stephen with him.'

Leo reached over and kissed her, very gently, on her cheek. 'I'm sorry too. I'm sorry about everything that happened between us, and that you felt you couldn't confide in me. Friends again?' His face was hopeful, boyish, without a hint of his customary sarcasm and arrogance.

She laughed, the years peeling back. 'I'd like that. We need to sort this mess out first, find Bethan, and find out who killed Ellen. You realise, we're left with Huw, Penny or Paul, don't you? Jesse is dead, and I refuse to believe he did it. Rhodri, I don't believe he tried to kill himself, I think he was targeted too. And you, and me, well, we didn't do it, did we?'

The words hung in the air between them, and they stared at each other for a long moment.

'I'll have a shower while you make your calls,' Leo said abruptly.

Sophie answered on the first ring, and launched straight into conversation. 'Where are you?'

'Leo's place.'

A long silence. 'I see. Interesting choice. Are you all right?'

'Perfectly, thanks.'

'Good, especially good after that fuck-up last night. Firstly, as you know, Ellen's parents were informed yesterday. They have asked that any of Ellen's friends that might try to call round, are politely told where to shove it. The FLO officer is with them now.

I can understand their sentiments, and I know you will too. DI Hevis, my colleague, has a team still down in East Wood, but we've lifted the body and taken it to Cadrington. Next, I had a call from the hospital. It should have come in earlier yesterday, but they were busy with a big RTA and someone forgot to pass a message on… Anyway, Rhodri should make a good recovery, but when they examined him they found something odd. Someone has drawn on his body.'

'Drawn?' Ava sat upright, pulled the duvet around her, staring out into the darkness. 'What do you mean?'

'I've never seen anything like it, but someone has used a sharp knife to draw pictures along his torso, and down his legs. I'm sending you over the photos now.'

'But why are you sending them to me? I can't do anything. Like you said yesterday, I need to stay out of it…'

'As well as the pictures, your name is on his body. This is a message to you, Ava. Take a look and tell me if it means anything. Think really hard.' Sophie's voice was sharp, and impatient. In the background a babble of voices and echoing footsteps suggested she was down at the station in Cadrington.

'Fuck.' The photos came up on Ava's screen as she put Sophie on speakerphone, and she scrolled down in silence. Rhodri's poor, pale, skinny body was exposed on a hospital bed. There was an IV drip in both arms, and he was still on oxygen. It must have been a very sharp knife, and just the point used, she thought, trying to be objective. The wounds were not deep, but scarlet threads of colour. His torso was decorated with flowers. Flowers? Ava turned her phone around and zoomed in to get a closer look. It must have taken a while to get all this artwork done…

Childlike flowers entwined to form a heart shape on his abdomen. In the centre of the heart was her name. The same flower pattern was repeated down his thighs, but his back was different. Big, coarse scratches along his lower back area, and words not pictures:

'Remember me.'

'Any thoughts?' Sophie broke through the silence, her breathing quick and light. She was clearly desperate to solve this.

'Sick bastard?' Ava offered, shaken and shivering under her covers. 'Sorry, I don't know. Obviously "Remember me" is just a repeat of the previous messages, but all these flowers, fuck knows. Is Rhodri conscious? Has he said anything?'

'No, still out of it. They say it could take a few days before he comes round, and even then they aren't sure how coherent he'll be. Shame about the drawings – if anything jogs your memory, let me know.'

'Sure. Um, Sophie… do you have Huw in custody? I got a message from his girlfriend, Isabell. I have no idea how she got my number, but she was pretty threatening. It doesn't bother me as such, I just wanted to know.'

'Huw is helping us with our enquiries. I can send uniform down to have a word with her, if she's hassling you.'

'And Bethan?'

'We can't get anything else from the photographs, but we're doing everything we can. Right, got to go, speak to you later, Ava.'

Dawn was streaking the blackness with silver darts, and Ava stayed where she was until Leo emerged from the shower. Should she tell him? She would, she decided. She needed someone to trust. Surely if Leo was behind all this, he would have killed her by now. It was poor logic, but her brain was floundering with this latest development. Huw? Paul? As she had said to Leo, the field was narrowing.

If it was Paul, did Penny have any idea? When Penny had told her about the night Ellen died, what had she said? That she was terrified it was Paul, and that was another reason she lied… She might be in danger if the killer was Paul, and she didn't have any idea, but could he physically have done all this, given his advanced illness? Too many questions. 'Leo, I need to get going. Can we go and find the truck?'

'Sure.' His eyes tracked down her naked body, appraising. 'You might want to get dressed first, though. It's pretty cold outside.'

'Funny. I just spoke to Sophie and there's been a development I need to talk to you about…'

* * *

Although they discussed the weird drawings on Rhodri all the way to the truck, Leo couldn't shed any light on the flowers, and appeared revolted by the idea that someone might have drugged Rhodri and then carved a message on his body.

'Huw might have just about had time to do it, before he picked up Paul,' Ava said, thoughtfully, one hand on the door handle as she prepared to drive the truck back to Aberdyth.

'Well, if that Sophie woman has her hands on Huw at the moment, he won't be able to wriggle out of it. Let me know if anything else happens. Maybe we could head over and visit Rhodri later. If he wakes up, he might tell us stuff he won't tell the police,' Leo suggested.

'Maybe. Send my love to Stephen when you get to camp, won't you,' Ava said.

He smiled. 'Of course. I'll ring you later and let you know what's happening. If I have to stay and get on with filming, you could take Penny with you.'

'Good idea.'

The snow was falling steadily again as she drove back towards the village, turning left up the hill to Paul's farm. The sheep were huddled under the shelters and a blue tractor was dragging a trailer of hay across the valley. Hills that normally decorated the horizon above Aberdyth were now shrouded in grey and purple fog. Was it her imagination, or was the snow getting worse? Her son had asked her to find Bethan. It was the only thing he had ever asked of her, and for his and Ellen's sake she must get the girl back alive. It was almost as though her conversation with Leo had swept away the tangled cobwebs of emotion that had been hindering her brain. Now she felt sharp and alert.

At the farm, Penny was equally shocked by the idea of the drawings on Rhodri's body, and the news of Huw's detainment. Paul, she said was still sleeping off a hangover, and the men were out looking after the stock. 'There's a weather warning out for blizzards tonight and tomorrow. So much for global warming, I can't believe this is April! I need to go and visit Uncle Alf, just in case we get snowed in for a bit, but you can come over again later if you like?'

'Oh, I'll come with you if that's okay?' Ava said quickly. She needed to talk to Penny away from her husband. 'I'd like to see him too.'

'I suppose you can, but he's in a pretty bad way. He's had MS for years, as you know, but he has dementia as well. He won't recognise you, and it's quite hard. He's not at all like you'll remember.' Her forehead was furrowed, and her expression was anxious.

'It's fine,' Ava told her, putting her cup down, and snagging the last of Penny's plate of home-baked flapjack. 'You are just the world's best cook, Pen. Good thing I don't live round here anymore, I'd always be hanging around your kitchen!'

Penny laughed at that, but there was a shadow of sadness in her eyes. 'I wish you did live round here, lovely.'

'Maybe you should come and visit? I'd love to show you around LA,' Ava told her.

'That would be great! I just need to pack up a few bits for Uncle Alf. I take him his favourite soup a couple of times a week, and biscuits and things. Do you want to wait in the hall? The signal is crappy up here, so you can use our phone to make any calls if you like.'

'Thanks, Pen.' Ava left Penny to it, wandered into the hallway, and, after a moment's thought, rang Jackie again. Although she had left her several messages since the news of Ellen's death, and she knew from Sophie that a memorial service was planned, neither of Ellen's parents had been in touch. She could understand that. It was the ultimate betrayal. Part of her wanted them to shout, to be angry and sad, and mourn their daughter properly, but shutting her out was probably the only thing they could do.

The phone went straight to voicemail, so she tried the landline. It rang and rang, before a man's voice finally answered. Peter.

'Peter, please don't hang up. It's Ava.' She waited, holding her breath, listening to Penny locking up the house, packing her bag. There was a pile of books and papers on the hall table next to her. Scribbled notes and numbers.

'What do you want, Ava?' His voice was cold, icy as the snow drifting past the window.

'I'm so sorry, Peter, so terribly sorry. If I could go back and do things differently, I would… But I can't. There is something I need to ask, though…'

'I think any asking should have been done years ago. Do you have any inkling of what we are going through at the moment? Jackie is in bits. We trusted you, and you lied to us. Our daughter was attacked and murdered, and you, her best friend, helped to cover it up.'

'I know, and there are no excuses.' She was just going to have to try this, because she clearly wasn't going to get a second chance. 'Peter, when Jesse said he was going to tell you about Ellen, did he say he had to check something, or check with someone?'

'What do you mean?'

'Exactly what I said. Can you remember? It could be important.'

'Ava, I don't think it's sinking in, so I'll repeat myself – your best friend is dead, killed in some reckless game that you were also part of, if I understand correctly. Our beautiful daughter has been dead all these years, buried yards from our house. All the time, I hoped she had just run away, that she might be married, might have children and be enjoying life, even if it was a life without us. Do you understand any of that?'

Tears were blurring her vision, and one dripped onto the papers stacked on the table. She brushed it away with a shaky finger, smudging the scribbles. Her finger froze. Doodles, not scribbles. Someone had doodled flowers around a phone number. They were more intricate than the basic scratches on Rhodri's body, but the style was the same. Peter was still talking, his voice raw with grief. She let him continue, it was the least she could do.

Carefully, phone wedged between her shoulder and cheek she sifted through the paperwork. More doodles, little flower sketches, and notes. Penny was calling she was nearly done.

'Peter, I can never go back and change things. I wish I could…'

'I wish you could too. Goodbye, Ava.' He hung up.

'Sorry, lovely, I found some old magazines when I was sorting through the loft the other day… What's wrong?'

'Oh. I was just speaking to Peter.' How the hell was she going to do this?

'Oh. I saw Jackie yesterday and she looked right through me. I don't blame her though, I totally hate myself for what we did. Mrs Evans at the shop told me that they already put their house on the market, and they're renting a house in Somerset. Apparently, they are going straight after they have some kind of proper burial for Ellen.' Penny's own eyes were wet. 'One stupid mistake and you wreck lives. I wish so much I could turn the clock back.'

Ava hugged her, and deliberately sent the whole pile of paperwork cascading onto the floor. 'I'm so sorry! Let me pick these up for you.'

'No bother. You always were clumsy, Ava. I need to sort that pile out anyway.'

Ava took a breath as she stood up with the sheaf of scribbles. 'These are pretty. Who draws flowers while they're working?'

Penny smiled. 'Paul does that. He doodles on everything, the big loon. It's either flowers or stars. Not very manly, is he?'

Ava forced a laugh. 'I didn't know he was artistic?'

'His dad would have gone mental if he knew Paul liked drawing, wouldn't he? It was always all about the farm. His mum was a bit arty though, I think… Look, Paul did a few watercolours a couple of years back…' Penny waved a hand at the wall by the stairs, and Ava peered at a few landscapes. 'They were pretty good, actually. No flowers, though.' Her gaze sharpened and she looked back at the doodles. 'Ava! These are just like the ones on… on Rhodri.'

Ava watched her carefully. 'Yes, I thought so too. Is Paul still asleep?'

'Yes, I just peeked in on him. But what does this mean? You think Paul hurt Rhodri?' Penny's voice was shrill.

'Perhaps. What do you think?' Ava said quietly.

'I don't know. Surely he wouldn't…' She put a fist to her mouth, eyes wide, and cheeks colourless. 'I can't deal with this, Ava, I really can't.'

No, but she would take this new evidence straight to the police, Ava thought. Penny was shivering now, fiddling with her keys, passing them from hand to hand. 'Shall we go then?'

Penny nodded, clearly surprised, but Ava wanted to think. Was Paul capable of all this, or was she looking at two or maybe three perps working together? Paul and Huw as bully boys and Penny, perhaps under duress, as the secret-keeper.

* * *

They drove in silence, neither commenting on the scrum of people around East Wood, or the big white tent, which was only just visible among the darkened tree trunks. The snow was lying thickly on the road as they turned up the lane to their destination.

The residential home was clean and bright. Nothing could disguise the lingering smell of piss and disinfectant, which reminded Ava of the precinct back home, but there were pots of fresh flowers, and big pictures of seascapes dotted around. The two women were shown up to a large, tidy room, with a hospital bed next to one wall. Penny was clearly a welcome visitor, and the predominantly foreign staff seemed friendly and efficient. Before they had got to the lift, Ava caught a glimpse of a living-room area, where various residents were propped on sofas, chairs and wheelchairs. Some gazed blankly into the distance, others were knitting, and one man appeared to be reading a book upside down. The air was hot and fetid, despite a few windows cracked open in the passages.

'Ava, we'll go in and say hallo, and then if you don't mind going out whilst I feed him…'

'You have to feed him?'

Penny smiled, misunderstanding. 'Of course not, but I like to when I can. It makes it a bit more personal. Even though he doesn't recognise me, I really hope on some level he does know it is me. Does that sound mad?'

Ava touched her arm. 'Of course not.'

Alf Thomas was sitting in a brown tweed armchair next to the window. The immaculate room was stocked with books, magazines, Lego creations, and a bowl of fruit. Two big framed prints of the valleys hung above the bed.

'Hallo, Uncle Alf. Look who I've brought to see you!' Penny said brightly, leaning down to the shrunken old man and pecking his cheek.

'Hi.' Ava moved into his sightline and smiled. She was shocked at his frail appearance. It was a far cry from the big, athletic man she remembered yelling down the football field. His shoulders were slumped, eyes rheumy and pink and a line of drool was hanging from the corner of his mouth. The thick brown hair was gone, replaced by a thin layer of greying mouse, and the stubble on his pale cheeks and chin was white.

Alf Thomas gave no sign he had heard, or even seen, either of them. He stared resolutely into the middle distance. The freezing valley and snowy roofs of Aberdyth stared back, half-hidden by the gusts of snow that fell sideways across the window.

Penny was bustling around, unpacking the bits she had brought, needlessly tidying the room, plumping the bed pillows and chattering away. Ava walked over to the window, feeling slightly sick. You could see Leo's house from here, and Ellen's... She turned to Alf and smiled again, opening her mouth for some mundane pleasantry, but his face had changed. He was looking directly at her, focusing hard.

He reached out a shaking hand, pointing a bony finger at her, moistening his lips with his tongue. 'Y – y – you... are Ava.'

'Yes.'

Penny put an arm around his shoulders, speaking slowly, and carefully. 'Darling, do you remember Ava? She and Ellen were my best friends at school.'

His eyes moved to Penny, and the stuttering continued. 'Y – y – you... and Ellen.' It was clearly an effort to form the words.

'That's right.'

Alf Thomas was looking past Penny now, bewildered, but hanging on to whatever thread of memory had been thrown up by Ava's appearance. 'W – w – where is... Ellen?'

Penny bit her lip and cast a worried glance at Ava. 'She died, darling. I told you. She died a long time ago.'

He seemed to accept this, but the agitation increased as his gaze tracked back to Ava. 'She looks like h – her.'

'Who, Ellen? Well, a little bit I suppose, but only because they both had long dark hair.'

'P – p – pretty. S – s – special.' Suddenly he sank back in his chair, slumped with apparent exhaustion, eyes almost closed, frail chest heaving.

Penny held a glass of Lucozade up to his mouth, fitting the straw between his lips. He took it noisily, dribbling some of the liquid out the side of his mouth. 'That's so good he recognised you. Some days he doesn't say a word, or calls me Judy or Sarah or something,' she said sadly. 'Do you mind popping downstairs whilst I just give him some of that soup I brought? It's homemade and his favourite, but he does get so messy when he eats, and he gets a bit agitated if he thinks anyone is watching. I'd rather do it alone.'

'Of course.' Ava was longing to escape but felt guilty. 'Lovely to see you, Uncle Alf.' He had always been 'Uncle Alf', and all the kids called him that, even though he was only actually related to Penny. It was tragic that such a larger-than-life man had been reduced to a dribbling shell of humanity. The pleasure and hope she had seen in Penny's eyes whilst the old man was speaking made her realise how hard it must be to see a loved one like this.

One of the carers escorted Ava down to a little waiting room, and she checked her phone for messages. A text from Leo that made her smile, and a load of emails, mostly junk. One from Jack acknowledging the photos of Rhodri she had sent him. She probably shouldn't have done that, but she knew how he was with a case – he would pursue it to the end, and he might come up with something useful. She didn't have to tell Sophie if it came from him.

Penny said little on the way home, simply asking where Ava wanted to be dropped off. She jumped out at the B&B, boots crunching in the deepening snow, and turned to watch Penny drive slowly and carefully back down the hill.

Mrs Birtley was hoovering her living room, and Ava carefully removed her boots on the mat. Standing on one leg, she lost her balance and grabbed at the rack of coats next to the door. Swearing and righting herself, she saw she had pulled out the sleeve of a green Puffa jacket. Surely Alex had been wearing this when he left after her interview?

Mrs Birtley, alert to the noise of someone trashing her neat hallway, bustled into view, lips pursed. Ava jumped in quickly. 'Mrs Birtley, wasn't this Alex Jennington's coat?'

The other woman pulled her glasses out and stared at the Puffa. 'Yes, it was. My goodness, Ava, I thought I gave all his things to the police. I suppose if he hung his coat here it would have got lost among all the others. These coats and the boots are old ones I keep for visitors, so I don't really take a lot of notice of them.' She was rattling on, clearly horrified at her blunder.

Ava cut into the chatter. 'Don't worry, I'll take it to the police myself. I'm on my way there, I just stopped to pick up a few things.'

Mrs Birtley opened her mouth, and then closed it again, and unusually for her made no comment as Ava picked up the coat and ran upstairs in her socks.

Obviously, Alex had not been wearing this on that fatal night. Ava, without much hope, began to search the pockets. Nothing but a packet of tissues in one, and a half-eaten tube of Polos in the other. But the smaller, inner zip pocket yielded gold.

With shaking fingers Ava unscrunched the paper. It looked like a torn page from a notebook, with a list of names. Sara Blackmore, Andrew Menzies, and two she didn't recognise, had been crossed off, but right at the bottom Coach Thomas was circled firmly in black ink. There was a telephone number scrawled next to his name.

Without thinking, she tapped out the mobile number, and waited, heart pounding. The phone rang for ages, until a male voice answered. Without waiting for her to speak, he told her to fuck off.

'I've got nothing else for you. That was all a long time ago and I'm different now.'

Before he could put the phone down, Ava spoke softly. 'I'm a friend of Alex Jennington's. I don't want to get you into trouble…'

The line went dead. She quickly called back, but the phone was switched off. Fuck. She really hoped she hadn't just screwed that up.

Another text made her phone buzz, and she looked quickly at her messages, hoping the man had had second thoughts.

Cylch o gylch o rhosynau,
Poced llawn o flodau,
Atishw, atishw, ac yna syrthiodd i lawr.
'Ring, a ring o' roses, a pocket full of daisies.
A-tishoo, a-tishoo and then she fell down.'

Chapter 31

Mum came into the living room once when I was trying on a new outfit. It was a white silky fairy outfit – every little girl's dream. She saw me half-naked, with his hands on me, turned, and walked right out again. The ultimate betrayal. I think I knew then that I would have to kill her.

Uncle Alf all but ignored her by then. Occasionally he yelled at her to take a bath, or clean up her mess of empty bottles, stale cigarette ends, and crisp packets. Mostly I cleaned up, and as she slipped further into her addiction, I was forced to care for her too.

I waited… By my eleventh birthday, Uncle Alf was starting to lose interest in touching me, although he still photographed me. He still used me as bait and cover on our trips into town. Who would suspect a man shopping with his cute little niece? I watched and waited. Soon I knew how the drugs worked, and had started to experiment with them myself.

It seems strange I never thought to kill Uncle Alf, but even then I knew how to pick my opponents. There was no point in starting a game I couldn't win, and he was simply too strong and powerful.

Mum progressed from a human being into a fat, yellow, doughy lump. She could barely make it off the sofa. When it was time for her to exit the game, I executed my plan with precision.

Uncle Alf may have suspected, but as I think back now, his opinion of me was so low, he would never have imagined I could kill anyone. And of course, there was our shared secret. He treated me as a prized business acquisition, but never as anything else. I was there to be used. I suspect that if I hadn't killed Mum, he would have done it himself in the end.

Now I see that fate kept him alive for a reason. I've enjoyed torturing him, and I'll carry on doing it right up to his miserable death. Every moment of my childhood that he destroyed, every second of the other children's torment, he is paying for.

Under the guise of concerned niece, I can revel in the fear in his eyes as he sees me coming. The terror in his face warms my blood as I force onion soup between his lips. The carers are so impressed when I make him a nice flask of homemade soup. I make sure it is a flavour he hates, and then I make him eat it. A small thing, but a real pleasure.

I am careful never to leave any marks, but I read up on pressure points and torture techniques – some of my regular customers were very helpful. For him, my regular visits are indeed tortuous, and that is exactly how it should be. I have won. The last dice roll set him on one path, me on another. It gave me back control.

When Jesse came to me, after he'd decided to tell Ellen's parents the truth about their daughter, I was so sympathetic that he could never have imagined what was really going through my mind. The trouble with both Jesse and Alex Jennington, was that they had hit on the truth about Alf Thomas. It wasn't just Ellen's secrets they wanted to uncover, it was my own.

Jesse and Rhodri had both been victims of Uncle Alf's photography studio. They were tough kids from broken homes, and Rhodri had been in and out of care since he was five. My uncle knew how to pick his victims. So Jesse was leaving, and he wanted to come clean about Ellen, but he also wanted to come clean about Uncle Alf. He tried hard to persuade me to help him. I pretended enthusiasm, whilst planning how he would die.

The PI, Alex, stumbled into my territory accidentally. He managed to find a source in Cardiff who knew my uncle. Maybe it was a fellow trader he had pissed off, or an unsatisfied customer, I don't know. Anyway, the result was the same. The man was a convicted sex offender, and Alex told me that he thought it was an obvious link for any PI to try, especially with the advancement in technology. He told me he had put pressure on the man to reveal others in the area, and Uncle Alf's name had come up. Alex wanted me to confirm the rumour from his source that my uncle was 'interested in young girls'. His English accent annoyed me in the same way Ava's American one does. Of course, it was a short route from a suspect paedophile living in the same village where a girl disappeared, to Alex deciding he may have been responsible for Ellen's 'running away'. He was so eager, excited, his pale eyes bright, and a vestige of personality lighting his colourless face.

It was a shame, but actually these little annoyances make my life more interesting. It has occurred to me that I've probably killed enough people to earn the title of serial killer. This does not sit well with my legacy, so I'll keep most of them quiet. They might wonder, but they'll never know.

'*Wyt ti'n gofalu, Ava Cole?*'
'**Do you care, Ava Cole?**'

Chapter 32

Ava sat in the bleak little interview room at Cadrington police station, a steaming cup of coffee in her hands. Time was running out, and the frustration at being blocked from actively investigating, from joining the team, was tearing her apart. This morning, she had been more confident, happy that her 'work head' seemed to have returned, but now, she seemed to be no further forward, and still locked out in the cold. It had been hard going on the roads to get down here, and darkness crept across the valley by half past two. She knew from his text Leo was also at the station, 'helping with enquiries', but she resisted the urge to ask. The DS she remembered from Alex Jennington's murder scene sat on the other side of the table. He grinned at her when she asked if there was any more coffee.

'You're probably the first person ever to want more of that stuff. The DI will be back any second, so I'll get you a cup in a bit.' He flicked through the folder in front of him.

Sophie walked back into the room, slamming the door, and sitting down opposite on one of the scratched, grubby plastic chairs. 'Okay, anything at all is going to be useful, so just take me right back to your childhood. We'll walk through everything. There's a clue here and we're not getting it.'

'Do you think Bethan is still alive?' Ava asked.

The other woman sighed. 'Normally after this length of time, I think we would both agree the chances of that would be fairly low. However, in this case, let's say I hope so…' She tapped a pen against her teeth, pulling a funnel neck jumper tighter around her body. 'It's bloody cold in here. Right, Bethan – yes, I think she is alive. The killer is trying to draw you into finding her. If she was dead already, surely the game would be over.'

'They sent me to a body last time,' Ava pointed out. 'What did Paul say about the doodles on their telephone pad?'

'One of my DS's called it in just now. Paul says they were his wife's work. Penny swears they were his. He's obviously in a pretty bad way, mostly self-inflicted after the other night, but we need to go carefully given his condition. The press are out to get us as usual, and me having worked Ellen's original case is an added stick to the fire.'

'I think, if it is him, he must be threatening Penny. She loves him so much, she'd do anything for him. Even when I was with him, I could see there was something between them. I was a mistake, and she was the real thing.'

'What if the doodles are Penny's? Let's just say we've been dismissing the obvious. Penny was in the wood that night, killed Ellen, and she has had every chance to kill both Jesse and Alex Jennington.'

Ava was shaking her head. 'Pen loved Ellen. And are you forgetting she was apparently assaulted?'

'Could have been made to look sexual… Or it could have been Paul and Penny covering for each other, maybe? I'm just throwing it out there.' Her green eyes were calculating, watchful, searching for any stray thread.

'I don't know. But you should have seen her with her uncle this afternoon – making him soup, fussing over him. She's always been like that, so bright and happy. Unless Penny saw Paul attacking Ellen, and as you say, helped him cover up a rape.

269

Besides, I'm not sure she'd have the strength to kill a man, she's tiny. Actually, what am I saying? Okay, personally I can't even compute it might be her, but professionally I'd have to say everyone is a maybe. Did you get anything else from Alex's notes about Uncle Alf?'

Sophie lit a cigarette. 'Not really. He was clearly convinced from fairly early on that Ellen's disappearance was down to foul play, much as I was all those years ago. With the new evidence that you brought forward regarding Ellen's murder, I am hopeful we might be able to question Mr Thomas, but his condition will make that difficult. We're tracing that phone number you found too. Pity you had to call it.'

Ava ignored the reprimand. 'You think that Uncle Alf, or this other man, might have killed Ellen? That it wasn't one of us after all?'

'I think there is a strong possibility that this "other man" may prove to be the missing part of the puzzle. If we had known at the time that Ellen had been sexually assaulted and murdered, we would probably have been able to solve the case fairly quickly.'

The guilt was back, flushing Ava's cheeks, making her voice croaky and uncertain. She had failed Ellen but she wouldn't fail Bethan. Uncle Alf. The name seemed to be branded in fire above the desk. She shoved the image away. If he had been involved in Ellen's death, he was certainly not involved in Bethan's disappearance.

'Right, let's get on with this. Huw is talking to one of the PCs now, and of course he's asking all the same questions. Huw is shouting about everything. His solicitor is getting pretty pissed off with him. Doesn't mean he has anything to hide, obviously. We need to find this bloody girl and nail whoever is behind this. I mean, if we can't work it out from such a small pool of suspects, I might as well retire now.'

'Okay, I'm ready.' Ava took a deep breath, inhaling smoke, fighting to keep her hand still and not reach for Sophie's packet.

It took two hours, and by that time they still hadn't discovered anything useful. Ava checked her phone again, but there was nothing.

'Shit, come on, Ava, flowers and hearts.' Sophie shoved another cup of coffee across the table, paused to answer a call, and then hung up sighing. 'Nothing on the photographs of Bethan, and it looks like the team down by Big Water had to go home early because of the weather. The only caves mapped around here have now been searched. We've been up to your parents' old caravan park and there is nothing, the same with the old kids' playground, the outward bound centre and the derelict houses off the new estate. No holes underground, no cellars or anything. Come on, Ava!'

'The only thing that comes up is primary school. We used to scratch doodles like that into the desks, and maybe send notes to each other,' Ava said helplessly. She was exhausted and frustrated at her inability to help. Her personal involvement was a hindrance, preventing her usually fertile brain from churning out answers.

Sophie leant back in her chair, tugging at the collar of her red shirt, rubbing tired eyes. 'All right, let's give up for tonight. Go home and see what they come up with next. I've sent someone to look at the old primary school. I'm sure you already know, but Leo has been in all afternoon. They've resumed filming, but I wanted his take on the night Ellen died again.'

'Okay, thanks. I'll probably be staying at Leo's place again tonight. I feel safer than at the Birtleys.'

Sophie gave her another hard look. 'Right.'

* * *

Leo gave her a weary smile as they met outside the police station. 'Shit, I need a drink after that. Race you back home?'

'Is that okay? Me staying with you, I mean… I did drop in at

271

the Birtleys' and get some things.' Ava bit her lip, colour flooding her cheeks again.

'Of course. I hope that old truck can get up the hill to my driveway or I'll have to tow you again.' He grinned at her, snow-flakes settling in his dark hair.

She spent the whole journey with her eyes riveted on the road in front, bumping slowly down snow-clogged lanes. But her mind was far from her driving, still desperately trying to place those flower scribbles. She was also thinking about Leo.

It was so weird the way their relationship had progressed in the last twenty-four hours, but she didn't stop to analyse. When they arrived back at his house, his housekeeper had made up another room for Ava, complete with toiletries, bathrobe and even slippers.

'So how did your interview go?'

He pulled a bottle from the rack and uncorked it, not answering until he took a sip of wine. 'It was harsh. Are you sure they don't think I did all this, Ava? I feel like a prime suspect. My legal team are not happy, and my PA just called to say all the nationals want a quote. Thank Christ the snow is keeping them all away at the moment, but when the contestants go home they're going to make a killing, sorry – wrong word, on media appearances and exclusive interviews.'

'I don't know if you are still a suspect. Sophie is good, but at the moment all she has to go on is us lot, and the messages I keep getting. Hell, if I was really clever I could be behind all this and sending them to myself for cover.' She took the glass he handed her and smiled.

Leo raised his eyebrows. 'You're not that smart.' His smile was teasing.

'But every question leads us closer to Bethan. Sorry you had to go through that, and I know you're desperate to carry on with the filming, so at least you got clearance to finish it. I reckon anything we can add, any tiny detail or memory will help at this point. Even knowing something that might not be important on its own, when you add it to the bigger picture, you get clarity.'

He was smiling at her. 'I can see why you're good at your job, Detective Cole.' Then his voice changed. 'I can't believe Coach Thomas might have been involved in Ellen's murder though.'

'He might not be. It might be a friend of his, or a business associate, but clearly there is a link. Alex got close, and whoever he was pushing for information silenced him.'

'Shit, and we were so convinced it was one of us... I suppose they'll ask Penny if she knows anything, but Coach Thomas will never understand if they question him. I mean, you said you'd seen the man, Ava. He can hardly speak now.'

'I know.'

They sat in silence, but it was an easy peace rather one filled with awkwardness. Ava curled up in a fleecy throw that was draped across the sofa, tucking her long legs under for extra warmth. The big, fat candles that were lit on the windowsills scented the air with peppermint and rose. 'Wow, Leo, you are spoilt – this is like a luxury spa or something.' She didn't mention sleeping with him and he didn't ask. Perhaps this was meant to be closure or something. The spark between them was still there, but it had dulled to a comforting glow, making it stronger, less antagonistic.

'Well, you know... I've got an idea. How about I cook you dinner and we catch up properly, just talk about fifteen years of stuff, nothing to do with Ellen or Bethan?'

'You're thinking our sub-conscious might hit on something important?'

'Nope, I just think it would be nice.' He grinned at her. 'Plus, I'm a great cook and I want to show off.'

Ava sank deeper into the overstuffed sofa, and crossed her long legs. 'Sounds great, I do like to be pampered. Actually, I don't really. My girlfriends are the ones going to spas and pamper days, and I go down the gym for boxing, or up in the hills hiking. One of my best friends lives out in Long Beach, so I drive down there and we go to a great place on the corner of Ocean and Pine for lunch. Burgers and fries with a Bloody Mary.'

He was laughing, but his eyes flickered over her body. 'Seems to be keeping you fit. I thought you were going to say you went to some healthy place where they just drink wheatgrass juice or something!'

Her phone buzzed and they both froze. 'It's just a text from Penny. She's pretty cross about those doodles, and she wants to know what the police are doing with Huw. Apparently, his girl-friend is speaking to the papers. Silly cow, that's all we need.'

Leo rolled his eyes and began assembling ingredients on his countertop. 'Trouble is, Huw has always had a temper, hasn't he? His women have all left him, and he can't see why.'

'Do you mean he hits them?' Ava was shocked.

Leo shrugged, shredding cabbage, and slicing bacon at speed. The knife glinted in the bright lights of the kitchen, a contrast to the soft glow from the candles at Ava's end of the room. 'I don't know, but he might have done. He'd never touch the kids. I know it might seem like we're all still really tight, but I only catch up with the boys when I'm down here. It's more the history than anything. They all came up when I was at uni though...'

Ava curled her legs under her and hugged a furry cushion. 'I know. Penny told me. She told me about the girl who was raped the weekend they all went up. You went to the same bar she did.'

Leo stopped what he was doing and laid the knife carefully onto the board. 'It was such a long time ago, and there was never any suggestion it was me. I did wonder why the police brought it up. Did Penny say she thinks I did it then?'

Shifting loyalties, Ava thought, wriggling deeper into her sofa. Three days ago, she would have defended Penny to the death, but was she now going to abandon her friend over some scrib-bles? In work she always went with her gut... 'I don't remember.

We were just brainstorming and catching up. It was a passing comment.'

Leo grinned, taking a frying pan out of a high cupboard. 'Sure it was. Is that your phone again?'

She reached for it, and picked up her wine glass for a refill. 'Sophie?'

'I just heard from the hospital that your friend Rhodri has taken a turn for the worse. They've moved him into ICU and they're working to get him stable again. The heroin he injected was mixed with something else, and at the moment they aren't sure what. Any more messages from our perp?'

'No. Shit, I wonder if I should go up to the hospital, but as he's still unconscious…'

'I wouldn't. No point, and there will be press hanging around. You staying at Leo's is going to make them even more excited. I'm packing up for the night now but call me if anything happens.'

Ava ended the call and relayed the information to Leo. Delicious smells were wafting from the kitchen area and her stomach growled.

'We won't do any good by charging up to the hospital. Do you think we'd even get to see him?'

'Probably not,' Ava admitted.

'Well then. Here, eat this… I'll open another bottle of wine, and we'll do that catching up thing.'

'Okay, sounds good.'

* * *

Ava slept late, woken by Leo thumping on her bedroom door. She felt muzzy-headed and lethargic. The huge window opposite her bed showed the skies loaded with grey and purple clouds. Tiny spatters of snow were already spinning through the sky.

'Coffee. I thought you'd like a lie-in.'

'Thanks, Leo.' She yawned and checked her phone. Twelve

messages. While she drank she scrolled through. The last one made her sit up. She flung back the covers and narrowly avoiding spilling her coffee. 'It's another message from our friend.'

'What does it say?'

'It's in Welsh.'

'Fuck. I can't remember any of it. Can you translate it?'

'Maybe. Give me a minute.' She was hastily Googling the words, dragging her mind back to the language of her childhood. It was only at primary school that they had been taught Welsh, but many of the older inhabitants of Aberdyth switched fluently between that and English, so the children had copied them. 'Okay, I think I've got it.' She read it out loud:

'You lose, you snooze, and she's sleeping right now. Do you want to lose her, or will you take a dare? Ava Cole, how does your garden grow? With silver daisies, and long pretty grass, all planted under the hill.'

Chapter 33

As I said, it wasn't just me. As coach of Aberdyth Football Team, Uncle Alf had access to all the local kids, and he picked up others from the care homes in Cardiff. The ones who slipped between the cracks, the ones who social services tried to keep up with but failed, or the street kids desperate for warmth and money. They were his. He played the game carefully and picked on those he had a chance of using.

I watched, sometimes baited, and hoped that the kid would realise what he was really like. This friendly, cheerful man with the heart of a monster.

Rhodri was one of his earliest prey, and Jesse too. But not Ava or Ellen. They were too confident, too protected. That's why I was so pleased when Ellen found her own way to my uncle. Ellen, so cool, so confident and in control, was falling for a paedophile. She was being taken in by a man who controlled an empire of sick porn and made his living preying on children. And she invited herself in, the stupid bitch.

The drugs cupboard was impressive, well hidden but accessible. I found myself intrigued by the effect different drugs could have on different people. It could make you sleepy, or horny, or crazy, just by mixing different substances. Having experimented with the drugs myself, mostly against my will, I began to share them with my friends. When I discovered I could mix the various substances, with more interesting results, I used them to control my friends.

If Uncle Alf noticed his stash going down, he never said anything. I was bigger now, but still useful, and besides, he still showered me with gifts and new clothes. Everyone said I was so lucky to have him to look after me when Mum died.

When Leo or Paul asked where the drugs came from I brushed it off, saying they were from a friend in Cardiff. The trips to town were well known now, and I would return with more new clothes and an air of sophistication. Nobody ever knew how hard it was to be special, and how I longed to be ordinary like Ava and Ellen.

And so it continued. Uncle Alf found more kids to photograph, and started going on trips abroad for 'IT conferences'. He employed Mrs Birtley to give the house a 'onceover' and look after me when he was away.

It was hilarious, but I was still under sixteen, so he played by the rules. The fact that he let nosy Mrs B anywhere near the house was proof his business had moved away from Aberdyth.

I toyed with the idea of telling her, just to see her reaction, but I liked her bullying me into eating a full roast dinner, or telling me off for coming home late because we'd all been out in East Wood, or down near Big Water. She never liked me, but her husband did. All men enjoy looking at me, but he is different. He stutters, and struggles, is ugly and slow in many ways, but what I feel for him is close to love. Not love, because I can't, can I? There was a time, and it was like this with Ava too, that he looked at me a bit differently, and asked if I was all right.

I'm not sure if Mr B ever guessed, but he arrived at the door just after my uncle had finished a photography session. I was still dressed up, still a bit woozy and I saw his concern, as he dropped off some part for the truck. It was the day after, on my way to meet Ava, and catch the school bus, that he stopped me.

His concern never went any further, but it was almost as if he knew. He went out of his way to be kind to me, and still does to this day. The fact that he is different and people laugh at him makes no difference. He is the only person in Aberdyth who was ever perceptive enough to suspect something was wrong. As far as everyone else was concerned, Uncle Alf rode in to save me from my crazy, alcoholic mother.

'*Gallai wedi bod chi, Ava Cole.*'

'**It could have been you, Ava Cole.**'

Chapter 34

The snow was blinding. It stung Ava's cheeks and whipped her hair around her face. Her eyelashes were clogged with the tiny whirling flakes, and she yanked her scarf tighter around her neck, pulling it up to shield her face against the rising blizzard.

Sophie, bundled up in a black coat, struggled towards her. 'I'm going to have to call the teams in. This weather is impossible, and if Bethan is outside in this she'll have died of exposure long before we get to her.'

Ava nodded. She couldn't speak. The conditions were extreme, and the wind was funnelling down the valley, creating a wild vortex of snowflakes. The blizzard showed no signs of abating, and there was no point in trying to search when it was impossible to see more than a few feet in front of your own face.

'Are you sure that this is the right place?' Sophie asked.

'Well, the message referred to my garden, so it would have been either here at the caravan park, or down by the school.'

'Nothing around the school. That was easier of course, but up here... We'll just have to wait until the weather turns again. Where's Leo?'

'Up at the camp. They got a snowplough in to clear the tracks down to the main camp. Lucky they did spend a load of money on those luxury trailers, or everyone would be freezing to death. As it is, he reckons they can turn it around, and go with the weather for extra impact. He's going to try to cram in a few episodes worth of filming and see if he can get the show out on time after all. The contestants have been pretty pissed until they started filming again. He said nobody showed any special concern for Bethan, apart from Stephen, obviously, who is going crazy with worry.'

'It must be tough being so near your son, but not being able to talk with him. How about Leo? None of my business, but are you and he a couple again?'

'No. We're just catching up. I don't have any strong feelings for him one way or the other, and believe me, if this was down to him, I would be as quick as you to drop him in it.'

Sophie nodded. 'I believe you. Now let's get the hell out of here and get warm. We can't do anything else at the moment.'

Leo's house was silent, and Ava caught up with her emails. She drew maps of the village, plotting her garden and the primary school plot. There were no daisies in the woods, and it was bloody freezing outside, so likely even the early spring flowers had been iced to death. She was missing something. She hit her iPad and dragged up everything she could on Paul and Penny's business. Hiding in plain sight, was a phrase her boss often used. If Uncle Alf had known about, or been part of, Ellen's death, had Penny known? Would she have told Paul, the love of her life? Probably. What if Alex hadn't been killed by the original perp, but by Paul, to protect Penny from family scandal?

It was a long shot, but the doodles on Rhodri's body tied both Paul and Penny to his assault. And Bethan? She was dating Stephen. Maybe they didn't approve of the union? Oh God, if she had lied about Stephen's parentage, who else might have lied? Was Bethan even Huw's daughter… Too many questions and not enough answers.

On impulse she called Zach, the tech whizz at LAPD, and explained her idea. He agreed to do some digging and get right back. 'That was what you called it when you cracked the trafficking wasn't it – the shadows underneath? Well, see if there are any shadows underneath any of these websites, names or email accounts, and we could be closer to finding our mispo.'

'Sure, Ava, like I've got nothing else to do today, and it's only eight in the morning,' Zack complained, but Ava could tell he was hooked. Anything that couldn't be explained, that everyone else was stuck on, was the perfect challenge for Zack.

It began to get dark just after she fixed herself a sandwich, and she kept a lookout for Leo's headlights. He had told her he might have to stay the night at the camp if the snow got worse.

A loud clang made her jump, and the security lights flickered on. Probably one of the press had managed to get past the gates. Phone in hand, she went to open the door, peering cautiously through the spy hole first. The security light was still on, but she couldn't see anyone. There were footprints leading to the door and back though, and she peered at these as best she could without venturing outside. Large prints, made with the type of hill boots they all wore.

There was a parcel on the step. Warily, Ava drew it inside, shutting the door behind her. She opened the brown paper wrapping, almost holding her breath, heart racing, her hands shaking. The fragile length of dried flowers was wrapped in tissue paper. There was a note at the bottom, but her attention was caught by the blood dripped in a regular pattern across the daisy chain. It wasn't dark and discoloured, faded like the brittle flowers, but fresh and red, smelling slightly sour.

Gingerly, trying not to touch the paper any more than she needed, Ava unfolded the note;

'Ydych chi'n credu mewn hud, Ava Cole?'

It wasn't a hard translation, but Ava double checked with Google, just to be sure;

'Do you believe in magic, Ava Cole?'

She remembered then. It wasn't about gardens after all, it was about that magical little place they had discovered one summer. She and Penny had found it first, roaming the hills around Big Water after a swim, and Ellen had suggested it was a perfect place for a BBQ. The boys quickly joined them and if she had to remember one golden day of her childhood, when you get that warm glow of happiness, this would have been it. And this had to be where Bethan was.

Ava grabbed her coat and her phone, which had burst into life, flashing up Sophie's name.

'Hi. Good timing,' Ava said, still eyeing the daisy chain. Her heart was still thundering and her palms sweaty. Quickly, she explained about the package.

'Holy crap, who would have thought?' The DI gave a low whistle. 'Right, I'll sort things out my end. The bad news is that apparently due to a snowdrift on the Brockford Road, Aberdyth is now cut off from Cadrington until they get the snowploughs out tomorrow morning, so nobody is going anywhere. Not Penny, not you or Bethan.'

Bethan. 'That's the only thing that doesn't fit. There are no caves near that daisy meadow we found,' Ava said wearily. She took another look at the darkness, the floating flakes, defeated.

'Are you on your own?' Sophie asked.

'Yes, I'm still at Leo's. He said he might have to stay at the camp tonight, so they can wrap up filming tomorrow. Of course, if he was coming back he'd have come round via the road and not been able to get through anyway.'

'All right, well sit tight. He has a security alarm, doesn't he?'

'Yes,' Ava said again, her mind flicking over possibilities.

'The forecast is better tomorrow, and the snow clears by about 4 a.m., so at least we'll have clear skies. I can get the road clear as soon as it's light, and we'll take a team down to the hill. It's directly behind the hill with the zip line on, you said?'

'I need to be there really, to guide you.' It sounded feeble even to Ava's own ears.

'You are not to go near that place. We know where to go, and we know she must be underground, so we will throw all our resources into finding Bethan. Separately, I will send a few officers and DI Hevis over to Paul and Penny's farm as soon as we can get through on the road. Understood?'

Translated, if it needed to be any clearer, DI Miles wanted her to stay the hell away and not interfere. She did understand. She was a civilian messing up the case and she needed to butt out and let the professionals get on with their job. 'I get it.'

'Any problems, developments, ring me. I'll be on this number all night.'

Ava rung off, and stared at the daisies, lying pathetically in their tissue paper nest. Almost immediately her phone rang again, and when she glanced at the caller ID, her stomach clenched. 'Hi, Penny... How's Paul doing?'

'Hi, lovely! Much better, thanks. Oh, and Leo told me that they're wrapping filming tomorrow so Stephen can come home. I wondered if you'd heard anything from the police? You know, about releasing Huw – Isabell is going mad trying to cope with those twins on her own.' She sounded so normal, chirpy and happy, her worries swept away. Why was she so happy? What had happened to set her mind at rest? Ava could picture her bustling around her big kitchen, tidying, cooking dinner, phone wedged between shoulder and chin, blonde hair swinging. But she was definitely fishing.

'No, sorry. They haven't been back in touch since I was interviewed.' Something like anger burned at the back of her mind, as she listened to her friend's voice. Penny was involved, she had to be, but was the anger she felt directed at the other woman, or was she furious with herself for being so blind? Her emotions had clouded her judgement.

'Oh... Are you okay, Ava?' There was nothing but concern in her voice now.

Ava chose her words carefully, working on instinct. 'I am just so worried about Bethan. You know, with this snow, I haven't been able to run at all, so I might go out early tomorrow morning.'

Silence. Ava could hear the chink of cutlery, and there was the faintest sound of music in the background now too. 'Pen?'

'Sorry, Paul's lying down, and I thought I heard him call out. You be careful if you go running tomorrow, the going will be treacherous down around Big Water.'

'Yes, that's what I thought too.'

'It *is* Paul, sorry, lovely, got to go. See you tomorrow sometime probably.'

She was still clutching the phone when Zack got back minutes later. 'Got something for you.'

'What is it?' She clutched the phone so tightly it made a white indent in her palm.

'A shadow. A faint one, but the kind of software I use can hack most things. So the original photographs of you, and then the ones of your mispo, all come back to the same account. I'm ninety-nine per cent sure about this, but it's like joining dots.'

'Zack!'

'The name on the accounts is Paul Jones. The same name is linked to all the aliases and the emails you sent me, even the ones from that bakery business.'

'Fuck.'

'No worries, mate, anytime.'

'Sorry, Zack, you are a genius. Thank you and I owe you a drink.' Ava tried to control her voice, but panic and disbelief were making her dizzy. It was one thing to suspect, but another to have it confirmed. Paul had taken Bethan. Either he was working with Penny and Huw, or he had threatened either or both of them to keep quiet, because there was no doubt in her mind that Penny was part of this. But why were they doing it?

Ava stood next to the dark window for a long time, watching the steady snow fall, the security lights flick on and off, and thinking of the boot prints on the gravel. Had Paul dropped the parcel off whilst Penny created an alibi? They would have no idea Jack's team of cyber-crime experts had blown their cover, but the undercurrents in her conversation with Penny were definitely not her imagination. Something had soothed her earlier fears. What the hell could it be?

She checked the weather on her phone, thought of Bethan, alone, injured, hypothermic, imprisoned underground, and then she sent a quick text to Leo.

'*Assume you stuck at camp. Spk soon x*'

Out the window she could see the snowflakes whirling sideways in the wind. It was dark, but the urge to do something, to save someone, was desperate. She hesitated then, finger skimming over her contacts list, but eventually she decided that nobody else needed to know. It was time to finish the game, and whatever Sophie said or thought, she knew the killer wanted her present for the finale. She felt sure Paul, or Penny, would not allow the game to finish, except on their terms. The more she considered this, the more she felt that this had been the case all the way through.

It was personal.

Chapter 35

It was Leo I wanted really, but anyone could see he was obsessed with Ava. She wouldn't have anything to do with him at first, telling Ellen and I that he was arrogant, but I always knew. We sat on Ava's bed and talked and giggled, and her eyes glowed, cheeks reddening when she said his name. Ellen often tried to shut me out of these talks, to persuade Ava not to have us both over for sleepovers. But Ava was fair. She liked me, and she liked Ellen. Ellen had the edge because she was brash and bold but I was cute and funny, so she tolerated me. It was a strange group dynamic.

One day we were out exploring round Big Water, and in a dip behind the hill, we found a magical place. It was a sheltered spot and the long grasses were mixed with a meadow of big white daisies. They were so pretty, and their subtle peppery scent mixed with the smell of summer sunshine. Soon we were making daisy chains, and as Ava fastened one around my neck, I felt her cool fingers brush my neck. A thrill of excitement ran through my body, and Ellen was sat there looking piqued because Ava hadn't made her one yet. I fell in love with Ava at that moment. She chose me first, not because I was special, but because she liked me too.

Those friendship bands became the craze next summer, and we all got off on exchanging plaited cotton. Leo gave Ava a band of leather with two tiny seashells attached on a silver ring, and suddenly all the boys were wearing them too. That's why it seemed right, when I saw Ellen's lifeless body, to pluck her bracelet from her wrist, and her hair toggle too. Ava had made the bracelet for her, and Ava had borrowed the hairband. I wanted nothing of my girl to touch a dead body. I popped them quickly in my pocket.

Paul was my second choice. Like my uncle, I became adept at picking my prey, at picking up a weakness I could use to win the game. Ava was my secret fix, but Paul would be my rock.

The whole 'True Lies' thing was Leo's idea, but I embraced it wholeheartedly. They all appreciated my courage in doing dares, my willingness to discuss sex and fantasies. I was careful never to seem too knowledgeable, but I could hold the whole group spellbound simply by alluding to something most of them had never done.

Paul also appreciated my short skirts and skimpy tops, but more, he enjoyed my whispered suggestions. Even then he had that edge, or weakness, that I was looking for. We enjoyed the same things, and traded what he thought were innocent fantasies. I suggested a few things, promised a reward, he did what I said. It was like training a dog. A good-looking dog. He enjoyed the things I did to him so much, he was willing to overlook the fact I knew a whole lot more than he did, and he never asked how I learned my trade.

I was there that night, watching and waiting, enjoying the scene. The simmering resentment I had felt at being pushed aside earlier vanished as I pulled a camera from my pocket. Ellen and I had a row that afternoon about one of the 'True Lies' dares. Nothing serious but she called me immature and a child. She even suggested that I should be excluded from the night. Me, who had experienced things most adults should never go through.

I knew she was texting Uncle Alf, and I had assumed that it would simply come to a point when she became one of those kids he brought home to photograph. He wouldn't need to drug her drink because she was already in love with him. I thought she was already a bit old for his tastes, but I suppose she was new, and that was more important. Perhaps he had a client with a specific request. Sometimes that happened.

Ellen was a terrible drama queen, and she had supposedly secret rows with my uncle. I would listen in on the other phone or sit outside the door as she 'dropped the football shirts off'. As far as I could gather, she wanted him to run away with her, which was laughable. They still weren't having sex, and it was clearly driving him crazy. All his usual methods were impossible with a girl like Ellen. Her parents were formidable, and she would blab at the slightest hint of scandal. She was an oddly selfish girl, always the centre of attention, and she certainly had some magic when it came to boys. And men. They wanted her, and she teased them.

That evening she and my uncle had arranged to meet on the edge of East Wood. We would all be there anyway, on the other side, doing our usual Friday night party thing. He may have said he would run away with her, he may have just agreed to a secret meeting to finally get what he wanted. Either way, Ellen would get what was coming to her.

I gave Paul a bag of pills to hand out, watched Ava laughing in the firelight, and set about making sure the others were so off their heads they could hardly stand. We talked about dreams and dares and life after Aberdyth, and Rhodri strummed his guitar. I waited.

Ellen was late, probably taking a long time tarting up her appearance. I revelled in the fact the others had already taken the drugs, done dares, and she had missed out this time. Leo was kissing Ava, which was worthy of a photograph. After a while, I watched Paul instead, clicking carefully as he laughed and talked with Huw. Then I was with Paul behind the oak tree, his hands on my body. The empty cans of lager sat next to the roaring fire. A bottle of vodka rested on a tree stump.

After Ellen had arrived, done the zip line dare, and sat down, she was the centre of attention as usual. Ava was unconscious, keeling over soon after Ellen arrived, but after a quick conversation with Leo, Ellen didn't seem bothered that she had passed out. She should have been looking after her supposed best friend, but now she sat in the torchlight, laughing with Paul and the others. The light caught her fall of shiny hair, her dimples, and shyly touched on her high breasts. She was obviously wearing nothing under her green vest, and they liked that.

Paul came over to me for another quick grope. I pressed myself against him and kissed him long and hard. But I was keeping an eye on Ellen, and she was getting edgy, fiddling with her phone and checking it every few minutes. She was arguing with Jesse, but I couldn't hear what they said.

It was so easy. I watched and waited. There were a lot of 'what ifs' in this particular game, but fate was with me. Ava stayed passed out, Leo accepted another pill, went off for a piss in the woods. He was still stumbling around when Paul started kissing Ellen. There was a protest from Jesse, as I thought there would be. But he was easily silenced. I watched, they laughed and cheered and watched.

Up until then I hadn't been quite sure what I would do, apart from watch, of course. Now I knew. After another argument with Jesse, safe in the darkness, Ellen crept away from the firelight and into the woods. I followed her, whilst the others stayed, semi-comatose on the other side of the wood. I think Jesse called out, but the others were laughing, and I heard more cans opening. The music was turned up, but Rhodri wasn't accompanying on his guitar.

He was waiting by his car, smoking, and they did the usual kiss. I took a quick photo. The photos were pretty blurred because of the darkness, but he'd left the car headlights on, so you could make out faces. He switched the lights off, locked the car, and slid an arm around her shoulders as he drew her deeper into the wood. Then they were talking urgently. She wanted him to run away with her, go to Cardiff like he had promised. It might then still have been okay, but she threatened to tell everyone he had been seeing her since she was fourteen. I think she even said the word 'paedophile', and of course that did not go down well with my uncle.

It was over very quickly, although she fought back pretty hard. It was a hard lesson to learn, but it was done. He was moving away from her, breathing hard, zipping up his trousers, when she leapt up like a cobra striking. Her own clothes were all torn, and her knickers were halfway down her thighs, but she was swearing at him, threatening to tell the police, her parents. At first he laughed, then he grabbed her arm and pulled her close again. I could hear the venom in his voice, but she pulled back and lashed out at his face.

I don't think he meant her to die, and by the time I realised what was happening it was too late. I had only wanted to see the light on her face when it happened. I wanted to see the terror, the helplessness in that camera flash. She wasn't special like me, but this was her chance. She deserved it. He took pictures, and I took my own pictures. Mine have been under the floorboards, but he sold his as usual. I was surprised he dared, with Ellen 'missing' but he was so cocky, so arrogant and sure he couldn't be caught. He ripped her knickers away for his own trophy drawer. His was overflowing, my own collection just beginning.

It was so quick, Ellen's murder, I couldn't have stopped it. Would I have done? Yes, I think I would have tried. This was not part of the game, but somehow fate had decided for me.

Her body was still in his torchlight. I could see the marks on her neck. She was as limp as the ragdoll Uncle Alf bought me for my eighth birthday.

He was breathing fast and swearing under his breath. I could see him glance over to where our party was, almost hear the swift calculations in his brain. He picked her up, ran past me, and threw her down in the very middle of the path that led back to our clearing. My uncle chucked an armful of leaves across her body and ran back to the car.

It was the strangest thing, as I always saw him as so calm and in control, but I think this time he actually panicked. This was something that wasn't in the plan, and it was his good fortune that my friends reacted the way they did. Although, I suppose within my uncle's calculations would have been his realisation that he had a body, and the police would find and examine that body. He wore gloves, and I know he always used protection when he had sex, so did he hope there would be no physical traces that led back to him? I'm still not sure to this day why he just threw Ellen's body down and fled, but it was interesting the chain of events he set in motion that night...

I could hear the engine revving as he drove up the hill. It was very quiet this side of East Wood, and for a bit it was just me and her. Back on our side of the wood, I could still hear laughter, screams of laughter, and loud music, but it seemed to come from so far away that it could actually have been another dimension.

I wasn't sure what to do, but as I stood undecided, Jesse stumbled towards me. He called out, something about having been looking for Ellen. He was totally out of it, so instinctively I pulled him in for a kiss – my ultimate distraction technique, and one that has always worked with Paul. He was shocked, I could tell, but he kissed me back, because his brains were addled with chemicals and alcohol, or maybe he'd always had a thing for me. To our left, the body lay on the path, sprawled for anyone to see, but I kept kissing Ellen's boyfriend.

It was Rhodri who first discovered the body, who yelled at us to help him, and Rhodri who picked her up and ran back towards the firelight and the safety. Jesse and I ran screaming after him, and there were real tears pouring down my cheeks. I could taste the salt, and suddenly I was shaking uncontrollably.

Jesse, his hood thrown back now, was still crying as she tried to wake her up. Leo was shouting that there was no pulse, like he was a doctor or something. Ellen was gone, and they were panicking.

The arguing, the shouting, turned to hushed whispers. Huw, backed by Leo, was telling them what to do. It seems utterly ridiculous, the decision they made, we made, now, but at the time, it seemed entirely sensible. We would get on with our lives as though nothing had ever happened, and there would be no police, no parents, no explanations or accusations. Huw was always a big boy, muscular and brutish. His entire large family of brothers, cousins and random relations lived down in Lower Street, and he would threaten anyone who crossed him with 'his family'. Many of them had a history of brushes with the law, and we were terrified of them.

So when Huw, angry, and probably more terrified of what his family would say to him than what the police might do, was backed by Leo's charm and manipulative persuasiveness, we were swayed.

It was nothing to do with me, but fate had interceded to change our lives, and to save Uncle Alf from retribution. I was puzzled at the time, but now it all makes sense. Fate was keeping a dice roll for him alone, and it means far more than a few years in prison. Uncle Alf exists in his own personal hell, from which the only escape is death. He is bewildered that I hurt him, just as I was all those years ago when our positions were reversed. As for that night when Ellen died – it was done, and I held the balance of power. I decided, after much thought, not to tell anyone what really happened. It gave me more control, and I enjoyed seeing them all so terrified, creating their own stupid nightmare that would haunt them all for years to come. Because nobody else knew that there were nine of us in the wood that night. I kept my evidence and waited.

Chapter 36

'Hi, Ava! Are you okay?'

Ava wiped sweat from her forehead and spun round. 'Shit, Pen, you scared the life out of me.' The six-mile run from Leo's house down to Big Water had been hard, but the snow was packed tightly so for much of the way her trail shoes had been able to get enough grip for a reasonable pace. She had fallen a couple of times, into innocent-looking drifts that were actually a couple of metres deep, but she was in good shape. The bait she had laid earlier had been taken and the final stages of the game could commence.

'Sorry, I came down with the Land Rover, but I had to leave it at the top of the track. It does well in the snow, but there is a massive drift down by the gate. We're missing about thirty sheep, so I'm out looking this side of the hill, and Dwaine, he's the shepherd, is out the other side. Sometimes the daft beasts come down this way because it's lower, and a bit warmer, but if they huddle they can get trapped in the snow and… I don't have to remind you, do I? You lived here!' Penny's blonde hair was pulled back in a ponytail, her cheeks slightly pink from the walk up the hill. She had a green waxed jacket with big pockets, and she carried a small red rucksack over her shoulder. 'I heard the snowplough out early this morning. Paul's at the hospice until four, so I really hope they clear it by then. Ava, is something wrong? It's not those freaky text messages again, is it? Have the police said anything about the suspect?'

The two women stared at one another, and Ava could feel the tension stretching between them as she didn't answer immediately. She would wait for Penny to make the first move, and hope that her knowledge would be enough to keep her one step ahead. Had Penny really come on her own, or was Paul hiding somewhere?

'Yes. I had another message, and I think I might know where Bethan is. It's just over the hill.'

'Just over the hill? Surely that was already searched.' Penny snuck a wary glance across the white landscape, and shoved a hand into her pocket. 'Ava, I know you've been really stressed out lately, and I can see why, but this person is dangerous. We can't go trying to rescue Bethan ourselves.'

So, she was still playing the happy wife, still pretending. Ava mirrored her, answering as though she too believed that Penny and Paul had nothing to do with Bethan's disappearance. 'I have to. Penny, she could die! That's if she hasn't already.'

* * *

Ava had waited and waited, as the feeble stabs of morning light crept across the darkness, for any sign that the police were on their way. In the end, frustrated beyond reason, she had called Sophie, who told her curtly that the road was still blocked and the helicopter was rescuing a couple of climbers off the side of Naddglyden.

For another hour she had paced Leo's silent house, checking her phone for updates on the road. But the local authority website and social media feed merely informed her the road into Aberdyth was still blocked. She would wait, she would not do anything to screw up Bethan's chance of rescue. And then the next text came in, again in Welsh, and this time accompanied by another photo-graph. With an effort, she translated:

'*If you leave a flower without water for too long, it starts to die. If you leave it too late, and the sun comes out, there is nothing but blood on the stone. Time's up, Ava Cole.*'

Naturally she had scanned the photograph for signs of life, but Bethan was stripped naked again in this one, hands and ankles tied tightly, and the cave was bare of any supplies.

'Sophie, I'm sending you a message and pic,' she had told her quickly. She waited on the line for the DI to look at the message contents.

'Fuck! This bastard is really playing for fun today, aren't they? Okay, we'll be maybe another hour. The hill is unstable, so it's tough going for the road team clearing the snow. The good news is, the helicopter crew just cleared from their last job, so they'll be up here as soon as they've refuelled. Just keep me updated.'

'Will do.'

Ava had rung off and got ready to go out. Remembering the conversation, the sheer sweat-dripping frustration in Sophie's voice, weighed against the horror she had felt at doing nothing to save Bethan, Ava shivered, suddenly aware of her cold feet, her numb hands. Her running gear was designed to keep out the cold, and yet let her body breathe, and it was expensive kit. Bethan had been naked in the photographs...

* * *

Penny frowned. 'Ava? What makes you think you know where she is?' A weak ray of sunshine slid through the layered grey cloud and sliced a path of gold through Penny's hair.

'I had another weird message, I told you. Come on.'

The two women started up the hill, Penny swinging her red rucksack onto her back.

It was tough going. The snow here had blown up into great hard-packed ridges, and by the time they crested the hill, they were both panting. Ava's stomach growled, reminding her she hadn't eaten since last night.

'I need to rest a minute – sorry, Ava, I'm exhausted. Paul was in a lot of pain last night, and then the stupid sheep missing this morning… Paul's been so vile the last few weeks, I really do think he's struggling with it all more than he lets on.'

Wary, Ava looked over her shoulder and reluctantly slid to a halt as Penny unzipped her rucksack, but she still seemed so normal, and there was no sign of anyone else on the hill.

'Here, I'm going to pick up Stephen after this, and I made this for him, but hell, if we find Bethan, I'm sure he'll understand. He's been going out of his mind with worry, poor love. I think they have a snowplough and gritters trying to clear the main road, so I suppose the other contestants will be driven back to the hotel in Cadrington. Are you all right, Ava?' Penny took a blue and silver flask from her bag and unscrewed the cap. 'Beef soup. I made it this morning. Go on, you might as well, and I know how much you liked that stew the other night. I've got biscuits too.'

Hesitating, her smile frozen on her lips, Ava realised how hungry she was, but also how stupid she would be to accept the drink. Her mind flashed back to the spiked drink at the pub. Who had done it – Penny, Paul, or even Huw? But Penny was watching her, her own smile lighting her face, waiting for Ava to take the cup. 'Actually, Pen, I've had a bit of a dodgy stomach the last couple of days, so I might stick with the biscuits, if that's okay?'

Penny shrugged. 'Of course, lovely, all the more for Stephen. The amount teenagers eat these days is shocking. I'll have to get some extra food in for when he comes home.'

Ava stayed alert, muscles tense, scanning the daisy meadow. At this time of year, and covered in snow, there was no trace of the idyllic pocket of flowers, but she could gauge the area she needed to search, and it wasn't large. Somewhere under the snow, if she had guessed correctly, Bethan was dying. If she had to tear every tussock out by hand she would find the girl and bring her home. Meanwhile, what to do about Penny?

The blonde woman opened a tin of biscuits and offered them to Ava, before pouring herself a cup of soup. She was still smiling, still chattering about Stephen, and how she really hoped Bethan was okay. There was no urgency in her voice or mannerisms. 'Do you remember how I had that little leather book for pressing flowers? We brought it down here, didn't we, for the beautiful daisies.'

Ava did remember, and the memory stuck in her throat, clogging it with emotion at the image of three children picking flowers. How had it come to this? It was tough, but to keep her going, and to appease Penny, she ate a couple of flapjacks, and was just about to swing the conversation around to the daisy meadow again, when her phone rang. She glanced down. 'Sorry, I need to get this.'

'I got your email about the latest message. Sounds like it's nearly time to finish the game,' Jack said. His voice was faint and the weak signal made the line buzzy and indistinct.

'Yeah, I got that too.' Ava kept one eye on Penny, who was munching happily, and clearly not in a hurry to get on and rescue Bethan. Her own heart was thundering against her chest, and her breathing was short again, the icy air almost painful as it hit her lungs in sharp, anxious bursts.

Jack continued. 'Right, I have some more… information that might help, and although I have Sophie's details, I thought I'd call you first…'

'I'm listening. You're really faint, the signal is so bad up here.' In her mind's eye she saw the bloody daisy chain, coiled like a snake in the tissue paper. Was it Bethan's blood, or the killer's? If it was the killer's that would mean they had identified

298

themselves, and after all their cleverness, it must be deliberate. Did they want to be caught? Was that how the game ended? She moved a little way down the hill, away from Penny, but she could feel her friend's eyes on her.

'So, Zack told you we traced the person who was putting the photographs up. We've got more now. It was slightly odd in the end, almost as though this perp started off trying to cloak their identity, but then led us along a trail right to their own website. It's a whole site dedicated to sick porn, and snuff videos. All kinds of fucked-up shit.' Jack hesitated.

'Go on.' Ava indicated to Penny that they needed to get on, rolling her eyes in an attempt to convey boredom at the person on the other end of the phone. But this mattered, she could feel it, and the sweat on her forehead wasn't just from the climb up the hill. 'The site is linked to Penny's Bakes and Makes. She's Paul's wife, isn't she? All the emails and photographs linked to him, but this is a direct hit on her.'

Ava froze, heart hammering, and then covered her reaction quickly, zipping her running jacket up tighter, stamping her feet. She dragged up a picture in her mind of Penny's bright colourful site, and heard her light, pretty voice explaining that Paul made the website because she didn't understand technical things... and Leo did the photographs. 'Tell me how.'

Jack sighed. 'So, the tech guys tell me this kind of site often lives right underneath a legitimate site. Hard to describe, but imagine an island – your wholesome sand and palm trees on top, but underneath you got a load of sharks and weed...'

'Very lucid. I get you,' Ava said dryly, desperately trying to process this new information.

'This dark web site feeds off the same images as the legit one, JavaScript, and whatever – not my thing as you know. You go onto the legit site, you click a specific image selection – in this case, it's a photograph of a cake, and then an icon – and it takes you down below to the sick shit. A couple of things that stand out – it's her site, but the website and all the email accounts are registered to her husband. Did you...'

The signal gave out and she swore, apologised to Penny and explained it was a work call. She rang him back, hoping it would connect... Fuck, she was going to have to stop the soft approach and hammer Penny. All the time she tried Jack's number again, she was scanning the hill below for signs of Bethan. Underground. There must have been a hidden cave entrance they had missed when they explored up here as kids. Or perhaps an old mine entrance had opened up in the years between her escape and now. It did happen. She remembered that there had been a big news story a while back about a whole house disappearing into a sinkhole, because so many mines were never mapped.

Jack was back, and she gripped the phone so hard it hurt her palm through her glove. 'Lost you for a minute. Now, it could be that they are in this together, or he could be using her as a front. You said he's been diagnosed with terminal cancer? It could be the trigger that started all this off. Say he was responsible for the rape and murder of your friend, and say his wife doesn't know, but suspects...'

'Oh really? Well, maybe. Look, I need to call you back later, I'm right in the middle of something.' Ava's mind was racing. Could it be Paul, or was this a team effort between husband and wife? Had they brought her back for this all along?

'Are you with someone?'

'That's right – just a girlfriend.'

'Paul might or might not be your perp. You're with her, aren't you, the wife?' Jack said sharply. 'Does Sophie know where you are? Do you want me to update her?'

'Yes she does, and yes please, as soon as you can. Thanks, speak later,' Ava said quickly. Penny? No way, and yet it fitted in so many ways. But she wouldn't be doing it alone. If Paul was involved, it must be because he attacked Ellen that night. Fuck, Penny... She felt nausea creeping up her stomach into her throat, and beside her, the blonde hair shone in the sun, the pale green eyes fixed on hers...

'So. who was that?'

'It was just my boss back home. We're halfway through a tricky case and he wanted my take on it.'

'Oh.'

'Do you remember the daisy meadow, Penny?'

Her face lit up. 'Yes, I do… It would be right below us on the side of this hill, wouldn't it? Do you think Bethan is there? That would have been searched, wouldn't it?'

'Yes it was, but I think she is being kept underground.' Ava met Penny's gaze. Again, there was nothing but a pretty farmer's wife, a soon-to-be-bereaved wife. Her childhood friend. 'Penny, we need to find her!'

Still no reaction from the blonde woman, so Ava started to climb. She could hear Penny following her but didn't look back. They slithered down the hill, grinding to an unsteady halt approximately halfway down. This side of the hill, as they sank beneath the snow, was matted with bramble cables and bare scrubby vegetation, and the usual muddy ruts that caught unwary boots.

Ava jumped onto a ledge of jutting rock. Nausea made her head swim, but she brushed the feeling away. There was nothing obvious here, after the fresh fall of snow, and yet she was sure this was the place.

'Could the place be a bit further over?' Penny asked doubtfully, dumping her rucksack on the ledge next to her friend.

'I don't know, it might be. What do you think?' Ava challenged her, her voice sharpening. 'Where do you think Bethan might be, Penny?'

'I don't know. How could I? It's you who have been getting the messages, isn't it, lovely, so it must be up to you to find her.' Penny was smiling blandly, charmingly, with no hint of fear or sadness.

So that was it. She glanced quickly down to check her phone, which was now displaying the 'no signal' icon, but still displayed the map she had saved earlier. 'I'm thinking a natural fissure in the rock that is well hidden from the outside, or possibly even an entrance to some old mine workings. We need to check every bramble patch, and every ledge from here downwards. What do you think?'

'Oh, I think you're pretty clever to have thought of that,' Penny said softly and started moving to the right, shoving aside clumps of snow, parting the scrub, scanning along the rocky outcrops. 'Let's see now…'

Ava let her lead, whilst she was pretending to search further up. Penny wanted her to find Bethan, so she would trust that if she couldn't find the cave, her friend would guide her. They searched for a few minutes when Penny suddenly shrieked. 'Oh my God, Ava, get over here!'

Elated, Ava abandoned her search area and ran towards her friend. The nausea returned, making her head spin. She forced the feeling away. Gut instinct had been right. Unless it was an extreme coincidence, which she didn't believe, Penny had rung last night to gauge how things stood. Penny and her husband had decided she would come down and meet Ava after the last message, and pushing towards an unknown end goal, Penny would show Ava where Bethan was. The question was, now what?

Penny was excitedly tearing at undergrowth with her gloved hands, chucking up mud-laced snow, 'Look! It's an opening, but it has boards over it. It must be an old mine entrance or something. Do you remember that one we used to go exploring in over Manrith way?'

If you didn't know where to look, it would have been almost impossible to think that the snowy ridge held an underground entrance. In normal circumstances the SAR teams would have covered this area with more advanced equipment, and probably discovered something, but the weather had been on the perp's side from the beginning. Ava felt herself sway and frowned, putting a hand out onto a stunted hawthorn to steady herself, but Penny was still moving grass and mud and didn't appear to notice. 'Penny, I know,' Ava said quietly.

Penny swung round, breathing heavily, a smudge of mud on her forehead, her cheeks red from exertion. 'I know you do. It certainly took you long enough. You started off well, but, goodness, lovely, you could have saved Bethan days ago.' She shook her head sorrowfully.

Ava froze, tense and incredulous. To have her admit her guilt, with about as much emotion as if she was ordering bread at the shop, was sickening. 'So tell me, because I'm having trouble with this. You were my friend.'

'Oh, I still am your friend, Ava.' Penny chucked another tussock of brown, winter grass down the hill. She paused, and met Ava's gaze. 'I will always love you, but there are things I need to do.'

'Is Bethan alive then?' Ava checked that the rucksack was still way above them, balanced on the ledge. Penny's coat was slim-fitting and belted. The pockets couldn't possibly conceal anything more than a small knife. Whilst Penny was obviously moving towards a very definite goal of her own, she seemed to be taking Ava to Bethan, so unless that changed, she would keep things civil, even though her stomach was churning with horror. As she spoke, Penny was nothing but a pretty, empty shell, devoid of emotion.

'Oh yes. She's not in a good way though. You'd better hurry.' Penny heaved the last board away and threw it into the snow.

'Is Paul with her?' Ava enquired.

'Paul? Of course not. He's at the hospice like I told you.' She laughed suddenly. 'It's just you and me, lovely, and that is how it has always been.'

'Did you kill Alex?'

Penny ignored the question, placing a gentle hand on Ava's arm. 'This is where it all started you know, so it is so lovely we can finish in the same place.'

'What do you mean?'

'Ava, you made me a daisy chain.' The green eyes were wide and innocent, lips slightly parted from exertion, but there was something behind the expression, some hardness, or wildness that had never broken through before.

Ava took a step towards the dark hole and Penny smiled approvingly. It was a tunnel, just wide enough to crawl along, giving off into blackness. The air smelled of earth and dead things. 'I still don't understand why you would do this. Did you kill Ellen?'

'So many questions, and you're always harping on about Ellen, aren't you? Yet you made my daisy chain before you made Ellen one. I have loved you, Ava, as much as I could love anyone. Paul has been my rock, and you were my fix, and now for one last time I have the both of you together again. One last time. You see, on the outside everything has always been perfect, but underneath I am rotten, and squirming with maggots. You look shocked. Now, I can hear that helicopter too, lovely, but we have a few more squares to cover before we get to the finish, so we need to get a move on. The police will be here soon, but they can't come yet. I've planned it all so carefully... Ava, are you all right?'

* * *

Was it night again? Ava's head was thumping, and she groaned. Her eyes were gritty, so she raised her hands to rub them, child-like. Her fists bumped wood. Slowly, clarity returned, but the darkness remained. She tasted musty wood, earth and damp on her tongue, and as she shifted a foot, that too knocked up against wood.

Memory returned, and snatches of Penny's soft voice urging her forward, into the darkness, her arm around her shoulders, and her just wanting to lie down. Panic flooded her brain, and she jerked both feet downwards, fists hammering upwards, eyes wide in the darkness. She was locked in a box. What the fuck had happened to Penny? She yelled her name, but the air inside her box just seemed to get a little hotter, a little harder to breathe.

The box was just big enough for her to lie on her back. If she raised her hands, she had maybe fifteen inches until her nails scraped wood.

The memories burned in her mind, and suddenly she was thirteen again, locked in a box under East Wood, whilst outside Huw counted down the minutes remaining. It was 'True Lies' all over again. But how long would she leave her in here? Surely she had been telling the truth when she said that the game wasn't over. How long before the air gave out, and where the fuck were the police?

Ava searched her mind. She remembered nothing else. The helicopter had been circling though, the rotor blades thunderous in the silence of the icy valley. Sophie and her team knew where she was. It wouldn't be long.

The back of her head was very sore. Was there blood? She couldn't reach to check it out, but she managed to turn her head so her cheek pressed against rough wood, easing the pain a little. The nausea and the dizziness had come on before she even entered the cave, hadn't they? In trying to coax Penny into taking her to Bethan, making sure she didn't upset her, she had eaten the biscuits. Had they contained a drug? Had Penny hit her as well? She tried yelling for Bethan, then for Penny again.

The silence was ominous, the minutes ticking by. Furious, she kicked out at the box again and again. She tried to distract herself, much as she had done years earlier, playing 'True Lies'…

* * *

'You really gonna do it, Ava?'

'Of course. I'm not scared, if that's what you think.'

'I wouldn't dare.' Penny was looking on with wide eyes, but Ellen pushed her to the side.

305

They were all watching. The darkness swirled around the wood like a living thing, and in front of her the box gaped like an open wound. Leo was grinning, a cigarette hanging from his fingers. 'Go on, Ava, you lost, babe, so in you get.'

She did.

The lid was thumped closed and the claustrophobia hit. She couldn't breathe. She could hear laughter, followed by a thump of earth on the lid of the box. She jumped, heart pounding so hard it felt like her chest would burst.

Outside they counted down her time underground, and she blocked the terror and counted with them, visualising the numbers in her head as big neon digits.

'10, 9, 8, 7… oh, the watch has stopped. Sorry I need to start again…' Huw was laughing.

'Huw! Just fucking get on with it.' That was Rhodri, his voice edged with worry.

'Okay, all working now, 10, 9, 8, 7, 6, 5…'

* * *

Ava had no idea how long she'd been down there. It was too dark to see her watch, and every breath seemed magnified a thousand times. She could do this. If she was right, Bethan had a chance as long as, she, Ava, played the game.

She must have passed out again for a while, but a sound of digging, a spade hitting earth and clinking off rock, roused her.

'Hallo? Who is that?' No answer. She still didn't know for sure that Penny was working alone.

'Penny?'

The noise abated, and she thought she heard the clunk of boots. Then silence again. She screamed, but her screams echoed around inside her head. Then another sound caught her attention. The buzz of a phone receiving a message. What the fuck? How was there a phone signal underground? Unless she wasn't far from the entrance. Hope surged through her, giving a fresh burst of energy. Without thinking further, she thrust her hands upwards again and this time the roof of her prison moved. Just a little. Desperation gave her strength, and she shoved as hard as she could. The lid of the box moved sideways and she sat up, head spinning. It was still dark, but there was a torch on the floor, casting a beam of yellow light onto her phone.

Ava crawled out of the box, inching towards the phone, grabbing it and pulling it close. There was a signal, very weak, but there was a signal. She hit the number for DI Miles, and waited, propping herself against the cave wall.

'Ava? Where are you?' Her voice was distorted, and she asked something else but she couldn't make out the words. 'Ava?'

She took a deep breath. 'I'm in an old mine working under... It's obvious, the entrance hole to the tunnel is... I... Penny is... Hallo?' But with a buzz and a bleep, the phone gave out again.

Ava shoved the useless object in her pocket and picked up the torch. Her knuckles were cut and bleeding from battering at the box. She slowly swung the light around. It was a large cave, with a passageway passing through either end. She studied the two exits, trying to work out what to do next. A wrong move, and it could cost Bethan's life, and her own. And at every turn she expected Penny to appear from the darkness, knife in hand. It was then that she saw the chalk message on the wall.

'CONGRATULATIONS, AVA COLE. NEXT QUESTION. AFTER LEO WENT IN THE BOX THAT NIGHT, WHAT DID HUW HAVE TO DO BEFORE ELLEN ARRIVED?'

Chapter 37

Ava touched the spidery handwriting with a fingertip. What night? It must be referring to the night Ellen died. She forced her thoughts into order. Leo hated the box, so his punishment in 'True Lies' was quite often to get in it. Huw was pretty good at playing the hard man, but there was one time the act slipped, and it was, if her memory was right, the night Ellen died, the night she was late to the party. Fuck, she hoped it wasn't a re-enactment of that particular game. Paul had especially enjoyed that, she remembered suddenly, her breathing quickening.

It was the one time they got Huw so scared he 'nearly wet himself', so he told them afterwards. Penny had tied a cord around his neck and pulled until his breath came in gasps, just for a few seconds. That had freaked him out. What had they been thinking? Of course, the drugs and alcohol had been partly to blame, but how had a bunch of teenagers even come up with that? It made the sickness in her stomach rise as bile in her throat. Was that Bethan's fate, or her next ordeal?

In a panic of indecision, she scanned the passageways. The one to her right was empty, but the other had a bunch of daisies placed right in the middle. Where the hell did Penny get daisies in the snow? She bent down and touched them with a shaky finger. They were fabric, immaculate and perfect, but fake.

The tunnel was musty, but dry, and the walls were uneven with the marks of old mining scarring the rocks. Ava walked cautiously forward, instinctively checking her phone every few strides, although she knew it was useless.

The path led steeply downwards, a little to the west, cutting deep into the hillside. Occasionally smaller paths wound off into the darkness, but she followed the main tunnel, peering at each intersection for any clues. Sometimes she called out, 'Bethaaaaan! Penny!' and her own voice flung mocking echoes around the tunnels and caverns.

The police would be at the entrance to the tunnel by now, but images of Bethan hanging by her neck drove her on. Penny and Paul? The names seemed to be branded on the walls in front of her. Penny had only admitted her own guilt, but could one person really be responsible for all of this? Then there was Ellen's murder... She stopped abruptly as the gleam of water caught in the torch beam. Thick, oily and foul smelling, it was a huge underground lake, presumably in a vast cavern which had seen much working.

There was no other way around, and no other way out. She would have to swim. Ava hesitated, then hauled off her windbreaker, zipped the phone carefully in a pocket and tied the whole thing to her neck, as high as possible. The torch went swiftly between her teeth, and she waded in, feeling carefully for each step.

Four strides in and the depth dropped suddenly off a ledge and she was swimming. The thin yellow torch beam waved wildly, casting grotesque shadows across the walls. Her own breathing sounded loud and the sound travelled around the cavern. She even wondered if she could hear her own heartbeat in the deep, dark caves.

The water was freezing, and she gasped and floundered her way across. Eventually, when her body and limbs were numb with cold, and the stench of deep rotten things threatened to choke her, she felt her feet touch the rock again. Slowly she struggled up a steep ramp and into the next tunnel. The path wound upwards this time, still breaking on into ancillary workings, but the main artery held true. There was no sound but her laboured breathing and the squelch and thud of her feet and clothing.

As she rounded yet another bend, she heard a noise ahead. Someone else was struggling for breath, and there was another sound like a box being kicked over, hitting the rock with a bang.

'Bethan?' Ava called.

Only her own footsteps echoed mockingly back, but the desperate breathing became a wheeze and then a gurgle. She ran, rounding the turn into another larger cave.

Bethan was hanging by her neck from an old piece of machinery. Her eyes were rolling back, her tongue hanging out, and her hands were still clawing at her neck, but weakly.

Without thinking, Ava jumped up onto the rusting metal pulley and yanked at the rope, trying to free the girl. 'Bethan, I've got you. Just keep breathing…' Her fingers were shaking as she fought to untie the rope from the metal ring, but the girl was heavy, and the rope tight and wet. 'Fucking hell!' Ava swore. 'Bethan, stay with me…'

She looked desperately around for anything to hack through the rope, a convenient rusting tool… but there was nothing, and Bethan's eyes were closing, her hands dropping limply. Then her eyes followed the rope back and she realised it was a pulley system. She could wind the wheel and lower the girl to the ground. The rusty wheel turned easily, and almost sobbing with relief Ava scrambled over to the girl, checking for signs of breathing. 'Bethan, can you hear me? It's Ava. You're going to be all right.'

The sound of clapping made her spin around, crouched ready to spring at her attacker.

Ava jerked round. 'Stay away from me, Penny. It's over, and the police know exactly where we are.'

Penny was smiling. She held out her hand, and the torchlight picked out a glimmer of silver. A knife. 'Do you want to take this knife, Ava Cole? It's the same one I used to cut you that night I spiked your drink. Your cut was real, but they aren't all real. Remember that. Perhaps I might have got carried away once or twice, but generally it's mostly been froth and fantasy. All you have to do is get the other person to believe… I've really enjoyed our final game.'

'Penny?'

'I asked if you wanted this knife?' Her voice was sharp.

'Put it on the floor.' Bethan was breathing, but it was slow and faint. Her skin was icy cold. Ava kept her voice steady, low and encouraging, despite the fact she was shaking with cold, and her muscles, stuck in the crouching position, were cramping painfully.

'Okay. Here it is then.' Penny smiled encouragingly and held the blade out, tempting Ava to come closer.

'Just put it down on the floor. Has it all been you and Paul?'

'I said come and get it.'

There was no way Ava was leaving the girl on the floor unprotected. 'Tell me why you did it, Penny. I want to understand, because I'm having trouble believing all this is actually happening.'

Penny frowned. She seemed to be listening, to be engaged, and Ava prayed she could keep her talking until the police arrived. Surely they would find her soon, and in the meantime she would keep Bethan alive. She had to, for Ellen and for Stephen, and also at the back of her mind, she finally acknowledged, for herself.

'I've left you a gift, Ava, and it is a good one. Everything is explained by my final gift, because that is the way I want it to end. There is nobody else involved. It has been me all along.'

'Did you kill Ellen?'

She smiled, face lighting with amusement, and the charm that was her trademark. 'You dafty, of course not, and neither did Paul. In fact, all that panic was for nothing. My uncle killed and raped Ellen. He was a paedophile, you know. All through my

311

childhood and beyond, I've been tied to him, and his business. You never guessed, did you?'

'Fucking hell, Penny, why did you never say anything? You knew who killed Ellen, and you were being abused...' Ava pressed one hand to the cold stone floor, still crouching, brain spinning. This changed everything. 'You mean, when Huw and Leo made us all bury Ellen, we kept quiet for your uncle...' She almost couldn't breathe with the sheer horror of past events, at her blindness. It was fine to be a fucking excellent detective when your own emotions, your own people weren't involved, but she had let all these things cloud her judgement, both then and now.

'It was odd how a random chain of separate events could screw up so many people's lives, and yet the man who was responsible for so much of it walked free. I've thought a lot about how we almost certainly saved Uncle Alf from becoming a convicted paedophile and murderer. There must have been some evidence on Ellen's body they could have used, and we whisked it away. How funny is that? But as for telling someone... Come on, Ava, don't be stupid. Who would have believed me? He came into Aberdyth like a knight on a white horse to take care of Mum and me. The social workers, the police, the football team, he fooled everyone. Nobody would have believed me,' she repeated dully, before brightening. 'But I always knew I was your best friend, and you knew it too. We didn't need Ellen. No, don't look down at her, we're almost finished. It took you a while to figure out the daisies, but I knew you'd get it in the end. I had loved you since you came to Aberdyth, Ava, and because you made me the first daisy chain, I knew I'd finally found someone who loved me back. You did love me, didn't you?'

'I... I do love you, Pen, and I wish you'd told me all this before. I could have helped, done something to stop it.' The words sounded genuine, and her chest was tight with emotion, but again Penny frowned.

'Nobody could have helped me.'

'But you still visit him in that home, and care for him… How do you do that?'

She laughed. 'I don't really care for him at all. I would have liked to have killed him, but for some reason, even when I realised he was growing physically weaker, I just couldn't. It would be easier for him to have died. She's still breathing, isn't she?'

'Yes.'

'I'm glad. Goodbye, Ava.'

'Penny, where are you going?'

She laughed, as though surprised at her friend's stupidity. 'To finish the game, of course.'

'Don't go. We can work something out…'

Her mood changed quickly. 'Don't tell me what to do. This is my game and my rules. Did you mean it when you said you loved me?'

'Of course.'

'Even after knowing what has happened?'

'I don't really know what has happened, do I? I'm still trying to take it all in,' Ava said carefully. She could hear something, definitely. Quite far off, but the noise magnified along the ancient tunnels. Help was coming. She squeezed Bethan's hand. The girl's fingers were limp and icy.

Penny heard them too, and her eyes narrowed in the torchlight. She moved so quickly that Ava hardly had time to shield the girl at her feet. But Penny was trying to leave, and the other tunnel was right behind where Bethan lay.

'Penny, we can work something out. I can help you… You've always been special to me.' Floundering a little, Ava's only thought had been to keep them all alive until the police arrived, but clearly her choice of words had triggered a reaction. 'Penny?'

Her face contorted with horror and fury, Penny struck, slashing the knife across Ava's arm. 'Bitch! How could you say that? After everything that's happened, I thought you were different…'

Ava, hampered by her need to protect Bethan, initially let the knife bite across her arm, absorbing the fierce sting, and hoping her layered clothing would take some of the force. She dodged, and felt the other woman's hot breath on her face, her knife hand zinging past her ribs, tearing fabric again and again.

'Penny, stop!' It soon became obvious that Penny seemed to have forgotten Bethan's existence, her whole being focused on punishing Ava. What the hell had she said to trigger this? She searched desperately for something to say to defuse the situation, but the fight was taking all her battered resources.

They faced each other again, circling like animals, each looking for the other's weakness. Penny feinted to the right, then struck at Ava's chest, missing as they locked in combat. Ava shook a fist free and hit her right between the eyes, at the same time seizing the knife handle. It was slippery with blood or sweat she half-noted, but she held on with grim determination.

But Penny moved quickly and drove the knife deep into Ava's stomach. She dropped, clutching her abdomen, feeling the wet ooze of blood, the burning pain as the weapon hit its target for a second time.

Ava was lying on the hard floor, eyes closed, clenching her teeth against the pain, when Penny leant down to her. She tried to roll away, but the other woman held her head fast, hands either side of her cheeks. She dropped a brief, hard kiss on Ava's lips. 'Congratulations, you earned the knife. *Nos da*, Ava Cole.'

And then she was gone, running down the tunnel, footsteps drumming on rock. Ava summoned all her ebbing strength and rolled over to the discarded knife. With fumbling fingers she cut away all traces of the deadly noose from Bethan's neck. Realising the girl had stopped breathing, she yelled for help, again and again.

Ava tilted the girl's head back to open the airway, and listened. Nothing. She started to pump Bethan's chest. One hand over the other, fingers linked, her own blood sticky on her hands;

'One, two, three, four...' No point in trying for breaths. She was struggling to stay conscious herself, and the pain in her side made her clasp a hand to the wound. More important to keep blood pumping round the body, than waste time with breaths that might never make it, she told herself. Even with only one hand, she was doing something to keep her alive. 'One, two, three, four…'

It seemed to go on forever, the counting, the darkness, her own blood slippery on Bethan's body, before she finally heard answering shouts behind her. She began to yell again, 'Help – over here!'

The cavern was quickly crowded with uniformed officers, search and rescue teams, and paramedics. Powerful searchlights lit the space with a bright artificial whiteness, and the blood shone brightly on the stone floor.

Ava clamped a hand over her wound, left Bethan in safe hands, and started up the tunnel Penny had vanished into. The DI was yelling at her to stop. Ava let out one last breathless scream, 'Penny!' before collapsing on the rocky floor. From behind her she heard urgent medical talk around Bethan's body. 'She's got a pulse… She's back.' Thank God for that, Ava thought, vaguely aware of a medic pushing her hands away to get to her wounds, of an oxygen mask being strapped to her face. *Thank God I managed to save Stephen's girlfriend.* Her son's words danced in her brain. '*You fucked up being a mum, so, Detective, why don't you try and do what you're supposed to and find my girlfriend.*'

It was a shame she hadn't got to know Stephen, a shame he hated her so much…

She drifted, woozy, but Penny's face stayed with her. That perfect, perky little girl, whose pretty face had concealed a monster. It wasn't her fault though. All those conversations made sense now. She had planned it, planned the game, and planned all those conversations – to ease her conscience, or justify her actions? What made a killer like Penny? Her mother, or Uncle Alf, or was she just born with a random gene?

It was a question Ava had often asked during her career. Was it nature or nurture? She just never expected to be asking it about one of her friends. She was cold now, so cold she could cry, despite the foil blanket they were wrapping her in. She needed to go home. She had made her peace with Ellen. It was time to go home... Ava closed her eyes.

Chapter 38

So here we are. The last square on the board, the last roll of the dice. If I'm honest, now the moment has come, I want to carry on. A tiny piece of me is crying like a scared child, or a child who is piqued at losing their favourite game. It's never happened before, losing so close to the end. My very last move, and I don't even have to move from this square to make it. My choice.

Looking back, I know that now is my time to reflect, to prepare for what's ahead. Fuck that. My first could be described as a mercy killing, and so too could my last. I wonder what my mother would think, if she knew how I spent my adult years. Perhaps I'll meet her on the other side, in the light and the warmth. If I do, I'll be sure to punch her in the face.

At least I'm not teetering on, pathetic and trampled underfoot by those who are stronger. I am not like she was, and I took my revenge on him. I've had some good games, and I've played the perfect wife and mother. I've had plenty of money. What else is there?

So, I've decided to take a running jump off the board, before the other players can catch up. Silencing that flicker of fear, I take a deep breath. The air is icy, the flakes whirl and spin. A dance of death and music playing just for me.

Ava Cole? She won't be far behind. This was all for her. I'm sure she'll work it out eventually, when she sees exactly what I am leaving her – she's a clever girl. Not as clever as me, but who is? She'll figure out all our heartfelt, girly conversations were actually confessions. She knows me better than she thinks, or less well than she believes. Who is to say which? I can hear my own high-pitched laughter echoing back at me. It's just a game.

I rattle the pill bottle, breathing slowly, relishing the feeling of being alive. The snow skitters sideways now, inviting me to play. I can see faces in the ice crystals settling on the rock, and daisy chains are threading in and out of the icicles at the entrance to my cave. The scent of summer is returning, and I know it will be all right.

I unscrew the bottle, my fingers clumsy with cold, and swallow the tiny pink capsules. The effort hurts all the way down to my gut, as though, even now, my body is still fighting.

The snow is deep and soft, virginal even. The daisy chains are swinging in the cool breeze, and the muffled silence is just for me.

I can taste my own blood, and I know fate is right behind me, tongue lolling, waiting for the kill. I'm not cold anymore, but the fire has gone from my belly. Slowly, I make my way towards the edge of the hill. The steep drop is cloaked in white, the vicious rocks gentle now, waiting just for me. Far below is the treacherous black gleam of Big Water. The air is sweeter up here, and my mind spins as I take in the vast, lonely, frosted landscape, my kingdom and my grave. I will step off the edge and fall so very far, for such a long time, I think.

And afterwards what will happen? I can see their faces more clearly now; My mum, Jessica and the others, are waiting with Jesse. But not Rhodri. And Ava? No, Ava will be up here soon, and she will know that I have won. Or maybe she won't. I didn't mean to hurt her, but perhaps I was meant to take her with me? I wonder if Bethan is alive. I don't much care. I suppose that

Stephen will be upset, but that's life, kid. My love and hate has gone, and peace floods my mind.

Slowly, as the whiteness deepens, I step out, off the last square of the board, and start to fall. My prettiest princess dress floats around me, skirts billowing, lifting with the force of my leap. My beautiful golden hair tangles across my face, tears freeze on my cheeks. My feet and legs are bare, but that's what makes me special, makes the boys happy...

'Three little girls, sitting up a tree,

Kissed all the boys,

But no one loves me.'

I can hear her shouting for me now, but it's too late. I have won after all these years.

Gem drosodd, Ava Cole.

Game over, Ava Cole.

Chapter 39

The grave was a slash of yawning darkness in the spring-washed grass of the graveyard. A mix of mourners milled around in the light rain, but not all of them really cared, apart from Stephen. In the last two weeks he had buried a mother and a father, neither of whom were actually his kin. He remained unaware of his parentage. With the graves fresh and raw, now was not the time. She hated to be lying still, after everything that had happened, but Leo had kept the secret long enough. Let her son mourn the man who had been his father, before they told him the truth about his biological parent.

Ava blinked hard, but a few tears slid from under her dark lashes. The tears were for all of them, for eight children playing in the woods, for the years of lies. Her son glanced round and smiled at her. It was a genuine smile, the kind she never thought she would have the right to. But in a funny way, she felt she had finally earned it. On Stephen's other side Bethan, white-faced and big-eyed, was staring at the coffin. Her collar was turned up to hide the bruising on her neck, and her bulky red puffy jacket hid her skinny body. Luckily, she was young and fit. The doctors said that had saved her life during her time in the freezing caves under the hill. Physically, she would be okay. Mentally,

Ava knew she would remember what happened for the rest of her life.

DI Miles was watching from a respectful distance, and Ava raised a hand in recognition. The other woman nodded and mirrored her action. The earth was being shovelled back into the ground now, thumping hard against the wooden coffin. She winced. Strange that Paul should go so quickly after his wife, or perhaps not. Penny had been the vital heartbeat that drove him. He had long ago lost the fight against cancer, but it seemed she had almost been keeping him alive by her very presence, her denial that he would die.

Ava had been with him when he died, and he fell asleep with a half-smile touching his lips. It was enough.

* * *

Back at the Birtleys', Ava quickly finished her packing, snapped her case shut, and took a last look around the room. She would go to Leo's place tonight and collect the things she had left there. Her heart gave a painful jerk as she noticed a small pink box on the bedside table. It wasn't hers. Surely it hadn't been there this morning.

She reached for it, sliding shaking fingers around to prise open the lid. A memory stick lay on a bed of white foam. No note. There was nothing else. A footstep outside her door brought her swinging around, hand automatically going to her hip.

'Oh, Ava, I see you found the box. Good, I quite forgot that Penny gave it to me last month, just before we knew you were coming. She said that I must give it to you when she was gone. Very cryptic she was, but of course I never imagined that she meant gone, gone, you know, as in dead… I thought she might move away after Paul died.' The old man rubbed his face, sniffing loudly. 'I always did have a soft spot for little Penny, and I never liked Alf Thomas. How did we never guess, Ava? That poor child.

There's been a lot in the papers about how evil she was, planning this, and making money out of misery, but everyone forgets that she was corrupted first.'

'I know, it doesn't justify what she did at all, but I do know what you mean. You couldn't have known what was going on. Please don't beat yourself up, Mr Birtley. Did... did Penny say anything else when she gave you this?'

He shook his head. 'No. Just what I told you. Anyway, safe journey, Ava. I have no doubt we'll see you again next time you visit young Stephen.'

On impulse, Ava leant over and kissed his cheek. 'Thank you.' She didn't have the heart to tell him she would never come back to Aberdyth. Stephen wanted to head to England for university. Their relationship was still in the early stages, but at least she had been able to give him the money without causing offence, presenting it as funding for his degree. His acceptance, and the tiny smile he gave her, told her that there was hope. Ellen's parents had made their feelings pretty clear, and she didn't blame them. They were holding a private memorial service for Ellen, before they too moved away.

When Mr Birtley had gone, Ava rang Leo, then Stephen. It seemed right that they should both be present for Penny's last gift. It seemed even more fitting that they should meet at her house.

* * *

Stephen opened the door, red-eyed and frowning. 'You said she left a USB?'

'Yes. Can we go into the office?'

They booted up the computer and slipped the USB into the slot. Leo was drumming his fingers on the oak table and Ava told him sharply to stop. He glanced up, grinned briefly at her, and without thinking, her hand slid onto his shoulder. She couldn't

322

predict whether they had anything but possible friendship, but Leo had already casually mentioned he would be spending time in LA over the coming months.

'It's just her bakery website...' Leo said squinting at the screen.

'No. Look there's something at the bottom right, a tiny square in her logo. That shouldn't be there,' Stephen said, pointing.

Ava clicked on the pop-up, and the screen went black, then red swirls started appearing. 'Is it a virus? There isn't anything she could want destroyed on here. The police have been through all her files. Oh, shit, it's the dark web site underneath, isn't it?'

'More than that. There are hundreds of files on this stick, all dated and named. I can bring one up – look, names, phone numbers, addresses. Who are these people?'

The documents were neatly arranged, with website links, passwords, and hundreds of names. Some were highlighted, others had information missing. A separate folder held photographs, and another contained videos. Clicking on a couple, Ava winced and glanced at Stephen, but he just shrugged, and pushed her hand away as he carried on looking through. His face was a careful blank, but his brow was furrowed, and he kept rubbing a nervous hand through his wild hair.

'That's Penny.'

'Yes.'

'And that's Rhodri, and Jesse.'

'Yes.'

'And there are so many others...' Leo's voice broke and he coughed to hide it.

They were silent for a long time, abandoning the photographs, and scrolling through the documents.

'I could be wrong, but I think Penny's last gift is enough evidence to take down a number of paedophile rings. I assume from the things she said, and from what she did to me, that she continued with the family business, but if you look at the dates on a few of these, she was never involved in child pornography.

The pictures she used on these sites are old, and of her...' Ava blinked back her own tears. 'The women in these newer photos are all older. I'm not saying that makes it right, because it sure as hell doesn't. She was making money out of sick bastards who got off on the idea of torturing and abusing women. But I think I know what she meant when she said "everything isn't as it seems". I asked about the cut on my leg, and she said mine was real, but others weren't, so perhaps this lot are just make-up and Photoshop? I mean, if this many women were suffering serious GBH, or even dying, on a regular basis in Cardiff, the police would have noticed! She was too clever for that.'

Leo ran his eyes down the files. 'Bloody hell, she must have infiltrated hundreds of these websites to get this much evidence. This list of names and contact details runs over five pages. The Major Crime Team, or whatever DI Miles is involved in, are going to have a field day.'

They sat in silence for a moment, Leo's arm around his son's shoulders, both of them leaning close to Ava. Ava couldn't get the photographs out of her mind. Penny had gone home to this for years and years. No wonder she was damaged. Damaged so badly, she came up with a whole new twisted logic to explain her behaviour and make herself feel whole again.

Paul had been her rock, but when it became clear he was terminally ill, that had shaken Penny. Jack had been bang on with his theory.

She had never killed Uncle Alf, because he didn't deserve the easy way out. She needed to make him suffer, but Ava thought from their conversation that it was more than just being able to torture him on a weekly basis. She was inextricably linked to him, unable to free herself from his business, or his life. Or was it that Penny had simply told herself one day she would get revenge on all of them, her uncle included, and he needed to be alive for that?

Ava called DI Miles. 'Hi, Sophie. Penny has left us a parting gift. Let's just say it is far more palatable than her other gifts. This will keep you guys busy for months.'

'Cryptic,' the other woman said dryly. 'Care to give me a clue?'

So Ava told her about Penny's legacy. 'I'm at the farm now, so I'll wait until you get someone over here, shall I?'

'Sure. Bloody hell, who would have thought?'

'I know.'

'We found a few other things when we searched the house. You should know that there was a stash of evidence that ties Alf Thomas not only to Ellen's murder, but also to a string of other offences. Penny obviously kept it all after he went into the nursing home.'

'I still can't believe she knew, but never told anybody. I'll speak to you later. Thanks for letting me know about Uncle Alf.'

Leo made coffee, and Stephen scrolled through his social media. None of them spoke. It was too much, too many horrors. Restless, Ava wandered back into the office, opening random drawers, and peering into cupboards. Nothing of interest, and the police would have taken anything anyway. She wondered what evidence Penny had kept to convict her uncle. Trophies probably, maybe photographs. Had she always intended this, or did she think about blackmailing him when he was lucid?

'What are you looking for?' Stephen appeared at the door.

'I don't know... Something special. Where would she have kept something that she really treasured?'

The boy shrugged, his brow creasing. 'Dunno... Oh, maybe in her dressing table. There's a wind-up music box in there. She used to show me when I was younger. It's got some Disney princess character that dances when the music plays. I'll show you, if you like.'

They went together up the wide staircase, and in the bedroom Stephen hunted around for a bit before bringing out a box. 'Look, she kept it in here.'

The music box was packed tightly against something else. A

chequered game board and a couple of dice fell out with a clatter. Several wooden playing pieces rolled under the bed, but Ava was looking at something else. A little book right at the bottom. The book Penny had mentioned they had as kids, for pressing flowers. The summer they discovered the magic meadow near Big Water, all the girls had a pungent little book of dead and dying squashed flowers.

Ellen had tired of it well before Ava and Penny. Ava opened the book with gentle fingers. The pages crackled, but right in the centrefold was a fragile line of daisies. It was smaller than the one Penny had sent to her, and would most certainly have fitted neatly as a floral necklace.

She could almost feel Penny's warm breath on her hand as she placed the flowers around her neck, see the glow in her green eyes, and the pure, untainted happiness in her face. Her clear voice came from nowhere and everywhere.

'I loved you then, Ava, and because you made me the first daisy chain, I knew I'd finally found someone who loved me back. You did love me, didn't you, Ava Cole?'

Tears were streaming down her cheeks now, as she sat alone in a shaft of sunlight, smoothing the last page of the book with unsteady fingers. The writing was clear and strong, and she hardly had to think to translate it:

'*Sut byddwch chi'n cofio fi, Ava Cole?*'

'**How will you remember me, Ava Cole?**'

Acknowledgements

So many people helped and supported me whilst I was writing this novel, so huge thanks to the following:

The team at my wonderful publishers HQ, HarperCollins, including Nia Beynon, who is an absolute pleasure to work with.

Thank you to Abi Truelove, Mick Oakey, and Charlie Plunkett for championing my early works, and to The Crazies, and The Kick Ass Girls for your literary naughtiness and genuine encouragement.

Just before I sent this book out on submission, I visited The Author School, run by Helen Lewis and Abiola Bello, and their enthusiastic support and friendship has been invaluable. Thank you also to my fellow authors – I have met so many wonderful writers over the years, and your advice and support is something I cherish.

Thank you also to Eric and Dee at Singularis for sharing their knowledge and experience of police work and film crews, and for reining in my imagination when I went too far!

The Welsh language features as a strong thread throughout this book, so many thanks to my Welsh 'cuz' Julie Lord for correcting my Welsh in the first drafts, and to Jill Crocker for use of her Welsh dictionary.

Having started my writing career whilst working as cabin crew all those years ago, it seems apt that I polished the final draft of *Remember Me* on a flight back from LAX – thanks to the wonderfully encouraging British Airways crew on that flight for keeping me plied with cups of coffee as I worked through the night.

Huge thanks also to the bloggers, the readers, retailers and librarians, whose support is so vital. Thank you for buying my books, for reading, recommending and reviewing. I couldn't do it without you.

Last but not least, I owe huge thanks to my wonderful family. My gorgeous boys, James and Ollie, who give me unfailing support and encouragement. My lovely husband, who is always happy to discuss the best ways to murder someone, and get away with it. To my parents, who are such an inspiration, and have never, ever told me to give up writing and get a proper job!

Dear Reader,

I started writing *Remember Me* after the birth of my first child, whilst I was suffering from PND. After writing an outline, I put it to one side, and eight years later, revisited my idea. Previously, the ideas were too raw and too painful, but as time has gone by I have been able to see more clearly, and fit the story together. Ava's strength and vulnerability reflects pretty much every woman I know. At times, we all have things we simply can't cope with, or process, and at times, we all need to ask for help. It is the asking that is so difficult.

I applaud the current trend for speaking out about mental health, for making it a priority, and for chasing away the preconceived ideas that have often previously surrounded it.

I do hope you enjoy *Remember Me*.

Kindest Regards,

D. E. White

Thank you for reading!

Thank you so much for taking the time to read this book – we hope you enjoyed it! If you did, we'd be so appreciative if you left a review.

Here at HQ Digital we are dedicated to publishing fiction that will keep you turning the pages into the early hours. We publish a variety of genres, from heartwarming romance, to thrilling crime and sweeping historical fiction.

To find out more about our books, enter competitions and discover exclusive content, please join our community of readers by following us at:

🐦 *@HQDigitalUK*

f *facebook.com/HQDigitalUK*

A   *lso looking for authors to*
jo   *e submit your manuscript*

ollins.co.uk.

you soon!